LARGE PRINT
F Levinson
Levinson, Robert S.
A rhumba in waltz time

A RHUMBA IN WALTZ TIME

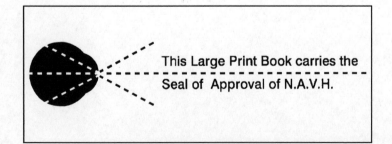

This Large Print Book carries the
Seal of Approval of N.A.V.H.

A RHUMBA IN WALTZ TIME

ROBERT S. LEVINSON

THORNDIKE PRESS
A part of Gale, Cengage Learning

GALE
CENGAGE Learning®

Detroit • New York • San Francisco • New Haven, Conn • Waterville, Maine • London

GALE
CENGAGE Learning®

LIBRARY OF CONGRESS CATALOGING-IN-PUBLICATION DATA

Levinson, Robert S.
  A rhumba in waltz time / by Robert S. Levinson.
    p. cm. — (Thorndike Press large print mystery)
  ISBN-13: 978-1-4104-4543-8 (hardcover)
  ISBN-10: 1-4104-4543-7 (hardcover)
  1. Motion picture industry—Fiction. 2. Murder—Investigation—Fiction.
3. Metro-Goldwyn-Mayer—Fiction. 4. Hollywood (Los Angeles,
Calif.)—Fiction. 5. Large type books. I. Title.
PS3562.E9218R48 2012
813'.54—dc22   2011044246

Published in 2012 by arrangement with Tekno Books and Ed Gorman.

ALWAYS FOR SANDRA
and
In Loving Memory
IDA LEVINSON NISLOW
February 9, 1912–June 27, 2010

CHAPTER 1

December 1933

Prohibition and my future as an LAPD detective ended within a month of each other, after a nineteen-year-old MGM starlet who'd been celebrating her option pickup with Benzedrine and sidecars at an Echo Park dive was assaulted by a couple *cholos* in the backseat of the Chevy convertible she'd parked in the garbage-riddled alley behind the bar.

A pair of cruiser cops crashed the scene.

The *vato locos* fled.

Instead of chasing after them, the uniforms threw the blowsy, stripped-down blonde looker into the cruiser and aimed for Central Division at City Hall.

That night, working the cold spaghetti and warm beer shift out of Hollywood Division, I was at Central following up on a series of mob-inspired murders that had spread to Central's jurisdiction, when they waltzed in slap-wrestling the handcuffed girl. She was half-naked in torn clothing that revealed a flat chest smothered in nasty bruises and bite marks, and her desperate Orphan Annie eyes punctuated a battered face stained with mascara.

They led her to the desk sergeant, where the beefier of the pair, whose belly hung over his uniform belt like an island of Jell-O, said, "This one's a whore no more tonight, Maxie."

"Unless you'd like us to deposit her in a holding cell and one of us hold down the phone for you, while you do some fancy interrogation," his younger and trimmer partner chimed in, his ferret-like face gushing with delight.

Both cops laughed like they'd just invented humor.

I might have thought better than to involve myself, but common sense and good judgment — never my strongest attributes — had been at their weakest since my wife left me a year ago. They had been further bound and blinded five minutes ago in the parking lot by the two quick tastes from the flask I kept under the seat of my unmarked, next to my throwaway .32 revolver with the numbers filed off and my lifetime stash of Pep-O-Mint Life Savers and Sen-Sen.

I said, "Knock off the crap. Just make the booking."

Until they heard my snarl of a command, the two cops weren't aware anyone had come into the station house behind them.

Big Belly wheeled around, a nasty look on his Porky Pig face, getting ready to say something nastier, when he recognized me and broke out a fake smile.

"Just joking around is all, Blanchard. We caught the bitch chipping over in Echo, her and a bunch of Pancho Villas who ran off."

The girl made an undecipherable sound and struggled to raise her voice above a whisper. "I was raped, and these bulls didn't try catching the guys who done it. They told me they'd let me go if I gave them both blowjobs. I told them to try blowing each other, not something they liked hearing from me."

"Shut up, bitch!" Ferret-Face's voice overrode hers. "Don't go making it worse on yourself."

Big Belly shook his head. "The bitch is lying, Blanchard. Been threatening trouble since we saw her panties down around her ankles. Going on about being some movie star, knowing big, important people, and how if we didn't let her go it was aces and eights for us."

9

"Why don't you uncuff her and get your sorry asses back on the street? I'll finish it up from here."

Ferret-Face said, "You're not gonna believe this damn slut over two of your own, are you, Detective? Or you out to steal our pinch, that what this is really about?"

Maxie the desk sergeant frowned and gave his walrus mustache several anxious tugs. He knew me and my temper well enough, had seen it in action when it was fueled by booze and anger. He bounced into the conversation before I could answer Ferret-Face. "Do yourselves a favor, boys. Uncuff her like Chris said, get the hell back on the street hoping he forgets your badge numbers by the time the sun comes up and the milkmen start their rounds."

Big Belly and Ferret-Face exchanged body language and silent communications.

"Okay, okay," Big Belly said. He held up the key to the cuffs like it established some bond between us and freed the girl, who spit in his wake after he turned and took off with Ferret-Face.

She pushed back her hair, adjusted her clothing, and used the back of a hand to brush away the tears washing her mascara-blackened cheek. "Thank you," she said, in a whisper hampered by a phlegm-filled

10

throat. "Thank you, thank you, thank you, and God bless you."

I should have let it end there and taken her home.

Instead, I took the girl's statement.

A mistake.

Big, big mistake.

Being an honest cop and being a smart cop, they're not necessarily one and the same.

By daylight I'd gone back to the bar in Echo Park, found the starlet's car and a few witnesses to confirm enough of her story to recognize she'd been telling the truth, enough to have her sprung uncharged to the custody of a baggy-eyed lawyer with a gimp left arm who had been dispatched to Rampart by MGM after I advised Maxie to call her agent and explain the situation.

Afterward, I filed a report, expecting it to lead to an investigation that would cost those two miserable excuses for law and order their jobs, their pensions and, maybe, earn them a deserved Northern California vacation at San Quentin.

It didn't go down that way.

Less than twenty-four hours after filing the paperwork, I was sitting across the battered, jacket-filled desk of an LAPD assistant chief, who was instructing me to forget what had happened as if it never had happened.

Angered at the order and fortified by a mouthful of Pep-O-Mint Life Savers, I said, "The department is already dirty enough, so it's not like I'm adding anything new, Chief, just unloading four or five hundred pounds of garbage."

"Dirty? That's how I'd classify what you're trying to do to your two brothers in blue, assholes though they might be."

"They're not my brothers, Chief. They're two horny sons of bitches who should be introduced to the justice system. *Justice.* The word ring any bells?"

"And the horse you rode in on, Blanchard. For Christ's sake, it's not like they went down on the Virgin Mary."

"Tell that to the girl."

"She was up to here in bennies." The assistant chief moved his hand horizontally to the bridge of his bulbous, blue-veined nose. "And up to her fucking gills in booze —" Paused dramatically. "— like you are three-quarters of the time, Blanchard." He eased back in his chair and laced his fingers over his stomach, pushed out an insincere smile. "Somehow that's never caused the kind of paperwork that could get you in deep waters."

"Why does that sound like a threat, Chief?"

He leaned forward with his elbows propped on the desk and made a pyramid with his fingers. "Maybe because that's the way I meant it? You try to make ka-ka for me and, so help me, Detective, I will make ka-ka for you."

I weighed the consequences through a sleepless night and came down on the side of law and order.

Every internal call I tried led to a dead end.

I turned to pals I'd made at the newspapers by shelling out inside tips that helped me stir pots that needed stirring and brought them page one bylines.

Their memories were shorter than Singer's Midgets.

More dead ends.

Not one favor in the bunch at the *Times, Herald Express* or *Daily News.*

A glimmer of revelation came from an assistant city editor at the *Examiner,* whom I had once rescued from some potential knee-breaking debts he'd run to the moon playing the ponies with one of the bad boy bookmakers operating up Topanga Canyon.

"Chris, it's your word against the Blue Wall of Silence, and that's not even good enough for fifty words on a back page across from the classifieds," he said. "You have a bone to chew, but no red meat for the likes of a news hound like me. Make it a meal and maybe it'll happen."

"Like what, Smokey?"

"Like the obvious, the actress confirming what you put into a report that I'll bet is nowhere to be found, anybody from the press comes looking. Get her talking and maybe you have a story worth a headline in 72-point type. But you won't find her, and if you do, you won't find her ready to spill. Understand what I'm telling you?"

"You're saying it's also the studio, Metro, sweeping this business under the rug."

"No rug that I can see, not here, pal. All that's on the floor here are cigarette butts and spilled coffee."

No rug.

No actress, when I went searching after her.

Not at the home address I had for her, a villa-style garden apartment complex on Beachwood, in the shadow of the HOLLY-WOODLAND sign.

Neighbors hadn't seen her for days.

14

Only a runaround at MGM, where I got a different story from everyone who took my call. She was on location; not sure where or what production, sorry. She was visiting her family; no, not in L.A., not sure where. She was in New York, in seclusion, preparing to audition for a play; no, sorry, don't have any other details.

January 1934
The New Year arrived, with it notification that I was being suspended, on charges of insubordination and chronic drunkenness.

I celebrated by getting drunk.

Woke up from the bender to a summons scheduling me for a disciplinary panel that included the assistant chief.

Thought about going on another bender.

Instead, turned in my badge and gun, beating that conniving son of a bitch to the punch —

Then went on the bender.

After sixteen years on the force, the best I could expect was a pension that would not buy more than a bag of peanuts and a cloud of cotton candy at the circus.

A call from Louis B. Mayer's office at Metro-Goldwyn-Mayer changed that —

His private secretary, Ida Koverman, inquiring in a voice as proper as a senior

15

prom corsage if Mr. Blanchard would be good enough to meet this afternoon with Mr. Mayer.

I didn't know Mayer, only *of* Mayer, that Mayer was the studio's vice president of production and possibly the most powerful man in the movie business, given he presided over the most successful movie studio, made more money than his mogul counterparts at the other studios, and played benevolent "Uncle Louie," accomplishing with his iron fist only what he couldn't achieve through crocodile tears.

I doubted there was a screen test in the offing.

About his absent starlet, maybe?

Unlikely, but curiosity is a prime addiction of the underprivileged.

Mr. Blanchard said he'd be honored.

I reached Culver City and the studio about fifteen minutes before our three o'clock appointment, parked my battered '32 V8 coupe in the lot and studied the billboard on the grass knoll before crossing to the administration building. It was advertising an upcoming movie called *The Thin Man,* starring William Powell and Myrna Loy. I'd read the book it was based on, by an old Pinkerton hand named Hammett; not bad.

The Art Deco building was situated next door to a sedate funeral home. Mayer's second-floor suite was reached through an inner office occupied by four secretaries that fed into the inner office Ida Koverman shared with her own private secretary, elegantly furnished like a set from one of the studio's drawing room comedies.

Several people were waiting for an audience — looking anxious, nervous, like they were sitting out a jury verdict — in cushioned armchairs or straight-backed chairs from the reign of one of the French King Louies, not Metro-Goldwyn-Mayer's Louie, the Russian-born son of a scrap metal peddler.

The only face I recognized belonged to Chester Morris, a regular in a lot of the MGM cops and robbers movies that were always on the lower half of a double bill with a movie starring Gable or Tracy or Shearer, or one of the other big names at the studio that boasted "More Stars Than in the Heavens." Wearing a look of practiced resignation, he managed a brief smile and a nod after he caught me studying him, but converted it to a sneer when Koverman ushered me ahead of him into the august presence of Mayer.

If the outer office was the bees' knees,

Mayer's was the whole damn hive.

I felt I was stepping into a scaled-down version of the throne room of the Czar of all the Russias. Mayer, a good fifty feet away, didn't seem out of place behind an ornately carved, curved desk etched in gold.

He rose to welcome me, stretching out his arms as if anxious to embrace a long-lost brother. "Thank you, thank you for coming, Mr. Blanchard." Each word carried its own punctuation. The tip of his smile stretched almost to his ears. He gestured for me to take the empty visitor's chair.

The other chair was occupied by a gent I'd occasionally seen at the station house, Mayer's head of publicity, Howard Strickling, the studio's "fixer."

It was whispered around the LAPD that Strickling knew everybody who mattered and where the bodies were buried — supposedly having buried a few himself — and over the years had rescued more than a few stars and others from personal or career disaster, what he'd once been overheard calling "life's little inconveniences."

No problem too small.

No secret too scandalous.

No crime too heinous.

No solution beyond his shadowy reach, or

18

so went the legend building around Strickling.

"You know Howard here, Mr. Blanchard? Howard Strickling."

"As well as I know Lamont Cranston," I said.

Strickling smiled. "The spotlight is for our stars," he said, revealing a modest stutter in an otherwise soft-spoken, well-modulated voice that carried overtones of his West Virginia roots, and let his gaze drift over Mayer and out the picture window.

He was stylishly dressed in a custom-tailored double-breasted sky blue pinstripe, matching wide tie and pocket handkerchief, and black wingtips that could double as a shaving mirror. Mid-thirties. Full head of impeccably cut black hair. A golf course tan. Handsome short of leading man looks; more a guy like Ralph Bellamy, who'd lose the girl to Gable or Tracy in the final reel.

Mayer by contrast was in his early fifties and homely as a gnome, or how I was ready to bet a gnome would look if he looked like Mayer. Short of stature. A receding hairline. Steel-rimmed glasses perched on a prominent nose. A thick body disguised by the world's most expensive haberdashery.

He smiled delightedly, and grazing his eyes on me, said, "Well, boys, I'll get right to the point." Pushed forward, shoulders hunched, and finger-locked his hands on a desk dressed in an intercom, telephones and an array of paperwork. "I hear how you did us a good deed, Mr. Blanchard; Chris, if you'll permit me to call you Chris?" I nodded, not for a minute thinking the decision was mine to make. "I believe good deeds should never go unrewarded, Chris."

"What good deed was that, Mr. Mayer?"

"A modest man, Strick. I like that about Chris. . . . Our sweet, young actress and her unfortunate encounter with two officers of the law, of course."

"I was only doing my job."

"And it cost you your job," Strickling said, barely loud enough to be heard.

Mayer said, "And it cost you your job," delivering the line with the passion of a Barrymore. "That should not have happened, Chris." He slammed a fist on the high-gloss surface of the desk. "That was not right. That was not fair. That was not justice. That was not the American way." He turned his mesmeric stare from me to Strickling, who nodded agreement. "And not just my opinion, either."

He rose and, arms locked behind his back, paced a small circle on the elaborate Persian rug behind the desk.

"Strick here has told me how you could've left our little girl without a career and my studio with her new movie coming out that could've put us in some red ink but good after what I think the Bible-thumpers and the fish eaters would be doing and saying with their rantings and ravings."

"Those thoughts never entered my mind, Mr. Mayer. Your little girl did wrong, but those two cops did worse. I didn't get dumped for helping to spring her or because I wanted to give you and her movie a happy ending. I wanted those two rotten apples out of the basket."

Strickling nodded. "Mr. Mayer knows that, Blanchard."

"I know that, Chris," Mayer said.

I said, "When they came after me, I went looking for your little girl, because no one was going to believe me without her corroboration, but she was as reachable as the moon." I turned to Strickling. "Your handiwork, Mr. Strickling?"

Strickling shrugged.

Mayer said, "My champion horses don't only win at the track, Chris." He threw a mouthful of teeth at Strickling, who pushed off the compliment.

I was beginning to feel like I was in the climax of an MGM movie, the only one who hadn't read the script. I rose and adjusted my jacket, preparing to scram out of there.

"Sit, I'm not finished yet," Mayer said, poking the air with an index finger. I sat. "A favor is a favor no matter what, and that's what you did for us and, Chris — I want you to come work for me." His head bobbed up and down so furiously that his jowls danced. "Explain it to Chris, Strick, what I have in mind for him."

Strickling jumped on his cue. "Mr. Mayer believes you would be the perfect one to undertake special problems here at the studio, as they might occur," he said in a noncommittal tone.

"Isn't that what you do, Mr. Strickling?"

Mayer answered for him. "Strick does what he has to do, a lot better than anyone knows," he said, "only Strick got his hands full watching out for me with the stars and the *shleppers* who don't know enough to stay out of trouble. I got other things need watching out and worrying about, and I need them handled by somebody who is honest and who I can trust."

"And you think that's me."

"I know that's you, Chris. I had Strick ask around before I sent for you. He said you had a good reputation, but I wanted to be absolutely certain."

Strickling said, "You would be surprised about some of the people who vouched for you, Blanchard."

"For instance. Care to name names, Mr. Strickling?"

"In time, maybe."

"Mr. Mayer, I don't hide evidence and I don't pay off cops to look the other way, if that's what anyone is thinking. I don't do rhumbas in waltz time."

Anger flashed across Strickling's face, vanished as quickly. "And I don't do booze for water," he said, his words hissing like a steam cleaner.

Mayer said, "Boys, enough!" He pinned me with his stare again. "Chris, I wanted to, I could've put in a call to the highest reaches, the highest reaches, and you would have been back on the police force in no time at all." He snapped his finger. "Like so. And you might even have been promoted. Louie Mayer knows when to give out favors and when to get them, but I wanted you here, Chris, all favors aside. It's not for you, just say so, and I'll say *Thank you for your time in coming on over here,* shake your hand and walk you to the door. Why? Because then you'll be a foolish man in my estimate and I got offices full up already with foolish men. Besides, I don't ever beg, you understand?"

He seemed on the verge of tears, stroked at his eyes, clutched at his chest like he was struggling for breath —

As good an actor as I'd heard.

But there was truth in what he'd told me and, besides —

My only other option was unemployment.

And I did love the movies.

They were my passion.

"What's it pay?" I said.

"You were a hundred percent correct, Strick. Chris is not a foolish man, but he is a practical man," Mayer said, cackling. He made a performance of looking to Heaven for a number. The one he chose was about five times what I had pulled down every month as a Detective One.

"That's every week, not every month," Strickling said, as if he'd read my mind. "It pays a lot of alimony."

"You really do your homework well, Mr. Strickling."

"One can't ever be too thorough."

"The job might turn out to be interesting," I said. "I could try it for a while."

"Welcome to our family," Mayer said, offering a handshake.

Four years going on five, I was still at MGM.

CHAPTER 2

Wednesday, November 9, 1938

Not quite midnight.

I couldn't sleep.

I stared out my bedroom window cursing the dry, hot winds battering the panes, kicking up dust that obscured my sixth floor view of the nondescript light show that was the downtown Los Angeles skyline. I looked across the room at the decanter of rum on the dresser, lovingly; decided it was a lousy way to cure insomnia, same as it had never helped me any other way. I tapped a Lucky from the pack on the night table and lit up, picked a shard off my tongue and considered the glowing tip with distaste, wondering why I still smoked; wondering why I couldn't shake off what happened earlier today in Superior Court.

Damn it.

There wasn't any doubt the guy working in the costume department stole Metro-

Goldwyn-Mayer cross-eyed, not in my mind or the jury's unanimous vote that would be sending him behind bars for two to ten on grand theft. He'd overreached attempting to peddle exotic furs from MGM movies like *Saratoga, Libeled Lady* and *Mannequin* to Che Castillo's Pawn Emporium at Main and Third. Che, who owed me from the years I was a cop and helped him duck some misdemeanors, recognized the studio's inventory tags and got on the horn to me.

That wasn't it.

It was his wife, of course, the way she looked at me while I testified and later, sitting outside the courtroom during the five minutes it took the jury to reach a verdict, how she stood over me accusingly, like I was the thief, not her husband, saying, "I got cancer eating me up is why he did it, money for the doctors, money for the medicine, so now that's no more and soon me neither, so tell me, Mr. Blanchard — what's to become of our four children with also their papa gone from them. Who looks out for them now? Do you?"

In that minute, I hated myself as much as she hated me, this fragile woman with dark circles and dehydration lines around her helpless brown eyes, wasting away inside a cheap summer dress.

I had no answer for her.

Not then.

Not now.

Tomorrow?

Tomorrow, maybe —

After I explained the circumstances to Strickling.

It might be one of "life's little inconveniences" too small to warrant his personal attention, but maybe he'd agree to make a few calls. With Strickling you never knew. No matter how close anyone ever got to him, it never felt close enough to be real. Strick was his own best friend and everybody else a means to an end, except for Mayer, to whom he was totally devoted —

Or so it appeared.

Strick.

Tomorrow.

I popped a hopeful smile, stubbed out the Lucky in an ashtray overflowing with butts and considered crawling back to bed and giving shut-eye another chance. The stale white sheets weren't inviting.

I thought, okay, maybe a hot bath.

Halfway to the bathroom I heard the doorbell sound.

Again.

Then a tentative tapping on the door that increased in volume and duration.

Cursing Walter the night doorman for letting someone upstairs unannounced, I threw on my robe, crossed into the living room and yanked open the door without first checking the peephole, ready to rain curses on my unexpected midnight caller, at the same time welcoming any distraction that might help me unburden my mind, however temporarily, of that hapless woman and her four kids.

Marie MacDaniels, her gorgeous face red, puffy and tearstained, was using the doorjamb to prop herself up. Mascara ran down her classic high cheeks. Her lip gloss looked chewed through. Her girl-next-door body telegraphed its usual hint of promise inside a low-cut, coal black dinner gown. A strand of matched black pearls dressed her swan's neck. A posh fox stole trailed behind her on the tired carpeting of the apartment hallway.

She was barefoot and she was drunk.

"I killed him," she said in a tremolo that rose to a wail. "I killed him, Chris."

I pulled her inside before any of my cat-eared neighbors woke up and came to investigate; closed the door and threw the chain lock.

"I did it, Chris, I shot him," Marie said. "He's dead. Dead with no face. Face all gone. And the blood, the blood — "

Her voice burbled into incoherence and she exploded into tears, holding onto me like a life preserver. I half-walked, half-carried her into the kitchen and settled her down on the one chair with arms. Anything less, I had visions of her tilting onto the linoleum.

"Hold on while I brew us some coffee," I said, grabbing after the percolator.

She strapped herself into her arms. "What do I do, Chris? I never killed anybody before."

"And now?"

"Day. I killed Day. Shot him. He was going to hit me and he was saying all these terrible things about me, the louse. Terrible things that just were not true. Not true. Not true."

Day Covington.

Marie had married him a year and a half ago.

He was a poor man's Ronald Colman, who couldn't act his way out of the cheapo pictures he made for Monogram and Republic, seven-day wonders that usually had reviewers wondering how he managed to keep working.

Marie had been having better luck with her career since landing in Los Angeles from Chicago. She was twenty-four, pretty in a wholesome way that appealed to Middle America. Her perky, girlish charms, garnished by a dusting of freckles across a milky complexion, disguised a sophisticated, sexually hungry woman whose tastes often ran to the exotic.

Trained in classical drama, Marie fared better with casting couches than casting calls, was "discovered" by an MGM talent scout, and now was halfway through a basic seven-year contract co-starring opposite Baxter Leeds in the *Battling G-Men* series of popular programmers, playing his bright-eyed girlfriend, a Watson to Leeds's two-fisted Holmes.

She and I had hooked up two years ago, four years after my wife stormed out on me suddenly and without an explanation. It was a brief, torrid affair, Marie taking pity on a guy who needed more than a dog for a friend.

After a while, she recognized I was starting to confuse lust with love.

She let me down gently and moved on to another lover or two, or three, or more, before she fell hard, quick and for real for Day Covington.

We'd remained friends, fallen into an easy camaraderie, me often accompanying her, at her request, whenever Marie was sent off on personal appearances, using the time to trade studio rumors and gossip, catch up on each other's latest secrets, me sometimes wondering to myself what would happen if I ignited the old torch and tried again, but —

This killing business was a new wrinkle in an old suit.

"Tell me about it," I said, calling over my shoulder.

"About what, baby?" she said, her voice cutting through her alcoholic haze.

"About killing Day."

"I did, yes . . . killed him. He attacked me, baby. Came after me, so I took out my gun — this gun."

Her hand came out of her clutch purse holding a small, nickel-plated, engraved automatic. I charged across the kitchen and twisted the weapon from her hand. It was a .25-caliber Vest Pocket Colt, sneered at as a lady's gun, but more than capable of killing a man.

"Just making sure there isn't another accident," I said.

I picked up a kitchen towel and held the gun in it.

Dropped the magazine, saw two rounds were gone.

Pulled back the slide and ejected the bullet in the chamber.

At least one bullet fired.

I sniffed the barrel.

Fired recently.

I wrapped the pistol in a towel and stashed it on an upper shelf.

"How long ago did you shoot Day?" I said, keeping my tone conversational and calm, as I'd done before in a thousand interrogation rooms.

"Tonight. We were supposed to go out to dinner, but we started arguing about his gambling, that we never seem to have money. We'd both had a couple of cocktails, and he said . . . he said things about me and I said some things back. He came at me. I took the gun from my purse, closed my eyes and pulled the trigger. . . . I didn't see him or hear him fall or anything. I turned and ran out the door without looking back."

"What time tonight?"

"Seven . . . no. Seven-thirty. We were supposed to be at the Biltmore at eight, but . . ." More tears. Broken off as swiftly as they'd started. "Can I have a drink, baby?" Her voice sobering.

"Not a good idea. Here. Coffee's on. Drink it black." She grimaced, but obeyed. "What happened between then and now,

Marie?"

"I went ahead to the Biltmore and I got stinko. Polluted. Four sheets to the wind. Then, when I got back home, I saw Day was laying there, his face all blood, nothing but blood. All over the carpet, and — "

"Stop, Marie. Stop. Now!" My command startled her to silence. She took a thick swallow from her coffee cup. I said, "Who were you meeting for dinner?"

"Eve Whitney. She's —"

"Baxter Leeds's secretary in his *Battling G-Men* movies."

She wagged her head. "Our *Battling G-Men* movies, Baxter's and mine."

"Of course."

"And Eve's been my very good friend for, oh, for ever and ever. She was with some boy she just met, and she's trying to decide if she wants to fall in love with him."

"So you went to the Biltmore and had dinner with Eve and this boy. He have a name?"

"Whatever. I don't remember. I mostly drank. And a couple of bars after the Biltmore. I was kind of a wet blanket, so I left them and came home to . . ." Her hand shook, splattering coffee on her lap. She didn't seem to notice. "I loved him, Chris. I loved Day."

34

"Finish your coffee," I said, excused myself and headed for the bedroom closet.

I found a tie and knotted it, pulled on a sports jacket and hat, then crossed over to the bedside table and retrieved the rubber-gripped .38 Colt Detective Special I kept there, its trigger guard cut away, hammer spur and rifle front sight bobbed, and hitched up my shoulder holster.

Returning to the kitchen, I said, "Pull yourself together, kitten, and let's us take a ride. We'll use your car. I'll drive."

The wind was blowing hard, strong enough to drown out the hum of the engine, and occasionally rocked her flashy Graham-Paige as we traveled east from my place at the Ravenswood Apartments on Rossmore to Cahuenga, then north about a mile to the Covingtons' relatively new Craftsman bungalow that sat close to the street.

The porch light was on.

Lights were on behind the drawn window curtains.

I drove past the bungalow and around the block, scouting for signs of police.

None.

The neighbors' homes were dark, the poorly lit street deserted.

I pulled in to the curb, cut the motor.

Marie was slumped against the passenger door, staring into space.

I told her, "Come on."

"I can't go back in there, baby. Please don't make me."

"All right, but stay put. Don't do anything to draw attention." I pocketed the ignition keys as a precaution and slipped out into a wind blowing shrubbery like a man whipping a reluctant horse. On the front porch, I wrapped my handkerchief around my hand before testing the door. It was unlocked. I inched it open and stepped inside.

The living room in what could have been any young married couple's first home was full of expensive-looking furniture. The table surfaces and the fireplace mantle were covered in ornate, sterling silver–framed photographs, most of Day Covington in various roles; the rest, candid and posed photos of Day or Marie with other movie stars of higher rank, most appropriately inscribed.

A man's body was sprawled halfway across the room, face down.

Spilled blood had pooled and was turning the beige rug black.

I did a quick tour through the rest of the house.

Every room was tidy; nothing disturbed.

The rear door off the kitchen service porch was locked.

Back in the living room, I knelt beside the body and turned it over. One arm flopped limply, short of the blood pool. I eased it away and touched the stain with a fingernail; confirmed it was still damp.

Day Covington was wearing an open-necked shirt, ascot, slacks, and half-boots, all expensive-looking — precisely what a young actor would choose for a casual night out on the town.

At thirty-two, he was eight years older than Marie.

Handsome.

Not much else to him.

I'd run a make on Day after Marie found me at lunch in the MGM commissary and whispered the news in my ear, how they had fallen madly, passionately in love and were going to get married.

He was from upstate New York.

From upper-middle-class money.

Had gambled away his modest inheritance by the time he met Marie Willens, his future bride.

He'd had some minor roles in summer stock and a few Broadway walk-ons and bit parts, including three lines in the 1929 disaster, *Young Love,* whose director,

George Cukor, brought him to Hollywood for a screen test in the early '30s, after Cukor himself moved west and scored big time as a movie director. The test didn't go well, no contract was offered, and Cukor, probably motivated by guilt, called around to friends, asking that they cast Day; nothing fancy, maybe just enough to cleanse Cukor's conscience.

Whatever his shortcomings as an actor, he had a decided talent for secretiveness, apart from the gambling and a proclivity for partying and wholesale whoring, pastimes regarded as acceptable staples of the business. Sharing with Marie the few minor stains I found on his personal scorecard would likely be hooted away by her as the jealous rant of an ex-boyfriend.

I studied Day's face.

He'd been a handsome man, a bit weak in the chin, but now there was nothing but a mask of gore. The mortician would have his work cut out for him if Marie was foolish enough to ask for an open-casket funeral service.

I leaned in closer to the body and counted the neat bullet holes.

Six.

I exercised caution rummaging in his pockets, found a wad of crisp new twenties among the more worn notes. Some coins. Keys on a fob with a small metal ship labeled NEPTUNE. A wallet containing his driver's license, some business cards, some torn-off ticket stubs printed SHUTTLE, and three checks, each for twenty-five dollars from:

THE PHOTO SALON OF OTTO ROTHMAN
Photographer to the Stars

Another check in an inner compartment was for five hundred dollars.

The name on the signature line drew a silent whistle from me —

George Cukor.

I pocketed all the checks and the shuttle boat stubs, restored the wallet to Day's hip pocket, and repositioned his body as I'd found it.

I walked the room before leaving, stopping at a classic Victorian picture of a stag at bay. The glass was starred, a hole in one of the wolves' heads, and, in the wall behind the picture, a neat .25-caliber bullet hole.

Back at the Graham-Paige, Marie was staring dully at the porch light as I slipped behind the wheel.

"You found him?" she said.

"Yes."

"Dead."

"Yes, but you didn't kill him, kitten. You shot a wolf."

"I don't understand."

"Your shot punched a hole in that deer picture you have hanging on the wall. Someone waltzed in and shot Day after you took off for the Biltmore. You came back drunk as a hoot owl, found him and understandably thought the worst."

"You're saying that only to keep from calling the cops on me, that's it, right?"

"That would make me an accessory after the fact, and that stupid I'm not. . . . You think you can drive?"

"I've never been *that* drunk. Why?"

"A really good friend, someone who'll stand by you no matter what?"

"Yes, there's —"

I aimed a palm at her.

"Don't tell me anything," I said. I opened the door a crack, so the interior light clicked on. Pulled a card from my jacket pocket, wrote down a number and handed it to her. "I want you to drive to your friend. Have your friend drive and park the car seven or eight blocks away and leave it there. You stay there the night and tomorrow you don't go anywhere. Nowhere. Call me on the number I just wrote down at three in the afternoon; no sooner, no later. It goes straight to a phone in my office, not through the switchboard. You'll do this for me?"

Marie thought about it, sucked the air from the car. "Okay. For you." She crossed her arms over her chest. "What about you? How will you get home?"

"I've got business to take care of first. After that, I'm sure there'll be lots of people wanting to give me a ride, one place or another." I inserted the ignition key in the slot and angled myself out of the car.

Marie slid across and looked at me with a scared expression, her face chalkboard white. She turned the key, pressed the ignition and put the car in gear. Let the clutch out with a jerk and took off.

I waited until she turned the corner and was out of sight before starting back for the bungalow, had reached the porch steps when I heard a car pulling up and its motor quit, turned to see Howard Strickling stepping out of the long, black Packard Twelve sedan.

He surveyed the street in both directions before joining me, wondering in the soft, emotionless voice he'd mastered as a means of commanding full attention, "What are you doing here, Chris?"

I answered Strick's somber expression in kind and, consumed more with concern for Marie's future than mine, risked an unwelcome show of insubordination suggesting, "You go first, Strick."

He spent a moment or two thinking about it.

"Certainly, why not," he said, flicking a patently false smile.

CHAPTER 3

His stutter less pronounced than usual, Strick said, "Somebody phoned, gave me this address, told me there had been a murder involving one of our contract players. That right?"

"Day Covington. Shot at close range with a small-caliber pistol."

"Dead?"

"Deader'n Frank Shaw's career in politics."

"Our former mayor is still a good friend of ours, as is his successor, Mr. Bowron."

"You've never lacked for friends in high places, Strick."

"The low places, too. . . . Our Marie MacDaniels' husband, so it was she who shot him, that right?" He answered his own question with a nod and manufactured a grin that seemed to indicate he enjoyed the probability.

I wasn't surprised, remembering what

Marie confided in me once upon an affair, how Strickling had suggested her career might advance more rapidly if she joined him for a weekend at Lake Arrowhead.

She had declined his come-on, and he never raised the subject again, but it was after that she didn't get the plump roles she was rumored for in big-budget movies opposite Gable, Tracy, Taylor, and Powell, roles that could have helped elevate her to major stardom.

Rejection never sat well with Strick.

Revenge was more to his taste, like the sight of blood to a bullfighter.

Tipped off to the truth by Mickey Rooney during a lunchtime romp in the Mick's dressing room, Marie invaded Strick's office, cried crocodile tears through an apology, lobbied for forgiveness and the opportunity to make amends — right then and there, if he chose — and displayed her sincerity by spreading open the regal fur coat she'd borrowed from wardrobe.

"I was naked as a jaybird," she told me, "ready to give him my all, but whatever hard-on he had for me, it wasn't in his pants. Strickling looked at me like I wasn't even there, got up from his desk and left without saying a word. Last I saw of him, ever since. The influence he has with all of

44

those big shots, from Louis B. Mayer on down, I hate to think what'll happen when my contract's up for renewal."

"Strick treats loyalty like the eleventh commandment, so he'll do what's best for his personal god, Mayer, and for MGM," I said.

"You've been getting pretty tight with him, baby. Maybe you could put in a good word for me?"

I told her I would, but never did, disinclined to trade my own good standing with Strick for a place on his shit list. The guilt nagged at me, sure; still does. But survival is a priority in this town, and I needed his good will and patronage. Strick knew I'd been close to Marie, probably too close, and that was fine with him, as long as I routinely proved I was closer to him.

I wasn't immediately sure what had adjusted my attitude here and now.

Maybe it was what I sensed was Strick's enjoyment at the concept of Marie facing a homicide rap, where he had been all business when called upon in the past to clean up messes involving bigger Metro names than Marie MacDaniels.

Like the so-called suicide of producer Paul Bern, whose movies included *Grand Hotel* and *Anna Christie,* in '32, after Bern's marriage to Jean Harlow. Like the cover-up he'd choreographed after Harlow's own death in '37, supposedly from uremic poisoning. Like those nasty deaths at Nazimova's Garden of Allah on the Sunset Strip that stood to rupture the careers of Johnny Weissmuller and Mitzi Miles, Gable and Loretta Young, if Strick hadn't swept them under the table; me taking care of some of the delicate details.

"Marie believes she shot and killed Day, but it's not necessarily the case," I said. "There are complications."

"Complications?" It wasn't what Strick expected to hear and it showed in the way he pulled in his manicured eyebrows, creating an expression that combined curiosity with concern. "Spell them out, Chris. I need to know if Metro is open to problems that require delicate handling."

"Besides the usual delicate handling?"

"If by that you mean looking after the best interests of your girlfriend —"

"Ex-girlfriend."

"Your ex-girlfriend — yes, of course," Strick said. "She's one of ours, after all, so maybe these are *good* complications you're about to share with me?"

Before I could answer, a police cruiser skidded around the corner, its red spotlight glaring, siren howling, and braked to a stop behind Strickling's Packard.

I knew the two plainclothes detectives who jumped out wearing cheap dark suits that almost matched and tan hats that looked as if they'd been sat on: Eddie Vassily and Elmer Troy.

During my cop days they'd been motor-cycle cops in the traffic division, famous for having smashed up a handful of Harley-Davidson hogs between them. How they had managed to score detective status was a question that defied a rational answer, but was a major contributor to locker room humor.

Vassily was an overweight six-footer in his thirties with droopy eyelids, a banana nose and flap ears — the better looking of the pair.

Troy, Vassily's age but a few inches shorter, was a redhead with keyboard teeth, who looked like he should be toting a cheerleader's megaphone, not an LAPD badge, or the service pistol he had out and was aiming at us.

"Both of you! Don't move!" Troy shouted, loud enough to get the neighborhood dogs barking, his voice like chalk screeches on a blackboard.

I said, "Put the gun away, Elmer. We're on

your side." He looked puzzled, but held his aim. "It's Chris Blanchard, Elmer. I'm here with Howard Strickling, who runs the publicity department at Metro-Goldwyn-Mayer."

Strickling threw them a wave. "Hi, fellas," he said, as if he'd just added two new best friends.

"Metro-Goldwyn-Mayer, huh?" Troy ran his tongue around his lips and slipped the pistol back into his shoulder holster.

"The Fixer himself," Vassily said, filled with awe, like he had been introduced to royalty. "You got some good reason to be out here this hour of morning with Blanchard, Mr. Strickling?"

"A phone call saying there was trouble here at the home of one of our brightest and most talented stars, Marie MacDaniels," Strickling said, taking command.

Troy said, "Yeah, the *Battling G-Men* picture shows; some looker, that one."

Vassily gave Troy a *Shut up* slap on the shoulder. "Trouble, you say? What kind of trouble, exactly, sir?"

"A shooting, Detective. We were weighing whether to try entering the premises when you arrived, concerned for Miss MacDaniels' safety and well-being. Isn't

48

that so, Chris?"

"So, Mr. Strickling, and it's possible the gunman might still be in there," I said.

At once, Troy had his gun out again.

Vassily yanked his two-inch .38 from a hip holster. "Stand back out of the way," he said, and jerking his head at Troy: "C'mon, Elmer."

They went up the sides of the walk and flattened themselves on either side of the unlocked porch door.

Vassily booted it open.

The door clattered against the inside wall.

Something fell over and smashed.

The detectives waited out possible shots from a gunman before Vassily ducked inside, his automatic waving back and forth like a drunk's finger, Troy at his back like they were Siamese twins.

Troy materialized back in the doorway within a minute or two, announcing, "The place is clear, except we have ourselves a *corpus,* dead as a dodo bird, but it ain't the *G-Men* dish. Eddie's calling it in now, so you'll need to stay until we get your statements."

"Please let Captain Travis know I'm here," Strickling said. The idea of advising the head of LAPD's homicide division appeared to unhinge Troy. Strickling saw it, too. He said, "I guarantee you, Officer, it will bring you and your partner gold stars in your jackets."

"From Ray Travis or from you?" I said, dropping my voice to a whisper.

"It's certainly chilly this time of morning," Strickling said, turning up the collar of his elegantly styled cashmere overcoat, a fit as perfect as his "Fixer" nickname.

He was at it now, of course.

Fixing.

But exactly what he was fixing I couldn't be certain.

About twenty minutes crept by before three cars screeched up to the MacDaniels residence: a black and white, an unmarked black four-door Ford and a new silver La-Salle four-door.

Travis stepped out of the LaSalle, made a beeline for Strickling and shared a hug and a double-handed shake. For me it was a perfunctory nod and a "Blanchard," said with all the warmth of a Siberian blizzard.

Travis, a lean, hard man in his late fifties who seldom smiled, was one of the few high-ranking survivors of last year's City Hall scandal that brought down Mayor Shaw and Police Chief James Edgar "Two Gun" Davis, who had promoted and protected graft, payoffs and cops on the take.

He had a reputation for being utterly incorruptible and lately the reform element was talking him up for chief, but I saw him in another light. He might be honest, sure, but he also had a reputation inside the Blue Wall for not being particular how he got suspects to cooperate.

Before resigning from the force, I'd had a few encounters with the cop who some called "Rubber Hose Ray," none entirely unpleasant; a couple more since coming aboard at MGM. There was something about him I disliked, not sure what, any more than I knew why he seemed to hold me in contempt, but Strickling liked him and so did Mayer and a lot of Metro big shots in Mayer's "college of cardinals," especially MGM vice president Eddie Mannix, Strick's frequent partner-in-cover-ups.

Travis had no problem cooperating with the studio where it didn't involve any major violation of the law, Strick mentioned matter-of-factly the time we were dealing with a bushel of traffic tickets amassed by Joanie Crawford, *major* coming across to me as the operative word.

The tickets disappeared and shortly afterward Travis earned a few dollars doing a walk-on in one of Joanie's movies, *The Bride*

Wore Red, something I classified to myself as a minor payoff for a minor violation. It wasn't Ray Travis's first screen bit and, judging by his walk-on here, it wouldn't be his last.

Strickling said, "Thanks for coming, Ray. It always works better when someone of authority is on the scene."

"I heard that for the first time from King Vidor, when he was directing *The Texas Rangers* with Fred MacMurray and Jack Oakie over at Paramount."

"Your scene with Lloyd Nolan was something. Almost a shame you chose to be a policeman instead of an actor."

Travis digested the compliment with a smile and got down to business. "So, what say we head inside and see what's what?" he said. "Stay behind me, boys, but be sure not to touch anything."

We tracked forward, followed by the four plainclothesmen who'd emerged from the unmarked car carrying black cases, adding to the jumble of remarks from residents who had been awakened and drawn from their homes in robes, wrappers and hurriedly tugged-on clothes by the police sirens and general commotion.

Troy and Vassily were in the living room

prodding and prying around the body when we entered.

Vassily took hold of Day Covington's arm and rolled him onto his back, exposing the ruins of Day's face.

"Oh my Lord in Heaven," Strickling said softly and pushed his way back out of the room.

Troy looked up and spotted Travis, and leaped to his feet issuing a half-salute. He said, "We got here as soon as you called, Cap'n. The scene was deserted, except for these gentlemen."

"And him, Cap'n," Vassily said, pointing at the corpse.

Travis said, "Turn him back over, the way you found him, Vassily. You should know by now you don't mess with a crime scene until our photographers are done."

Vassily apologized and obeyed the command.

"Whose footprints are those?" Travis said, pointing at imprints in the damp stain on the rug.

Troy said, "Afraid that was me, Cap'n." Averting Travis's deadly stare, he stepped over to the coffee table, grabbed an antimacassar, and wiped away the blood stains on his shoes.

Travis said, "The victim have a name?"

"The name that comes with the address," I said. "Covington. Day Covington."

"And Marie MacDaniels, then. The wife. Where's she at?"

"Not here."

"Thanks, Blanchard, but I'm not due for another checkup on my 20/20s until next year." He called to Strickling, "Strick, Marie MacDaniels. One of your people, right?"

Strickling stepped back into the room, making a show of concern while avoiding a look at the corpse. "She is, Captain Travis. One of our highly regarded contract players, a bright future certainly ahead for her if this tragic misfortune doesn't interfere."

Department Speed Graphics were popping flashbulbs, casting temporary patterns of traveling light and darkness over the crime scene. Strickling noticed one aiming in his direction, waved it off and turned his back to the lens.

Travis said, "You know we always have to figure the spouse as a prime suspect in situations like this one here, Strick. Money problems. Career conflicts. From what I know of him, Covington was quite the swordsman about town, so add jealousy and revenge to the list."

"No apologies necessary, Captain. Whatever direction this turns, be assured you have the complete cooperation of Metro-Goldwyn-Mayer, and mine, of course. Do your job professionally and thoroughly is all we ask or expect, no matter what, isn't that right, Chris?"

"As rain."

"Would you know to tell Captain Travis where Miss MacDaniels is at present?"

"Would if I could, Strick, but I'm here because she called me, not the other way around. I have no idea."

Travis said, "What's she drive? I'll have an APB put out on her."

I shrugged and flipped my palms skyward, like I'd failed trying to track a distant memory.

Strickling was more helpful. "It's a Graham-Paige, Captain Travis."

Travis lifted a shaggy eyebrow. "One or both of them doing that good or is Mr. Mayer paying his contract players better nowadays?"

"Ego has its own reality, Captain. I lost count years ago of how many actors drive cars beyond their means. . . . You mind if I tell the press boys when they call that Marie is grief-stricken over the senseless murder of her husband and cooperating fully with you and your men?"

"And tell 'em to spell my name correctly,

especially when you're talking to that Parsons dame down at the *Examiner*." Travis made it sound like a joke and got a laugh out of Strickling, but his face told a different story. He got off seeing his name and puss in print. Turning to me, he said, "Blanchard, anything I should know about what Miss MacDaniels, Mrs. Covington, said had gone down here when she called you? You once were a real cop, remember?"

"Nothing," I said, at the same time remembering things about having been a real cop that I'd like to forget.

CHAPTER 4

Thursday, November 10, 1938

"Chris, come in and sit," Louis B. Mayer called from behind his desk, his arms embracing a three-foot width of air, "but whatever you got to tell me is so urgent, Strick here, he's already told me." Mayer's head nodded vigorously. "This Coverdale business, that right?"

Strickling corrected him: "Covington, L.B." He was standing to Mayer's left, a half shadow in the recessed lighting of the boss lion's den. "Day Covington."

"Day, what kind of name is Day?" Mayer said, ignoring the correction. "If he was one of our family, I'd have told you to figure out a truthful name that looks good up on a screen, that people remember and can be comfortable with, like . . . like . . ." He dismissed the subject with a flick of his hand. "Dead is dead, so the only place the name matters is on a tombstone." He seemed to weigh his own mortality for a few moments. "Chris, you see in the newspapers how big a story it is already, this murder business?"

He pointed at the final street editions of the *Times* and the *Examiner* and the early editions of the afternoon *Herald* and *Daily News* spread out on the desk and picked up the *Times.*

"Big," Mayer said. "Big, big, big. All of them, and on page one, but not as big as what's happening overseas in Europe, that damned Hitler. Getting bigger and bigger since that damned Hitler, damn him, marched into Czechoslovakia, and now this *Kristallnacht* business. Mark my words, Chris, it will cost us the European market before it's over." He'd made a business observation, but I thought I saw something more personal moving across his misting eyes. "Strick has done a fine job of not getting us so involved, this Coverdale business, and I don't want it getting so big it hurts us." He put down the newspaper. "That so, Strick?"

Strickling turned back from the window, gave me a half-smile and a nod.

I knew what the papers were saying. Before heading for the studio I had checked them over my usual morning black coffee and sinkers at the Hollywood Ranch Market, up Vine Street from my place at the Ravenswood.

I also knew what they weren't saying.

They weren't saying Day Covington's wife, Metro-Goldwyn-Mayer actress Marie MacDaniels, was the principal murder suspect.

She was mentioned, of course, and the *Examiner* had spotted a glamour shot of her on the page twelve story jump.

The stories reminded readers she co-starred with Baxter Leeds in the *Battling G-Men* series and quoted LAPD Homicide Bureau Captain Ray Travis saying in what was described as a careful, but emphatic voice: "We would like to talk to Miss MacDaniels about her husband and this unfortunate occurrence, but she is by no means a suspect at this time. We understand she is out of town, visiting relatives, and hope to hear from her as quickly as she learns of the tragedy."

I recognized Strickling's fine hand, the "Fixer" collecting on another favor, and I asked him about it.

He shrugged. "You were there. You heard. Travis understood at once there was no earthly reason to brand the poor girl before he had a chance to talk to her."

"I also remember you going along with the idea she was the most probable suspect. You have a change of heart since last night?"

"No change, Chris, any more than I believed you when you said you don't know where our girl is. I don't particularly care for Miss MacDaniels and I have a feeling in my gut that she's guilty as sin, but my feeling doesn't matter a twitch when it comes to my job. Travis knew without having to be told it was better to leave the book open until Mr. Mayer could hear all about it and decide what belongs on the page."

"And Travis on the silver screen again, the likelihood of another walk-on for him in another movie here?"

"As it so happens, Woody Van Dyke's newest. Casting will be calling Travis later today. Woody's directed him before, so he knows how to handle him."

Mayer said, "And, meanwhile, we got us a nice plug on *Battling G-Men* that don't hurt us any. Later, turns out she did the murder, we'll have one of our fine young contract players groomed to take over the role opposite Baxter Leeds. You were suggesting who, Strick? The redhead, that Ball girl? Not that Laraine, who's tied up with Dr. Kildare, or the English girl in the trees with Tarzan, that Maureen, who I got bigger thoughts for."

Before Strickling could answer him, I said as emphatically as a dog who's treed a squirrel, "Mr. Mayer, Marie MacDaniels didn't kill her husband."

Strickling snorted. "What else do you have to sell, Chris? The Brooklyn Bridge?"

I ignored him. "Mr. Mayer, no matter how bad you might hear it looks, I'm certain about it. Marie did not kill Day Covington."

Strickling said, his voice coiled like a cobra: "The fact that the two of you, you and Marie, used to play it like Nelson and Jeanette, could that be clouding your opinion?"

"No more than the fact Marie never let you step up to the plate."

Strickling glowered. His mouth opened, but no words came out for seconds that played like eternity. Finally: "More snake oil, L.B."

Mayer motioned him quiet. He gave me a curious sideways glance, removed his glasses and burnished the lenses with his Countess Mara silk pocket handkerchief. I took his silence as an invitation to continue.

I had intended to tell Mayer about Marie's admission she'd fired a single shot at Day and that the six slugs in his body couldn't have come from her .25 Colt, but —

Not now.

Something about Strickling's reaction — I wasn't certain what — changed my mind.

Mayer said, "So, Chris, explain yourself. I'm waiting." His voice and expression mildly curious, what I knew from experience was his calm before the storm.

I lied. "She told me."

Strickling hooted.

"This isn't *The Thin Man,*" he said derisively.

Mayer squinted at me, replaced his glasses and raised his chins; gestured me to say more.

The outer office door burst open before I could, and a voice boomed dramatically, "L.B.! Sorry I'm late for our appointment!"

It was Mayer's son-in-law, David O. Selznick.

Mayer closed his eyes and scowled. "David, we don't have an appointment."

"So, thank God, then I'm not late. I would rather die than keep you waiting, L.B."

The gruff, burly, towering hit-producer at RKO, MGM and for the past two years down the boulevard at Selznick International Studios was never intimidated by his father-in-law. He had fled Metro fed up with the wags who suggested he owed his position to his wife, Irene, not his ability to crank out hits like *Viva, Villa!*, *Manhattan Melodrama*, *David Copperfield* and *Anna Karenina*. He'd since answered them with money-makers like *The Garden of Allah*, *The Prisoner of Zenda*, *A Star is Born* and *Nothing Sacred*.

Selznick's flair for high-stakes gambling and the good life — along with the little white pills that kept him high in constant wing-flapping motion — had recently brought him back to papa-in-law, trading distribution rights on his much-anticipated *Gone with the Wind* for much-needed financing and Gable as his Rhett Butler.

"Something exciting to show you," Selznick said, charging up to Mayer's desk with a nod for Strickling, bare acknowledgment for me. He settled to Mayer's left and called, "All right, Nancy, dear. It's curtain time for Mr. Mayer."

The young woman posed in the doorway, Ida Koverman's hand on her shoulder, hesitated. She was in her early to mid-twenties and clearly unused to being a commoner this close to the throne.

"C'mon, c'mon, cookie," Selznick said, his smile generous and his hand beckoning like Sousa working a marching band. "Mr.

Mayer won't bite. Anyway, not right now."
He winked.

"Davey, you know I don't appreciate that kind of talk," Mayer said, reining in the fury I spotted in his eyes before advising the woman, "It's all right, you. Enter. It's okay, Ida. She's most cordially welcome."

Ida retreated two steps, allowing the woman to move tentatively into Mayer's lair, and closed the door.

"L.B., Howard, say hello to Nancy Warren," Selznick said, ignoring me.

Mayer nodded to her nervous smile.

Strickling smiled politely.

I half-rose from my visitor's chair and said, "Blanchard, Chris Blanchard. I work here."

"He helps me out," Mayer said. "So, what's going on here, what's this all about, Davey? I don't have the world for you right now."

Nancy Warren sashayed forward with a fashion model's grace, a figure to match; a slender five-eight or five-nine in three-inch heels, in a cotton dress the color of maple syrup that stopped about eight inches above her trim ankles. Cloth-covered buttons down the front curved over her breasts and quit under a wide, dark brown belt emphasizing her slender waist. Contrary to the

64

short-cropped mode of the day, she wore her strawberry tresses long and loose past her shoulders. Her vivid, iridescent green eyes were her best feature on a high-cheekboned face barely touched by makeup, adding to a kind of quiet beauty that could easily stand up against the painted faces on the lot.

"Nancy, come around here by me," Selznick said. "Let Mr. Mayer see what we've brought him."

Nancy moved to the desk, tilting her body slightly to inch by Strickling — who did not seem to mind the brushed contact — and passed the folder to Selznick.

Selznick swept aside the newspapers, settled the folder on the desk and flipped it open, revealing an inch-thick sheaf of brown foolscap, only now saying, "Is it okay to use your desk, L.B.?"

"Just so you don't use my private toilet," Mayer said, shading the rebuke with a flash of smile as he looked at the first page.

"I promise," Selznick said, taking an oath with his right hand. "You've already taken enough shit from me on *Gone with the Wind.* but I wanted you to share this new excitement from this fresh, young and astoundingly talented girl, an artist of the first rank who has brought to our production — "

"Davey, Davey, you are beginning to sound like one of your damned, page-after-page, go-on-forever memos that I can't get anybody to read anymore, not even on a bet. Just tell me what you're saying."

Selznick was notorious for his memos to production people that often ran to more than a hundred pages on subjects as minuscule as the length of Dietrich's eyelashes or the width of Freddie March's ties. His conversations weren't much shorter, sharing the gift of golden gab that had made his older brother, Myron, the town's most feared agent.

Now he raced through a review of the work being done on *Gone with the Wind* by his production designer, William Cameron Menzies, and art director Lyle Wheeler before pausing for a deep swallow of air and to confess, "But you know that already, L.B."

"Of course I know, so that must be why you are telling me all over again? Listen, Davey, our deal says point blank clear in black and white you have to tell me, but you don't also have to tell me what you told me, or haven't I told you that already?"

Selznick's head bobbed while his palms held off another interruption.

He said, "You remember how you requested —"

"Told."

"How you told me you'd like me to think about bringing on board another art director or two, not because Bill and Lyle were bad, but to speed up the process?"

"So?"

"I listened to you, L.B., because you also know these things, and one thing led to another thing and to this young girl, Nancy here — already employed in your studio's own art department. Look at her sketches, L.B.! Look! Look! See if she is not adding another dimension to this movie all the world is waiting to see."

"Like all the world is still waiting for you to find our Scarlett O'Hara."

"In due course, L.B. Due course. We've tested Davis, Crawford, Jean Arthur, Chaplin's live-in girlfriend, Goddard. Our nationwide talent hunt isn't over yet, and we continue getting reams and reams of publicity thanks to my Russ Birdwell and your own Howard." He flooded Strickling with a smile.

Mayer said, "I still want you to think about the Tarzan, you remember?"

"That little O'Sullivan scamp? How could I ever forget her, even without you to remind me?" Selznick said, trying to be gra-

67

cious and failing. "For the moment, however, look at what your own Nancy Warren has achieved."

He started to put an arm across her back.

She moved away without making a show of it.

Mayer rummaged through the drawings and sketches, grunting and making undecipherable sounds, sometimes stopping to inspect one at closer range; sometimes nodding, sometimes not; never giving any clue to what he really was thinking until he finally said, "These are some pictures you have here." Like an art critic admiring the frame instead of the painting. "Strick, have a look."

"My opinion would be worthless, L.B., especially next to yours," Strickling said, ever the political creature. "You know publicity is my game. I leave the creative work to the creators, like David."

Mayer said, "You, Chris?" Not as much a suggestion as an order.

I took the folder from Mayer and leafed through the pages.

Selznick took long note of me for the first time and was displeased. "The man is an ex-cop, L.B. What in God's name could he possibly know about anything creative?"

"I've been to a museum or two," I said. "I

even know how to spell Picasso, easier than I ever knew how to spell Selznick, Mr. Selznick."

Mayer said, "Besides, he's my ex-cop, Davey."

Selznick threw me a dirty look.

Years ago, when I was still in uniform, I'd responded to a call from the Biltmore Hotel and wound up booking Selznick on a drunk and disorderly, indifferent to who the foul-mouth protester was and misspelling his name as "Selsnik." In no time at all, an RKO lawyer had seen to it that the charges were scrubbed, and I had to send Selznick a written apology.

The first time he saw me on the MGM lot, he tried and failed to get me fired. He had carried the grudge ever since, maybe that's why Mayer had asked for my opinion. It was another way to spank Irene's husband, whom he still privately cursed for leaving the studio to go independent, putting him in a category with the silk glove salesman Goldfish, who changed his name to "Goldwyn," but never, never, Mayer would spew, was a part of Metro-Goldwyn-Mayer.

I finished checking out the sketches. "They're okay," I said.

"So much for Mr. Bernard Berenson

here," Selznick said, adding fresh curves and dives to his roller coaster eyes.

"Only my opinion, Mr. Selznick."

"And worthless, if you want mine," Nancy Warren said, snappish as a pit bull.

She anchored her hands on her hips, elbows akimbo, tipped back her shoulders and challenged me. "I'd like to know what you in your infinite wisdom feel is wrong with them," she said.

I imagined her rich, throaty voice, sweet and smooth as honey fresh from the tree, under a more pleasant circumstance.

"What I see is close, but no cigar, Miss Warren, seeing as how close only counts in horseshoes."

"A horse's ass should know."

Mayer was displeased. "Girlie, no need to use profanity."

"I apologize, sir, but I don't ever stand still for insults from the uneducated. I did not want to be here, you know? Mr. Selznick wanted it. He said it was a good idea for us to meet in person."

Selznick said, "It still is, sugar. Forget Blanchard. He's at the crayons and coloring book stage." He threw me another sneer.

"What I said hasn't anything to do with the quality of your sketches, Miss Warren. Your likeness of Gable is topnotch, Gable to his jug ears and the tiny mole on his jaw, but otherwise —"

Selznick cut me off. "Stow any more the insults, Blanchard. L.B., how about we continue this discussion later?"

"Later is good."

"C'mon, cookie." Selznick started around the desk.

I closed the folder and stood to hand it over to him.

Nancy, trailing in Selznick's shadow, bumped into his backside, pushed him forward, and verged on tripping over her heels onto the plush carpeting.

I caught her in time, kept my arms around her until certain she had recovered her balance. She felt good there, like she might even belong there under other circumstances.

There was something I liked about this Nancy Warren.

A lot of something.

I wasn't sure what.

She pushed me away, hard.

"You're welcome," I said, offering a peace smile.

"You're not," she said, and sailed out in Selznick's wake.

Heading for the *Wizard of Oz* set, I ran

Nancy Warren through my mind like an endless loop.

Heard her voice.

Saw her soul inside the shimmer of her angry eyes.

Knew I wanted to see her again.

Had to see her again.

Already feeling how it had been with Marie MacDaniels and not since.

The set was quiet, except for a few crew members touching up some zigzagging yellow path that ran from one end of the soundstage to the other. The producer, Mervyn LeRoy, was huddled with the director, Victor Fleming, alongside Hal Rosson's camera, both locked in conversational frowns that barely eased when they saw me. Little Mervyn said something to Fleming and hustled over, his head shaking like the '33 quake.

The *Oz* set hadn't been on my agenda for today until one of LeRoy's assistants ran me down, all frantic-eyed, saying LeRoy needed me pronto.

"Thank you, Chris, you made good time," LeRoy said, extending his left hand for one of those Hollywood mirror-image handshakes that seemed to be a secret code among celebrities. "We have us a problem, Chris, and L.B. said for me to take it up with you."

I waited while the cherub-faced producer sucked up a few gallons of air.

"Chris, you know Tyrone Powell?"

"Tyrone Power?" I said, thinking I'd heard him incorrectly.

"No, Tyrone *Powell*. One of the performing midgets and dwarfs we hired that damned Singer to bring in for the *Oz* shoot."

Singer's Midgets was a major attraction on the international vaudeville circuit. MGM needed all of them for the movie, as well as any other midgets and dwarfs Singer might know about. According to Louella O. Parsons, it was the first time that many little people had gathered together. Many had never realized they weren't the only small humans in God's domain until they checked in at the Culver Hotel.

"We had to shut down after a couple of setups this morning and another one after the lunch break," LeRoy said. "This Powell's critical to the next scene, but he's nowhere to be found. It turns out nobody has seen him since last night."

"You couldn't just use another dwarf?"

"Midget. The little prick is a midget. And, no. He was established yesterday with Judy. We need him for a two-shot before we strike the set."

73

"Have you checked the dresser drawers at the hotel, you know, like that Sluggo kid in the *Moon Mullins* comic?"

"Hah. Hah. Hah," LeRoy answered, not meaning one *hah.* "We finally found the little hemorrhoid-helper, and now we need you do to something about it."

"Where and what?"

"Sleeping it off in the Culver City jailhouse."

"Mervyn, isn't getting him out a job for Strickling?"

"Same as I was thinking when I got hold of L.B. He said something about Strick being off the lot somewhere and to have you handle it. You know what I think, Chris?"

"What's that?"

"No offense, but I think L.B. felt this emergency was too small a job for Strick."

CHAPTER 5

Tyrone Powell was one unhappy midget.

He sat grumbling alongside me, sometimes louder than my Ford V8, which was sounding like it needed a new muffler. Again. The third one this year. Russ Collins, who built Andy Hardy's hotrod, thought the problem had something to do with excessive back pressure and constantly promised to get it fixed right *next time.* Meanwhile, the V8 could outrun any police car and most of the old bootleg specials trafficking around L.A.

"Go ahead, say it," Powell said as we approached the Metro gate. "Say what's on your mind, wonder how dumb I could have been to get myself into this kind of screw-up. Dumb? How does crazy sound? Insane? Better? Closer to the truth." He began moaning.

I said, "Not here to judge you, Mr. Powell. I was sent to spring you from the jug, get you back here for your scene with the Garland kid."

Hal Hollenbeck, the sleepy-eyed guard, recognized me and pulled back the gate.

I returned his salute and toothy smile as we passed through and slowed down for the crawl south to the *Oz* soundstage.

Powell had perked up at the mention of Judy Garland and momentarily forgot his moaning, telling me, "You know they strap down her tits? You know that? And she got great tits, too, for a teenager. I copped a peek into her portable when the door was open and I was waltzing by."

He licked his lips and let a momentary smile slip over his handsome face, pushed back his thick black hair.

I figured Powell for mid-to-late twenties, same as Bob Taylor, who he resembled, but looking about ten years younger than Bob and like one of those miniaturist paintings on ivory or in lockets that I'd seen two or three months ago at the Natural History Museum in Exposition Park; a bit more cherubic than Bob, or even Tyrone Power.

He was stylishly dressed in a smartly cut blue suit and patent leather shoes that glistened with a spit shine, somehow having missed whatever chaos had wrinkled his shirt, rumpled his suit and put to brown death the wilted red carnation boutonniere that matched his bloodshot eyes.

He caught me stealing glances and, adjusting his red bow tie, said, "It's oke to stare."

"Sorry."

"No, really. It's oke. You did real good for me with them cops and don't think I'm not grateful. You were one of them once, that the story that drifted my way?"

"Not one of them. I was City of Los Angeles police, a detective. The ones who arrested you are from Culver City."

"You had no respect for them, did you? Don't answer, you don't want, but I could tell by the way you handled them. Oh, all nice and sweet talk, giving them sneak preview passes to the Norma Shearer picture to jolly them up while you sweet-talked me out, but I could tell."

"What makes you say that?"

"A true gift, same way some people can go into basketball. I've gone the world fifteen times over with that lying, thieving, cheating, conniving Singer and his barrel of midgets, doing the kind of mind-reading act the late Mr. Harry Houdini once caught and admired when we played a split week at the Paramount."

"Then I don't have to tell you about Culver City cops."

"I heard from a wino in the tank last night. He said the cops in this town are more twisted than pretzels, even more than the cops in Los Angeles."

"Is he also a mind reader, the wino?"

"A girlie boy, but I straightened him out in a hurry. Like with you, I send out very positive signals is all. So do you. I like you. I'll bet you were never one of the crooks, Mr. Chris Blanchard."

"Maybe too honest for my own good," I said, and immediately wondered why I was being so candid with somebody I didn't know. I have friends, who hard as they try, still don't know my middle name. Hell, I liked the little guy; simple as that.

"Herbie Duntz, that's me," Powell said, as if recognizing I had names on my mind. "That totally corrupt *I owe you and will pay you back with interest* Singer said it wasn't so hotsy a name for the show business when he saw me feeding slop to the pigs on my folks' farm back home in Boise and sold me a bill. He said, *You know who it is you remind me of, Herbie? Tyrone Power, the actor. Maybe you should be our own Tyrone Power, what do you say? Let us think on it after the contracts are signed.*" Powell dropped the thick European accent he had adopted. "He bought me from my folks, paid fifty dollars cash money and a pack of promises, bought me for less than an old gray gelding, and I was 'Tyrone Powell' quicker than you can say Jack G. Robinson."

"And here you are and here we are," I said, pulling the V8 to a stop alongside the soundstage door. "Mr. LeRoy and Mr. Fleming will be pleased to see you."

Powell's fat-fingered hand flicked away the advisory.

He showed no intention of getting out of the car.

I could tell he had more on his mind.

Whatever it was had him making sad noises again.

He said, "Don't you even want to know what got me into this mess and the pokey, too?" Tears formed at the inside corners of his sad eyes. Before I could answer him, he was telling the story.

Last night he'd gone to the Culver Dog Track and bumped into Ben Siegel, the Brooklyn mobster who'd moved west and into Beverly Hills and was using a boyhood friendship with the actor George Raft to paint himself as an upright citizen.

Anybody who read the newspapers knew the true story, that Siegel was the co-founder with Meyer Lansky of the notorious Bug and Meyer Mob — "Bug" as in

"Bugsy." In spite of his leading-actor looks and painted-on charm, Siegel was a cold-blooded killer with a hair-trigger temper in a mob that had expanded its goals and reputation as Murder, Inc. He had strong ties to local crime through Red Shapiro, Jack Dragna and others; his fingers in a variety of vice and gambling pots, like dog racing.

I knew Benny better than the newspapers. Like him, I was one of the Brownsville boys. I'd grown up with him and other thugs back in New York, two years ahead of Benny, and like Benny had turned to the gun, but on the legit side of the law.

I said, "I have a few minutes, Mr. Powell," and switched off the ignition. "Tell me about Siegel."

Powell swallowed hard. He said, "I admit I had a few too many by the time I got to the track. I was loop-dee-do and heading for the ten-dollar window when I ran smack into this slick-looking dude's tight ass. So, oke, maybe I said a few things I didn't, shouldn't have, but so did he."

"Like what?"

Powell assumed a Brooklyn accent, about ninety-five percent thicker than the accent I had managed to correct over the years, and quoted Benny: *Please watch where you are* going, sir.

"I can see where that would get you riled. So, you said?"

"His polite manner didn't fool me one iota. I said, *What do you think, wise guy, that I purposely steered my smeller into your Grand Canyon? Who do you suppose you are, anyway?* I saw immediately he didn't like that."

"Good catch. And he said?"

"Nothing. It was this gorilla with him. Big goon with a face like a bad accident. He says to me, *Be careful with that sloppy mouth, freak. This is Mr. Benjamin Siegel.*"

"And you said?"

"My prayers. I know who Siegel is, and one good look up at his face — and sure enough it was him. I may have been drunk, but I wasn't stupid. Quick as a wink, I said, *My apologies, Bugsy. . . .* Who knew how much he hates that nickname?"

Powell waited, wide-eyed.

I gave him a two-handed, palms to the sky, *Things happen* gesture.

He said, "I see little pockets of foam forming at the sides of his mouth, and he says, *I am gonna accept your apology, you ugly little Chihuahua, after you get down on all fours and bark for me. Gimme a woof-woof, which is all you cockamamie dwarfs are good for anyways.*"

"I don't read you as someone who woof-woofs for anybody, Mr. Powell."

"Keerect. What I did was kick him in the balls; hauled back my size three brogans and put two in his side pocket. Siegel howled, went down and grabbed his *kishkas* like he was scared his peter would fall off. I was straddling him in a flash, determined to strangle the insulting bastard. I was doing a good job of it, too, until a sharp, hard, slam-bang pain at the base of my neck turned the whole world the color of India ink, and I came to in the pokey, puking in a bucket."

"There was nothing in the paperwork, nothing I was told by the Culver City boys that mentioned Siegel, only that they got the call about a D&D, a drunk and disorderly, at the track."

"All of it truth, s'help me, even if you never see it in Ripley's *Believe it or Not.*" He was raining sweat and made a whimper of a noise. "Siegel is probably going to have me killed, you think?"

I shook my head. "Don't take this personally, Mr. Powell, but I expect Ben Siegel has bigger fish to fry." Powell gave me a plaintive look. "How about I call around, make sure you're in the clear. I know a name or two that can square it with Siegel."

"You'd go and do that for me?" His eyes tightened as his delicate features turned into a question mark. "Why? What's in it for you?"

"It comes with my job at the studio, Mr. Powell, like getting you back here in one piece for your scene with Judy Garland."

Powell spent a few moments thinking. "Herbie, I'm Herbie to you," he said, his smile obscuring the rest of his face. "I like you, so we are going to become great friends. Great, great friends. Pals. Buddies. Whether you like it or not."

He was out of the car and dashing into the soundstage before I could answer.

I checked my watch.

Almost three o'clock.

Grimaced.

I had to race to my office or risk missing my phone call from Marie MacDaniels.

My office, on the ground floor of the administration building, had last belonged to a casting director with a roving eye and hot rocks in his pants. The incongruously plush leather couch pulled out into a bed, whenever he was in the mood to pull out something else and had handy an ambitious young actor eager to learn the business from him.

I left the office as I found it after moving in, except for putting Yale locks on the two filing cabinets — one of which held a decent selection of alcohol — a cruciform lock on my desk and a private phone line in a desk drawer.

I stared at the phone for an hour and a half, sipping away at the two fingers of rye in the glass beside it, waiting until 4:30 to admit Marie wasn't planning to call. I finished the rye and took off for the set of *Battling G-Men in Havana,* the newest programmer in the series that had turned profits for Metro over the past four years.

These low-budget movies, like the *Tarzan*s, *Andy Hardy*s and *Dr. Kildare*s, often made more money than the bigger, more expensive titles buffered by the big star names. Louis B. Mayer could spot a trend faster than he could make one, and he'd ordered a unit to produce the *G-Men* titles when he saw what Warner Bros. had done with titles such as *Public Enemy, Little Caesar* and other modern morality plays that made stars of Cagney, Robinson, Muni and Raft, only he wanted them made fast and sloppy, like the five-day wonders churned out by Harry Cohn and Columbia over at low-rent Gower Gulch.

While I understood the popularity of the

Battling G-Men, I was no fan of the star, Baxter Leeds, who portrayed stupidly intrepid Field Agent Thomas Harrison II.

He had been cast in the lead because the boss didn't want to waste even a Walter Pidgeon, Jimmy Stewart or Bob Young and instructed producer John Mahoney to pick a day player from the ranks. Mahoney, a master at cutting budget corners, knew there were only two months left on Leeds's twenty-dollar-a-week contract. Anyone else would have cost at least a fin more.

Leeds's six-foot height, Santa Monica tan and pencil-thin mustache put him in the same minor category as Warren William, Warner Baxter and Cesar Romero until *Battling G-Men* made him a star, although at a much lower altitude than the real stars in the MGM heavens.

Not to hear Leeds tell it, of course.

As his stock and salary rose, he developed an ego that hung from his mouth like a goiter.

Gable and Tracy were flukes to Leeds, his own Oscar only a role or two away.

He went from being tolerated to being despised, especially by the *G-Men* crew.

I'd had one of my worst times tracking the grip on the catwalk who barely missed Leeds's thick, slicked-back locks with a ball peen hammer after Leeds had accused him of being a "Red Commie bastard." The grip's nickname was "Polack" and he'd fought with Pilsudski against the Bolsheviks, but his accent had sounded Russian to Leeds.

Polack was sacked in a show of appeasement to Leeds, with promises of criminal prosecution. I put in a few quiet words to a few people, Howard Strickling among them, and Polack was back working on the lot three weeks later, hiding inside a full brush beard and reassigned to the new *Maisie* unit.

At the *G-Men* set I went looking for Marie's friend, Eve Whitney, on a hunch that Marie headed to her place the night of the murder. Eve played Leeds's feisty, bold, bright and brassy secretary, "Bright Eyes," where Marie played his adoring girlfriend, "Jane Conway."

Eve might know where Marie was now.

I waited for the red shooting light to go out before passing through the heavy-set doors and tracked around the flats in time to see Eve walking off. I started after her, but Leeds caught me and brought me to a halt.

"Just the man I want to see, buddy." Leeds called everybody "Buddy." It saved him from having to remember names. "Do you have the time?"

"Not really," I said, trying to be cordial.

He stopped in the middle of our hand-shake and stepped backward. "I suppose you would have the time if I were that lush Tracy or the so-called King."

"Okay, fine," I said. I knew the house rules, and one was: *Do not upset the actors unnecessarily, not even turds like Baxter Leeds.* "What gives?"

Leeds checked his back before moving in close enough to whisper in my ear. "I hear things when I'm in town, like last night on the Strip, at the Mo, catching dinner and the show," he said, his baritone as mellow as a summer sky.

"Like?"

"Like Franchot Tone?"

"Yeah, I like Franchot Tone."

"You know that's not what I mean, buddy." He took a few seconds to swallow his temper. "He wasn't there with the Crawford bitch. They're an item, you know?"

"I know."

"He was there with Eddie Bromberg, you know? J. Edward Bromberg. And with Morris Ankrum." A smug look came over his even tan and he swiped an index finger across his mustache, first one side, then the other.

"What am I missing, Mr. Leeds?"

"Buddy, buddy," Leeds hiss-whispered at me. "Bromberg and Ankrum. The talk around town is they're both full-fledged Commies. I'm betting Franchot Tone is in it with them."

"Especially with a name like Franchot."

"Make fun, buddy, but consider — he's brought out here from New York, where he knows those robin red breasts from. He's an original member of that Group Theater crowd, and we know from where they stand. Group of flaming pinkos is what they are — and worse."

"Maybe Bromberg, Ankrum and Tone were also catching dinner and the show, like you?"

"I don't think so, buddy, not when you put the two and twos together. Something should be said about it."

"To Parsons or Hopper, and let them know that the information came from you? Sorry, Mr. Leeds, but that's more a job for Howard Strickling, so maybe you should tag him."

Leeds's head wagged left and right, and he found a way to get another inch closer to me. Whatever he'd devoured for lunch smelled like garbage. I found myself breathing in spurts, whenever his face briefly turned away, trying not to be too obvious.

"Not that at all," he said, his breath raining on my nose. "I know how close you are to Mr. Mayer, and Mr. Mayer is the one who should learn this. He's about to approve Tone's casting opposite Garbo. Garbo. That's quite a risk to take with a known Commie."

"And I might also mention to Mr. Mayer how right Baxter Leeds would be for the part?"

Leeds smiled, clasped his hands in front of his narrow chest and bowed Charlie Chan style. "I would owe you a big one, buddy. Baxter Leeds has a good memory and would remember who helped it happen if the G in *G-Man* came to be the G in *Garbo's Man.*"

"Gotcha," I said, tapped my temple and turned it into a finger salute while backing away. "Leave it to me."

I had no intention of saying anything to Mayer and Leeds wouldn't have the nerve to bring it up himself to the boss, or he'd have already done so. His heroism was confined to the script of the *G-Men* pictures. Mine to the good guys of the business, like Franchot Tone, who, the day we were introduced, said, "Chris, you ever see me getting too big for my britches, please tell me to go fuck myself."

The door of Eve Whitney's trailer was half open.

She recognized my voice and invited me to join her.

Her reflection in the dressing table mirror smiled as I pulled the door shut.

Eve had oversized angular features, arranged like one of God's private jokes, that could get an audience laughing with a blink of her large, take-no-prisoners, dark brown eyes. There was nothing exciting about her shapeless body, usually stashed inside office attire that would win instant approval from prudish J. Edgar Hoover himself. She was a bottle blonde who never tried to bottle her urges; quick enough to handle any insult or flash of wit a script called for; as smart and savvy in person as any of the characters she played.

Eve hoisted her beer bottle, told me to find a brew for myself in the small service refrigerator, slid half the long neck into her mouth and tilted back her head.

I declined, lit up using the butt anchored in the lip of Eve's ashtray, plopped onto the narrow sofa across from her and pushed out a tube of smoke from the corner of my mouth.

She finished her swallow, finger-wiped her lips and, hoisting the long neck, said, "Every time I take a swipe I remember Milton Berle's shlong. Like you wouldn't believe, Chris. And Chico, crazy Chico. Better than any beer. That one's a Coney Island Red Hot. It must be the kosher thing."

"Wouldn't know, Evie."

"Yeah, you are definitely no — " She changed her mind. "I never did you, did I, Chris?"

"Never."

"Not even after — you know? To say thank you?"

"Not necessary, then or now."

"Marie always said you were grand when the two of you were an item. Are you grand, Chris? If so, maybe you wouldn't mind proving it firsthand sometime?"

"Sometime," I said, not meaning it, even if she did.

It had been our running gag, although Eve was usually more subtle about it than now. She was either a little looped on the beer or on something else. I heard traces in her smoke-starched voice and understood the glaze in her eyes. Reefer, maybe. Probably. But reefer was none of my business unless somebody decided to make it so.

I said, "You hear from Marie, Evie?"

"Why did I know you were going to ask?" She took another lick from the bottle. "We shot around her. Fucking G-Man Thomas Harrison Two simply claimed the baby's close-ups for himself."

"If Marie was going to call anybody, it would be you. Maybe even stay with you last night?"

Her expression gave away nothing.

"The stories in the newspapers, Chris, all over the radio . . . bad for her?"

"Not as bad as they make it sound. Did she give you a jingle? Maybe tell you where she's parked now — or is she still parked at your place?"

"No," Evie said, overemphasizing the word, anxious to make sure I believed her.

"To what?"

"To everything you said."

"I have to talk to her, Evie."

My eyes caught hers and refused to let her look away.

She finally managed to break the connection and looked around the trailer.

It was full of stuffed animals. Eve collected stuffed animals. Anybody who read *Photoplay* or *Modern Screen* knew that.

She settled on a teddy bear in a sailor suit

that dominated a corner and kept her eyes away from me.

"Marie didn't do it, Chris, no matter what the news hounds say anymore."

"Tell me something I don't know, Evie."

"I mean, she had every reason to put that son of a bitch Day Covington away for keeps, seeing what he always was putting the baby through, her never knowing from one minute to the next where his cock had been or what color stain he might be bringing home to their silk sheets . . ." She shifted her gaze to a teddy bear in a tuxedo. "Oh, hell. I'm saying too much, am I not? Am I not, Chris?"

"Say a little more, Evie."

She wheeled around on her seat. "Okay, so maybe this is something you should hear."

A knock on the door beat her to her next thought.

I expected it to be the AD telling her she was needed on the set, or maybe the makeup girl come to administer a touch-up.

Neither.

"It's Howard, Eve. Howard Strickling."

Eve made a face and, as quickly, opened the dressing table drawer and stored the beer bottle on its side. She double-checked herself in the mirror and nodded at me. I took it as a cue to open the door.

Strickling moved inside, showing no surprise at my presence.

Eve said, "Howie, baby!"

He answered her smile and turned to me. "Chris, I can't say thank you enough for suggesting Leeds corner me and tell me all about Franchot Tone's plan to seize control of our government."

"I owed you one, Strick."

"Another one. We still haven't reconciled the business with Polack." He thought about it. "Maybe what I should do is arrange for Polack to get back on the *G-Men* picture and give him another ball peen hammer." He didn't show it often, but he did have a wry sense of humor.

"You in there, Strick?"

I recognized the voice and the face that came with it: Captain Ray Travis.

"That Baxter Leeds is quite the yapper," he said, stepping inside the trailer and acknowledging Eve with a head curtsy and his name.

"Travis? Ray Travis?" She was thrown momentarily, and then lit up like a klieg. I expected her to say she knew his name from the news stories, but she fooled me. "We did a picture together, didn't we, Ray Travis? You fingerprinted me in *Bombay Rain*."

94

Travis's stone face cracked into a smile. "And I brought you your luggage into the hotel suite in *A New York Scandal.*"

Eve nodded. "I was pretty good in that, too. . . . So, tell me, how's your career going, Ray Travis?"

Strickling hurried to say, "Ray is not a full-time actor, Eve. He's a captain with the LAPD's homicide bureau." Eve snapped her fingers. "He's come around to ask you a few questions about Marie MacDaniels."

"This seems to be the day for it," she said.

Strickling turned to me. "You don't mind giving us some privacy, do you, Chris? I suspect Captain Travis prefers working without an audience."

I shot a glance at Eve.

She was moving her head sideways, but Strickling's expression made it clear I had no bargaining room.

I said, "The pleasure's all yours, Captain," and slipped out of the trailer, hoping — whatever Eve might know about Marie — she wouldn't tell the cop before she got around to telling me.

CHAPTER 6

Friday, November 11, 1938

A parade was blaring its way through the arid heat of early afternoon and the crowded sidewalks of Hollywood Boulevard, celebrating the twentieth anniversary of Armistice Day, the ending of the War to End all Wars.

I was stuck in my Ford, in the thick cross-traffic heading north to Sunset, letting it idle and trying not to notice the climbing temperature gauge. Hollywood High loomed on my left, putting the Photo Salon of Otto Rothman directly across the street.

A decrepit Chevy Coach dodging from the curb almost took off my fender.

I grabbed the space, locked the car and ambled up the half block to Rothman's building, large and freshly painted in a spiffy beige, his name in fancy gold lettering above a discreet "Open" sign.

A forlorn bridal attire shop was on one side of the studio, on the other an empty front with "For Lease" chalked across the display window. That got me thinking:

No depression for Otto Rothman. Every aspiring actor or actress who sleeps through the night clutching pillows for Oscars will always need portrait and publicity pictures on the cheap.

Giant blowups dressed Rothman's five display windows: a young man, debonair in a tux and high hat; a young woman in soft-focus, lips parted in longing; a sad-faced little girl in a Shirley Temple gown; dueling portraits of the sisters and unfriendly rivals Joan Fontaine and Olivia de Havilland that made me bet myself they'd both be much too grand a year from now to traipse the boulevard for a session in front of Otto Rothman's lenses.

He had lost his high ranking and most of his reputation as a studio gallery hotshot a few years ago, with it the status stars confuse with talent.

He'd worked for Paramount, RKO, then Warner Bros., resigning from each after about a year, the reasons never spelled out.

After coming across his card in Day Covington's wallet, I'd pressed to learn why the photographer had fallen off those payrolls. The closest I came to an answer was from a secretary I'd once briefly dated, a gossipy brunette with crystal green eyes, who worked at RKO in accounting.

She told me over the phone, "There's nothing outrageously wrong in his personnel file, but people constantly complained about Otto. They said being photographed by him was like, well — volunteering for a Peeping Tom."

I said, "Selma, did Rothman every try anything with any of them?"

"Try anything? You mean like you never got around to trying with me, Chris?"

"My loss, Selma."

"I'll say," she said. "The file says only once and not much then. Someone said he wanted to know if they'd be interested in him shooting an art portfolio. Art studies. For free."

"Free meaning . . . ?"

"Free meaning *free,* but art meaning *naked.*" I grunted into the phone. "What was interesting about that, Chris — it was an actor he asked, not one of the typical horizontal honeys. In this town, that kind of proposition's like getting stopped for speeding, so Otto wasn't banned or anything."

Calling around, I also heard that Rothman got occasional studio work, generally from those along Cheap Row, or on recommendations from talent agents who needed a set of stills for some new client's publicity package.

I didn't pick up any other hint of scandal.

No one knew anything to connect Rothman with Day Covington.

I was wondering about the twenty-five-dollar checks Covington received from him as I turned the studio doorknob.

The door was locked.

I knocked once, then louder.

No answer.

He was in the darkroom, maybe?

Maybe up at the parade?

The lock was a standard Yale.

I fished out two small L-shaped bits from my wallet, pushed one into the keyhole, then the other, moving them slowly, gently, back and forth, trying not to look too intent to any passersby, someone leaning on the doorway waiting for a bus. I hid a grin when the tumblers clicked back; slid inside and eased the door closed, thinking: *If Rothman is inside, I'll tell him the door was open.*

Soft floodlights illuminated the anteroom that ran the width of the building. A small black metal counter sat in the center of the room, behind it a sliding door that led into the studio. Giant photos dressed the walls. Classy black leather couches formed a waiting area. *The Hollywood Reporter, Variety,* magazines like *Vanity Fair, Collier's, Saturday Evening Post* and *Vogue* were stacked on glass-topped tables.

I called out, "Hello, Mr. Rothman."

Silence.

I wrinkled my nose at the smell of carbon tetrachloride and thought it odd —

I'd never heard that cleaning solvent was used in photography.

I pushed back the sliding door and entered the large back studio. There was the usual array of lights on stands, a large studio camera on a tripod and —

A body lying on its back next to the camera.

A supremely large man burst through a curtain to my right, in the act of bringing down a blackjack.

I threw my fedora in his face, spun right, ducking, hands lifting.

Threw a block at the man's forearm.

Drove a right into his gut.

The man coughed out a bellyful of air that smelled like Listerine and head-butted me. I stumbled back, recovered as the man came at me again. Snapped two fast jabs into his florid, round face and connected a right cross to the stomach. Danced in ready to drop the man. He swung the blackjack wildly. It caught me on the shoulder blade hard enough to flash needles through my body.

I stumbled back and tripped over a lighting cable.

Went down hard.

Banged my head against the door behind me.

The man sprinted for the back door, fast for someone carting that much bulk.

Rolling to my feet, I chased after him.

He passed through the door and slammed it hard.

I yanked my gun out of its shoulder rig, charged through the door, saw the man race down the alley and dart between two buildings; heard the grind of a car's starter; rounded the corner in time to see a blocky Dodge gun away; looked for numbers as the car pulled onto Highland and disappeared. The yellow license plate had been muddied over.

I leaned against a brick wall recovering my breath; stashed the gun and rubbed my left shoulder, trying to ignore the pain; heard cheers and the faint strains of "Washington Post March" coming from Hollywood Boulevard; lit a Lucky and swallowed a lungful of smoke; noticed my hand was trembling; remembered the carbon tetrachloride; flipped the Lucky away after three quick drags; went back inside the studio, locking the door behind me.

The body sprawled on its back next to the expensive Deardorff portrait camera in the big studio proper had to be Rothman. He fit Selma's description of the photographer: slender, tweedy, with teeth that could eat a tomato through a tennis racket.

I touched one arm, lifted it.

It was stiffening.

Rigor mortis setting in?

Did that mean the big guy had killed Rothman, then hung around in this heat, for — what? — at least three hours?

There was a bullet wound almost in the center of Rothman's chest. I studied it, hoping to find a nice, neat little hole, like there'd been in Day Covington. No such luck. Instead, I found a raggedy tear from a high-caliber pistol.

"Strange, strange, stranger," I told myself, and walked into the studio.

To the right of the outer waiting area was a small, curtained makeup room, from where the big man had come charging at me. Inside were two two-gallon tins of carbon tet, one half-dumped. I put the lids back on them.

Next to the tins was an electric timer with

a plug on one end and a conventional light socket on the other. Screwed into the socket was an electric bulb with a tiny hole taped over after the bulb had been filled with black powder.

I recognized how simple detonation would have been.

Set the timer and plug the socket into the wall.

The timer ticks down, current goes through the circuit to the bulb, and —

Flash!

The carbon tet goes up and, a few minutes later —

So does the studio.

The detonating mechanism is destroyed in the fire.

Along with Rothman's body.

The door opposite the makeup room opened onto a hall that led to the store's far side, then turned right and ran to the back wall.

Photographs mounted along the walls — a sampling of Rothman's *art studies* — inspired a silent whistle. Some were simple nudes, some couples. Sometimes men and women. Sometimes only men. Sometimes only women. Lots of hugging and caressing.

I surveyed the faces.

One I was sure was Luise Rainer, one of

Metro's major stars, posed with a man I didn't recognize. Another was certainly Joanie Blondell, who loved to show and tell, or so I had heard from pals over at Warner Bros. Another was a fresh-faced starlet I knew, but I couldn't remember her name. There were Cary Grant and Randolph Scott in swimming trunks, sitting cozily side-by-side on a diving board. Someone who looked like Claudette Colbert, wearing a look of sultry interest, was staring up at a blonde who had her ample assets on full display.

The photos went on and on, rows of them.

Common sense told me Rothman wouldn't have let just anyone back here to see them. Most were too suggestive for that, although none were even vaguely illegal. Erotic, yes, but not overtly lewd, nothing to inspire mass outrage and a demand for prosecution by the district attorney.

On display for who, then?

For Rothman and his cronies to appreciate and gossip over?

Cronies like Day Covington?

I went from room to room down the hall.

The first was a neat, orderly darkroom illuminated by the glow of a red safety light. The 8 × 10 prints on the dryer were of a curvaceous brunette in her late twenties wearing various expressions and skimpy outfits against a variety of backgrounds.

Next, a storeroom full of photo supplies and cameras.

Most of the cameras were what a studio photographer would be expected to have, Linhoffs and the like, even a couple Speed Graphics, but there were four 35mm Leica B's on a shelf, useful for news shots and family candids, not quality studio work.

The last room held a small desk and Rothman's files, neatly enveloped, row upon row organized by year. Almost every envelope had a different-colored stripe, black, green, orange, blue; here and there an unmarked envelope. The files on the next-to-bottom shelf had been ransacked and spread on the floor. Near the shelf were two unopened carbon tet cans. I knelt and sorted through the files. They dated from 1938, but none were later than June, suggesting the files from July to November had been taken.

I returned to the waiting room, examined the counter area, and came up with the company checkbook and a stack of ledgers, tall, narrow, bound in light green cloth, some with colors daubed on the front: black, green, orange, blue.

I headed back to the file room with the ledgers.

Two hours later, I had Rothman's system figured out.

The black-coded ledger corresponded with black-marked envelopes and held portraits or head-and-shoulder publicity shots of actors and actresses. Appointments, billings and expenses to agents, a studio or the client himself, were neatly listed in the black ledger. In the blue ledger were precocious child actors, either brazenly posing or looking like they'd rather be on a playground. The blue ledger listed parents, guardians, other adults connected with the children and the finances.

The orange ledger reflected assignments from architects eager to memorialize their creations before their clients ruined them with furniture, children, life in general; commercial products; here and there an expensive, overproduced show business–style wedding. Green was for outdoor pictures, the ledger listing the expenses of trips to Hot Springs, Arrowhead, Yosemite Park, Palm Springs and other vacation areas, explaining why Rothman had the 35mm Leicas. The most recent entry logged a visit to San Diego, where Rothman and an unidentified "model" stayed in a suite at the Hotel Del Coronado across San Diego Bay.

When the prowl was over, I realized I'd

discovered —

Not much of anything of value.

Except, of course, a dead Otto Rothman.

I glowered at the rows of neat envelopes, ran what I'd seen through my mind.

Snapped my fingers at the memory of something I'd given short shrift.

I went to the shelves, rifled envelopes until I found one that had no color coding, only a number on the outside and on the inside a thick sheaf of 35mm negatives in clear paper sheaths. No proof sheets.

I held one strip of negatives up to the light.

Blinked.

Took a closer look.

Two people were entwined on the strip.

I was pretty sure they were naked.

I found another envelope without color-coding, no proof sheets, only negative strips in clear covers. These showed a naked man with a pronounced erection, his hands behind his head. One pictured the man and the back of a second person, probably male, whose short-haired face was buried in the other guy's crotch. The third, fourth, fifth and sixth shots had variations on the pose.

The film in all but one of the unmarked envelopes was 35mm.

Easily transportable.

Easily hidden.

I thought: Bingo!

Blackmail.

But who was Rothman blackmailing who'd turned murderous?

I went back through the studio, pretending away the serious pain in my shoulder as I searched for something that might answer the question.

Hidden behind the photos on the walls, maybe?

Nothing for a while, then —

A built-in wall safe hiding behind a photo of a delectable Clara Bow wearing a nice smile and nothing else. I pulled the handle and the safe swung open. Empty.

Maybe under a loose floorboard? No loose floorboards.

Hidden niches in walls? None that I could find.

Hidden in the base of lamps? All the lamps were sleek, modern poles.

Secret compartments in desks? No.

Overhead? Nothing in the high-ceiling studio but the real roof.

However —

The three other rooms had false ceilings.

Back in the darkroom, I turned on the normal light and, looking up, spotted a small, square hatch. I pulled over a stool, climbed up on it, pushed open the hatch, and felt around.

My face lit up like a premiere at Grauman's Chinese.

I brought down a ledger and a three-to-a-page business checkbook.

I returned to the file room and compared them against Rothman's filing system.

Scattered through the stubs for mostly small amounts were the twenty-five-dollar checks made out to Day Covington, most written over the past two months. There were also several large withdrawals written to "Cash."

Rothman's current balance was a squeak over ten thousand dollars.

I thought: *A nice, quiet, profitable business. Until the guns started going off.*

The ledger was organized around the pornographic envelopes, but the numbered entries showed only initials; no names.

There were at least two hundred sets.

Number 124 had the initials EF.

EF for Warner Bros.' dashing Robin Hood, Errol Flynn?

I found envelope 124 and scanned the negatives.

There were three people in each shot, two women and a man, all naked. I couldn't tell if the man had Flynn's mustache. The prim entry in the ledger said: *Client declined to involve himself with project, other than to request ten copies of each shot for personal use.* There was no indication Rothman had complied with the request.

Other entries had dates and dollar amounts. Most were for ten or fifteen dollars, spaced three or four months apart. The earliest was 1931, the most recent October of this year.

I thought: *A very careful man. He never took enough dough to seriously hurt the person, make them desperate enough to go to the law or grab a gun, but enough to make a tidy little profit over time.*

So what happened?

What did Rothman finally do wrong?

Did Day Covington somehow set the murders in motion?

Playing a hunch, I ferreted out envelope 109, assigned by the ledger to JH, who had made larger payments than the others — up to seventy-five dollars — until 1937, when the payments stopped. The envelope held pictures of a naked man and woman enjoying each other.

The woman was Jean Harlow, one of Metro's biggest stars, who had died under suspicious circumstances in '37.

The photo angles masked the identity of the man.

Producer Paul Bern, her dead husband?

Movie star Bill Powell, who never stopped loving her?

The gangster Longy Zwillman, another of Harlow's longtime lovers?

I remembered the check for five hundred dollars from George Cukor that I'd found on Covington. I checked ledger entry GC. The largest amount paid was fifty dollars and only paid once or twice a year since 1933.

The GC envelope was 98. It was missing from the files. Nothing anywhere to link GC to Cukor, who'd be directing *Gone with the Wind* as part of the financing deal worked out between Mayer and Selznick.

Cukor and *Gone with the Wind* . . .

The combination pulled me to gossip that had lingered for years on and off the Metro lot, about Cukor and Clark Gable, one of those twisted stories that grow stronger with continued repeating and the passage of time, and to the possibility of a ledger entry for —

CG.

Two payments each of $40 in 1939, but —

No envelope.

No way to determine if CG was Gable.

I shook my head clear of imagined photos

of Metro's biggest star, "The King" himself, the nation's number one box-office draw, tangled up in Rothman's art studies, and moved on to checking through more files and pulling all the unmarked envelopes.

Found more than a few faces I knew from the MGM roster of contract players.

Lit up a Lucky and tried sorting out my thoughts:

Otto Rothman was a blackmailer, somehow in cahoots with Day Covington. His racket rumbles along quietly and successfully for quite some time, years, until something turns sour. Both are murdered by someone they'd been blackmailing.

The killer is someone with a lot to lose, who doesn't kill in the heat of anger and knows what he or she is doing; probably a he with connections to the bad guys, because the scene here smacks of a pro and pros rarely cotton to a woman.

The big guy who attacked me with the blackjack shows up a couple hours after Rothman's murder to destroy evidence. He's at least a semi-professional torch man; an amateur would have slopped gasoline around, tossed a match and taken off.

Can it be what we have here is gangster action, maybe Longy Zwillman, angry after discovering he had co-starred with Harlow in kinky photographs? Probably not. Zwillman never hid his affair with Harlow. Besides, more than a year after her death, why would Zwillman even care? He might be prouder of those photos than any of him that ever hung behind post office glass.

My thoughts were getting me nowhere.

I quit while I was behind, did some tidying up and went to the phone.

I dialed and waited for Ida Koverman to put me through to Mayer, who got on the line after keeping me on hold for three or four minutes, a trick the Hollywood crowd uses to define pecking order.

He picked up, saying, "You need to make it snappy, my boy. I'm in the middle of important business."

I said, "Mr. Mayer, I wanted you to know immediately. The studio has some very large and serious trouble on its hands."

A guttural sound moved from the back of his throat to my ear. He'd discovered over the years that I was never one to minimize or overstate a situation. He said, "Fine, all right, go ahead. My important business can wait."

My next call was to the cops, an anonymous tip-off about a dead body and where to find it, and afterward I double-timed it out of there.

By nightfall, Rothman's murder was front-page news, but the "Photographer to the Stars" was not a big or important enough name to overshadow coverage of the Armistice Day parade. Many of his old clients were mentioned, but there wasn't a single MGM star among them; nothing to link the studio to the crime; no reference whatsoever to Rothman's wall of art studies.

CHAPTER 7

Saturday, November 12, 1938

I invited Nancy Warren to join me for dinner and the floor show at the Coconut Grove for two reasons: her skills as a sketch artist and my need for a sketch being the one I mentioned, and my fascination with her being the one I kept to myself. Truth be told, that's the one I felt strongest about. I could have gotten the sketch I wanted from any of those artists working in Cedric Gibbons's department at Metro or on the Ocean Park amusement pier.

Getting a decent table took more than making a reservation and showing up on time, unless you were a government hotshot, a Mayer or a Warner, or a famous face that would draw notice and score a mention in tomorrow's Parsons or Hopper column.

The maitre d' waited, his expression as bland as a shark circling a fat swimmer. He eyed the sketch pad Nancy held; lifted an eyebrow. I palmed him a twenty. *"Merci beaucoup,"* he said, a smile oiling its way across his features. "Your table down front is ready, M. Blanchard." He bowed, led us through the packed Grove to a small table near the bandstand and seated her first.

"Bonsoir," he said, bowing.

"Au 'voir, vous cochon avidité," Nancy said, smiling brightly.

The maitre d', looking confused, circled away.

I said, "Would it surprise you to find out he's from Milwaukee and speaks about as much French as I do? I sense you insulted him, yes?"

"I called him a greedy pig."

"How diplomatic of you."

She checked out the room. "Is everything in this damn town for sale, like him?"

"Not everything. Some things are for lease, and I'm for rent on a regular basis."

She laughed a little while I gawked at her with admiration.

She had on a royal blue floor-length figured taffeta gown, gathered with a sash at the waist and full sleeves in the middle of her upper arm.

I was decked out in what I call my "working" tuxedo, the one that had been hand-fitted by a studio tailor at Howard Strickling's orders, cut to allow for my .38's shoulder holster, presently sitting on the bureau at the Ravenswood. I'd learned long ago that guns not only spoil the hang of most suits, but are about as much fun to wear without reason as a chunk of pig iron in a trouser pocket.

"I sense you don't like Hollywood a great deal," I said.

"Not much, but I like to eat and I'm not much for breadlines or Hoovervilles."

"There is that to worry about these days."

A waiter arrived, anxious to take a cocktail order, his eyes widening for an instant when Nancy said, "Bourbon and branch over a lot of ice." I went for rye, bonded, with a water back, and the waiter vanished.

Nancy said, "I just showed you I'm no lady, right?"

"I didn't know there was an approved cocktail list for ladies."

"Most certainly is. Manhattan. Daiquiri. Sidecar. Pink Lady. Anything with crème de menthe. Martini, if you're considered daring. Sherry, maybe."

"So why did you order what you did? If it's because you're from the South, you do a damn good job of hiding the accent."

"Try Portland, Oregon. Bourbon and branch, because I swore a couple of years ago that if I came back from where I was I would never drink anything but American and cold."

"And at the time you were drinking . . . ?"

"Subtle, Mr. Blanchard, so very subtle. You are a good detective. At the time I was drinking rotgut Spanish grappa in a ditch, getting strafed by Fascists."

"You went to Spain?"

"I did," she said, bitterness in her voice.

The waiter brought our drinks. I lifted mine in a toast, saying, "This marks a first for me — the first time I've ever bought dinner for a Communist."

Nancy looked at me carefully, searching for something beyond my smile. "I'm not a Party member any longer," she said. "I joined as a secret member while in Paris, made a unilateral resignation on a dusty road outside a cruddy little hole called Zaragoza."

"You went over as . . . ?"

"As a volunteer from the North American Committee to Aid Spanish Democracy. Nice people, who didn't seem to realize, or care to realize, who ran the show. Those of us in the Party considered ourselves pretty clever, letting the liberals do our work while we stayed in the shadows. Surely, we were all very clever," she said, bitterness on the rise. "I was an acceptable volunteer because I was a comer in the Party. But I was not enough of a big shot so it'd matter if I walked into a bullet. I drove an ambulance when I got over there — not the one Hemingway bought for us — and I nursed. Then I lost my ambulance in that grand screw-up last fall, along with some other things I thought were important.

"I had already learned that the Party took good care of its own, but nobody else, something I learned about in Spain. You happened to think differently than what your friendly local commissar said was the official Party line, you could find yourself very dead, with a nasty little bullet in the back of the neck. That kind of thing, done by the people you believed were heroes, wrote Paid to my idealism. When I got out from the hospital, I decided it was time for Nancy Warren to go home and get on with her own life."

"As . . . ?"

"As an artist. Not a commercial artist. You saw and, in spite of what you said, I'm pretty damned good. But there's a lot of pretty damned good, some pretty damned better, artists out there on relief. . . . A friend of my father's, a professor up at Reed College, heard MGM needed artists to help producers understand what they were producing. So, I came on down and here I am, one of Louis B. Mayer's wage slaves."

"Not forever, not the way you're talking."

"I'm saving up hard. I want to go back to Europe, to Paris. This time not playing Boadicea, but painting, painting what isn't there, but what I see; what I saw as long as I was able to stay in France, before I had to go to Madrid." She drained her drink, found the waiter with a look that signaled one more. "Don't worry. I won't get sloppy drunk on you. . . . Let's talk about something else. Let's talk about you."

"Not my favorite subject."

"Try."

"Not much to say, really. Family's Irish, Anglo-Irish, actually. My dad didn't like what he saw in Ireland, soldiering with the King's Occupation Army. He married a local colleen and got himself to America and on the New York police force. I grew up wanting to be a cop, but definitely not the way they played it around Brownsville, where the pols had the cops in their back pockets. I took off for L.A. and joined Two Gun Ed Davis's cop shop, which shows you I'm not exactly the brightest person, moving from a corrupt frying pan into the main furnace. The short of it — I learned the way

120

the world works without needing to go to Spain. The end."

The waiter brought Nancy's drink. She thanked him, touched it to her lips and set it down. "You still haven't explained your offer of dinner here in exchange for my doing a sketch of someone, who you're yet to tell me about," she said. "Couldn't you simply have me out on a date, or am I guessing wrong?"

"If you were guessing right, would you have said yes?"

"The Coconut Grove beats staying home and washing my panties."

"It's work," I said.

"A sketch of a friend or a stranger?"

"Strange enough. Someone I ran into recently; rather, who ran into me with a sap." I described the big man to her, leaving out the circumstances.

Nancy listened intently without opening her sketch pad.

The waiter returned offering menus. She ordered the T-bone, green salad, French fried potatoes, and a 1928 Chambertin, explaining, "My father's influence. He taught me that wine's first job is to be red, second to be French and third to be Burgundy."

I went for the sweetbreads, new potatoes

with butter and parsley and the steamed baby carrots, asking her after the waiter departed, "You get enough of a description from me to start drawing?"

"Your getting sapped makes me a sap for more details. Tell me something worth gossiping about. I'll guess it has something to do with Day Covington's murder and his missing wife, Marie MacDaniels."

"No."

"No or no cigar?"

"No is good enough."

"No gossip, no sketch, Mr. Blanchard. . . . Seeing as you are Mr. Mayer's private bloodhound and he's probably paying for this oh-so-expensive evening, it has to be the photographer in Hollywood, Rothman. Better?"

I made a production of lighting a Lucky.

"I remember a quote from the *Herald*," she said, and recited: *"Captain Travis of Homicide announced that some photos found in Rothman's studio were the property of the Metro-Goldwyn-Mayer studio and returned to MGM. Howard Strickling, director of publicity, said they had evidently been stolen in unguarded moments and, to prevent the slightest embarrassment to anyone in the Hollywood community, would be personally destroyed by him."*

I aimed a stream of smoke at the artificial palm trees that decorated the Grove's interior, leftovers from Valentino's 1921 idol-making *The Sheik*. "You must be a whiz at memorizing poems," I said.

"Does Rothman's murder tie into Day Covington's murder? I'll bet it does."

"You're too clever by half. I'll have to take you to the ponies next time I go."

"Were the photos really destroyed or is Howard Strickling keeping them in a safe place, against some future need to keep one of Mr. Mayer's stars in line? Maybe someone like Marie MacDaniels? That sounds like something the Fixer would do, don't you think so?"

"I think it's none of your business."

"Neither was Spain, it turns out. . . . You ask me, the photos were dirty and Rothman a blackmailer who got killed for his pains. They don't get killed for photographing a star at the wrong angle, like that Claudette Colbert, who won't let a camera get anywhere near her left profile."

"There are wrong angles and there are wrong angles."

"The story they were telling over on the Selznick lot was that Marie MacDaniels done the deadly deed on her husband after he found out about the photos and blackmail, why the cops are anxious to talk to her. Rothman breathing his last. Also her handiwork?"

"Maybe in the movies," I said.

"Art imitates life, or is it the other way around?"

It was clear Nancy wasn't going to let go of the subject without some satisfaction, so I told her enough of the story while we lumbered through our meal to get her doing the sketch I needed —

How I stumbled onto Rothman's *corpus* when I went to his studio to investigate a rumor he was in possession of photographs that belonged to Metro and discovered the big man preparing to set fire to the studio.

It wasn't entirely the truth or much of the truth, but it rang true enough to satisfy her.

She flipped open her sketch pad, retrieved pencils from her mesh bag and began to draw quickly, showing her work to me half a dozen times and taking a few corrections without comment.

Finished, Nancy passed the pad across the table and waited out my verdict.

"That's him, to a T," I said, and pointing at her dinner plate, "to a T-bone. . . . Well done enough for me to take to some friends on the Arson Squad."

"Well done enough to earn a dance?" The

orchestra had taken to the stage and was moving from the last notes of "Nice Work if You Can Get It," while the spotlight caught a gracious, shy Freddie Astaire at a prime table, into "Pennies from Heaven," which had Nancy shedding tears.

I helped her from her chair and onto the dance floor, asking, "What's the matter?"

"We used to sing that in Spain . . . when we were getting bombed." She put a hand on my arm. "Sorry. I'll stop doing the Un-American Legion stuff. I promise."

She danced well and felt even better pressed against me, her breath tilting at my ear, the sweet scent of her perfume dazzling my mind with a hint of better things to come past her sketch and my half-truths. The next number was "A Ghost of a Chance," and I thought: *Yeah, maybe I do stand a ghost of a chance with her.*

I kept a close rein on her waist heading back to our table.

She didn't resist.

Two men were in our seats.

They were sleekly dressed, but everything about their tuxedos was a little too much: too much lapel, too much satin; gigantic diamond studs; heavily pomaded hair immaculately slicked back; nails as well groomed as their overripe smiles rang false.

I knew both of them, but not the massive side of beef who looked like a bouncer hovering in the background.

"Nice seeing you again, Chris," the smaller, handsomer of the pair said.

"Wish I could say the same, Benny." He studied me for sincerity, found it absent and let his smile lapse. "Nancy Warren, this is Ben Siegel, the well-known mobster. His friend here, you probably recognize — Georgie Raft, who only pretends to be a mobster, in those Warner Bros. movies not good enough for Robinson or Cagney."

Raft threw his eyes to the glitter ceiling and shook his head. "C'mon, Chris, ixnay with the insults. They're uncalled for."

"Calls 'em the way I sees 'em, Georgie. . . . Benny, anyone with nerve ripe enough to mention you're getting bald? Your forehead is growing higher while your morals couldn't possibly sink any lower."

Nancy gripped me by the wrist, her way of telling me to stop goading him.

Siegel, his face glowing red under a modest desert tan, glared hard at me and said, "Chris, I come over to talk to you, feeling nothing but good will toward you. Why do you want to behave like this toward me, somebody you know since boyhood? I never done a thing to upset your apple cart. Ever."

"Because I know you since boyhood? Because I know what you were back then and what you became, no matter what kind of picture you've been painting in this town? You talk about apple carts, perfect for someone who's rotten to the core."

Nancy tightened her grip and begged under her breath, "Chris, please. Enough."

The side of beef took a step toward me.

Siegel waved him back.

Raft spoke up. "Jesus, Chris, Ben's only come out here tonight to do you a favor."

"Leaving would be a favor, Georgie."

Siegel got up from the chair and stepped into my face. "Okay, I catch, so let's put it this way — I come to tell you there's nothing there for you with this Rothman guy you're wrapped into. The people he made angry are major players with no interests in this town and long gone back East, which is where Rothman made enemies out of them. They took a while finding him, is all. Rothman's got nothing to do with anything at Metro-Goldwyn-Mayer or in L.A."

"That's it?"

"It. A friendly tip from me to you, because you got enough work cut out for you already, what with all them Commies running around the lot and some of the drug addict actors keeping you busy; who knows what else makes up your blue plate special."

"To show you I'm grateful, I promise to keep quiet about your run-in a few nights ago at your crooked joint of a dog track with one of our actors."

"The fucking dwarf, you mean?"

"Midget. . . . You hear about that, Georgie? He got beat up at the track by a midget. Took half a dozen Culver City cops to rescue Benny."

"Dammit, that isn't what happened." A blue vein started pulsing on his forehead. His right hand slid into his jacket, toward the armpit.

Raft paled. "Come on, Ben, let's not start anything."

I said, "No, Georgie, fine by me. Let him start something." Moved my hand inside my tuxedo and held it there. "Waiting on you, Benny."

The side of beef moved again, anxious for a signal from Siegel.

"Your big mouth's gonna get you killed one of these days," Siegel said, making every word count.

His hand came out empty. He turned and stalked off, trailed by the side of beef.

Raft gave me a look, shook his head, got up and scurried after his mobster pal.

There was a knot of silence around Nancy

and me, people at other tables staring. I ostentatiously took a handkerchief from my inside pocket and blew my nose. A woman laughed shrilly, breaking the tension.

"I need a drink," Nancy said, sitting down. Her hands played with her face. "He was going for a gun, wasn't he?"

"He was thinking about it."

"And you. Could you have outdrawn him? Would you have?"

"With my handkerchief?"

"You mean you don't —"

"Come on, Nancy. Who goes to the Coconut Grove for a gunfight?"

"Ben Siegel," she said. Looked around. "Where in hell is our waiter?"

A coffee and a cognac settled her down barely more than some of my answers to her questions unnerved her again, especially how I'd come to know Benny long before I became a cop.

"He and I grew up in the same part of the world," I said. "Brooklyn. Brownsville, where you have three career choices — being a cop, being a crook or being professionally blind to what goes on around you. He was a year younger than me, a first-rate hellion and already carrying the nickname Bugsy. We didn't get along from the time

129

we met."

"How so?"

"He and two of his friends decided to jump me one night when I was coming back from helping my parish priest shingle his roof. A territorial, Catholic versus Jew kind of a thing, not uncommon then or now in the old neighborhood. Benny thought he was be-all, end-all as a boxer. He told his friends stand back while he taught the fish eater a lesson. I taught him otherwise in a hurry. He pulled a knife. I got it away from Benny and beat him up some more; tore off his pants and tossed them on top of a tenement fire escape. He got his friends involved then, had them hold me down while he worked me over. I suppose I was lucky he only used me for a punching bag. I swear I saw murder in his eyes. I saw it every time afterward when we crossed paths, in Brownsville and later here in L.A. He's a first-class psychopath, that one."

"Making you brave or stupid tonight."

"A little of both, maybe. Maybe, showing off for you."

She ignored my puppy dog expression. "He told you to forget about Rothman. Why? Why would he track you down here for that? What's his involvement, a big-time gangster like him?"

"Big, but not in the same league as Luciano, Genovese or Lansky. He and Jack Dragna are the Syndicate's clout here on the Coast. Benny would love to be a movie star like Raft. He gets himself invited to everybody's parties, but nobody's ever going to cast him in anything — unless it's playing a corpse, and the shoot's something like one of our own *Crime Does Not Pay* shorts."

"You haven't answered my questions."

"They're also my questions," I said. "I'll be looking for the answers."

"You look too hard and maybe you'll get yourself killed."

"Would it make a difference to you?"

Instead of an answer, she gave me a look that could have meant anything I wanted it to mean and retreated into her glass of cognac.

I raised mine and toasted, "To life."

She looked up approvingly and echoed the toast in a warm whisper.

The orchestra had returned from a break and was into the first notes of "I Only Have Eyes for You." Without asking, I came around the table, helped her onto her feet and guided her to the crowded dance floor.

She held onto me like a favorite toy.

Had me wondering how the night would end.

Wishing it never would.

CHAPTER 8

Sunday, November 13, 1938

I woke up the next morning with Nancy sprung from my dreams but still on my mind. Both of us too exhilarated from shared unspoken emotions — or maybe simply too tipsy from our last rounds of cognac — I'd driven out to the beach, where we watched the Malibu waves for a while, talking in insignificant generalities, nothing important, as if fearing a wrong question would cause a response disastrous to our budding relationship, or so I chose to tell myself.

I got her back to her garden apartment in the Echo Park area before sunrise.

At the door, we stared at one another for an hour past eternity before she tapped my nose with her index finger, brushed my lips with hers — more than a friendly kiss, but not much more — and cooed, "I'm available next time you need a sketch, dinner optional," before disappearing inside.

I had a fitful time before falling asleep, trying to decide if I was sorry or glad she hadn't asked me in, or if I should have invited myself in for a nightcap.

A nightcap.

Hah!

Nightcap — a polite word for what was aching at my mind and body.

On reflection, I was pleased at how the evening concluded.

It augured well for a realistic future in the land of make-believe.

Or was that only my own make-believe?

I struggled out of bed one body part at a time and found the kitchen.

Orange juice, black coffee and a boiled egg on toast later, I was feeling better; feeling like a beer chaser before deciding the business I had on tap for today merited a clear head, my wits about me, because of the delicate nature of the conversation I was already practicing in my mind.

I showered, shaved, splashed on some bay rum and dressed carefully — an oxford cotton shirt, no tie, sports coat with subdued checks — after considering tennis whites that might work better at integrating me into the crowd I'd be joining.

I left my place around eleven, drove through the glare-hung streets around palm fronds that had been blown down during the night and trash cans the hot, dry November afternoon winds were rolling along like lost tumbleweeds, past a scattering of kids, ball players and dedicated picnickers in the public parks.

There already was a circus of cars outside George Cukor's estate on Cordell Drive in Brentwood when I got there.

I parked my V8 among Cadillac convertibles, Packard Twelves, a few cabriolets with bored chauffeurs, two bull-nosed Cords, two Duesenbergs, and a smattering of real peoples' automobiles and crossed over to the entrance gate in the high brick security wall.

A muscular young man, quite blond-haired, quite good-looking and quite aware of it, was lounging just inside the Spanish wrought ironwork. He strutted over, his baby blues giving me a cautious onceover. "Yes?"

"Here to see Mr. Cukor," I said, sliding my calling card through the bars.

He studied it. "Your name and nothing else on it, so how will Mr. Cukor know what this is about?"

"He'll know the name."

"If this is about business, you're here on the wrong day for it. Mr. Cukor devotes his Sunday afternoons to his special friends."

"I said he'll know the name." I tilted back my shoulder to give Blondie a glimpse of my .38 Detective Special at rest in its holster.

He lost his officious grin and opened the gate. "Follow me. I'll give George your card, but don't say you weren't warned if he tosses you out on your ear."

"To ear is human," I said.

The gag was wasted on him.

He led me up steps into the courtyard, past terraces and carefully watered plants into a garden studded with classic marble statues, asked me to wait here, and sped along his merry way. The bar at the far end of the courtyard was being tended by two colored waiters. Forty or so men lounged around, talking and laughing in quiet, confident voices. Some wore bathing trunks, others casual outfits.

Cukor's Sunday parties were reputed among those who knew the whispers to be true to always mix actors and others from all levels of the business with social luminaries from New York and Europe. I recognized some of them. One familiar face belonged to a prominent MGM banker, who was standing in an alcove, engaged in intense conversation with a scantily clad boy-man best described as beautiful.

The only two women around were in the pool. One was the writer Salka Viertel, who saw me and waved before racing the other woman, Garbo herself, across the length of the pool. It was not until they went up the steps to the deck that I saw both were naked. Garbo moved in close to Viertel and engaged her in a hug and modest kiss, picked up a towel from a deck chair, and began drying off Viertel's back.

"Excellent, Mr. Blanchard, how you kept your eyebrows under perfect control," George Cukor said, smiling, his voice as calm and cultured as always, indifferent to the fact I had crashed his party and most definitely was the only outsider among his guests stepping out of the closet this delicious Sunday. He pumped my hand vigorously. "Can I assume important studio business brings you here on a weekend, some urgent matter on L.B.'s agenda?"

"I hope not, Mr. Cukor. It's about the late Day Covington."

"Oh?" His smile thinned and went away. "Perhaps we had best go inside, Mr. Blanchard."

He wheeled around and waddled up the

137

steps to French doors feeding into an oval-shaped room that reeked of success. The walls were covered with tan suede, the ceiling painted a lush blue, the fireplace a marvel in copper. A huge beige sofa curved with the walls, and behind it was a dramatic picture window that looked out onto the gardens. The chairs and pillows were done in green and opal. Fine European and American art was on display everywhere, added testament to his exquisite taste and moneyed status.

Two familiar-looking middle-aged men dressed for tennis sat thigh to thigh at one end of the sofa, engaged in an intense conversation that carried across the room.

"Of course we've got to stop the bastard," the balding, bulkier one with pale skin the color of ivory said. "We didn't at Munich, and now he thinks he can ride roughshod over the world."

His friend, slimmer and more muscular, with brooding eyes and a hawkish nose overhanging a big-boned chin, his voice a mellow sax to the other's blaring trumpet, said, "Germany isn't our problem."

"It damned well's going to be, mark my words. First they savage the Jews, next they'll come after us, and after that —"

"Girls, please," Cukor called over. "Out-

138

side with your League of Nations debate about Herr Schickelgruber and how to deal with his insanity. I need to borrow my room for a bit, if you don't mind fading yourselves into the sunshine." He directed them to the French doors.

They smiled acceptance, locked hands and glided out.

Cukor closed the doors behind them and signaled me to take a seat.

I plopped onto one of the dark brown club chairs surrounding a glass coffee table smothered in a display of arts and architecture books and magazines and issues of *Daily Variety* and *Hollywood Reporter.*

Cukor strolled over and stood with his hands behind his back, studied me through his tortoise-shell eyeglasses like he was framing and lighting a scene. He was in his late thirties, a paunchy five-eight or five-nine in height, heavier than the last time I saw him on the Metro lot, a testament to his penchant for Hungarian food and rich desserts.

He had overgrown features, a large nose and overripe lips, a pouch of fat below his chin that made him sensitive about his appearance, but no one who spent longer than five minutes in his company ever thought him ugly.

Louis B. Mayer, in spite of his conservative bent and constant preaching of family values, had elected to ignore Cukor's sexual leanings. He'd made him one of the highest-paid directors in town, at seventy-five thousand dollars a year on a three-picture contract, a reward for turning out hits like *Dinner at Eight, Little Women, David Copperfield,* and *Camille.* Every actress on the lot clamored to be directed by Cukor, and he was David O. Selznick's first choice to tackle *Gone with the Wind,* although there were rumblings that Gable was unhappy about that and had sworn publicly that he'd "never work for that God damned faggot."

I'd last dealt with Cukor about a year ago, when he and a friend had a set-to with four sailors at the Long Beach Pike while prowling after what his cloaked society called "rough trade." They were badly beaten, ended up in jail, and shutting up the incident cut a large hole in Howard Strickling's budget.

I was sent by Mayer to bail out Cukor and his friend, get them home undetected while Strick negotiated the payoffs. Seeing Cukor's battered face enraged me, and I tried to get someone in authority to jail and prosecute the sailors. The cops laughed at me, and the ship's captain who commanded the four sailors, eyes and fists ready for a tussle of his own, shouted me down, saying, "My men have every right to beat up any queer they run across, any time they want. That what you are, one of them pansies?"

I kept my temper, told him, "I'm somebody who's never been able to understand why it mattered what other people do when they're by themselves, so long as they don't push their ideas on other folks."

"Yeah, and you probably voted for Roosevelt," the captain said, and ordered me off his ship.

Embellishing his reputation as one of Hollywood's most gracious and congenial hosts, Cukor said, "Cigarette, Mr. Blanchard? Feel free to help yourself to the brand of your choice." He pointed to the sterling silver tray on the table.

"Thanks, no, Mr. Cukor. Trying to cut down."

"Coffin nails, to be sure, but we all have to go sometime or other." He sank into the club chair across from me, selected a Pall Mall from the cigarette tray and lit up with the jeweled sterling silver table lighter. He took a delicate puff, let it escape his lips and said, "You're a welcome visitor here anytime, but what is it about Covington that brings you to my domain this fine Sunday?"

"The check you gave him for five hundred dollars."

"Yes, I did do that." He took a deep drag from the Pall Mall. His hand trembled slightly. "Sad about his dying the way he did," he said, not sounding particularly sad, an unconvincing downturn to his mouth.

"He was blackmailing you, and that was the payoff, the five hundred, in exchange for photographs of you that, for obvious reasons, you didn't want made public."

Cukor seemed unsure how to answer and used the cigarette as a bridge, tapping a Florsheim while taking a series of nervous drags and firing puffballs of smoke across the room.

After a minute or two, he said, "You're a most loyal and trustworthy fellow, Mr. Blanchard, so I will answer you as honestly as I can. Yes, blackmail, but — pardon my French — the little prick wasn't after me. The pictures were of a close friend of mine, and no, I shan't tell you his name. Suffice it to say, it's a name you would recognize at once."

"Unnecessary, Mr. Cukor, unless it were to become an important issue in a court of law."

"Heaven forbid." He smashed out the Pall

Mall in the ashtray and dry-washed his hands. "And this is between us, if I understood you correctly? L.B. is a tolerant man, but blackmail might be too much for him to accept even of me, especially if it related to my friend and a murder."

"Mr. Mayer pays my salary, but I'm acting for myself here." It wasn't entirely the truth, but I'd learned during my LAPD years that the truth doesn't always serve a truthful purpose. "I'm looking to help an old friend of my own, get her out from under suspicion of murder."

"His wife, Covington's wife. The lovely young girl who stars in one of the studio programmers."

"Yes. Marie MacDaniels."

"The police and, it seems, MGM appear to believe she might have done it."

"The police and MGM think a lot of things."

Cukor managed a thread of a smile. "They do, don't they."

"Tell me about the photographs."

"Of Day Covington and my friend, which may also account for the shadow of suspicion falling on your Miss MacDaniels."

"You're saying Covington —"

"Liked it both ways, yes."

The little light bulb over my head flicked

on. I suddenly understood what Eve Whitney meant when she mentioned the stain Covington might bring home to his silk sheets. Covington never oozed that inclination in my presence, and if Marie knew or suspected anything, she hadn't shared it with me.

Cukor said, "Covington was in the habit of convincing his lovers — whether male or female — that it would be kinky to take pictures, using a couple Leicas he kept around the apartment exclusively to memorialize his liaisons."

I flashed on the Leicas in Otto Rothman's studio.

"Unbeknownst to me, my friend became lust-ridden with Covington about a year ago and agreed to smile at the birdie," Cukor said, his expression darkening. "Damn fool idiot that he is." He caught my smile before I turned my head and sent a hearty laugh into the air. "I know, I know what you must be thinking, Mr. Blanchard. Who is Cukor to be calling anyone names? Someone who whistled at four sailors and paid the price. The pot calling the kettle black."

I took a flyer. "What can you tell me about Otto Rothman, the photographer who was murdered in his studio?"

"And not a very good one, certainly no

144

George Hurrell or Clarence Bull. You can be more direct than that with me, Mr. Blanchard. Yes, I did know Otto Rothman and, yes, it developed he was a despicable ally of Covington, partners in malice."

Cukor reached for a fresh Pall Mall.

I joined him, pulling a Lucky from the tray.

I popped a string of smoke rings to his shafts of smoke, easing back in the chair, crossing my legs at the ankle, allowing him as much time as he needed to construct his memories.

"It starts with Covington and goes back years," he said. "I was directing plays in Rochester, New York, when we met. He was in love with theater more than theater was ever going to love him. He had more money than acting talent, and we had a brief fling, long ended and forgotten by me by the time I was brought out here by Metro-Goldwyn-Mayer and won my wings.

"I thought I'd heard the last of Covington until I received a wire from him in late '31 or early '32, telling me he was in desperate straits over gambling debts and hoping I could help him out with a film part or two. Out of sympathy, I set up some jobs for him and wired, *Come West, young trick.* He was part of my circle before he made friends of his own and disappeared from my life until one evening I came to rue, when we found ourselves at the bar at Musso & Frank.

"I had just ended a relationship a little explosively and not at all on my terms. He oozed friendship and understanding, and shortly we adjourned to this modest apartment of his. Next morning, dragging myself to the loo, I noticed a closet door open and inside, aimed at the bed, a Leica camera on a tripod, for Christ's sake. I had no need to ask what that was about. I shook Covington awake and told him he was *persona non grata,* I never wanted to see or hear from him again, and fled. Foolishly, I stormed out of there without first demanding he hand over the film."

"Where Rothman comes into the picture."

"Not immediately. A year or so later. Rothman called me, advising he had fallen into possession of certain photographs."

"You and Covington."

"Precisely. He said he planned to retain the photos in his film history archives and was I interested in making a small contribution to help ensure that the negatives were not ruined through inadequate storage? No mention of blackmail, but extortion nonetheless. For as modest a sum as he wanted, it wasn't worth going to the authorities, exposing the situation publicly and endangering my career. Rothman never asked for more than twenty dollars at any one time — fifty dollars once or twice — and I only heard from him a couple times a year."

"I know."

"You know?" Cukor seemed startled, but quickly regained his composure. "How do you know?"

"You weren't his only victim. Rothman kept coded ledgers and envelopes stuffed with negatives for everyone he was blackmailing. Dozens upon dozens of celebrities. In the ledger, against the initials GC, he logged the amounts you say you paid him, but not the check for five hundred dollars that you made out to Covington."

"When he contacted me, I caught the impression Covington was voyaging out on his own, where he and Rothman had shared the miniscule proceeds from the photographs with me."

"And probably a lot of other couplings of a private nature, all adding up to a nice profit for both of them every year."

"Five hundred dollars is a lot of money, but it's what one does for a friend whose own financial circumstances are not as flush as one would like." Cukor's mind wandered briefly. "He would do the same for me, were our circumstances reversed," he said, like he was trying to convince himself.

"How did you get the check to Covington?"

He took my question the wrong way, bolted upright in the chair and fired a harsh look at me. "No, Mr. Blanchard, I didn't deliver it to his home and while I was there use the opportunity to murder him. Were it my doing, I'd have devised some manner of death far more horrible and painful for that sad excuse for a human being."

"I'm here for you, not against you, Mr. Cukor." I removed his five-hundred-dollar check from my billfold and offered it to him. "Otherwise, the police would have this, and you'd be downtown fielding questions from them."

He caught his breath, took the check and studied it. "The bastard thought it would be oh, so cutesy to make the transfer at Musso & Frank. When I arrived, he was half into his cups, tottering on the same damn barstool as the last time." He lit the check with the table lighter and watched it burn in the ashtray, smiling as it turned to black ash. "Sorry about my bad manners, losing my temper that way, Mr. Blanchard."

I waved off the apology as unnecessary, drawing an appreciative smile, and pulled out Nancy Warren's sketch of the big man. "Recognize him, Mr. Cukor?"

Cukor examined the sketch, shook his head. "A face in the Central Casting crowd at best; by comparison, makes Wally Beery look like a matinee idol . . . I suppose it would be expecting too much to believe you also brought the envelope you mentioned, with the negatives?"

"The envelope was empty, Mr. Cukor, one of many empties I discovered."

"Oh, dear me," he said. "And my friend. His envelope? Also empty?"

"Impossible to answer, seeing as how you haven't shared his name with me."

"Yes, of course. How foolish. Let me see what I can do about that."

CHAPTER 9

Walter, the Ravenswood's doorman, rang me at five minutes before six asking if I was expecting Mr. Haines. I was, I said, and granted him permission to allow Mr. Haines use of the elevator. Walter had mustered out of the Great War as a lieutenant colonel and remained a stickler for chain of command.

"Yes, sir, thank you, sir," he said, and within a minute or two I was at my door greeting William Haines, a great star of the silent screen, one of only seven to be billed above the title by MGM, who easily made the transition to talkies as star of the studio's first talking picture, *Alias Jimmy Valentine.*

He was an interior designer now, decorating the homes of many of the stars he'd once acted opposite, who had continued a quiet friendship with him after scandal closed out his acting career. Among his clients were Joan Crawford, Claudette Colbert, Carole Lombard, Lionel Barrymore,

Marion Davies, and George Cukor, who had arranged for our discreet tête-à-tête with a phone call earlier in the day.

I held out my hand for a shake, got a bear hug instead, as if we were old friends, followed by a generous greeting in a booming voice that carried strong traces of Haines's Virginia birthplace. He stepped back and sized me up. "You look far too decent and honest to be working for Louie B., the Mayer of Metro, to whom I owe a deep debt of gratitude for giving me a future by burying me and my past."

I understood Haines's meaning.

In '33, on one of his frequent forays downtown to Pershing Square, Haines picked up a sailor and took him to a room he kept at the YMCA. Shortly, the house detective and L.A. vice cops burst in, arrested and handcuffed the men. Strickling managed to hush up the incident, but an outraged Mayer hauled Haines into his den and roared a demand, that his star choose between his lifestyle and his career. Haines, ten years into a relationship with Jimmie Shields, his stand-in and live-in lover, chose the former. Mayer tore up his contract and made favor calls around town to all the other studio bigwigs that guaranteed Haines would never work again.

He and Shields bought an antique shop in Manhattan Beach and expanded it into the interior design business around a Haines concept that came to be fashionably famous as the Hollywood Regency Style.

However, old habits die harder than bindweed.

In '36, a neighbor accused them of propositioning his young son. The police were called in, but the charges were dropped after Strickling quietly came to their rescue at the personal behest of Joan Crawford, who he quoted to me as saying: *Billy and Jimmie have the happiest marriage I've ever seen in Hollywood.* A short time later, they moved out to Malibu after they were attacked and beaten by the White Legion, California's homegrown Ku Klux Klan.

Haines followed me into the apartment, humming an invented melody as he ran his eyes over the walls and furnishings, cutting into it with a clucking sound that grew increasingly louder and despairing. "Definitely, Mr. Blanchard, this place could benefit from a woman's touch. Unfortunately, Jimmie and I are booked solid far into next year."

"I hope that's not the reason Mr. Cukor gave you when he arranged this meeting, Mr. Haines."

"It's Billy, please, and no — it's the reason I gave Jimmie before driving in from the beach. A favor for George. Easier for him to understand that than my confessing it had to do with that horrid Day Covington. He doesn't know, you see, and it's nothing I ever want him to know. We've both already had enough misery to last a lifetime."

Haines's soulful eyes plea bargained with me before he moved over to the wall dominated by a group photo of me and my teammates at the old LAPD Revolver and Athletic Club in the Chavez Ravine chunk of Elysian Park that later became the Police Academy. He adjusted the frame. "Better," he said, and helped himself to a spot on the sofa as I took inventory of him.

Haines was a six-footer, approaching forty and as trim and fit as I remembered him from his movies; glowing with suntanned health; perfectly groomed hair capping a high, intelligent forehead. He drew a gold cigarette case from his Italian cut sports coat and offered me an English Oval before lighting up himself. Waited patiently for me to speak while I torched a Lucky with my Dunhill.

"Tell me about the five hundred dollars Mr. Cukor loaned you."

"The five hundred, miniscule in relation

153

to the debt of gratitude I owe him." He nodded accord. "Go back about five years, before I ceased to exist at the studios. I was invited to an organizational meeting of what became the Screen Actors Guild by Ralph Morgan, Frankie's brother. It was him, Karloff, Alan Mowbray, Jimmy Gleason, Charlie Starrett, Bob Young, Lew Ayers, Fay Wray, Ginger, a bunch of others, among them this attractive wannabe trying to climb out of the B movie jungle, who fawned over me like I might be his avenue to bigger and better things. Well, his flattery inspired me to a bigger thing, for certain. We came to frolic on a regular basis, one or more liaisons captured by a camera I should have realized was too often all too available. This of whom I speak was, of course, Day Covington, who ultimately proved not to be one of the better things in my life and I cut the cord.

"We now dissolve to a week ago. Day Covington resumes unannounced in my life with a phone call, offering to continue keeping the photos and the negatives suppressed, safely under lock and key, for five hundred dollars. His timing couldn't be worse. Jimmie and I are having serious cash problems — we're currently a bit overextended, you see — and I certainly don't fancy giving

Jimmie a heart attack by revealing this sordid business to him. Pondering what to do, I remembered my dear friend George once confiding in me about his own horrible experience with Day Covington. I got on the phone to George. He volunteered to take care of the situation, and —" His voice quit. He clenched his face and suffered through a thought. "Dear me, you don't suppose that means for a minute George killed Covington, do you? That would be carrying the finest of friendships a step too far."

"I don't."

"That's a relief." He used a heel to extinguish the English Oval and dropped the butt into a side pocket of his sports coat. "When he phoned, George told me you might know the current whereabouts of those dreadful negatives and photographs, something about the photographer Otto Rothman?"

I explained to Haines in detail how Rothman and Covington had worked together. "I don't recollect any WH or BH in the Rothman ledger or any envelope for a WH or BH, empty or otherwise," I said.

"Or anywhere else?"

"Anywhere else?"

"Any other initials. . . . Covington took the photos he was holding out for blackmail,

155

but I did have occasion to pose for Rothman at his studio with — " He thought twice about using the name. "With Clark."

"Gable . . . there were two payments of forty bucks earlier this year by a CG. No envelope."

"Ours earlier and wholly innocent, I assure you. I've heard the same rumor as you, about Clark and George, lived the rumor about Clark and me. You get to be a star of his magnitude, you become fair game for the people who take great delight in building up an idol, then destroying the pedestal on which they've put him. These were publicity photos for some charity event sponsored by the Masquers." He filled the room with laughter. "It could just as easily have been Cary Grant, your CG, just as your GC might not have been George, but Gary Cooper. . . . Anything else?"

I handed over Nancy's sketch of the big man.

Haines recoiled at the image and gave me a puzzled look.

"Somebody you might have bumped into at Rothman's place?"

"Sorry, no. A dark alley, more likely."

The conversation, initially so promising, lapsed into small talk about George Raft before Haines prepared to leave. He had seen Raft emerge from a limousine and enter the Ravenswood ten yards ahead of his arrival, generating a smile and salute from Walter the doorman as he whizzed past him en route to the elevator.

"One of his periodic visits upstairs to see Miss West," I said.

"I thought he and Mae broke up long ago, when she became a bigger star than his ego could take," Haines said.

"There's breaking up and there's breaking up," I said. "Even I know better than to believe everything I read in the papers and fan books."

Haines greeted the thought with hearty laughter. "I put more faith in what doesn't make it to print," he said, rewarded me with a parting bear hug and air kisses on both my cheeks and volunteered a somber word of advice: "Really, fella, you must do something sometime soon about this place of yours. I haven't seen a disaster like this since Johnny Gilbert's career."

He was barely gone two minutes when the doorbell rang.

I thought maybe Haines had remembered something worth remembering.

Instead, I found myself staring at Ben Siegel's bodyguard, the side of beef from

Saturday night at the Grove —

Briefly —

Before he caught me in the chest with a punch that staggered me backwards and onto the floor.

"Mr. Siegel sends his regards," he said, and stalked after me.

His shoe connected with my rib cage.

Something went "crack" and an electric shock wracked me from head to toe.

He drew his foot back, ready to score again with his size twelves.

I managed to roll aside.

His shoe came down hard on the throw rug and threw him off balance, long enough for me to pull back up, haul off and deliver an uppercut to his lantern jaw.

I might as well have been punching a pillow for all the damage I scored.

He laughed off the blow and gifted me with another of his own.

It caught me on the shoulder, twisted me around and deeper into the apartment.

The side of beef kept on me like Joe Louis last June, when the Brown Bomber went after Max Schmeling in their rematch and KO'd the German heavyweight in two minutes and four seconds of the first round.

Only where was it written I had to be Schmeling, poster child for a Nazi Party boasting how no black man could ever beat their man, whose winnings would help build tanks back home?

Tanks, but no tanks.

If I was going to be anybody, I was going to be Joe, not some kraut stretched out on the canvas.

I imagined away my pain and turned to face him, my dukes up and motioning him to take his best shot.

He did —

A left-handed jab that sailed right through my defense and clipped me on the chin, followed by a right that crashed into my stomach.

My legs turned to mush.

I sank to my knees, my eyes straining to stay open, my ears assaulted by his high-pitched giggle streaming past a set of yellow and black teeth as crooked as his boss while he pulled a 9mm Smith & Wesson out from somewhere, crouched, and jammed the pistol barrel into my mouth.

He said, "Mr. Siegel, he says to tell you, next time you embarrass him in public will be the last time you ever do so in public again, unnerstan'? Nod once for yes, twice if you got a death wish."

"I understand," I said, only —

It didn't sound like me. Besides, I'd been

taught from an early age it was impolite to speak with a full mouth.

Walter the lobby doorman had sneaked up behind Siegel's guy, who withdrew the 9mm and shifted in his direction, but not fast enough to escape the billy club Walter kept under his desk and carried with him on his routine safety tours of the building.

Walter caught him with a hard blow to the temple that sent the side of beef off to Dreamland in a fetal position.

"You okay, Mr. Blanchard?"

I nodded, pressing hard against the one or two ribs I figured to be bruised, cracked or worse.

"He must-a come in past me after I started off to clock the checkpoints." He took a closer look. "Damn, if that ain't Mr. Raft's driver. Miss West won't like this, not at all, when she learns. I'll use your phone to call in the police, you don't mind."

"No police," I said, struggling to get the word out. "Call upstairs to Mr. Raft and invite him down to help get his friend out of here."

He threw away his hands and let me see that wasn't how he'd handle the situation.

"I swear on my mother's grave, Chris, I had no idea Ben was going to pull a stunt like this on you," George Raft said, after we'd finished depositing the side of beef into the limo and he settled himself behind the driver's seat. "Any time I've ever borrowed Spikes and this buggy, nothing like tonight's ever happened."

"His name's Spike?"

"With an 's,' Spikes, and more like a nickname. Goes back to when he was doing collections for the boys and sometimes had to threaten deadbeat customers to pay up with a sledgehammer and railroad spikes. Spikes never actually used the hammer on anybody, I don't think. . . . Once, but Ben covered the freight afterward to get Menchy Rosen back the full use of his hands and feet."

"Salt of the earth that he is. You're not doing yourself any good hanging out with Benny Siegel, Georgie."

"He helped get me out of the dance halls and onto the silver screen," Raft said, fiddling with the knot on his tie. "Otherwise, I'd still be doing dime-a-dance tangos and trots with sad old spinsters chasing cheap thrills back at Roseland. . . . I owe Ben big time, Chris. I'll owe him some more when I ask him to lay off you as a personal favor to me."

"I'd rather you ask him to ixnay any plans

161

he has in mind for Tyrone Powell."

"The dwarf you had the words over at the Grove?"

"The midget."

He made a face. "After, he couldn't stop raving like a maniac; madder'n I ever seen him."

"A personal favor for me, Georgie, and I'll owe you one."

Raft sighed in surrender. "He'll know I'm playing messenger boy for you, Chris, so no guarantees. With him you never count on anything for certain. Bugsy is plain old nuts, you wanna know the truth."

"I know the truth, Georgie. Believe me, I know. I'll take my chances."

I stepped away from the limo after we shared a tight handshake and watched as Raft accelerated past the speed limit heading north on Rossmore. A patrol car emerged from the poorly lit side street and appeared to chase after him.

Hugging myself against the damp night air, I headed back for the Ravenswood, quitting when I spotted the silver LaSalle four-door parked across the street, about five yards down. Captain Ray Travis of LAPD Homicide was leaning against the front fender, the brim of his hat snapped down over his forehead, the collar of his camel hair overcoat turned up, hands fondling a long-stemmed briar pipe.

I reversed direction and joined him.

"You can catch your death coming out in nasty weather dressed like that," he said, and plugged a corner of his mouth with the pipe.

"I could name a hundred nastier ways to die, Captain, but thanks for the tip. Aren't you a little off your beat?"

"Am I?"

"Beats me."

He almost smiled. "You're as quick-witted as ever with the words, Blanchard, but, in a manner of speaking — yes. You have become my beat."

"Care to explain?"

He took the pipe from his mouth and used his thumb to tamp down the simmering tobacco, smiled for real this time and said, "No, nothing I care to do right now, except to remind you things aren't always what they seem. You were a relatively fine, re-sourceful detective before you lost your way. Maybe you can figure it out by yourself."

"And if I can't?"

"I'll still be around," Travis said. "On that you can count."

"Rubber Hose Ray to the rescue?"

163

"That doesn't work for you, maybe you can get Errol Flynn."

"Captain Blood's too expensive for my blood."

"Then I guess you'll be stuck with Captain Travis."

"For more than a walk-on?"

"Unless I have to come running," Travis said, and left me standing there trying to figure out what the hell we were talking about.

He was on to me for something, but what?

Something to do with Covington and the missing Marie MacDaniels?

With Rothman, since I had no doubt my call to Mayer led Mayer to Strickling and Strick to LAPD, Travis and the news stories that failed to mention anything about MGM and its bounty of heavenly stars?

With George Cukor or Billy Haines?

With Benny Siegel or George Raft?

With —

Something or someone else?

Whatever else, I knew I was in for another restless night.

CHAPTER 10

Monday, November 14, 1938

I headed for the *Battling G-Men in Havana* soundstage after rifling through the morning mail and returning a call Mayer had directed my way from the people building the Hollywood Park Race Track he'd invested in with Jolson, Edward G. Robinson, Jack Warner and other movie colony turf nuts with cash to spare.

He wanted me to sign off on security features they had blueprinted for the track's clubhouse. I hadn't had time to check out the blueprints, but congratulated them on a job well done, promising myself I'd find them wherever I'd stashed them last week and take a look before the day ended.

I hadn't seen or heard from Eve Whitney since last Thursday, when she fell short of telling me whatever it was she thought I needed to hear once Strickling and then Travis showed up unannounced at her

165

trailer. She wasn't on the Friday production call sheet and there was no answer whenever I tried her home phone number.

On the set, crews were adjusting camera positions and lighting on a slow hustle while Hal Bucquet, the director, took Eve and Baxter Leeds through their blocking in a tawdry saloon, repeatedly reassuring Leeds he'd command the frame as he moved from there to here to there.

"That has my back to the camera when I reach the bar and order the rum and cola or whatever," Leeds said. "What do you say to that, buddy?"

Bucquet put on an Oscar-winning smile and in his proper English accent said, "I say that's where we'll cut to a reverse shot, you picking up the drink and offering a *Salud,* followed by a close-up of you taking an ample taste and lighting up the screen with your million-dollar smile."

Leeds liked that. "Genius," he said. "Buddy, your first *Battling G-Men* and you got me scared that we are going to lose you once Mr. Thalberg ganders at the rushes and your creativity."

While Bucquet played modesty to a fault with his star, he drew an understanding smirk from Eve, veteran that she was of Baxter Leeds's gargantuan ego.

She spotted me standing alongside the camera and tilted her head in the direction of her trailer.

I headed over and helped myself to a beer from the refrigerator.

She got there about forty minutes and a second long neck later.

Locked the door behind her.

Caught me by surprise with an embrace that ended with a smacker on the lips.

"That's from Marie by way of me," she said. "Were it my real thing, you'd be begging for more."

"In close-up."

"Closer than that. Face it, Detective Blanchard, all these years after the fact and I'm still a whore at heart. All the johns, my training ground for a prick like Baxter Leeds, you know what I mean?" She borrowed my beer and emptied the bottle; pulled two fresh ones from the refrigerator. "Here at the studio, at least, it's a producer or director's casting couch, slow and easy on the spine, not some quickie hit-and-run in a dark alley or behind some bushes in Echo Park."

"Didn't you once promise me to put all that behind you, Evie?"

"Put a lot behind me ever since, Detective, but since that's surely not what brought

167

you here — what brings you here?"

"You had something to tell me last week, before we were interrupted by Howard Strickling and Ray Travis."

"Howard and . . ." For a moment she had trouble placing Travis. "Oh, yeah, from *Bombay Rain.*"

"About Marie."

"Oh, yeah."

"I called you, but never could reach you."

"Oh, yeah."

She went after a smiling hippo from her collection of stuffed animals and pulled down the zipper on its belly. Extracted a glass container the shape and size of a lipstick, full of white powder I recognized immediately as cocaine. Tapped a small amount onto the back of her hand. Sucked it up a nostril; then a second time for the other nostril. Hid the tube back inside the hippo's belly and returned the hippo to her private zoo.

"Better," she said. "Where were we, sexy?"

It was my first indication Eve was using again, despite a promise she had made to me back when she was heavy into bennies, hooch, and an occasional spin with heroin, to break for keeps with all her bad habits. I should have seen the relapse in her eyes before now, recognized it was behind her distracted manner.

"About Marie."

"Oh, yeah . . . after Day Covington got murdered, Marie came over and had me get her to the boat, where she said she'd hang out waiting to hear from you. I was supposed to call and let you know. Sorry. I was all caught up partying with the pretty boy I was dating and my mind and body were somewhere else and the weekend just flew on by, whatever I remember of it, which isn't much, and please don't you get angry with me, Chris."

Anger right now would be a waste of an emotion. "You said 'boat,' Evie. Tell me about the boat."

"What's to say that you don't already know? The S.S. *Rex,* Tony Cornero's boat."

"Did you mention any of this to Howard Strickling or Ray Travis?"

"No, cross my heart and hope to die." She made the sign of the cross. "They kept on me about Marie, asking did I know where Marie was, but I played dumb, Chris. Not a word passed these lips, because the baby said not to tell anybody else but you."

"Strickling or Travis comes back, keep it that way, understand?"

"Cross my heart and hope to die," she said, like it was a new thought, and made the sign of the cross again.

She was tracking after the smiling hippo again when I left.

The S.S. *Rex,* a cruise ship moored three miles off Santa Monica, was billed by owner Tony Cornero, a mobster late of Las Vegas, as the world's largest, most luxurious casino, offering and surpassing all the thrills of the Riviera, Biarritz, Cannes, and Monte Carlo. Its location in international waters put it outside the reach of federal and state laws governing gambling, an assertion California's Attorney General, Earl Warren, intended to challenge in court.

The *Rex,* converted by Cornero at a reported cost of $200,000, operated twenty-four hours a day, seven days a week. It carried a crew of three hundred fifty, including dealers, waiters and waitresses, gourmet chefs, a full orchestra, the "Rex Mariners," and strategically placed armed security, and could host about two thousand gamblers every cruise, among them the ultra-elite of Hollywood.

I'm not a gambler, unless you want to count my ex-wife, who's cost me more in alimony than I'd ever want to toss away on blackjack or at the craps table, but I've been on board the S.S. *Rex* more than I've been to Vegas or Charlie Farrell's Racquet Club in Palm Springs since Cornero launched business earlier this year with three hundred slot machines, a five-hundred seat bingo parlor, six roulette wheels, and eight dice tables.

I was there with Mayer when the floating casino premiered with razzmatazz that rivaled one of Sid Grauman's opening nights, and I'm the guy they call whenever one of our stars goes out of control, creates embarrassing problems for himself or Cornero, and Strickling isn't available. The scenes are usually brought on by a combination of bad luck and too much hooch or some hoochie-kooch unhappy about being manhandled in one of Cornero's sin suites below deck, off-limits to anybody lacking a famous face or six-figure income. Of course, Cornero denies there's any prostitution on board, but getting too close to one of the downstairs doors uninvited will win you a gat in the face faster than you can say Jack Barrymore.

I got to Santa Monica shortly before eleven, wedged the V8 into a curbside spot on a side street rowed with cheap day rentals and hoofed to the *Rex* reservation booth on the pier, at the foot of Colorado Street, where two bits bought me a round-trip ticket for the twelve-minute water taxi ride. I scored one of the last seats, squashed between noisy tourists toting Kodak boxes and Brownies they wouldn't be allowed to use on board and silent gambling regulars wearing the look of chronic losers.

At the head of the gangplank, the ship's greeter, resplendent in a tuxedo and ship's captain hat tilted at a rakish angle, recognized me with a warm smile and limp handshake. I told him what had brought me out, and he dispatched an assistant to find Cornero, who arrived as his polite security goons finished frisking all the arrivals for weapons to ensure what they announced as the comfort and safety of Admiral Cornero's guests.

The ersatz Admiral was dressed to the expensive nines and smelled of imported cologne slapped over his five o'clock shadow. He led me to a far corner of the cocktail lounge, en route boasting that business was netting him fifteen grand or more a day, in a melodic voice that fit his undistinguished, dark good looks and bore strong evidence of his Northern Italy origin. "Not so bad for a poor immigrant from Lequio Tanaro not yet forty, and all of it legal, wouldn't you say, Chris? You know I put a hundred thou on the line, for grabs by anyone who proves there's a falsely run game here on the *Rex*. Safe as the dough inside my mattress, because every game is strictly legit. You don't not ever got to cheat when the law is on your side."

Waiting for our drinks — a split of Dom Perignon for Cornero, bonded rye with a water back for me — I listened to his foul-mouthed complaining about Warren trying to put him out of business, comparing him to Charlie-Lucky Luciano, Meyer Lansky and Frank Costello, the New York gang leaders who muscled him out of his Green Meadows casino in Vegas after he refused to cut them in on the profits. "I get the feeling they already got an eye on me here in L.A., what with Bugsy Siegel nosing around with that Yid nose of his. . . . So, Chris, not that it's not always a pleasure seeing you, but what cooks with Marie MacDaniels that brings you out today?"

"Pick up and delivery, Tony. I need to get her back to the studio for the picture she's making."

"Them *G-Men* movies, not bad. Not real, either, but she works her magic up on the screen, more than that *pezzo di merda* Baxter Leeds, who was coming here expecting to be treated like he's Vittorio Emanuele il Terzo until I told him no more or I toss him in the water for fish bait. Strickling made that one better before it came true. . . . Afraid I can't help you any, Chris. Marie ain't here no more."

"She's not here?"

"Not since Thursday. She come aboard Wednesday night with Eve, the broad from *G-Men* who plays the dopey secretary, and this kid Nicky. They park her in the lounge and shuffle off. She has five too many and passes out, so I have a couple of my boys deposit her downstairs in one of our suites, allowing how playing Boy Scout will earn me a marker with Strickling, you read me? Only, come morning, I'm hearing how her husband Day Covington, another *pezzo di merda,* you ask me, is dead, murdered, and she's incommunicado. I definitely don't need no incommunicado in my life, so I have one of my hostesses help her get her act together and sit her down at the ship-to-shore to call someone who'll come take her away, only turns out it isn't necessary. Someone shows up and off she goes."

"Who with, Tony? Strickling?"

"Nah — who shows up is Nicky, that same kid what brought Marie over with the other *G-Men* girl."

"You know him?"

"Nicky? Sure. Nicky Hartmann. A regular.

174

Been hanging out here almost since we opened for business. A young and good-looking stud like that, a catch for any lonely, well-heeled woman hurting for temporary companionship, you read me?"

"Did this Nicky say where he was taking Marie?"

"Away. After 'incommunicado,' the only word I cared about hearing."

"Any idea where I can find Nicky?"

"Surprised you have to ask, Chris. The way he's been telling it, he's at your place, MGM, working Teamster crews and looking to be discovered by anybody who can make him a star."

Back at Metro late afternoon, I tracked Nicky Hartmann to the transportation crew on the *Wizard of Oz* set. He wasn't there. He had clocked out early after receiving a phone message saying his mother had suffered a heart attack and was rushed to County General Hospital.

The hospital switchboard said there was no record of anybody named Hartmann being admitted today; no Hartmann anywhere among the patients in residence or in and out of the emergency room.

The home phone number the studio had listed for him was out of order.

The Teamsters local had the same number.

I charged over to the *Battling G-Men* soundstage, intending to confront Eve with what I'd learned about her date, her pretty boy, hoping she was straight enough by now to explain why it was Hartmann who retrieved Marie from the S.S. *Rex.*

Or, where Hartmann might have taken her.

Or, where I could find her.

Earlier today, Eve had pleaded a memory breakdown and beseeched me not to be angry with her. Well, dammit, I was angry with her now, or was I angry with myself for watching without protest while she dosed herself with coke and not pressing her harder about Marie?

Hal Bucquet was lining up Baxter Leeds's close-up with the actor's stand-in.

Eve wasn't in her dressing room.

Or anywhere.

Gone, but not forgotten.

Released after stumbling through take after take of the saloon scene with Leeds until she managed to get it right the fifth time, Bucquet told me. "I don't know which is worse," he said, "what this Sarah Bernhardt is doing to my budget or to my career. Bad enough Marie MacDaniels went missing, now I have to put up with her. I were Clarence Brown or Woody Van Dyke, I'd say enough is enough and quit the picture, but I'm not Clarence Brown or Woody Van Dyke. Not even a Sidney Franklin. Mayer wouldn't miss me, and I've never been certain Thalberg knows I exist."

Tyrone Powell was waiting for me when I got back to my office.

He was unrecognizable in a nonsensical costume full of clashing colors and patterns and a bald cap surrounded by patches of flaming orange hair.

His height gave him away.

He gave me *What can I say?* attitude with his face and hands, adding in his pipe-whistle voice, "Didn't have a chance to tell you hello when I saw you come and go from Munchkin Land, friend Chris. I was over in a corner reading to some of the twerp kiddies they're mixing in with us genuine Munchkins." He bounced onto a visitor's chair. "I heard later you were on the prowl for Nicky Hartmann, so I'm here to pay you back a little for a big favor received."

"So far only offered. Siegel and I aren't seeing eye to eye yet."

"Siegel and me, we'll never see eye to eye. What can I tell you about Nicky?"

"What do you know about him, Herbie?"

He liked that I remembered his name. "Been doing business with him almost from the day they parked us small fry at the Culver Hotel. I'm the *Oz* bookie. Nicky, he places the bets on the gambling boat over at Santa Monica and keeps twenty-five percent of the winnings for his troubles. Only time I haven't come out on the short end of a deal."

"It's important that I contact him. I heard he took off after a call came in about his mother suffering a heart attack and —"

Powell's laugh reached the ceiling. "That's one for Ripley, friend Chris, only bet on the 'or Not.' What he told me, he would be sneaking away for a hot date, someone he met on the boat, and I could think about joining him later for a hot two-and-a-half-some." He studied my reaction. "That was a joke."

I was in no joking mood. "What did he say about this hot date, Herbie?"

"Somebody I'd know on sight, he said, but he wasn't about to share the name."

"Did he say where?"

"No, but I know where. It's always the same where with Nicky."

"And where's that?"

"I'll go you one better," he said. "Give me

time to change back into a human being and I'll take you there, while I'm at it pick up a wad of jack he owes me."

Two hours later, I was traveling the ocean for a second time today, with Tyrone Powell on a ferry making the hour-and-a-half, twenty-two-mile trip from Long Beach to Santa Catalina Island.

Against a dark sky, Herbie's nonstop chatter and the gastric rumblings of several passengers railing against the choppy Pacific waters, I wondered if the hot date Hartmann had headed for was Marie and something else —

The ticket stub for the trip to Catalina matched the SHUTTLE stubs I'd found in Otto Rothman's wallet.

A coincidence, that Hartmann was somehow linked to Rothman as well as Marie and, by extension, to Day Covington?

I don't believe in coincidence, but I didn't know what else to call it.

For now.

CHAPTER 11

I hadn't been to Catalina Island in years, since the last month of my disintegrating marriage, hoping it might rekindle a flame that burned brightly on our first trip here, on our honeymoon. I don't know what went wrong over a weekend that started with promise and ended with me drunk as John Barrymore on his best day and my wife like some Babe Ruth using my face for batting practice, only that nothing went right then or afterward.

Entering the port town of Avalon was like trading the cold cement of a crowded city for a Mediterranean paradise inhabited by less than four thousand full-time residents even before dolphins glided through a bay full of sailing vessels and motorboats to greet us.

Herbie and I angled through the crowd of arrivals jockeying for taxis and crossed from the ferry landing to the Avalon Hotel three hundred feet away, where we would be meeting Nicky Hartmann in about an hour.

Herbie had called him before we left L.A., saying they needed to discuss making some changes in their business deal that needed urgent attention and, no, it couldn't wait until tomorrow on the *Wizard of Oz* set; of course, not mentioning he would be bringing company along.

The Avalon was one of Catalina's old line hotels, favored since the mid-twenties by the movie companies doing location filming here, a Craftsman-style structure full of luxurious trappings and a reputation for discretion where it came to the sailors among the stars who wanted their playtime shrouded in privacy. It's where Strickling reserved rooms for Metro's stellar Popeyes as often as he scheduled the Beverly Hills Hotel bungalows or a private cottage at Nazimova's Garden of Allah for landlubber stars and his private list of high-powered lawmakers sensitive to the periodic needs of Mayer and the studio.

The pleasant evening breeze and a temperature somewhere between sixty-five and seventy degrees kept us pinned to the hotel's patio overlooking the Pacific, trading stories about my life as a cop for his about the ups and downs of living a Lilliputian life, told in a self-deprecating manner that fueled the sadness and regret I saw hiding behind Herbie's eyes.

One bottle of Chablis became two bottles as too much time passed, and I began to suspect Hartmann wouldn't be showing up. Herbie had come to the same conclusion. His pudgy fingers tapped out a Morse code to his own impatience and, finally, irritation too big to keep to himself.

"Let's go," he said, easing off the chair and tugging at the hem of his sports jacket.

"If you're talking back to town, not as long as there's a chance he's on the island, Herbie."

"Not town, the Catalina Casino. That's where the bonehead hangs out when he's over here romancing his latest muffin."

We took an easy stroll to 1 Casino Way, music from inside the casino growing increasingly loud as we approached.

It was an Art Deco pavilion designed exclusively for dancing that, since opening in '29, had been drawing about four thousand people a night, who packed onto a white oak, maple and rosewood dance floor meant for five hundred couples dressed to the nines, hot to trot to music by the best of the big bands, including Glen Miller, Woody Herman and Jimmy Dorsey, under a dome a hundred and thirty feet tall, chandeliers by Tiffany, and vibrantly colored ceiling frescos decorated with twenty-two-carat gold leaf and sterling silver leaf.

Unlike the S.S. *Rex,* there was no gambling in this casino, or anywhere else on the island. Gambling was illegal, along with feeding wildlife, and harassing, harming in any way or keeping as a pet the rare species of Catalina Island Fox.

Over the next half hour we circled the ballroom, hoping against expectation that we'd spot Hartmann among the dancers on the crowded floor.

They were barely navigating to the Kay Kyser Orchestra's rendition of the Shep Fields hit, "Thanks for the Memory," when Herbie pointed us through a floor-to-ceiling door to an outside balcony, shouting to be heard: "I need a coffin nail."

Smoking, prohibited in the ballroom, kept the balcony a low-hanging, dull gray cumulus cloud, to which Herbie quickly contributed smoke rings from one of the six-inch Panatelas stored in the breast pocket of his blazer.

I fired up a Lucky and wandered around, searching for somebody matching the lean description I had for Nicky Hartmann. Instead, I caught myself squinting through eyes burning from the thick nicotine haze at the face I was certain had been captured in Nancy Warren's sketch of the big man who attacked me in Otto Rothman's studio.

He was staring at me with far more certainty.

He sent his smoke flying off the balcony and burrowed into the crowd, pushing, shoving and elbowing his way toward a door back into the ballroom.

I called for Herbie to follow me and fought my way in the big man's direction.

He had disappeared by the time I got inside.

"What was that all about?" Herbie said, shouting to be heard above the music, which had swung into a noisy rendition of Benny Goodman's "Sing, Sing, Sing" after Harry Babbitt's vocalizing on the quieter Bunny Berigan hit, "I Can't Get Started."

I settled on my haunches, cupped a hand to Herbie's ear and told him.

He asked to see the sketch.

I turned over the copy I was carrying with me.

Herbie unfolded the sketch, looked it over and handed it back.

"I know him," he said. "Karl Mueller. He does business with Hartmann."

■ ■ ■ ■

We quit the casino and headed for the ferry, Herbie explaining along the way, "I learned pretty early I wasn't the only one Nicky had deals with. He calls Mueller when he has a problem collecting on a sour bet or a debt of some kind or other. I told him to steer Mueller clear of any of my marks, that any make-goods he could take out of my share. It's cost me a Ben Franklin or three, but Mueller scared me from the first time I saw him, one day when he showed up on the set tracking after Nicky. We broke for lunch and off they went, Nicky saying Baxter Leeds would be waiting for them in his trailer on the *Battling G-Men* stage."

The last boat to Long Beach had sailed.

We crossed to the Avalon Hotel and grabbed the only available room, a modest ground-floor single with twin beds facing the village side and a step-down balcony onto a street full of noisy tourists.

Herbie flopped onto a bed without dressing down and was asleep within seconds, filling the room with a snore of kings that fractured any possibility of my catching a few hours of shuteye. I took the balcony out, fortified myself with boilermakers

185

served up at two or three of the bars that punctuated the district and squandered more time mingling with a shuffling crowd on the prowl for good times.

I searched among the faces for somebody matching Hartmann's description and for the big man, fancying myself after awhile and enough hooch as Inspector Slimane pursuing Pepe Le Moko through the streets of Algiers, the way Joseph Calleia had gone after Charles Boyer in the movie.

By the time I got back to the room two or three hours later, everyone was looking like everyone else, and I had decided I'd rather be Pepe Le Moko than Inspector Slimane, because Boyer was the one who got to woo Hedy Lamarr.

Herbie was gone.

Me, too many sheets to the wind to wonder or worry about his whereabouts, any more than he likely considered mine whenever it was he woke and found himself alone in the room.

I shrugged off Herbie's absence and collapsed on top of the bedcover, too lazy to turn off the lamplight, but determined to turn off my mind to a trip that shortchanged me on answers, only added another piece to the puzzle — Nicky Hartmann's connection to the big man in Nancy's sketch. Mueller,

Herbie had said his name was — Karl Mueller.

I was sweet-talking Hedy Lamarr into leaving the Casbah with me when a stirring sensation under the covers shook me out of my dream and back into the room. I rolled off the bed, threw aside the blankets and froze at the sight of the two rattlesnakes noiselessly prowling between the sheets.

They weren't large, maybe thirty inches from head to base, half the size of rattlers I'd seen on the mainland. One was a reddish brown with darker diamond-shaped blotches outlined in lighter-colored scales. The other was ash-gray with darker gray markings. Pale stripes decorated their heads.

Neither rattler had rattles; something I'd heard about the species unique to Santa Catalina.

I'd also heard the smaller the rattlers, the more toxic their venom.

I'd also heard that rattlers coiled when they were getting ready to strike.

These rattlers had coiled.

They appeared to be challenging me to make a move.

I wasn't biting.

Hopefully, neither would they before I made the only move that made sense to me, gamble that it was. Sweat rained down my face and from my armpits, gushed from every pore and bathed my body as I inched my hand inside my jacket and got a grip on the .38 Detective Special in my shoulder holster.

The rattlers held firm.

In a single move that broke the sound barrier, I whipped out the .38 and got off a shot that blew away the ash-gray rattler's head and left its body wiggling relentlessly. The reddish brown rattler sprang before I could get off a second shot. Its fangs penetrated my jacket and dug into the shoulder holster. It hung down to my thigh, trying to break free of the leather. I yanked the rattler off and flung it across the room. It crashed into the dresser mirror, dropped to the carpeting and was pulling itself together as I wheeled around, took two-handed aim and got off a shot that increased my head count to two. The body moved blindly across the room and stopped within inches of its headless pal.

The gunshots played against the noise of the street crowd and went unnoticed.

I spent what remained of the night fighting to stay alert in an armchair I moved and angled to give me a clear view of the balcony and the hallway doors, the .38 on my lap, ready to use on any other snakes — rattlers or the human variety — that might come calling.

CHAPTER 12

Tuesday, November 15, 1938

The phone buzz-sawed through my brain and startled me awake. I stumbled across to the nightstand and fumbled with the receiver trying to find my ear.

Herbie said, "Hit it on all six and meet me in the lobby, friend Chris."

I struggled to focus on the pink dial of my Rolex Turtle Centrograph, a gift from Strickling for an incident I handled involving Paul Kelly, who years ago had done hard time for manslaughter after beating to death the husband of Dorothy Mackaye, his actress girlfriend. I made some calls Strickling couldn't that allowed Kelly to finish a supporting role in *Navy Blue and Gold,* alongside Bob Young and Jimmy Stewart, and saved Metro a bundle.

The big hand and the little hand added up to eight in the morning. My body was stiff and my cracked ribs were sending me

an upgraded definition of the word "ache."
I blew my throat clear into my fist and said,
"Where you been, Herbie?"

"It's not where I've been, it's where we're
going."

"And that would be?"

"Where we'll be meeting up with Nicky
Hartmann and his hot date."

That snapped the last of the lingering fog
from my head. "*And* his hot date?"

"Marie MacDaniels. That the name you
been hoping to hear?"

I hit the bathroom, splashed my face with
wake-up water, finger-brushed my teeth,
papered back my hair, and sprinted to the
lobby.

Herbie wasn't alone.

The big man, Karl Mueller, was with him.

He looked bigger than I remembered,
scowled at me like unfinished business
through mismatched eyes, the left iris a
cocoa brown color, the right iris a gray-blue.

"He's oke," Herbie said. I was unsure
whether he was hoping to convince me or
himself. "Nicky sent him to find me and
bring me to him. I said I wasn't going
without you, so he got Nicky on the phone,
and Nicky said sure."

"Why can't Hartmann come here? What
happened to him yesterday?"

"He said it turned out he had unexpected company, in addition to his date from the gambling boat. He said tell you she's a friend of yours and would enjoy the surprise when you showed your mug."

"Did you get a name this time?"

Herbie said, "I wouldn't let him off the hook. It's Marie MacDaniels."

My adrenaline kicked in.

"If we are going, let us get moving," Mueller said, his meaty baritone tainted by a hint of accent.

Herbie gave me an *It's up to you* look.

I turned to Mueller. "Exactly where is it we're going?"

"You ask too many questions," Mueller said.

More questions needed answers, but it was finding Marie that had brought me to Catalina Island in the first place. "What do I have to lose," I said, recognizing there was one answer I would rank as wholly unsatisfactory.

Mueller's expression suggested he had read my mind. He flashed a mouthful of jumbo, nicotine-stained Chiclets, extended his hand, palm up, and said, "First I will need to have your revolver."

"My revolver?"

"From all appearances residing under the

bulge in your jacket, I would say."

"I don't think so," I said.

"Should I have said 'please,' is that why?" He turned to Herbie. "Listen to that. Now I am the one who is asking the questions." He twined his arms across his massive chest and waited me out.

I reached inside my jacket for the .38 and handed it over.

We climbed into a Mercedes-Benz 230 Pullman-Limousine and sailed into the rugged interior, sucking in twenty-three miles worth of fragrant trees and flowers on a well-worn road from Avalon to Two Harbors on the remote Isthmus side of the island.

A village with one hotel, one restaurant, one general store, and a school for the children of the less than two hundred people who made up the permanent population, I knew Two Harbors from *Mutiny on the Bounty,* which had filmed on location here, the beaches standing in for Pitcairn Island.

Mueller eased onto a secondary road, barely wider than a hiker's trail, and aimed for an isolated knoll that overlooked Isthmus Cove on the lee side and Catalina Island on the ocean side, a sprawling Craftsman manor hard to spot if you weren't looking for it. A half-dozen autos were neatly parked in an area fronting an elaborate patio overhung with a pergola and an assortment of plantings that further obscured the residence.

By the time Mueller finished making a career of parking the Mercedes in line with the other autos, somebody matching Herbie's description of Nicky Hartmann had stepped onto the patio wearing an open-collar shirt tucked into a pair of white tennis trousers and waved a greeting as he skipped down the steps. He wasn't tall. Adler elevators added an inch or two to his height, the way they served Georgie Raft, but he was trim and carried himself like an Olympic sprinter. He was deceptively boyish-looking, probably in his mid-to-late thirties judging by the laugh lines imbedded at his eyes and the quote marks framing a sensuous mouth on a sculpted face dominated by wide-set Adriatic blue eyes. His sun-bleached blond locks were cut pudding-bowl style. A row of thin, darker strands decorated his upper lip.

"Hey, partner," he said, dropping to eye-level with Herbie and pulling him into a fervent embrace. "Please tell me you forgive me for yesterday, Tyrone."

"You got the moolah I'm due, all is forgiven," Herbie said.

"Have I ever short-changed you?"

"Please, Nicky, I'm the one makes the jokes at my expense."

Hartmann feigned remorse, turned Herbie loose and put a palm to his heart, like he was pledging allegiance. "Never again," he said, rising. He offered me a handshake. "Welcome to you, Mr. Blanchard. I've seen you often on the lot, but we've never really met. I've been hearing wonderful things about you."

"Anyone I know?"

"And quite well, I gather — Marie MacDaniels."

"I understand she's here with you."

Hartmann flashed a look at Herbie, who turned away from me, saying, "He needed to hear that or he might not have come, Nicky."

I said, "What the hell's that supposed to mean?"

Hartmann said, "In due course, Mr. Blanchard, all in due course."

"Now, or —"

"Or what, Mr. Blanchard?" His tone darkened. "You'll hike on back to the village through unfamiliar terrain with a large population of Catalina rattlesnakes and scavenging foxes, whose bite brings with it the strong possibility of rabies?"

"I've seen your rattlesnakes, Hartmann." He didn't seem to know what I meant by that and turned to Mueller, who shook his head. "I didn't miss the two planted in my bed and sent to rattler heaven," I said, and reflexively reached after my .38.

Mueller laughed. He pulled back his jacket to show it was tucked under his belt. His own weapon was parked in a glistening brown leather hip holster.

Hartmann said, "And you're supposing that I'm responsible for them being there? Frankly, Mr. Blanchard, if I wanted you dead, you'd already be dead. In fact, I need you alive, so come, let's retreat inside and get down to business."

"You and I don't have business, Hartmann."

"Oh, but we do, Mr. Blanchard. We most certainly do. Why I was extremely set on Tyrone getting you to Catalina and up here."

Herbie didn't look the least bit apologetic. He scooped up a loose rock and tossed it into the brush, then fell in alongside Hartmann, who played tour guide while leading us to the house; me in the middle and Mueller bringing up the rear.

"The Isthmus is where smugglers settled

in the mid-nineteenth century," he said. "During the Civil War a small Union Army garrison was stationed here. The Banning brothers came along later. They installed the first telephone and wireless systems, built roads into the interior and, mindful of their privacy, built a remote, isolated home a lot like this one. It's not my place, if you're wondering, nothing I could ever afford on my modest salary. It's owned by friends who, like the Bannings, value their privacy. They allow me to use it free of charge whenever it's not otherwise occupied."

We entered at the end of the patio that fed into a two-story living room furnished simply and cheaply in bamboo, the wall space above all the French windows filled with mounted trophy heads of deer and bison, and moved through an enclosed sun-room into a room empty except for cheap pine tables arranged boardroom style, in a single row with matching pine chairs for twenty.

Hartmann settled at the head of the table, Herbie in an elevated chair to his right, me in the one on his left.

Mueller posted himself by a door across the room with a direct sightline to me. He pulled out a blackjack — the one I assumed he had tried using on me when we collided at Otto Rothman's studio — and smacked his palm with it a few times. Hartmann cautioned him with a hand signal, and Mueller responded like a pet dog. The blackjack disappeared back into a jacket pocket.

"Help yourself," Hartmann said, pointing to a selection of Riesling wines and a tray filled with a variety of crackers and cheeses on the table.

"Never before noon," I said, waving off the invitation.

Herbie filled a glass for Hartmann and poured one for himself.

"Nothing measures up to a fine Rhine white wine," Hartmann said. "Crisp. Dry. Aromatic and fruity. So many qualities to appreciate, more than with a *Spatburgunder,* wouldn't you agree, Karl? Tyrone?"

Mueller nodded agreement.

"Prost!" Herbie said. He tilted back his head, drained his glass in a single swallow and helped himself to a refill.

Hartmann took notice of the impatient melody I was typing on the tabletop.

"So, where shall I start, Mr. Blanchard? Any preferences?"

"About Marie MacDaniels. Where is she?"

He smiled to be polite. "That would be getting ahead of the story."

"The beginning, then? The beginning always works for me."

"You already know the beginning, the murders of Day Covington and then Otto Rothman."

"The real beginning, Hartmann, when, where and how you fit in — and why. Was it you murdered them or, more likely, Goliath over there?"

Mueller's grin suggested he took the accusation as a compliment.

"Not Karl, Mr. Blanchard, and certainly not me. I'm also a victim, but a different kind of victim. They worked a blackmail racket together, partners, as Tyrone and I have been in our modest bookmaking enterprise. Rothman took the pictures. Covington made the contacts and collected from their patsies."

"And there were naughty pictures of you you didn't want anyone to see?"

"I'm a nobody in the business, so who would have cared?" His eyes skipped around the room and settled back on me with an intensity that begged understanding.

"You making whoopee with one of your hot dates, someone like Eve Whitney, might have been worth the greenbacks they were demanding."

"To Eve, not me, but not that, either. I'm

speaking of a different kind of pictures that would have done in more than any hopes I have about being discovered and making a career for myself as a movie star."

"That gives you a motive for murder."

"Not as long as Covington and Rothman had those pictures."

"Tell me about them."

He waved off the request. "I'm getting there . . . I worked out this plan where Karl would get into Covington's house and search for the pictures while Eve and I did dinner at the Biltmore Bowl with Covington and his wife. Only Marie showed up without him. Next, I'm being paged to the phone by Karl. He says he's standing over Covington's dead body and what should he do. That so, Karl?"

"So." He made a gun of his thumb and forefinger and fired.

"I told Karl to do a speedy but thorough search for the pictures and then get out before company arrived. I gave him about an hour before I called the studio, said it was an emergency and I needed to speak with Howard Strickling."

"Why call Strickling? Why not the police?"

"I tipped the police afterward. Strickling because he's the studio's fixer, and this could be a situation that needed fixing for

Marie and maybe down the road do my career some good." He helped himself to a chunk of cheese and washed it down from a second pour of Riesling. "Karl said he'd given the usual hiding places a pretty good rinsing and came up empty-handed, so we set our sights on Rothman's studio, only with a different plan this time — convince Rothman to hand over the pictures, threatening to burn down the studio and the pictures with it if he failed to do so. Karl is somewhat of an expert in that area, you see, only he found Rothman dead."

"First Covington, then Rothman. Is it something you have to train for or does finding dead people come naturally to Mueller?" I fired up a Lucky and blew a ring of smoke in the big man's direction. "And I thought smoking was a bad habit."

Mueller forced a meaningless smile and did the gun thing with his fingers again.

Hartmann ignored my sarcasm. "Karl found where Rothman kept his hoard of negatives and prints, but too many to do a thorough search. He was preparing his little incendiary device when he heard you arrive on the scene and you had your little scuffle." He toyed with his wisp of a mustache. "Meanwhile, on the night of Covington's murder, Marie showed up unannounced on

Eve's doorstep, looking dreadful and begging us to take her out to the S.S. *Rex*. I fetched her the next day and brought her here, hoping she might be able to tell me what her husband no longer could."

"But you knew the negatives and pictures still had to be in Rothman's studio."

"*Thought,* Mr. Blanchard, not *knew.*"

"Something changed your mind."

"Yes. An unexpected phone call, a man, his voice muffled, announcing he was taking over for Covington and Rothman. He said he had the negatives and a fine set of prints and would contact me again shortly with new terms and conditions of sale. I was beside myself wondering how to proceed, when Tyrone came up with the excellent idea at the core of this friendly get-together with you."

His gesture invited Herbie to explain.

Herbie took on a look I'd often seen over the years, on cops and criminals about to betray a trust or a friendship; on success-driven actors and shirt-and-tie types who would rhumba barefoot on broken glass if they thought it would move them a rung or two up the ladder.

I showed him I knew and said, "C'mon, spill, Tyrone. What's the problem? Kitten got your tongue?"

He let my slam go without comment. "Nicky heard what you done for me about Bugsy Siegel, how you were a detective and wired almost as good as Strickling. Since you were already involved, I said why not let you carry the load for us on finding any negatives or pictures out there? He doubted you'd go along. I bet him you would, since I got the impression you were keen on Marie and we could just hold her for bait until you came through. After that, everything seemed to come together like it was meant to be."

"Thanks for the recommendation," I said.

Herbie bowed his head and found stains on the table to explore.

Hartmann said, "Do we have an understanding, Mr. Blanchard? If so, I'll describe what it is you'll be looking for."

"You'll get your answer after I see Marie, Hartmann."

"You'll see her after you succeed in locating and bringing me our negatives and pictures. Until then, my game, my rules. One misstep on your part and nobody will ever see Marie MacDaniels again." He stretched a phony smile into his cheeks. "What do you say to that, Mr. Blanchard?"

I blasted his smug face with a phony smile of my own.

"I say Marie leaves with me or you can go straight to hell, Hartmann."

CHAPTER 13

This time, instead of his blackjack or finger gun, Mueller pulled out a 9mm Luger from his hip holster, assumed a shooter's stance and aimed the four-inch barrel at me, his finger poised to squeeze the trigger. He looked for direction from Hartmann.

Hartmann, whose face had dropped anchor, resurfaced his composure and pushed out a heavy sigh. "Care to reconsider your intemperate decision, Mr. Blanchard, or shall I turn the dog loose on you?"

I took a gamble. After all, what did I have to lose but my life? I said, "Consider the consequences. . . . By now, Strickling must be turning the world upside down looking for Marie. Her absence is costing Metro hundreds of dollars a day. I get her back to the studio, the pressure's off me and off you. I can go about the business of finding you your goddamn pictures and negatives."

"What guarantee do I have you would

honor your commitment?"

"My word."

"Nothing personal, but I would want more than that."

"Whatever else, he's a man of his word," Herbie said. "Whatever else, he proved that with me."

Hartmann swept the air with a hand. "I didn't invite your opinion, Tyrone." Herbie dodged his scornful eye and turned to picking at his fingernails. "And what's to guarantee Marie won't say the wrong things and send the law raining down on me with a charge of kidnapping?"

"She'll listen to me. We're old friends. She trusts me. Besides, she'll be anxious as me to collar the person who murdered her husband, no matter what you and I think about Day Covington. Isn't that something else you'd like to see happen?"

This time I fired a finger gun.

Mueller gave me a nasty look, like I was auditioning for his job.

"You make an interesting case for yourself," Hartmann said, checking his watch. "Only now, I'm minutes away from a meeting, so my decision will have to wait for later, when I have more time to evaluate its merits."

He twirled a finger at Mueller.

"Come," Mueller said, holding a firm aim on me with the Luger while he opened the door; giving my back hard pokes with the pistol to urge me ahead of him up a narrow central corridor. Along the way we brushed past twelve or fifteen men who were casually dressed and toted a variety of attaché cases and doctors' satchels — Hartmann's meeting, I figured, and an explanation for all the cars parked outside. If there was any distinguishing feature they shared, it was the nod they had for Mueller and the suspicious look they had for this stranger in their midst.

"Here," Mueller said, halting me with a hand on my shoulder at an open stairway and giving me a directional shove. We headed down a poorly lit, rickety stairway leading to a stone-walled basement about twenty degrees colder than the ground floor level of the manor. "Through there," he said, indicating the kind of impenetrable, iron-hinged prison door Ronald Colman had passed through in *A Tale of Two Cities*. The door slammed shut behind me, followed by the click of a key turning in the lock and the sound of Mueller's footsteps clomping away on the concrete flooring.

I was imprisoned in a comfortably furnished room about twelve feet across, the side walls of the living area filled top to bottom with empty porthole shelves, suggesting the space had once been used as a wine cellar. The wall across from the door was invisible down a dark passageway of indeterminate length.

I thought I was alone until I heard a noisy declaration: "Baby!"

Marie raced into the light from the passageway, shouting my name like she had discovered lost treasure. Threw herself at me, strangling my arms with hers, her feet off the ground, saving the last in a series of greeting kisses for my lips. Led me to the deep-cushioned sofa and settled beside me, her hands tight on mine. Took a few moments to catch her breath and said, "Nicky said you'd be coming to pick me up when it was okay to show my face again, but one day became another and I kept getting fed excuses, baby, so I was finally scared that something was really wrong, especially this morning, after they moved me here from my room upstairs." She planted a cheek on my shoulder. "Gawd, I feel so much better now, now that you're here and all. Tell me everything's all right, baby. I need to hear it from you."

I wasn't going to lie to Marie.

I didn't have to say it.

She may have smelled it in my sweat.

"What's wrong, baby? What don't I know?" She inched away, drawing a tighter lock on my hands and moving them to a breast while she studied my face. Her heart was pounding. "Answer me, Chris."

"You go first . . . Nicky said I'd be coming for you?"

"From the time he picked me up from the *Rex* and got me to Catalina. He said he was doing it for Strickling and Strickling said to tell me you'd come for me once the coast was clear."

"Why didn't you phone me, tell me you were on the *Rex*?"

"I asked Eve to do it for me. Didn't she?"

"She said she was too involved sacking it with Hartmann and forgot."

Marie's eyes did a Betty Boop. "That's why I never heard from you before Nicky arrived saying Strickling wanted me to keep off the phone, just be patient and wait it out and — Gawd, baby, he's been playing me for a sap, that's it, isn't it? The son of a bitch has been playing me for a sap." Her eyes grew moist. Tears spilled onto her freckled cheeks. She let go of my hands and stroked them away. "What's the real story? Tell me."

The *real* story.

I didn't know the *real* story.

If I did, I didn't know I knew the *real* story.

I was saved from confessing that, at least for the time being, by the sound of the door groaning open wide enough for Herbie Duntz to slip inside the room.

He half-shouted my name and tossed me two keys on a black leather and enamel fob hawking Singer's Midgets.

I caught it on the fly.

Bouncing nervously, his words racing, he said, "No time to explain. Just flee this dump fast as you can, before they come after you. It's not safe. Down the other end, one key unlocks the door there. Stairs lead to the front of the house. The other key is for the Daimler Drophead *coupé;* two doors; green on black. Get back to Avalon and on a ferry to the mainland faster'n sound. Just do it, unnerstand?"

He hopped back and pulled the door shut, turned the key in the lock.

The suddenness of it all was confusing Marie, not that I understood what Herbie was up to, only that getting away from Hartmann and this place was advice too smart to ignore. I pushed up from the sofa, took her hand and pulled her up after me, and headed us for the corridor leading to the

210

back door.

"Wait," she said, pausing long enough to take off the high heels she was wearing the night of Day Covington's murder. Somewhere along the way, her outfit from that night had been replaced by a men's dress shirt, open at the collar and sleeves rolled up, and a pair of loose white tennis trousers like Hartmann had on, at least two sizes too large, belted Fred Astaire–style by a multicolored striped necktie. "Better," she said. "Let's go, baby."

Stepping into daylight, I saw the Daimler Herbie meant about twenty or thirty yards ahead of us, facing the road that got me here, nothing blocking its exit.

I checked around.

Nobody was minding the store.

A corpulent baldheaded gent in the sunroom, relaxing over a cigar, hands behind his back, was staring off into island side space.

"Stay close," I told Marie, and started for the car on a half-run.

Glancing over my shoulder, I saw the gent had turned and caught us in his sight. He used a hand to shade his squint against the sun and, at once, freed the cigar from his bite and looked to be calling out to someone

211

before he wheeled around and disappeared.

Marie kept up as I doubled the pace.

The Daimler was unlocked.

I jumped behind the wheel and turned the key.

No ignition.

I couldn't get the damn motor to kick in.

I checked out the window.

The gent with the cigar was on the patio, joined by a gang of ten or twelve men, maybe more — Hartmann and Mueller among them — and was using his cigar to point in our direction.

I failed on two more attempts at ignition.

The men were moving out of the patio and charging down the steps.

Mueller, his Luger drawn, headed the pack.

I dropped the emergency brake, threw the car into gear, jumped out, got a solid two-handed hold on the window frame, and pushed, commanding the Daimler to take traction from the modest slant down to the access road.

Marie understood what I was doing.

She hopped out and began pushing on the passenger side.

We weren't making headway, and then —

The Daimler started a slow roll forward.

Picked up speed.

The engine came alive as a bullet whizzed past my ear.

Mueller was targeting us from a shooter's stance, the Luger resting on the arm he had crooked in front of him, horizontal with the ground.

Marie and I crouched, quick-stepped onto the running boards and swung inside, pulling the doors closed.

I threw the car past second into third gear and floored the gas pedal.

Mueller's next shot thudded into the driver's side chassis.

The two shots after that pounded into the trunk.

I fought the steering wheel, maneuvering the Daimler into a straight angle down the narrow, rutted dirt road, yowling over the pain exploding at my rib cage.

Mueller's next shot shattered the rear window and dug into the back of the leather upholstery on the passenger side of the front seat, about where it might have struck Marie between the shoulder blades if the thick padding hadn't stopped the bullet.

I shifted the Daimler into overdrive, watched the speedometer climb to 40 mph as the manor disappeared behind us. Marie cheered loudly, punctuating every "wahoo" with a punch on my arm.

Any reason for celebrating was short-lived after a few minutes, when the rearview mirror revealed Mueller's Mercedes-Benz 230 chasing after us; Mueller behind the wheel; his face contorted like Lon Chaney's in some of those movies that, growing up, gave me nightmares.

He was closing the gap.

I clamped down harder on the gas pedal and got the Daimler up to 50 mph.

Mueller kept pace.

I managed 60 mph.

So did Mueller.

I took a curve on two wheels, leveled out and kept going.

Mueller hit his brakes, putting the Mercedes into a temporary tailspin that left him heading in the wrong direction. He executed a series of forward and back moves and was after us again, reaching some high-end speed beyond the 60 mph that was the best I could get out of the Daimler, no matter how hard I begged.

A mile or two short of the road that would take us back to Avalon, the car started sputtering.

I glanced at the gas gauge.

It read empty.

Maybe there is some angel assigned to agnostics.

The Daimler quit about twenty-five yards in front of a line of hump-shouldered bison crossing the road, each ten feet tall and weighing somewhere around twenty-five hundred pounds, forming a wall of brownish black fur that I might have crashed into with calamitous results.

Mueller wasn't as lucky.

He managed to navigate around me to avoid a crash, but his brakes weren't strong enough to stop short of the bison.

The Mercedes wheeled out of control, spun like a merry-go-round before it flew off the road and nose-dived into a deep ravine.

Marie and I hopped out of the Daimler and ran over to the hillside to check for signs of life, but the thick underbrush blocked any sign of the Mercedes.

She said, "Should we try to climb down there and —"

"And what? If Mueller is dead, we can't do him any good. If he's alive, he's got the gun, not us, so we wouldn't be doing ourselves any favors. We'll let the authorities know what happened when we get back to Avalon."

"He could be seriously injured, dead by the time help arrives."

"Aren't you listening? When did you

become Clara Barton? The man was trying to kill us, for Christ's sake. Chasing after us to finish the job." I cupped my hands around my mouth, like I was Rudy Vallee, and called down after Mueller. Got nothing in return. "I vote for dead," I said. Wheeled around and headed off, leaving Marie stung and silent.

She ran after me, shouting, "It would have been the decent thing to do."

"Keeping us alive is the decent thing to do," I shouted back.

That shut her down.

I suppose I could have explained what being the good guy in bad company can get you when you let your heart rule your head. In my cop days, it got my partner dead after he showed mercy to a fifteen-year-old kid we collared in the act of robbing an all-night liquor store, buying the kid's story about this being his first robbery, daddy out of work for months, mommy living with a fever, he and five younger siblings gone hungry for days. He got glassy-eyed and, over my objections, insisted we give the kid a second chance, if the kid promised us he'd stay on the straight and narrow. The kid promised, of course. My partner undid the kid's cuffs. The kid rubbed his wrists and showered us with words of appreciation before he pulled out a switchblade we'd missed on the frisk, ran it across my partner's throat and fled. I got off a shot that went nowhere and chose to help my partner if I could, rather than chase after the little prick.

Learn a lesson from that?

Yes and no.

A couple of years later I almost bought into a similar scenario, only this time it involved a brother detective I'd discovered was dirtier than a Hollywood Hills mudslide. He was running Sunset Boulevard prosties as a sideline, when he wasn't grafting from a madam or two, one of whom tipped me off after greed got the better of him and he raised the cost of his blind eye by half again. No way was he going to buy my silence, and I told him so. That same day, he was waiting for me when I got home after my shift, giving me a last chance to change my mind. He saw nothing he said was working magic and started to pull his Police Positive. I was faster getting to my weapon, and we turned into Johnny Mack Brown and Wally Beery facing off in *Billy the Kid,* only I hesitated at the idea of putting a bullet in him. He squeezed his trigger without hesitation. His bullet caught me barely an inch outside the kill zone. My shot was late, but better aimed, and killed him instantly. I dragged myself to the phone swearing I'd never make that mistake a second time.

I hadn't, and today there was nothing about Karl Mueller that made me want to risk my life or Marie's on the possibility of saving his.

We ignored each other tramping down about a mile and a half to the paved road to Avalon, where we thumbed a lift from a farmer carting a load of mule deer to market in his pickup, whose rich brown, leathered skin testified to his claim of having spent almost all his sixty-one adult years working under the island sun. He rambled on non-stop about Catalina's history, sharing stories in a way that bore the sound of many repetitions.

When we reached the ferry landing, I offered to pay him for his kindness.

He refused, suggesting that a kiss from Marie would be payment enough.

She embraced him and laid one on that lasted an eternity. He came away from it fighting for breath, giggling and boasting how she had made him feel like he was forty again, wondering if she'd like to try for twenty.

She did.

He left us smiling wide enough to hide the sky, warning me, "I want you to take good care of this lady of yours, you know what's good for you, or you'll have me to deal with."

We played a lovey-dovey game for his benefit, arms around each other's waists, until he was out of sight, then put space and silence between us marching across to the ticket booth, where I paid for the next trip back to Long Beach three hours from now.

There was a café with outdoor seating across the way.

I sued for peace, offering to buy her a meal while we waited.

"As long as I don't have to make you feel like you're twenty again," she said.

I detected a hint of a smile.

Correctly.

We were back on cordial terms by the time we'd washed down our hamburgers and French-fried potatoes with two pitchers of beer, holding hands across the table like sweethearts on the mend after she apologized for minimizing the threat Karl Mueller had posed and I apologized for coming off more arbitrary and hard-nosed than intended.

"It's never been your hard *nose* that appealed to me," she said, "especially back when." Her voice adopted a growl. "You remember, don't you, Chris — back when?"

I answered with a smile that recollected something, but wasn't meant to rekindle anything.

Some things are better served by memory, so better left in the past.

Besides, I had this new thing for Nancy Warren, growing like Morning Glories, fast and unmanageable. Marie's insinuating remarks had brought her to mind. I wondered how Nancy was. Where Nancy was. What Nancy was doing. When I'd see Nancy again.

"Don't look now," Marie said, as if she had managed to invade my thoughts. She used her chin to point to the ferry landing.

Passengers were preparing to board.

Tyrone Powell was among them.

So was Karl Mueller.

We turned our backs to the street until the ferry glided out of the bay.

I handed Marie the key to the Avalon Hotel room I had shared with Herbie and told her to double-time over while I traded in our ferry tickets for the next trip. "It's not safe out here," I said. "Hartmann could show up any minute hunting after us."

"What if he's waiting at the hotel?" she said, her fists tight with tension, shaking the air with invisible maracas.

"Scream 'Rape' and keep on screaming," I said. "He's too savvy to stick around or to try dragging you from the balcony down into whichever buggy brought him here from his hilltop hideaway." She looked uncertain. "Now, Marie — get up on your goddamn feet and get going," I said, playing tough cop, tougher than she'd ever heard me.

She pushed up from the table and took off, checking left and right as she carved a path around strolling tourists and through a lineup of taxis, whose drivers relaxed against their vehicles, smoking and trading animated conversation.

When I got to the hotel, Marie inched back a curtain to make certain it was me knocking before she opened the door, barely wide enough for me to pass inside before she threw it shut and slid the bolt lock back in place.

"I was getting real worried," she said, looking the part, her face mixing anxiety and fear. "You were gone so long."

"Ten, maybe fifteen minutes."

"It seemed like forever, baby."

She was down to her lace bra and panties. Her dress shirt and tennis trousers were in a heap on the floor. She saw me studying her. "Not what you think I'm thinking," she said. "I didn't need getting the outfit any sweatier than already, trying to shake the blues away." She plopped into an armchair and crossed her legs, did a thing with her hands and began some sort of chant. "It's the latest thing, called yoga; helps you to relax and leads to a greater understanding of yourself. Garbo swears by it. Taught in a class by a student of Krishnamacharya, Indra Devi, maybe you know that already?"

"I've heard of Garbo."

"Garbo does it alone," Marie said, making a nervous joke of it. "I hear Garbo does everything alone, if you get my drift, although that wouldn't explain her and poor Johnny Gilbert, would it?"

I was tempted to mention seeing Garbo dabbling with Salka Viertel on Sunday at George Cukor's poolside Bacchanalia, but Metro wasn't paying me to be some Parsons or Hopper. I changed the subject. "What do you know about that crowd visiting Hartmann?"

"Besides the fact they cost me my room, you mean, almost from when the first of them started arriving yesterday?"

"Not all at once?"

"Didn't I just say so?" She repeated this hummingbird kind of sound she'd been doing. "Like in twos and threes, maybe twenty in all? No rhyme or reason to them, but they say it takes all kinds. Heard some accents in the crowd. Got the usual looks from some of the older buzzards, but Nicky steered all of them away from me and me away from them, like their business was none of my business, which of course it wasn't."

"How about Tyrone Powell?"

"The Munchkin? No idea what's his story. Your guess good as mine. He showed up last night and was immediately welcomed like a brother. Next time I saw him, he was tossing you keys and instructions. Before, I only knew him from coming over to the set sometimes and going into deep huddles with that pompous asshole, my co-star. What's that all about?"

"He brought me to Catalina when he learned I was looking for you."

"Munchkins have a sixth sense?" She punctuated the question with a hum.

"He heard it from Hartmann. The two of them are tight as a drum, working a bookmaking sideline on the lot. He's clever enough and would have figured a way to maneuver me here if I hadn't spoken up first."

"Nicky and Eve hinted about the book-making at the Biltmore Bowl, but like it was all Nicky's business, no mention of the Munchkin, and — " As if she had suddenly remembered what else happened that night, Marie quit humming. She lost the glow that had been building and, in a voice thick with emotion, said, "Baby, I sometimes may play the fool, but a fool I'm not. I sense a connection here. You still owe me dialogue, so let's hear it. No time like the present."

She unlocked her silken legs, planted her feet on the faded carpeting and hunched forward with her arms resting on her thighs, her thin, manicured fingers laced, exuding an uninhibited sex appeal that played better in person than in her movies, why the plum roles kept going to the likes of Crawford, Harlow and Loy.

I lit a pair of smokes, stepped over and slid one between her lips before settling in a sitting position on the edge of the bed across from her, used up a few drags figuring the best way to clue her in to the truth, real and imagined, like maybe she'd be able to fill in holes in the score card.

"The way it's been shaping up, your late husband and Otto Rothman were making a tidy sum at blackmail," I said, and watched her reaction.

Surprise gave way to disbelief. She said, "Day would never, *never* have done that. He was a lot of things, baby, but he was no blackmailer."

"He was and they were, and it got them both killed. Rothman took the pictures of stars and others in compromising, career-destroying situations. Day negotiated the deals with their victims. Along the way they picked on somebody who decided it was cheaper to put his own personal twist on the saying 'Death before dishonor.' " I executed a string of smoke rings while she weighed my words.

"Nicky Hartmann, is that where this is leading? He killed Day and Rothman?"

"Not necessarily. Hartmann insisted otherwise to me. He was a blackmail victim, yes to that, and that's what drew him to us, he said."

"Me? Chris, I swear, all you are saying is hitting me like a Mack Sennett custard." She sucked at her Lucky. The smoke poured from the sides of her mouth like a fire-eating dragon. "You and I strutting our stuff for somebody's camera lens is nothing I would ever let happen, much less forget about. Ain't so, baby. Ain't so. No matter what or who Nicky Hartmann says he saw."

"Simmer down. Hartmann came after me to find and get him his pictures and any negatives from a third man, who contacted him saying they were in his possession now. You were Hartmann's bargaining chip. He intended to keep you a prisoner at the manor until I delivered the goods."

"Who's the third man?"

"No idea," I said.

"Cripes! What if you said 'no,' or what if you couldn't find the man or the pictures and negatives, what then?" She saw the answer in my eyes. "Dear Sweet Jesus. You truly believe he would?"

I used a heel to douse my butt and snapped it at the wastebasket, barely missing the rim by a few inches. "You saw what happened when the little fellow rescued us from the rabbit hole and the business with Mueller chasing after us."

"Why did the Munchkin even bother if what you're saying is so?"

"It's so, and I don't know, but if he and Mueller aren't in L.A. looking to find us and get us back in harness, I'd be the most surprised man since Alf Landon."

"Day and Rothman were also blackmailing this Landon guy?"

I couldn't bring myself to explain.

World affairs had never been Marie's long suit.

"And you were roped in because of me," she said.

She mashed her Lucky in the ashtray and sprang from the armchair, pushing me flat onto the bed, unbuttoning my shirt, smothering my face in kisses and insinuating her body against mine. "I need to thank you the best way I know how for coming after me," she said, gripping my arms and rimming my ear with her tongue. "And for rescuing and protecting me, baby. You good for it, baby, like the times we used to have?" She dug her tongue into my mouth, searching for my tonsils, making it impossible for me to give her an answer. "Remember, baby, remember? Ah, yes. Yes, indeed. I'll say you do."

Strickling had a studio limo, a Rolls Royce Phantom III, waiting for us when the ferry docked in Long Beach. "From your phone call, it sounded like you could use a little comfort, given the kind of day you described," he said, once I had followed Marie inside and the driver shut the door behind us.

He was lounging in the backseat over a bottle of Royal Crown Cola. Ray Travis was on the jumper opposite him, using his finger to twirl the ice cubes in a half-finished blood-red whisky.

"Help yourself," Strickling said, throwing a thumb at the well-stocked teakwood bar tray. "Cubes in the bucket."

Marie wanted gin and anything. Travis poured it for her, adding ginger ale and a lime twist. I filled a crystal tumbler with a double pour of what looked like scotch and turned out to be bourbon. It tasted fine and went down smooth as a baby's bottom, all I cared about right now.

"How's my girl?" Strickling said, giving Marie's thigh some friendly pats. "You've had all of us, from Mr. Mayer on down, worried by your absence. . . . Getting back to work tomorrow or another day or two off the call sheet — you decide what's best for you and I'll see to it."

More pats.

Marie inched her leg away and threw me an anxious look.

I said, "Nothing that a good night's sleep won't fix, Strick, with someone watching over Marie in case anyone shows up unannounced at her doorstep."

"You volunteering?" he said, framing a sly grin, like he suspected something fresh happening between Marie and me. The man certainly had a sixth sense about these kinds of things, but it wasn't everything probably trafficking in his mind right now. It shouldn't have been anything, but it was what it was, a tension buster, and she teased me later over my having called out Nancy's name several times before Mt. Vesuvius erupted.

Travis caught my hesitation. "You're not on the hook, Blanchard. I volunteered to stand guard duty after Strick called me with your update. It'll give me an opportunity to ask Miss MacDaniels some questions that still need answers about her late husband, Mr. Covington, isn't that so, Strick?"

"Once Marie is fully rested and up to the task, of course."

"Of course. And also about this kidnapping business."

I said, "You jake with that, Marie?"

She gave Travis a funny look. "Who are you, anyway? I recognize you from somewhere, don't I?" Strickling made the introduction. "Oh, yeah, the cop Baxter and I did a scene with in *Battling G-Men in New York.* You weren't bad delivering your line. I took you for a real actor."

"Thank you," Travis said. He repeated his line from the movie like he was starring in Shakespeare. "And now here I am again, only this time I'm playing the cop for real."

She blew out a pound of breath while her eyes roamed the Rolls' cream-colored interior. "I don't think I'm ready to spend a night back in the house. It's too soon after —"

"Of course it is," Strickling said, cutting her off. "I anticipated as much, so we'll be putting you up at the studio's cottage at the Garden of Allah. It's yours to use for as long as you need. We'll pick you up in the morning and deliver you back from the studio end of the day."

"And at Strick's request I'll have a team of my best men at your disposal around the clock," Travis said, "so you don't have to be afraid of this Siegel fellow or any other of this Nicky Hartmann's people getting at you."

"Thank you," she said, her voice a whisper, and lost herself to her gin and ginger ale while I swallowed what was left of my drink, retreated from the Rolls and watched it take off before I hoofed over to the public lot where I'd parked my V8.

A note had been slipped under the driver's side windshield wiper blade.

It was from Herbie Duntz.

CHAPTER 14

Wednesday, November 16, 1938

I'd been inside the Follies Theater only once since leaving the force for MGM, a night that Lewis Stone wanted to drop by one of his old stage haunts before he became a movie actor and say hello to Joe Yule. Yule was the top banana on the burlesque house bill and father of the son they shared, Mickey Rooney, Yule for real, Stone in the Andy Hardy movies.

Before that it was while I was working the vice detail, often to yawn through an investigation of some stalwart citizen's complaint about illicit, unlawful, illegal, unholy shenanigans happening onstage, demanded by City Hall politicians capitalizing on the opportunity to sound off in the newspapers about defending moral values and decency, usually while they were running for reelection.

We'd wind up carting off a few of the

girlies for the photographers' benefit, those whose g-strings and pasties were inclined to stray during a torchy dance number, inciting members of the audience to respond accordingly under an overcoat of discretion. They'd be back at the same old grind a couple of hours later, having made either bail or some of our hornier guardians of law and order, sometimes both.

Herbie's note in a large, precise script asked for a meeting here at midnight — ". . . just you and me, friend Chris. No tricks."

I got to South Main and Third about twenty minutes late and parked illegally in a loading zone across from the theater, in its glory days the Belasco, the nine-hundred seat home to plays produced and frequently performed by the revered Broadway star David Belasco. The marquee headlined Carrie Finnell the Great and "Red Headed Ball of Fire" Betty Rowland. Yule was still around, billed with Frances E. Dahl, Jo Ann Dare, June March, Gay Knight and Rita Cummings in hanging block letters one-third the size that also promised "80 On-stage, Mostly Girls, Including 40 Tentalizin' Co-Eds."

After my eyes adjusted to the dark and sour smells no amount of cleaning fluid could ever eliminate, I settled into a seat on the aisle at the back of the house.

Half a dozen leggy lovelies and as many less-than-lovelies were hip-switching off the stage to unruly whistles, applause and cat shouts from the fifty or sixty people in the audience discreetly spaced out in the front rows and along the runway, where they were guaranteed their twenty-five cents worth of sightseeing feminine pulchritude.

I couldn't find Herbie among them and wondered if my being late had made him figure me for a no-show and take off.

The house lights dimmed again and the candy butchers disappeared.

Yule and the comics took to the stage and were running through a tired baggy pants and rubber bladders routine that could have been written by Methuselah when a voice at my elbow said, "Bet you wouldn't-a been late if you were coming here to meet Gable."

I'd taken a side trip to make certain Marie was tucked in and under security watch at the Garden of Allah after picking up the spare Detective Special I kept in my office at Metro. This was not information I intended to share with Herbie, except to pat my chest and tell him, "I wouldn't be packing, either, I was here to meet Gable."

"But you are alone. I eyed you long enough to be certain."

"Can I say the same about you?"

"Mueller's sitting watch at the Covington house. He thinks I'm doing ditto at your haunt."

"You're saying Mueller doesn't know about the note you left me?"

"Isn't that what I just said? He knew about the note, the next notes would be from an organ playing 'Nearer My God to Thee' at my funeral."

"And Hartmann?"

"Running his meeting and waiting for word from us. We're not supposed to come back to the island without you and Miss MacDaniels, especially her."

"Which of course explains why you helped spring us in the first place."

"Of course not," he said.

We'd been talking slightly above a whisper, overriding the slim laughter from the comics doing a tired, overworked version of the courtroom sketch Clark and McCullough rode to the top of the burlesque heap. "Case settled out of court!" the fright-wigged judge decreed, slamming his gavel bladder, and the sketch went to blackout, pushing the tired pit musicians into a noisy introduction to a parade of strippers — no "tentalizin' " co-eds visible in the bunch — and eliciting whoops from the audience.

Herbie tugged at my jacket. "C'mon, friend Chris. Somebody's waiting down the road to share with you the whole truth and nothing but, and I don't mean the Wonderful Wizard of Oz."

The Pantry Café at Ninth and Figueroa never closed, making it a favored retreat of night shifters who kept downtown L.A. from looking any more abandoned than it was after stores locked up and businesses shut down for the day, transforming the City of the Angels into a ghost town of empty sidewalks and streets. Included in the mix of regulars that could be expected in the turnover period between midnight and 2 A.M. were cops on a Code 7; hookers taking a vertical break from the hotel claptraps that catered to short-term occupants; cabbies with time to spare until the next train pulled into Union Station; office building janitors and watchmen, ink-stained press operators from Hearst's *Examiner* and others trapped downtown who relished an off-hours breakfast or a thick New York steak grilled to perfection at a pauper's price.

I stepped inside and checked around for Herbie while the intoxicating smells of deep fried chicken and hash browns on the griddle pampered my nose, reminding me I hadn't had a meal since Avalon. The café was usually packed, tables shared by strangers who often struck up temporary friendships, solving all the ills of the world while sharing fresh bread from the bread basket and thick pads of butter, but not now. Twenty people were spread out among the Pantry's sixty counter and dining room seats, including two sets of uniforms at the fifteen-seat counter, feasting on the house in unspoken trade for the visible protection their paunchy presence guaranteed, the modern-day equivalent of beat cops walking off with an apple from the apple cart.

Herbie signaled me from his lonely table parked against the far wall by a terse thumb-and-finger whistle when I appeared to miss spotting his overhead wave through the grease and nicotine cloud stinging my eyes.

He was alone and, recognizing my confusion, said, "He's taking a pee-pee, friend Chris, so rest easy. Help yourself to a seat . . . no, not that one. He likes to face front with his back to the wall, so he can see anybody coming his way — Wild Bill Hickok style."

I said, "Until the night Hickok got to his poker game and his usual seat was taken, so he sat facing one door with his back to another. That made it possible for Jack Mc-Call to sneak up behind him and put a bullet into Hickok's head. Hickok was holding aces and eights, what came to be famous as the Dead Man's Hand."

"I loved that movie," Herbie said. "Gary Cooper as Wild Bill and Jean Arthur as Calamity Jane. She's some hot mama, that Jean, better'n anything tramping the stage over at the Follies. I could go for that creature in a big way, you know what I mean?"

The voice behind me said, "She's kind of eccentric, but nice, Tyrone."

It was Ray Travis.

He said, "I did a bit for Frankie Capra with Jean and Jimmy Stewart and Lionel Barrymore in *You Can't Take It with You* over at Gower Gulch last year. Have a swell picture of the two of us up on my wall, next to another real keeper, me and Bette Davis when we shared a close-up in *Dangerous,* the picture that won Bette an Oscar."

Herbie stepped aside so the cop could settle onto the chair facing out.

I was in the chair across from Travis, my back to the Pantry entrance.

We traded false smiles.

"You're not superstitious, Blanchard?"

"I'm not Wild Bill Hickok," I said. "I

always play the cards I'm dealt, even when I'm surprised by who's dealing them, like you, Travis. You're the last person in the world I figured Herbie was putting me with. Spill. What the hell's going on?"

His smile grew broader. He liked seeing me dumb. He pulled out a pocket tin of Stag and made a slow motion production of loading his pipe, tamping down the tobacco and thumb-striking a stick match. I popped a Lucky from my pack and leaned forward to share the match. He blew it out before I got there. Herbie reached over with a book match before I could congratulate Travis on repeating as my personal choice for Asshole of the Year, saying, "You want me to start, Captain?"

"I did, there'd be no need for this little meeting," Travis said. Herbie turned his face so only I could see him rolling his eyes while Travis made a show of searching the smoke-stained tin ceiling for inspiration. After another minute he said, "You've no idea what you're into thanks to Marie MacDaniels, Blanchard. The Day Covington murder. The Otto Rothman murder. Their blackmail enterprise. Tyrone here playing bookmaker with Nicky Hartmann on the MGM lot. All of it small change, part and parcel of a bigger issue, a threat to

238

our nation and the safety and well-being of all of its citizens."

Travis had taken on the sonorous tone of the guy who narrated the *March of Time* features I caught sometimes at one of the theaters specializing in all-newsreel programs, but was coming across as a third-rate Lowell Thomas, the voice of the Movietone News for 20th Century Fox.

"Enlighten me," I said.

He surveyed the room for privacy.

We were surrounded by empty tables, except for one occupied by an elderly gent in a rumpled gray sharkskin suit, slumped over and auditioning his snoring with his head resting on the surface, using his arms for a pillow.

Satisfied, Travis lowered his voice to a level that had me straining to hear him and launched into a detailed story that took him a little under an hour to tell.

He was good to his word. What he spelled out was definitely an eye-popper; nothing I would have guessed; some genuine surprises mingling with signs I would have spotted if I knew what I was looking for.

I said, "Why are you telling me this now, Travis?"

"I know your bark and your bite, how you stick with a case once your teeth sink in.

You know I've been monitoring you. You're so deep into this one now, I can't afford to keep you nosing around in the dark and possibly screwing it up, maybe get somebody else killed."

"Like me?"

"Like you? I loathe you — you were a disloyal cop — but I need you, Blanchard. Your country needs you. What do you say?"

I was still hungry when Travis left, taking Herbie with him.

We'd never gotten around to ordering.

The place was filling up with late-daters, the dance hall crowd from the Fenton Brothers' Roseland Roof, bar refugees, and blue collars who had either clocked out or were one-stopping on their way to a fresh work day.

A line had formed at the order counter.

I ordered a ham steak and eggs over easy with hash browns and a side of griddle cakes, a wedge of apple pie a la mode for dessert.

Returned to the table and moved around to the seat Travis had occupied, facing the entrance.

I was no longer alone when my order was delivered, having been joined by two sleepy-eyed nurses from Queen of Angels Hospital, whose white uniforms carried traces of fresh blood that made me think twice before splashing the hash browns with a layer of catsup. I shut out their operating room gossip and considered everything I'd learned from Travis and what my next moves should be.

The biggest surprise was the little fellow, discovering that Herbie Duntz was more than one of Singer's Midgets playing a Munchkin in *The Wizard of Oz.*

Herbie helped begin what Travis was calling on me to help end.

As the cop and later Herbie told it, Singer's Midgets were touring Europe when, during a stop for shows in Munich, Herbie had one drink too many after a performance. He staggered into a noisy beer hall by the River Isar, on the edge of the English Gardens, ordered a *seidel* of dark beer and settled at a marked table, whose brass plaque identified it as a table meant only for regular patrons, not a public table meant to be shared.

He was promptly set upon by a gang of Nazi brownshirts, who hoisted him over their heads like a gunnysack of grain, carried him out to an alley and beat and kicked him into a state of unconsciousness, screaming how midgets and dwarfs were God's mistakes, to be disposed of along with Jews, homosexuals and other freaks of nature.

The attack put Herbie in the hospital for six weeks — two of them in a coma — cost him the rest of the tour, and left him with a scar on his mind bigger than all those he had sustained on his body. Revenge became an obsession and turned into the proverbial *dish best eaten cold* when Singer brought the troupe to MGM for the movie.

While soliciting bookmaking customers, Herbie spotted Nicky Hartmann.

He had modified his appearance somewhat and was speaking accent-free English, but he definitely was one of the brownshirts who had led the assault at the Munich beer hall. If Hartmann remembered him, he didn't let on, maybe because beating up the drunk and the defenseless wasn't a one-time thing for him.

Hartmann surprised Herbie one day by inviting him out for drinks. Herbie went, figuring the closer he got to Hartmann, the faster he would be able to plan and execute a suitable revenge.

After a few hours of playing Good Time Charlie, Hartmann embraced him like a brother and proposed they become partners in bookmaking, sweet-talking a dozen reasons why, like Herbie wouldn't recognize they all were self-serving, Hartmann looking to pad his own pocket. After all, how bright could one of God's mistakes be — a midget meant to be disposed of along with Jews, homosexuals and other freaks of nature?

Hartmann, sensing his hesitation, suggested Herbie sleep on the idea. Herbie said he would, although he knew what his answer would be. The catch was figuring out how to say *Fuck you, you miserable shit* in a way that let Hartmann down gently and kept their pseudo-friendship working until get-even time.

The solution came the next day, when he was summoned from the Munchkinland set to the office of L.B. Mayer. Waiting for him besides Mayer, who was clucking away like a distressed father about to suffer cardiac arrest, were Strickling, Travis and a man dressed in mourner's black with an expression to match, who was introduced as Charles Cook of the FBI's Los Angeles Bureau and ignored Herbie's handshake offer.

Everything about Cook's appearance was average, from his height and weight, to an angular face that would stand out in a lineup only because of his Durante nose. His mellow voice had a studied correctness that sometimes slipped into mispronunciation, *bidness* for *business, excetra* for *et cetera,* or incorrectness, *irregardless* for *regardless, in route* for *en route.*

Herbie was sure some sore loser had reported him to the studio and he was about to be arrested, but he didn't understand why Cook was there, unless he'd missed the news that bookmaking was now a federal offense.

Strickling directed him to join them in the conversation area. He lifted himself onto one of the antique chairs, fluffed his orange hairpiece and tinkered nervously with his costume waiting for the boom to lower.

"Let's move this along," Mayer said from behind his desk. "I got rushes to watch and then I need to be in the commissary kitchen to supervise a fresh batch of my mama's own matzo ball soup in time for the lunch crowd. . . . You ever try some, Agent Cook? It's on the menu over there."

"No, sir, I haven't yet had that privilege."

"Strick will make the arrangement, you tell him when. You'll pass out from the pleasure. The balls are cooked under a broiler until they're crisp, just so, and served in a dark brown broth from a recipe handed down in my family for decades. . . . Your own Mr. John Edgar Hoover, he tried it and loved it when he visited me here, and took a container with him when he left. I still get thank-you notes from him."

Strickling got the meeting back on track, saying, "As you can tell, Mr. Cook, Mr. Mayer is anxious for you to explain to Mr. Powell why we're here."

"Words out of my mouth," Mayer said.

"So, yes, I'm a bookie," Herbie said. "If you're going to arrest me, arrest me, and let's get this over with."

"Arrest? Who said anything about arrest?" Mayer said, his eyes growing behind his glasses. "Strick, you know we can't have anything about this Tommy Harmon person leaking out anywhere, especially not to that *schmuck* — you should pardon my French — Nick Schenk in New York."

"Already taken care of, Mr. Mayer. Isn't that correct, Mr. Cook?"

"Correct, sir." Cook said, putting an ounce of pep in his voice. "I come with Mr. Hoover's personal assurance."

"I got to remember to fly him some soup," Mayer said. "The least I can do to tell him thank you. You can report to him it'll be on the way."

"I'll do that, sir, and, by the way, the name of the party under discussion is Nicky Hartmann, not Tommy Harmon. Tommy Harmon is the University of Michigan football star who has been breaking all manner of records on the field."

"You misunderstood Mr. Mayer," Strickling said, flashing the FBI agent a signal.

Travis, ever the angles player, said, "Mr. Mayer did say Nicky Hartmann."

"The two names, they don't even sound alike," Mayer said. "You spend any time at all on the firing range, maybe it's time to have your hearing checked, Agent Cook?"

"I'll do that, sir," Cook said, avoiding Mayer's fierce look.

Herbie finally spoke up. "What's Nicky Hartmann have to do with this?"

Cook said, "He's your partner."

"He's not."

Strickling said, "He will be, Mr. Powell, after you hear out Agent Cook."

Cook said, "Hartmann is a Nazi, Mr. Powell. A leader in the *Amerikadeutscher Bund,* the German American Bund, sent to the states by Hitler's deadliest henchman, *SS Reichsführer* Heinrich Himmler, to infiltrate and wreak havoc on our soil."

"With the nerve to work at my studio and pretend to be a good American while he and his filthy kind get ready to carry out their plans, that *mamzer,* you should pardon my French," Mayer said, spitting out the words, a fist railing at the concept. "I learned all this from Strick, I said, Strick, whatever it takes, L.B. Mayer and Metro-Goldwyn-Mayer got to help stop this business in its tracks. God bless America, how good it's been to me and mine." Mayer's tears were for real. There was none of his vaunted dramatics at work here.

Cook said, "Certain of Mr. Mayer's loyalty and devotion to our flag, we turned to Mr. Strickling, asking that he take every step necessary to keep Hartmann on the payroll, so we could monitor him at a closer range than before. In order to keep the FBI invisible at this early juncture, at Mr. Strickling's suggestion, we turned to the Los Angeles Police Department and his trusted ally, Captain Travis."

Travis locked his fists and waved them high, like a boxer being introduced into the ring at the Olympic Auditorium or Hollywood Legion Stadium.

"I still don't get it," Herbie said.

"We'd been looking for a way to get inside Hartmann's operation without rousing suspicion. The perfect opportunity presented itself last night, when Hartmann suggested the two of you partner up in your bookmaking enterprise."

"You'd be out of here faster than Stroheim, I knew that before," Mayer said. "The track, that's where betting belongs."

"It's more baseball and football, sir."

"Like the sport of kings isn't so important?" Mayer grunted and dismissed Herbie with a wave.

Herbie said, "How did you know that, about Hartmann wanting in, Agent Cook?"

Cook tossed him a palm. "We're the FBI."

"I wasn't going to say yes to him, for personal reasons."

"We knew that, too, including your personal reasons. We do our homework. It's why I requested this meeting and stamped it *Urgent* — to see to it that you do quite the opposite. You're our first and best opportunity yet to get inside Hartmann's operation."

"And if I say thanks, but no?"

"You won't look any better in prison stripes than you do in that funny costume they got you in," Travis said.

Cook said, "After that, federal charges — aiding and abetting a conspiracy targeted at the United States of America, a treasonable offense subject to the death penalty."

"That's not true. It would never be true and you know it. How can you do that?"

"We're the FBI."

■ ■ ■ ■

Herbie put off giving Hartmann an answer for a few days, while he was schooled in what to expect, what to do and how to do it. It came down to keeping Cook apprised of everything he saw and heard, following Cook's direction, and taking no action that wasn't first approved by either Cook or Ray Travis.

He countered Hartmann's proposal with his own, offering twenty-five percent of the take from bets Hartmann laid off for them on the S.S. *Rex* gambling ship. Hartmann unexpectedly agreed without hesitation — Herbie was prepared to make it fifty-fifty — and their partnership was activated on a handshake.

Shortly afterward, Herbie took to commenting on the day's news, expressing anti-American sentiments little by little, hoping to draw out Hartmann, who showed only mild interest, but contributed no complaints or observations of his own.

That changed the day Herbie exploded in the studio commissary over a bowl of L.B. Mayer's matzo ball soup.

"Good as it is, I should be boycotting this piss," Herbie said, lowering his voice when he saw he was attracting attention from Ann Sothern, George Murphy, Dan Dailey, Jr., Buddy Ebsen and some others at nearby tables. "Jew soup in a business run by Jews, who've never done anything for any minority but their own, especially now with that Jew president in the White House — Jewsevelt — and his 'Jew Deal.' "

"It's not so bad," Hartmann said.

"Maybe not bad for you, but try to see the world from my perspective, Nicky, and you'll understand soon enough. I've never felt this oppressed anywhere else that money-grubbing Singer has taken us. Not London. Not Paris. Especially not Germany."

"*Especially* not Germany? How is that, Tyrone?"

"From what I read in the papers, like today's *Times.* Quoting Mr. Fritz Kuhn, head of the German American Bund, on how the Nazi party of Mr. Hitler calls for a society of equals, not only in his country, but in the countries where he's spreading his philosophy."

"I've heard and read opposite opinions," Hartmann said, measuring his words. "I remember something about the unfair treatment of minorities, even people of your size, going back some years."

"Granted. I got my share of lumps, but that was then and this is now. I can only hope and pray that Mr. Kuhn and his Bund members will be successful in bringing Mr. Hitler's philosophy to our shores."

"Tyrone, I've never before heard you talk like this."

"I only wish more people were within sound of my voice, Nicky. Unfortunately, one voice does not a chorus make."

A man's shadow passed onto their table and stopped.

George Murphy stood over Herbie, arms crossed, a pained expression on his face.

He said, "I overheard what you been saying, fella, and I need to tell you it makes me sick to my stomach."

"Maybe it's the matzo ball soup," Herbie said, pushing away his bowl.

"Definitely you, fella. Whatever problem we have with the Commies, more and more it sounds like we have a bigger problem with you Nazi types."

"You must be a Jew boy," Herbie said. "Is that it?"

The plan worked.

Two days later, Hartmann invited Herbie to join him for supper at the Café Berlin on Brand Boulevard in Glendale, a half block south of the Alex Theatre, whose forecourt was a scaled-down version of Grauman's Egyptian in Hollywood.

Hartmann was no stranger.

The maitre d' greeted him with an enthusiastic air wave and a double-handshake, and he traded greetings with many of the patrons at the crowded circular bar on the way to the one unoccupied green leather booth in the dining room, where his arrival caused more waves and greetings, German substituting for English in several instances. There was an engraved brass plaque on the table reading "Reserved for N. Hartmann."

Cook had instructed Herbie not to ask leading questions, to wait for Hartmann to volunteer information. It came over the second round of drinks, after business small talk about the increase in bookmaking profits once Hartmann became involved.

"Tyrone, I have something to confess," Hartmann said.

"Our deal has me happier than a dog with two dicks, so if you been cheating me in any way, I don't want to know from it, Nicky."

Hartmann discounted the thought with a grand gesture. "It's about our profits, yes, but I have to tell you my share is not lining my pockets, the way I made you believe."

He paused, as if looking for the right words; ran a finger across his mustache and around his lower lip. "You remember our conversation about the *Amerikadeutscher Bund*?" he said, pronouncing the name in impeccable German. "The German American Bund?"

"Yes, of course," Herbie said, and raised his gin martini in toast. "More power to them."

"I belong, Tyrone. I'm a member."

"Go on, you're joking."

"Far from. I'm one of the Bund's proud leaders on the West Coast, dedicated to its principles and goals on behalf of Herr Hitler's Third Reich, so I was floored and grateful for all the true words you spoke; how you responded to that fool, Murphy; wanting to tell you then and there how my share goes to supporting the organization."

"Now I know you're joking."

"No, no, no, absolutely not. Many here tonight are also Bund members. We meet here regularly to keep up on the news from the Homeland and take up tasks that will lead to the greater glory when our philosophy overtakes the ranting of Franklin D. Rosenfeld and his kind." He let the thought sink in. "I invite you to join me in our undertaking and sincerely hope you will do so, Tyrone."

"You're serious."

"You're somebody I've come to know as a man of honor, somebody whose word is golden and I can wholeheartedly trust working alongside me to help achieve our goals and bring our New Order to America. So, what do you say?"

Herbie gave it a minute.

"Only if you let me contribute my fair share to the Bund," he said.

Herbie's first report to FBI Agent Charles Cook, using LAPD Captain Ray Travis as their intermediary, revealed that a house on Santa Catalina Island served as more than a getaway playpen for Hartmann and his women. It was where Bund leaders from around the country regularly gathered to coordinate their activities and advance plans for a major unified effort they called "Operation A."

Travis said, "That's a joke, right?"

"They don't smile or laugh when they say it," Herbie said.

"What else do they say?"

"This one time Nicky's taken me along, I overheard a date slip out from some of those Kraut lovers, next February 19, but no specifics. He wasn't ready to let me into the meeting, and I didn't hustle the question."

The date proved helpful.

Cook discovered through other sources that the Bund had rented Madison Square Garden in New York for that Sunday, when Fritz Kuhn would reportedly address twenty thousand or more members of his flock on a topic of vital international significance.

No one seemed to know what that meant — *vital international significance* — or if the Bund rally was tied in some way to the Washington's Birthday holiday celebration on February 22.

Herbie was instructed to do whatever it took to find out more.

He had no idea if what he discovered a few weeks later was tied to the rally: Hartmann was being blackmailed.

He took Herbie aside on the *Battling G-Men* stage and, his face red with rage, said he'd been contacted by Day Covington, who was demanding a quarter of a million dollars for certain negatives and photographs taken by Otto Rothman.

"If I don't come across, this two-bit actor says he's going to turn them over to the FBI, kit and caboodle. That would be a disaster. It's my fault, unintentional, but I would be disgraced. I cannot let that happen."

"Your fault?"

"I needed a cheap photographer to do the work, and this Rothman creature was suggested by Eve Whitney. He used to be important, she said, but no longer and could use the business. Cheap he was, dirt cheap, until the phone call from Covington."

"Rothman. A Jew? The name sounds Jewish to me."

"Christian. Believe me, I wormed the information out of him before I hired him, otherwise I'd have gone after someone else. Imagine if he were a Jew boy? The asking price would probably be double."

"Probably triple."

They shared a laugh that momentarily relieved the stress cloaking Hartmann.

Herbie said, "What are you going to do about it, Nicky?"

"Find the negatives and pictures or find the money and pay the ransom, whichever happens fastest."

"The pictures matter that much?"

"They are everything," Hartmann said.

He didn't volunteer why or what they showed.

Herbie knew better than to press hard.

Soon, Day Covington was dead — murdered.

Then Otto Rothman — dead; murdered.

And the negatives and photographs were

still missing.

Hartmann still desperate.

Herbie still in the dark where Cook and Travis were demanding more light.

Heading home, I played over and over in my mind what I had learned with what I already knew.

Not everything made sense.

I understood how Marie's desperate plea had led me from two murders into ugly world politics and a potential national threat of unknown dimensions tied to the German American Bund and a Madison Square Garden rally hardly more than three months from now.

I understood how blackmail had caused or, at the least, contributed to the deaths of Covington and Rothman.

I understood why Nicky Hartmann kidnapped Marie to Avalon and used her as a bartering tool with me, why Herbie's rescue of us wasn't as confusing as it first seemed.

I understood the involvement of Travis and Strickling, how they managed to be around at critical moments.

What I didn't understand —

I didn't understand what made the Rothman photographs so valuable, but would bet that, whatever they revealed, it had to be more than the kind of sexy stuff that lined Rothman's walls and the porn or near-porn that filled his files and provided an ongoing money stream.

The photos had to be worth the leap from chicken feed payments to the quarter of a million dollars Covington demanded, likely only the first in a series of demands. I'd been around enough blackmail action in my time to know the beginning rarely doubled as the end once a blackmailer buried his fangs into you.

In time, Herbie might be able to coddle their contents out of Hartmann.

Travis and the FBI agent, Cook, would be monitoring Hartmann and his Bund cronies, ready to strike when and if direct contact was made with the new blackmailer who'd clocked in claiming possession of the photos.

And me?

I could say I didn't understand why I'd agreed to stay in the loop, except —

Who would I be kidding besides myself?

Travis was right when he said I was in too deep to bow out.

My patriotic duty?

Sure, that.

But definitely still about where I started this rhumba —

Getting Marie off the hook on a murder rap.

CHAPTER 15

Thursday, November 17, 1938

I slept late, didn't get to the studio until late afternoon and headed straight for the *Battling G-Men* soundstage, anxious to corner Eve about Hartmann, who might have let slip what type of photographs he was chasing after when he asked her to recommend a cheap photographer.

She was on the call sheet, but not around.

The set was being struck and people packing to leave two hours earlier than the normal six o'clock quitting time.

Hal Bucquet was huddling by the camera crane with his cinematographer, Johnny Seitz, screenwriter Max Brand and Baxter Leeds, who was decked out in white tie, tails and top hat. Not one happy face in the bunch.

Hal made a despairing gesture and welcomed me over. "The last time I was going through aggravation here, somebody told me, *Smile, Hal, it could be worse.* Words to live by. This morning I arrived smiling and it got worse. Lousy enough I was shooting around Marie, who's yet to show her face again, now it's Eve who's disappeared."

"Disappeared how, Hal?"

"Look around, do you see her?"

"No."

"That's how. . . . We got two set-ups in before the lunch break. Afterward, she was gone — poof! — no word to anybody, leaving me with no choice but to shut down for the day or turn the picture into a collection of Baxter Leeds close-ups."

Leeds said, "No complaints here, Hal."

Hal missed the humor in Leeds's delivery and shot him down with a look. "I got an ultimatum from the front office. We shut down permanently unless Freddie can whip out some fresh pages on a new story direction overnight."

Freddie was Max Brand.

His real name was Frederick Schiller Faust, Brand one of nineteen pen names he used on his books and scripts. He was as American as jazz, born in Seattle, Washington, but growing anti-German sentiment had led him to disguise his family roots under layers of aliases.

Brand pushed a palm across his receding

hairline, removed the cigarette clamped in the corner of his mouth and ground it out under his heel. "A snap," he said. "We stay with the ballroom scene, only now instead of telling the Eve character he's off to take the Marie character for a whirl on the dance floor, he turns to a waiter and says, *Excuse me, please. Can you direct me to the gents? I'm desperate to take a king-sized dump.*"

Hal shook his head. "All of a sudden I have two comedians on my hands? This is my career, gents. The picture shutters, chances are fifty-fifty I'll be sent packing and next time you see me I'll be at Monogram telling the horses when to hit their marks."

"And me in temporary limbo," Leeds said. "I'll tell you what I think. I think the Commies are somehow behind this, Hal. They know where I stand on the Red Menace and it's not a gospel they want me spreading, not with all the fans I have out there. First Marie, and now Eve. You call it coincidence? I call it the premeditated sabotage of my career. Damn Commies."

Johnny Seitz spoke up. "Wouldn't it have been swifter and more effective if they just made you disappear, Baxter?"

"Surely you jest, Johnny. Hardly a breeze through the trees about Marie, even with a homicide hanging over her head, and Eve's less of a name than Marie. But me? The disappearance of Baxter Leeds would be headline news bound to turn out the full strength of Uncle Sam's army, especially once my great ally and defender of democracy, Miss Hedda Hopper herself, spoke up loud and clear in her column."

I said, "Hal, I can't say about Eve, but I might be able to locate Marie and get her back here to you."

"Tomorrow?"

"No promises."

"It would save me one hell of a lot of rewriting," Max Brand said.

"You writers, always thinking of yourselves first," Leeds said.

Hal looked at me like an answered prayer. "I'd be forever in your debt, Chris."

Johnny Seitz said, "Of course, you know, Chris — in Hollywood terms, 'forever' usually means twenty-four hours or less."

"Wonderful," Hal said, "now I have three of the Marx Brothers."

I gave my office a fast whirl before heading to the Garden of Allah.

Seven memos from Ida Koverman, spelling out requests from Mayer, nothing that couldn't hold for another day.

A phone message to call Strickling, who was now gone for the day.

Three phone messages from Eve Whitney, saying it was urgent she speak with me — no reason given. I tried her at the two numbers I had. No answer at either.

A handwritten note I almost overlooked, propped up against the exotic marble base of the Tiffany pen and pencil set Joanie Crawford gave me for my birthday three years ago, Nancy Warren wondering, *Whatever happened to Chris Blanchard?*

I stuffed the note in my pocket, grinning like Christmas had come early, and took off, one-stopping at Eve's place on my way to the Garden.

She lived in a low-rent section of the Wilshire District, where all the streets were lined on both sides with quaint Spanish-style duplexes and double-deckers with turrets meant to suggest medieval England or something like that, within walking distance of the Carthay Circle Theater.

I climbed the narrow tiled stairway to her apartment, knocked and, when that got me nowhere, tried the door.

It was unlocked.

I called her name a few times before entering.

The living room was inexpensively furnished. Dishes stacked in the kitchen sink and clothing tossed randomly around the living room and bedroom suggested she'd never be a candidate for the *Good Housekeeping Magazine* Seal of Approval. A percolator half-full of warm coffee and the smoldering remains of a cigarette in a mountain of butts in an ashtray told me she hadn't been gone long.

I stepped across the landing and rapped on her neighbor's door.

The woman who answered in an ill-fitting housecoat, her hair done up in curlers, air-drying a fresh coat of flaming red fingernail polish, appeared disappointed that I was there only to ask a question.

She'd seen Eve leave about a half hour ago with some guy, nobody she recognized from any of Eve's other gentlemen callers.

They were in a hurry, she said, traveling so fast the guy stumbled and almost took a dive down the steps.

"Anything else you notice?"

"Name's Dolores, good-lookin'."

"Anything else you notice, Dolores?"

"It was the noise got my attention," she said. "Otherwise, I'm not one for spying." She thought about it. "Yeah, one thing, maybe. Eve didn't look too happy taking off that way, even though it was one of those fancy-dancy, black as shoe polish Mercedes-Benz jobs."

The Garden of Allah, on the Sunset Strip at the intersection of Sunset Boulevard and Crescent Heights, had become the hotel paradise of choice for picture business types with a common interest in revelry, ribaldry and chronic alcoholism. A main building and twenty-five villas spread over three and a half acres of formal gardens, palms and other tropical trees played home to celebrated actors, musicians, artists and, farther down the status scale, authors like Faulkner, Hemingway, Steinbeck and Fitzgerald.

I threw a Pepsodent smile and a wink at Dusty, the middle-aged switchboard girl with Hindenburg breasts I'd yet to see without a Camel dangling from her mouth or ashes powdering the shoulders of the fashionable dresses that often came her way as thank-you gifts from residents who sought her out for more than their phone messages.

She smiled back and aimed a thumb across the modest lobby.

I turned to have a look and saw I was getting x-rayed by Jess Lowy, one of Ray Travis's boys, who looked out of place lounging on a divan that belonged on the set of one of DeMille's Biblical extravaganzas. I knew Jess from the old days. We had always been friendly, but never friends. No reason. That's how it happens sometimes, for anybody. He was never a dirty cop outside of the five o'clock shadow that hung on him like wallpaper and food stains on his tie, so it wasn't that.

He recognized me, tipped the brim of his charcoal gray felt fedora and signaled me over. Whispered, "Besides me, Travis has Brodie eyeing the front door to the cottage and McDonough around back on Havenhurst Drive, near the kitchen door. Your movie star's as safe as a bug in a rug. Got her autograph for my kids." Returned to attacking the crossword puzzle of his *Herald-Express.*

I double-timed my way into the courtyard and around the pool Alla Nazimova had ordered the builders to shape like the Black Sea, to remind her of Yalta, her birthplace. It was the silent screen star who transformed the hollow below street level, what once was a millionaire's dominion, into the drinkers' paradise that Louella Parsons's *Examiner* column revealed was driving Valentino's one-time leading lady broke.

I reached the studio's cottage and looked

around for Brodie before I pressed the doorbell. He was invisible, checking me out, I figured, from behind one of the towering hedges that surround a formal garden.

The door creaked open and Marie pulled me inside. "Am I relieved to see you," she said, the urgency in her voice traveling at the speed of light. She replaced the chain lock, flipped the light switch and double-checked that the thick drapes were fully drawn; threw her arms around me. "Something's wrong, baby."

"Tell me."

"I wanted to call the studio, let them know I was game for filming tomorrow, only the phone was deader'n a doornail. I couldn't get a dial tone, connect to the switchboard, anything. So I told this to Detective Brodie outside and he said stay put and keep the door locked while he went up front to check. That was more'n an hour ago, and he's still gone and the phone still isn't working and I don't know what brought you here, but I thank dear sweet Jesus for that."

"Did you report that to McDonough, the cop who's guarding your back door?"

"I tried. I called for him through the door, once, twice, three times, and never got an answer. Don't try selling me the idea he's hard of hearing. They're after me again, what it is, right?"

"Don't jump to conclusions."

"I've already jumped out of my skin, baby."

I unplugged my .38 from my shoulder holster and, half-hiding it by my thigh, told Marie to lock the door behind me, stepped out to the courtyard and headed for a survey of the formal garden area. A symphony of overlapping voices and laughter was growing by the pool as the first of the residents and friends gathered for another evening of free-form carousing.

I'd barely traveled ten yards when I tripped over Brodie. He was stretched out on the manicured grass, alongside the hedge, drunk as ten men. I'd forgotten what a booze hound Brodie was and how it had come close to costing him his badge. Travis saved his pension after he promised to reform, swearing on his mother's grave, his children's lives and his honor as a thirty-second degree Mason.

I parked the Detective Special and padded over to the lobby.

Lowy looked up from his crossword puzzle. "Everything jake?"

"Phone's not working."

"Heard that an hour ago from Brodie."

Dusty said, "Pacific Telephone will be out

to have a look in the morning, Chris. It happens a lot around here. Usually one of the writers who's stuck in a corner and decides to save what's left of the hair on his head by ripping the phone from the wall."

"Brodie needs rescuing, Lowy."

"Yeah," Lowy said, like he knew about Brodie's condition and didn't intend doing anything about it. "You happen to know a three-letter word for a very long time period?" he said, using his tongue to wet the stub of his pencil.

"Era," I said, turning to go.

"*Error?* That's five letters, Blanchard. What else?"

I did a fast walk on Sunset to get to Havenhurst, the tree-lined residential street a block west of Crescent Heights often used by Garden of Allah tenants and guests to park and enter the compound or a cottage without being seen.

McDonough's unmarked was parked across the street from the cottage's kitchen door. He was behind the wheel, his elbow hanging out the window and his bulbous nose buried in a *Black Mask* magazine. It took him more than a minute to sense somebody was standing over him.

"Christ, Blanchard! You scared the holy

crap out of me," he said, once he had his breathing under control, his husky voice clogged by years of a three-pack-a-day habit.

I popped a Lucky from my pack and offered him one.

He waved it off. "Between us girls, I caught a case of the Big C, my lungs, so I'm doing my damndest to cross the finish line on twenty — fourteen months down the line — and leave Gert and the brats the full pension, you follow?"

I snapped the Lucky in half and tossed it away. "Who else knows, Windy?"

"Some of our old gang, that's about it. Travis, he's been a prince, helping keep the word under wraps and throwing me easy bones, out of sight of the big brass downtown. I heard on the grapevine you were tied to this MacDaniels business. What brings you over here now?"

"Routine. How are you getting along with Marie?"

"She's desperate for my body, but I'm playing hard to get."

"She tells me she got nowhere trying to get your attention earlier."

He made a sour face. "Which time was that? It's like every hour on the hour she calls out my name and I got to trot on over and show off my face. Probably missed one while I was off taking a piss in the bushes. A regular Nervous Nellie, she is. Talk some calm into her, will you, Blanchard?"

"No, no, no, baby. Let him say that to my face. If he was pissing anywhere, it was on you." Marie was adamant. "It was only that one time I called for him, and I was scared silly, feeling like poor Thelma Todd must've felt the night they came after her and killed her."

"Nobody's going to kill you."

"Says you."

She lifted her hands in dramatic despair and turned the key in the back door.

I followed her through a kitchen that resembled a scaled-down version of the one in Judge Hardy's middle-America home into a sitting room full of overstuffed elegance out of a *Grand Hotel* suite, only slightly less dramatic than a dining room that was more upper-crust *Dinner at Eight,* the whole layout based on art direction by Cedric Gibbons.

She flung herself into a corner of the burnished leather sofa, wrapped herself in her arms and shook her head in slow motion. "This isn't working, baby," she said, and descended into silence.

I flopped onto a chair across from her and

said, "What you need to do is get your mind off this nasty business by going back to work tomorrow and surrounding yourself with friends."

It took her two or three minutes to answer. "Easier said than done, baby."

"Sleep on it. Get yourself a good night's sleep and then decide."

"A good night's sleep with the kind of protection I'm getting — one detective who disappears like Blackstone the Magician and another who claims to be taking a piss when I need him? Can't wait to see what the next shift brings."

"Look, safety in numbers. Hartmann wants me as much or more than he wants you, so would you feel better if I settle in for the duration?" I pulled back my jacket to show off the holster. "Me and Roscoe here?"

Marie didn't have to say a word.

Her eyes held the answer.

CHAPTER 16

We kibitzed about nothing in particular for the next hour, me looking to get her mind out of third gear and finally succeeding with some of the latest industry gossip I'd picked up around town and bum jokes I'd heard at the Follies Theater, like "Ball of Fire" Betty Rowland revealing, *I remember when I graduated from the School of Burlesque, I walked on the stage wearing a cap and gown and left wearing just two tassels.*

That one, one of the first I threw at Marie, relieved her tension enough to send her racing to the bathroom, knock-kneed to keep the dam from bursting en route; her laughter louder than the hoary gag deserved.

Lowy dropped by to announce a changing of the guard, slipping me a wink and a whispered *Don't do anything I would do* before I closed the door on him and returned to the kitchen, where Marie was whipping up a dinner with stuff scavenged from the refrigerator and the shelves. Nothing exotic, a meal built around salami, bologna and cheese double-decker sandwiches, a chili and beans concoction that tortured the roof of my mouth going down, a plate of sugar and chocolate chip cookies, and enough wine and beer to float the British navy.

"You deserve better for looking after me this way," she said, after we settled at the dining room table. "I owe you a night on the town, baby."

"With chili like this, who needs Chasen's?"

"I'm thinking Perino's. Caviar, oysters on the half shell, prime rib or a porterhouse steak or maybe a lobster or boned trout; creamed spinach; broiled asparagus. Fresh-made ice cream or sherbet for dessert. Naturally, an appropriate wine for every course."

"Naturally."

"How did I ever let you get away from me, Chris?"

"Just lucky, I guess."

"I mean it."

"So do I, sweetheart."

"Sweetheart. You haven't called me that in ages."

"Chalk it up to the *vino*," I said, hoisting

my glass.

Marie raised hers. "I'll take it any way I can get it," she said.

I'd been kidding.

I saw she wasn't.

I changed the subject, converting the conversation to every actor and actress's favorite topic — themselves. "I hear talk Selznick is considering you for a role in *Gone with the Wind*," I said.

Marie knew the trick. She smiled and wagged a naughty-naughty finger at me, but that didn't prevent her from answering.

"Past tense," she said. "A lot of loudmouth with David, but the sizzle fizzled when I declined his invitation to explore and enjoy the inner trappings of a Beverly Hills Hotel bungalow. Not that I ever gave up that kind of audition, but for cripes sake, he's married to L.B. Mayer's daughter. I go down on him, my career goes down with me if Strickling ever gets wind and tattles to the big boss — and no question Strickling would find out. He has more spies in this town than Walter Winchell. Besides, everybody knows David is a love 'em and leave 'em type, who makes promises he never intends to keep, so fat chance ever for me grabbing the role of 'Melanie.' "

"He has a British actress in mind for

Scarlett, I heard, and Olivia de Havilland for Melanie, if he can borrow her from Jack Warner."

"Larry Olivier's dish, Vivien somebody, and forget all the flack about a national search for the right actress that Russ Birdwell dreamed up. Olivia?" She fired her loudest laugh of the young evening. "Not Warner. David would have to borrow her from Errol Flynn. They're at it hot and heavy, so fat chance of that casting."

"Hal Bucquet sings your praises loud and clear to anybody who'll listen, and he's not the only one, sweetheart. I'm betting it's only a matter of time before you're up there with Shearer, Crawford, all those others billed over the title."

"Especially if that upstart Lana Turner gets hit by a truck. . . . Are you being truthful or telling me what you think I need to hear to show up for work tomorrow?"

"Both, maybe?"

"I would-a been happier to hear a lie, baby." She left the table and retreated to the sitting room, assumed that cross-legged yoga pose of hers on the sofa. I settled down next to her and said, "Marie, for what it's worth, I'm a hundred percent believer in your talent, and that's the God's honest truth."

She delivered a mother's kiss to my cheek and repositioned herself with her head nesting on my shoulder.

I was comparing her favorably to the Esther Blodgett–Vicki Lester character in another Selznick movie, *A Star is Born,* a dreamer who went from car-hopping to movie stardom, when I realized Marie had fallen asleep.

I managed to lift her into my arms and carried her through the curtained archway into the overripe bordello of a bedroom, the walls costumed in crimson silks, the ceiling mirrored over a circular bed the size of Rhode Island in the center of a floor layered in exotic Persian rugs on plush carpeting taller than uncut grass. The room resembled on a grander scale suites in the administration building where anxious starlets were groomed for stardom by Metro's cadre of producers, whose casting couches sometimes did more business than some of their movies. The air, as usual, smelled like a rose garden in full bloom, the source bottles of room freshener strategically placed around like rat traps, only meant to kill lingering sweat and other body odors.

I settled Marie on the bed and fled, fearing she might wake and invite me to join her. The temptation would have been overwhelming, again, like it was on Avalon, but all the Selznick talk had me thinking about Nancy; consumed by a desire, by the need to see her again. Tomorrow, I promised myself. I'd call her first thing tomorrow about us getting together. Maybe for dinner. Chasen's, maybe. Or, better — Perino's.

I tossed my jacket over the back of a chair, kicked off my shoes and stretched out on the sofa, my .38 within reach on the antique burl walnut coffee table. An hour later, I was still trying to catch the Red Car to Dreamland.

My mind wouldn't stop replaying the chain of events that had exploded rat-a-tat-tat over the past week, trying to recapture something I'd heard, something someone had said, that would hand me the key to unlocking the treasure chest of answers. I visualized a set of Russian *matryoshka,* the wooden nesting dolls; one inside another inside another inside another inside —

How many dolls had I reached so far?

Any?

How many more to go before —

Before what?

Before the murders of Covington and Rothman were solved?

Before the surviving blackmailer was uncovered?

Before the Rothman photographs were found and their contents revealed the crisis they'd created for Hartmann and his bunch of Nazi-loving morons?

Before I could get back to spending my time more comfortably and with less risk among the greats, near-greats and ingrates of the Show Biz in general, Metro-Goldwyn-Mayer in particular?

And there was Nancy Warren.

I focused on Nancy and was inventing our future together, felt myself easing into a dream, when a harsh noise coming from the direction of the kitchen snapped me back to real time, my heart doing a Krupa drum solo.

My imagination?

I reached over and gave it a minute, ready to grab my .38.

Heard nothing.

Another minute.

Nothing.

Wide awake now, I craved a glass of wine or a bottle of beer, maybe both, to help settle my nerves.

I rolled onto my feet and halfway to the kitchen, as an afterthought, grabbed a bronze Brancusi sculpture from its Carrara marble base, a sleeping head the size of a small grapefruit and heavy enough to crack a skull.

Turning through the kitchen arch, I saw the back door was wide open.

I switched on the light and saw why.

He was a distinguished-looking gent, a politician's suntanned face under a mane of snow-white hair, wire-rimmed eyeglasses enlarging hazel eyes, the left one drifting slightly off-center. He wore a bottle-green blazer over white linen slacks, highly glossed cordovan wingtips, like he could have been a costumed day player in some high-society picture set in Palm Beach or at a racetrack.

Except, the revolver he was aiming at me suggested otherwise.

"Put down that hunk of scrap iron," he said, sounding like Mickey Mouse.

I deposited the Brancusi on the kitchen counter.

"Key locks like the Door Master are easy pickings, so you never know who might drop in unannounced," he said. "Somebody should tell your landlord to order Safe-Guards next time."

"My billfold's in my jacket and my jacket's in the next room. You're welcome to take it."

"Like I need your permission?" His brow furrowed and he gave me a Popeye the

Sailor squint. "Besides, did I say anything about dropping in for mazuma, like a common thief?"

"Then I give up."

"Like you have a choice so long as I got this?" He held up the revolver, a snub-nosed Colt Police Positive. "I need you now to be the smart fella I heard you are and do what I ask, understand?"

"Who'd you hear that from?" I said, stalling for time, wondering how he'd gotten past the cop outside, wondering if he could squeeze the trigger faster than I could make a grab for the Colt.

Deciding he could —

Seabiscuit to my War Admiral.

Fools rush in where angels fear to tread.

I'm no angel and had no desire to become one, not yet.

Popeye said, "Where is she? Take me to her."

"Who?"

"Marie MacDaniels, I know she's here, so don't insult my intelligence or turn this into a game that would be bad for your health."

Call it chivalry or call it stupidity —

His bringing Marie into the game changed the rules.

"Miss MacDaniels is in the bedroom. Same noise that woke me woke her. When I

282

left her she was on the phone calling the cops."

"The phone's deader'n Kelsey's nuts; you're welcome. The quicker we get her, the quicker we can get out of here and on our way."

"Where would that be?"

"Where we're going, so let's get a move on." He thumbed back the hammer on the Colt. "Lead the way, brother."

Self-defense is like roller skating or riding a bicycle. Once learned, it's a skill you don't lose. Passing the counter, I got a grip on the Brancusi and in the same motion rolled around and whacked Popeye on the side of the head. Heard a noise like a sledgehammer cracking a coconut. Popeye dropped the Colt and followed it onto the linoleum, landing on his side and rolling over onto his stomach.

I stood my ground, telling him, "There's more where that came from, brother, you so much as try to reach for the gun or get up."

He didn't try to do either.

He didn't move at all.

I put down the Brancusi, swooped after the Colt and tucked it inside my belt.

Squatted alongside Popeye to check for a pulse.

He had one, but barely, like he was keeping his breathing a secret.

I was breathing hard enough for both of us.

The next dozen minutes were busy ones.

I zoomed into the bedroom, woke Marie, told her in twenty-five words or less what had happened and handed her Popeye's Colt, cocked and ready to fire.

I said, "Anybody but me comes through those curtains, aim and shoot to kill."

Her eyes ballooned. "I don't know if I can, baby."

"Try," I said.

Back in the sitting room, I grabbed my .38 from the coffee table and charged out the front door, strapping on my holster on the fly en route to the lobby. Paused to catch my second wind, bent over with my hands gripping my knees, before I told Dusty to get Strickling on the phone at his private home number and tell him I said to get here on the double; tell him to let Ray Travis know. Tell Travis we needed an ambulance.

She had a question on her face, but understood the urgency in my voice.

"Captain Travis? What's the story, Blanchard? What's happening I should know about?"

I turned around and saw Lowy's shift replacement staring at me gape-mouthed —

Eddie Vassily, all six-feet-zero of zero competence, his hand already slapping his hip holster. "Anything to do with MacDaniels?"

"Everything to do with her," I said. "Tell me it isn't Troy who's guarding the back door of the cottage."

"That would be lying."

I took off for the cottage, Vassily on my tail.

Bolted through the door, drew my .38 and headed for the kitchen.

Popeye wasn't where I left him.

He wasn't anywhere visible.

I moved back to the sitting room and called, "Marie, you okay?"

"Okay," she answered.

I told Vassily to stand guard outside the bedroom, triple-timed out the back door and across Havenhurst to the police cruiser I knew was a police cruiser, because Elmer Troy was asleep behind the wheel. That explained how Popeye was able to get in and out of the cottage without being seen.

I banged on the window to get Troy up. He rolled the window down and studied me like an intruder who had destroyed his sweet dream. He said, "What's it, Blanchard?

Anything happening I should know about?" And yawned into his fist, looking no more fogged over than he looked when he was fully awake.

Before I could give Troy the response he deserved —

A gunshot intruded on the quiet street.

I ran back inside the cottage, safety-stepped forward with an extended two-handed hold on my .38, and called out for Marie.

The answer came from Vassily, who screamed, "The goddamn bitch shot me, she shot me." He was hot-footing around the sitting room, a hand clutching his right forearm, blood spilling through his splayed fingers onto the rugs. "I step in to make sure she's okay and the goddamn bitch shoots me. Goddamn bitch could've killed me."

Marie's gunshot had drawn people onto the street and into the Garden of Allah court-yard, people whose curiosity was tempered by worried looks in the light of a half-moon standing guard over a flotilla of rain clouds sailing in from the ocean.

Many attributed the disturbance to a new robbery or burglary. There had been a rash of break-ins in the neighborhood, including one two weeks ago at Dorothy Parker's cottage. She'd gone around telling everyone, "At least they couldn't steal my career from me," to which Robert Benchley, another Garden resident, observed, "Metro-Goldwyn-Mayer beat them to it, Dottie."

A Havenhurst apartment-dweller who had been out walking her three Chihuahuas when the shot was fired reported seeing a man drag himself out of a cottage and struggle into the backseat of a car double-parked with its motor running before the driver raced off like some Wilbur Shaw at the Indianapolis 500. She wasn't sure which cottage it was, and Troy and Vassily — his bandaged arm in a sling — were obeying a directive from Ray Travis not to do, say or write in their investigation report anything linking the occurrence to Marie MacDaniels or Metro-Goldwyn-Mayer.

Travis, of course, was obliging Strickling, whose first words to him were *We'll keep this incident to ourselves, shall we, Ray?* before he followed me into the bedroom, where Marie was sitting on the side of the bed, frozen in time and indifferent to the world around her.

She saw it was him and said, "I could have killed him, Strick."

He smiled a cryptic smile. "Not if he killed

you first, so count your blessings."

"You would have liked that, though."

"I let bygones be bygones a long time ago, Marie. All I care about right now is for your safety and well-being." Spoken in a way that, if you didn't know better, commanded belief the same way the voiceover narration Strickling did for many of the studio trailers rang with honesty and conviction.

Marie wasn't buying. "Tell it to the Marines," she said, burying him with her eyes.

"I'm telling it to Marie, Marie." An edge had crept into his tone, but was offset by an indulgent smile. "Chris says you were getting ready to return to work before this awful business."

"Yes."

"Still?"

"If they're coming after me again, I'm safer on the set and surrounded by people I know than holed up here by myself, except for some cops as helpful as my Aunt Minnie, especially since I don't have an Aunt Minnie."

"After you? Nonsense. He was a burglar, who happened to choose the door to this cottage over any of the others. It's all the talk outside. Isn't that so, Chris?"

"All the talk, Strick."

Marie already knew better from me, but

played along.

"I'd like to get some sleep now," she said.

"Of course," Strickling said. "We want you to be as well rested as possible. Your call time is six. I took the liberty of arranging for Jack Dawn to come in and personally take care of your makeup. Think of it as a welcome-back present from Mr. Mayer." He turned to me. "Chris, you're staying, and you'll get her safely to the studio, right?"

"Right as rain," I said.

As if on cue, thunder exploded and a hard rain started slamming the cottage wall with windstorm force.

It was still coming down hard when I took off for Culver City with Marie, Troy and Vassily shadowing us by eight car-lengths in the predawn fogbound sky, as a safety precaution until I'd navigated the V8 through the classical Greek columns of the studio's main gate on Washington Boulevard. Under a blanket of black umbrellas was the usual crowd of extras rounded up by Central Casting, among them dress extras wearing their own tuxedos and tails, who would be taking home an extra buck or two. Also, a line of work-hungry hopefuls angling for any last-minute crowd slots that might open. And the usual run of Miss Podunk beauty pageant winners hoping to be noticed and yet to learn that a producer saying *Get down on your knees* wasn't extending an invitation to join him in prayer.

CHAPTER 17

Friday, November 18, 1938

Hal Bucquet greeted me like royalty after I deposited Marie with Jack Dawn at makeup. "Strick had one of his flock call ahead and slip me the word you'd found Marie, Chris. I managed to get here before the set came tumbling down." He introduced the set with a gesture, now, unlike yesterday, lit up like Jack Barrymore any day of the week —

A posh nightclub in Havana that defied reality in size and scope, enough tables and booths to hold half the city's population, its focal point a stage decorated like a rain forest.

"If the set looks familiar, it's because we borrowed it from Woody Van Dyke's last epic with MacDonald and Eddy, *Sweethearts*," Hal said. "The trees are courtesy of *Tarzan*. With a budget like mine, you make do. Beggars can't be choosers. Even the song Leeds performs is a hand-me-down —

Freed and Brown's 'Singin' in the Rain,' the fifth or sixth time it gets used in a picture since *The Hollywood Review of 1929*. That Artie Freed, I don't know what he's holding over Mayer and Thalberg. I hear he's in line for his own producing unit here."

I shook my head. "Nothing surprises me anymore around here, except that you have your G-Man hero on a stage singing anything," I said, earning a laugh from Hal.

"You'd think it's something the Communists cooked up, getting even for all the badmouthing they get from Baxter, but it's actually Freddie's snappy rewrite. Until Eve turned up missing, we had Bright Eyes accidentally going on while being chased by the bad guys and Thomas Harrison Two, Leeds, saving her with a last-second shot. Then we put Jane Conway, Marie, on stage, lip-synching to the same so-so version in the studio's library. Now, it'll be Thomas Harrison Two lip-synching to the version by Cliff Edwards and the Brox Sisters from the '29 *Review*." He turned dramatic on me. "Harrison races out onstage and joins the production singers and dancers thinking he's safe for the time being, but he is wrong. The murderous mastermind is in the house. The murderous mastermind sneaks out his pistol and prepares to fire before the final notes are struck by the orchestra. Jane arrives in the nick of time, barely seconds to spare. She whips out her pistol, gets off a shot and saves her boyfriend Thomas Harrison Two's life." He exhaled a mile of breath. "What do you say to that, Chris?"

The word "Hitchcock" slipped out of my mouth, like I'd just heard a variation on the climax in the chubby Brit's *The Man Who Knew Too Much.*

"What was that?" he said, cupping an ear.

"My hat's off to Max Brand," I said, at the same time worried how Marie would react when the revised scene was explained to her, considering what she'd gone through at the Garden of Allah and everything else since Day Covington's murder.

I expressed my concern.

Hal gave it a moment's thought. "She's a pro, Chris. Mark my words, Marie will weather the storm. The show must go on and all that. Come back later, when we shoot the scene. See for yourself."

He didn't sound entirely convinced.

I hit the *Wizard of Oz* soundstage next.

No Munchkins in sight.

None listed on today's call sheet.

A wave from Mervyn LeRoy, who was prowling the set, a castle interior getting touched up by a squad of painters.

Winged monkeys all over the place, bunched in conversation or engaged in card games or games of chess, some sitting off in a corner over a book, nothing you wouldn't expect from winged monkeys waiting to be called in front of Hal Rosson's camera.

I left and headed for the art department, wondering when I'd next be hearing from Herbie Duntz.

Nancy was engrossed over her drafting table, adding colors to a comprehensive drawing illustrating a woman searching among hundreds of Confederate soldiers lying wounded, dying and dead on the bloody grounds of a railroad station. I coughed to get her attention.

Startled, she mashed a brushstroke and obliterated some of the troops. Looked up and over, saw it was me, recognized my concern, smiled and, adopting a southern accent, said, "Don't fret, honey chile. I can bring them soldier boys roarin' back to life."

"I'll get out of your way, come back later," I said.

She put down her brush and eased the drawing aside, pressed a palm on her brow. "We're fine. I won't think about it anymore today. I'll think about it tomorrow." I gave her a queer look. "*Gone with the Wind.* You haven't read the book, have y'all? I'd heard there were people like you, who wouldn't know Tara from *Tobacco Road.*"

"Or *God's Little Acre,* don't forget *God's Little Acre.*"

"Careful — describing Mr. Mayer's studio that way could get you fired."

She applauded her joke like a little girl welcoming a clown to her birthday party before turning serious. "I was beginning to believe you were avoiding me."

"Like the plague." I pulled out the note she had left for me. "I intended to call you even before I saw this. Circumstances beyond my control got in my way."

She smiled. "But now you need something from me, right?"

"Another sketch. . . . How'd you know?"

Nancy dropped the smile and the accent. "I was kidding, but you're serious." She looked away and thumb-picked at her nails.

"You've been on my mind a lot and —"

"What kind of sketch?" she said, picking up a drawing pad and pencil.

"Nancy . . ."

"I said, *What kind of sketch?* What. Kind. Of. Sketch? I need to get back to work, so let's get to it, Mr. Blanchard."

"I can come back later."

"No, you can't, Mr. Blanchard."

There was no sense arguing with her.

The last woman I argued with was my wife, and what did that get me?

A Purple Heart and a divorce, not the Medal of Valor I deserved.

I closed my eyes and described Popeye, one detail at a time.

A little fix here, a little fix there, and in twenty-five minutes Nancy had caught Popeye perfectly on paper and sent on the sketch to the photo lab with instructions to print up a dozen copies for me, after which it would be my turn to try catching him for real.

"You're welcome," Howard Strickling said, his first words after showing up unannounced at my office and parking himself against the wall across from my desk, relaxed with his arms and legs crossed, like he owned the spot.

"What am I thanking you for this time?"

"Getting Bugsy Siegel off your case."

"I wasn't aware you knew he was on my case. Oh, wait, right. You're Howard Strickling."

He ignored my sarcasm, or maybe he took it as acknowledgment of his power. "Word travels," he said. "Fast since the two of you exchanged words at the Grove last weekend and a certain other occurrence at the Ravenswood."

That lit a bulb. "Georgie Raft been spilling beans?"

"Among others. George said something to Siegel about writing off any problems with you for old time's sake and, while he was at it, mentioned your wanting Siegel to let Tyrone Powell off the hook. I was invited to visit Siegel at the hacienda he's been renting on Rexford Drive for a little chitchat. I traded some payback due me on a few invitations and introductions I arranged for him and certain of his friends for his taking you and Mr. Powell off the books."

"Thank you."

"There is one condition, however."

"There's always one condition with Benny."

"He'd like you to drop by his place and apologize for your conduct."

"I'd like to find a pot of gold at the end of a rainbow. That's not going to happen either."

Strickling gave me a long, hard study, shrugged, and changed the subject. "Any new thoughts about last night's incident at the Garden of Allah, who that was came after you and Marie?"

"One of Nicky Hartmann's stooges, who else? But I have a bigger question, How did he know where to find us?"

"Travis thinks he had to be tailing you."

"Since when? When I took off from here aiming for Eve Whitney's place? Before that? Afterward? And how'd he know I'd lead him to Marie?"

"Maybe he didn't. Maybe he was hoping you'd lead him to Eve."

"No. He said Marie's name . . . Eve — is she still missing or do you have a handle on where she might be?"

"Still gone with the wind," Strick said. "No plug intended."

He turned and took off too fast for me to consider if he meant it or was putting his rarely seen sense of humor on split-second display.

I slipped onto the *Battling G-Men* soundstage minutes before the red signal light began flashing and eased into the director chair with Marie's name stenciled on the back. Hal Bucquet called *Roll 'em* on what the clapboard chalked as Take 2 of the nightclub scene, a master shot, but twenty seconds into the take shouted *Cut!,* mixing in a colorful series of obscenities about a boom light that had blown.

At once, Marie's makeup and hair people were attending her.

Baxter Leeds saw me and headed over.

"Our friend Marie and her outsized ego — unbelievable, buddy."

"No ego that I know of, Baxter," I said, thinking better than to add, *Compared to you, buddy.*

"No? Rehearsing the scene, I offered to show her how to hold her pistol properly, the way I always do, so audiences would really believe Thomas Harrison Two's girlfriend knew how to fire a weapon. I also tell her, *Pretend you're aiming at a damn Commie, like that damn Lionel Stander,* you know, who was the bad apple press agent in Selznick's *A Star is Born?* The role that should have been mine, if Selznick knew what he was doing."

"Maybe Selznick did you a favor, by not turning Baxter Leeds, a film hero, into Baxter Leeds, a film heel?"

"Or maybe he damn well knew I, Baxter Leeds" — tapping his chest — "could eat Freddie March alive in any scene together, the way Baxter Leeds chews 'em up and spits 'em out in the *G-Men* movies."

"How did Marie respond when you made your generous offer?"

"Get this. First she reminds me that Hal's

299

her director, not me. Then she says she got all the lessons she needed back when the two of you were an item and you took her out to some range in Elysian Park to teach her how to shoot and protect herself. Goes on and on about how, before you were finished, she could put a bullet in the space between your eyes from twenty yards away. That so, buddy?"

I thought about saying, "Sometimes Marie had to settle for one of the eyes," but before I could answer an assistant director raced over intent on dragging Leeds back onto the set.

"Positions, everybody!" Hal's A.D. called through his bullhorn. Leeds and Marie took their marks and the dress extras began filling in the tables and booths. "You, there, you in the bottle-green blazer," he called. "Not where you were established, so move it. Over there, in the booth with the Negro girl in the magenta dress, on her left." The A.D. repeated his direction, irritation licking at his words.

My eyes scanned the set to see whose confusion was causing the delay.

It was Popeye.

I pushed up and crossed the room, intent on getting within grabbing distance of him once the camera finished rolling on Take 3. I kept eyes on him instead of the floor, caught a toe in a tangle of electric wires and cables, and stumbled forward, crashing into a stack of flats that toppled noisily, drawing everyone's attention.

Popeye recognized me, leaped up from the booth and searched the soundstage for an exit. The door nearest him was clear across the set. He took off, pushing dancers aside, me in pursuit, my .38 drawn and raised, shouting for him to stop as people ducked out of the way voicing fright and confusion.

A panic-stricken, speechless Leeds blocked my way.

I gave him a shove aside that threw me off-balance and onto the floor.

I dropped the .38.

Marie snatched it while I was scrambling up, pirouetted into a two-handed grip and ordered Popeye to stop if he knew what was good for him; *wanted to stay whole* is how she put it.

Popeye looked over his shoulder, saw who it was barking at him and laughed.

"It's not a prop," Marie said.

Popeye, now only a few feet from the exit, ignored her.

Marie's shot caught him in the shoulder and twisted him around.

"You stop or my next bullet will turn your head into a bowl of borscht," she said, as calm as the sound of silence.

Popeye shook his head in disbelief and moved forward.

Marie took aim and fired.

Her shot ripped into Popeye's thigh. He crashed to his knees.

I seized the .38 from Marie and was bending over him in seconds, daring Popeye to move and calling for anybody to get studio security and a doctor from the infirmary in here on the double, in that order.

An emboldened Baxter Leeds stepped over to me and said, "If that foolish girl had accepted my offer to teach her, she would have shot him where she said she was going to shoot him." He moved on to the A.D., took the bullhorn and announced, "Everyone relax, the threat to your safety is past," raising his clenched fists above his head, as if it were his doing.

Marie was shaken, in a mild state of disarray.

I guided her to her trailer, assured her there'd be armed security posted outside the door on the possibility Popeye wasn't the only Nazi hanging around, and used her phone to get word of the incident to Strickling.

Surprise, surprise —

Strickling already knew and had alerted Ray Travis, who had alerted Cook, the FBI agent, who had a team on the way to pick up Popeye at the infirmary and transport him downtown for interrogation.

Marie's security arrived, a mass of muscles bulging inside a uniform that always made me think of the tailored costume guards wore in the Chester Morris–Wally Beery starrer, *The Big House,* and I took off for the infirmary to meet Travis and Cook's team.

Popeye was already gone.

He'd been patched up and released to the custody of a studio cop with instructions from Strickling to cuff him and bring him to his office.

I got on the phone to Strickling, complaining, "It would have been nice if you had bothered to let me know about the change in plans."

"What change in what plans are you talking about, Chris?" I told him. "It wasn't my doing and probably not our cop. Hold on." He was back on the line in two minutes. "Confirmed. Definitely not our cop."

I slammed down the receiver, grabbed a

transportation department two-wheeler and peddled back to the *Battling G-Men* sound-stage through the crowded streets, fearing the security guard outside Marie's trailer might also be a phony.

The soundstage was deserted, dark except for a safety light and a light filtering out from under the door of the trailer.

The security guard was still on duty, perched on the trailer steps.

He got up and moved aside for me.

Marie had changed from her costume into street clothes and was sitting on the floor of the trailer in that yoga position of hers, chanting.

She saw it was me and forced a tired smile. "We okay, baby?"

I knew the answer she needed.

"We okay," I said.

It was an easy lie.

"Then let's get out away from here, baby. I need to be somewhere else, anywhere but here."

Strickling, Travis and Cook's team, maybe Cook himself, would be arriving any minute. I was reluctant to get her to some-place safe before we could brief them, but the desperation in her voice dictated that the briefing could wait for now, while they could better put energy behind a search for

Popeye, who might still be on the lot.

Where to take Marie?

I'd figure that out once we were off the lot.

The guard saw we were leaving and insisted on accompanying us.

"Better safe than sorry," he said, nodding in agreement with himself.

I was parked on Grant Avenue, in the lot directly across from the administration building. Her buggy was closer, in an area on the sprawling back lot reserved for stars and other contract players, adjacent to the Overland entrance. That's where we headed.

"Over there," Marie said, pointing to the late-model candy-apple red Chevy four-door Master Deluxe in a space marked by her name on a hand-painted signboard, stuck between the almost identical midnight black Ford four-doors of Jimmy Stewart and Bob Montgomery. She dug the key out of her handbag and handed it over. "You drive, okay, baby?" and started for the passenger side, the guard at her elbow.

He was opening the door for her when Popeye limped out from behind Jimmy's car and batted him over the head with a lead pipe. The guard pitched forward. He fell onto the Chevy's fender and slid to the concrete. Popeye dropped the pipe and trapped Marie inside his good arm.

Cold steel pressed against the base of my skull as I chased under my jacket after my gun. The unmistakable voice of Karl Mueller — who'd been hiding behind Bob's car — warned, "I will end your life here and now if you fail to behave." He ordered me behind the wheel after I handed over the .38. Popeye shoved Marie into the passenger seat and joined him in the backseat.

When we reached the Overland gate, the attendant in the guard hut recognized the Chevy.

He waved us through, aiming a smile at Marie as we passed.

A couple of minutes later, at Mueller's direction, I pulled up to the Grant Avenue lot, pausing long enough for Herbie Duntz to sprint from behind the studio's Rolls-Royce Phantom parked near my V8.

"Seems like old times," he said, hopping into the backseat. "Definitely a small world."

Mueller kept me changing directions and frequently doubling back, making sure nobody was following us. Consequently, a cross-town trip to the Griffith Park area that took less than an hour under normal conditions took almost twice as long and often led to Herbie serenading us with words along the lines of *Follow the yellow brick road, follow the yellow brick road* until Pop-eye demanded, "Shut your big mouth!"

"Thank you, but my big mouth compared to what?" Herbie wanted to know.

Popeye had no answer for him.

"Because I say so," Mueller said.

Herbie resorted to humming under his breath.

I answered the fear gasps that escaped every so often from Marie with a gentle pat on her thigh. She would react by gripping my hand tight enough to cause me as much pain as my damaged ribs.

We passed through Hollywood on Sunset, turned south onto Highland, then east onto Fountain; Fountain to Cahuenga; south to Melrose; east to Gower; north past RKO and Columbia and across Hollywood Boulevard to Franklin; east to Western; north past Immaculate Heart and around the bend onto Los Feliz Boulevard heading east.

The poorly lit boulevard was a contradiction in civic growth and history, a rich mixture of homes ranging from elegant to imperial, a clutter of dirt lots overgrown with tall weeds and For Sale signs, fresh fruit and vegetable wagons, and fenced-off nurseries displaying potted plants, fragrant flowers of all varieties and placards asserting Japanese ownership as proof of quality.

The neighborhood had become especially popular with stars and studio executive types because of its proximity to Paramount, RKO, Columbia and, on the valley side of the hill, Warner Bros. and Disney. One private road south of Los Feliz led to the lavish estate of Cecil B. DeMille and, on a lesser level, his neighbor W.C. Fields.

I rolled down my window to draw in the perfumed smells of the park and caught a glimpse of the towering Griffith Park Observatory as we cruised across Vermont Avenue, past the unkempt mansion once owned by the late, hard-drinking criminal attorney Earl Rogers, a courtroom trickster and father of writer Adela Rogers St. Johns, whose scripts at Metro included *A Free Soul,* a courtroom melodrama starring Lionel Barrymore as a fictionalized version of daddy.

"Turn here and pull into the driveway," Spiedel ordered when we reached Griffith Park Boulevard.

He was talking about an imposing cement block building at the intersection, its facade bearing a marquee-type sign identifying:

THE SANCTORUM

A Temple of Wisdom
and Truth in All Things

"There's no place like home," Herbie said.

"Shut up, Powell. How many times do you have to hear it said?"

"Does *never* count, Herr Mueller?"

I headed down the driveway entrance to a road arm guarded by a meaty sentry dressed in a Hawaiian shirt hanging over olive-colored beachcomber chinos and go-aheads that put his dirty feet on full display. The bulge at his right hip said he was packing heat.

He recognized Mueller and Popeye with a hand salute out of *Triumph of the Will*, the Nazi propaganda film that made it look like Hitler had already won his wars and now owned the world, raised the road arm and directed me to a parking slot by the stairwell and an elevator that took a key to operate. We herded inside and took it down two levels. The door opened onto a narrow corridor ending at a thick steel door that needed four twists of a combination lock to open.

Marie and I were nudged inside. The door swung shut, leaving us alone in a cold, badly lit room the size of a two-car garage. No windows. Sparsely furnished. A concrete floor stained here and there in a shade of faded brown I came to associate years ago with dried blood. An interior door that lacked a lock of any kind and a doorknob. Overall, not a place intended for long-term residency.

I wandered the room, occasionally tossing words of encouragement at Marie, who had gone yoga in an oversized wrought iron armchair, her chant as desperate as the fright I recognized in her eyes. I was less bothered, maybe because I knew Herbie was out there playing his dangerous game, but —

How often can the cavalry ride to the rescue?

I was working out an answer that would favor us when the interior door slid into the wall and Nicky Hartmann stepped inside the room with a winner's smile, his finger on the trigger of a Beretta 1935 semi-automatic blowback. "So very nice seeing you again," he said. "Unfinished business we have — only this time joined by another friend."

He snapped his fingers.

Eve Whitney staggered through the doorway, followed by Mueller, and got a few feet inside before caving to the floor. Her face was covered in bruises. Her cheeks and lips swollen. One eye blackened. The other eye reduced to a slit. Her half-naked body bore red and purple bruises and welts, evidence of repeated beatings.

The door slid shut.

Mueller moved on her, picked her up and shoved her onto another of the wrought iron armchairs.

Marie raised the level of her chanting to override the sounds of anguish pouring out of Eve.

Hartmann said, "This time there'll be no running away by you. I get what I want one way or the other, or else."

I said, "Or else what, Hartmann?"

"If you don't already know the answer, I have been giving you far, far more credit for intelligence than you deserve, Mr. Blanchard. . . . Karl, please show Mr. Blanchard what I mean."

Mueller looked like he'd been granted a genie wish.

He stepped closer to Eve, drew back his arm and railroaded a fist to her nose. Her nose poured blood like a water tap had been turned on full force and streamed down her face. She slumped sideways in the chair, unconscious.

Fueled by outrage, I started after him, but was stopped short by a shot Hartmann drilled into the wall. Mueller moved to Marie and pressed his Luger against her temple.

She quit chanting. Bolted her eyes. Locked her hands in prayerful expectation.

Hartmann shook his head.

Mueller moved the Luger away from her.

Marie resumed chanting.

Hartmann said, "Assuming we now understand one another better, let's pick up where our earlier conversation on the island ended so abruptly and unexpectedly."

"You go first," I said. "I'd like to hear why you brought Eve into this. Earlier, you seemed to believe that taking Marie hostage would be enough to get me looking for your damn negatives and photographs."

"Insurance, but only after we came to experience difficulties with the two of you. I arrived later to the proposition that, since she was Marie's friend and your friend, it was entirely possible she could tell us something worth hearing. I suggested a brief encounter at her place during the lunch hour, lusty girl that she is. Next stop — here." He called over to her. "Correct, Eve?"

Eve groaned.

"She was at first reluctant, but we were able to inspire her ultimately to add to our store of information." He ate the canary.

"Isn't that so, Eve?"

She whimpered.

"I asked you a question, Eve. Be a smart girl and answer me, so Karl won't need to help you out again."

She struggled to make words, came close to something that sounded enough like *yes* to satisfy Hartmann. "What Eve shared with us was a significant piece of information that confirmed a suspicion and should make your task easier."

"I'm dying to hear this."

"I'd be more careful with my choice of words if I were you," Hartmann said, the joke in his voice offset by the malice in his gaze. "Eve confided in us that her dear friend Marie confided in her during one of their wilder adventures on the town that she was part of a profitable blackmail enterprise being conducted by her husband, Day Covington, and the photographer Otto Rothman. She swore Eve to secrecy, correct, Eve?"

Marie quit chanting. "No, no, not true," she said in a high-pitched squeal filling with alarm. "Me and blackmail? Evie, how could you make up such a story? How?" Eve struggled to make the *yes* sound again. "Chris, it's not true. Tell him."

"She says it's not true," I said, the best I

could do, no way of knowing if what I'd heard from Hartmann was a revelation or a fabrication.

Hartmann said, "And do you believe her? Based on your histories with these two women, you choose to believe her?" I had no answer for him. "Well, my sixth sense tells me she's telling the truth."

"Yes," Marie said, trembling. "Yes, I am. Yes. Yes. Yes."

"No," Eve managed.

Hartmann ignored her denial.

He said, "We have a proven method for curing liars of their lies. Karl, shoot Eve."

Mueller shoved the barrel of the Luger against Eve's neck, under her chin.

"Hold it," I said, and did a few abrupt steps and gyrations that drew Hartmann's Beretta and Mueller's Luger to me. "Maybe Eve was telling you the truth, and it's Marie who's the liar."

Eve made a noise.

Disbelief registered on Marie's face.

Hartmann said, "Explain. . . . What's that all about, Mr. Blanchard?"

I was stalling for time, pulling a bluff that might not be a bluff, but he didn't have to know that. "I'll explain, but first, I need to be alone with Marie."

He studied me in silence for a few sixty-minute seconds. Nodded. "Here is what's going to happen next. You will get your time alone with her. When I return, you will give me your final verdict, after which I will have you, not Karl, pull the trigger on the liar. Is that understood, Mr. Blanchard? It will be your choice. You will execute the liar for us."

CHAPTER 18

The interior door slid shut and I was alone with Marie.

She charged over, slapped my face and, banging her fists on my chest, demanded to know why I had put her life in danger. I grabbed her by the wrists and pulled her hands aside.

"Your life has never been out of danger since before they took us here," I said. "Or mine."

"And that made it all right to throw me to the wolves?"

"What would not have been all right was standing by and doing nothing, making no effort to keep Mueller from blowing away Eve's head."

"So now you'll be the one gets to blow away her head."

"Or yours."

"I don't find that funny, baby."

"I don't mean it funny, honey."

"*Honey.* That's a new one out of you. What happened to *Sweetheart?*"

"Too kind for somebody who sticks to a lie and is prepared to watch a friend die, instead of owning up to the truth."

"Dear sweet Jesus. You're saying I wasn't telling the truth?"

"No."

That wasn't entirely my truth, because of something I noticed that I'd pretty much forgotten about until now, Marie's facial tic, what my old poker playing cronies call a *tell.* Marie's tell was a tic at the right corner of her mouth that puffed her cheek briefly, ever so slightly, whenever she stretched the truth. You had to be looking for it or the tic could slip past you, but it had become more pronounced than ever here in this room.

I released Marie. "I'm saying give me something I can work with. Something I can use to sweet-talk us out of here. A lie, the truth, it doesn't matter. Right now we have nothing going for us."

She retreated to her chair and into the cross-legged yoga position. Shut her eyes. Chanted for an eternity. Said, "Okay, I knew about Day's blackmail racket. Lord forgive me, I went along with it. You want to live like a movie star, it's not possible on one of Metro-Goldwyn-Mayer's seven-year slave

contracts or the paydays Day collected doing piecework on programmers shoveled out
by the B-movie flophouses that called for
Day only when they couldn't do any better."

"How'd it go?"

"How do you think? He and Otto were
spiders who knew how to lure the flies to
their web. Otto had his studio and was a
smooth talker. Day had an open ticket to
George Cukor's Sunday weak-wrist soirées.
Photographs got taken sooner or later, and
you know or can guess the rest. Sex isn't a
spectator sport, especially for players who
cross the line, not in this day and age, baby."

"And that's the truth?"

"You said you wanted something to work
with from me, now you have something to
work with."

No tell.

I said, "Before we got away from him on
Avalon, Hartmann made it obvious the
photographs weren't about sex. He called
them a different kind of picture. What do
you know about that? What different kind
of pictures would be worth two hundred
and fifty grand, cause two murders and
almost a case of arson at Rothman's studio?"

"Tourist stuff."

"Tourist stuff?"

"Day told me Hartmann wanted pictures taken at something like a dozen places, Catalina and some others —"

"Some others like . . . ?"

"Day didn't say, only that he first learned about it later, when Rothman called all excited as Hades, saying he had taken pictures that he realized were going to make them a small fortune compared to the nickels and dimes they'd been making on the sex stuff."

No tell.

"Where are they now, the photographs and the negatives?"

"Rothman was a squirrel about everything, so your guess is as good as mine if he didn't have them stored at his place."

No tell.

"Maybe he turned them over for safekeeping to the third member of the blackmail team?"

"What third member? It was only ever Day and Rothman, or are you accusing me of having stashed them somewhere?"

"Did you?"

"No."

No tell.

I said, "When Hartmann comes back, I

need you to play along with whatever I tell him."

"What are you going to tell him?"

"I don't know yet."

Marie threw her eyes to the ceiling and crossed herself.

I played one idea after another to myself waiting out Hartmann's return.

It was like running on a treadmill.

None got me anywhere I needed to be.

One dead end after another.

Dead end.

Appropriate, after it struck me that no effort had been made to keep Marie and me from seeing where we were being taken. In my old world of Copperville that meant only one thing —

Hartmann had no intention of letting us leave the Sanctorum alive.

And where the hell was Herbie Duntz?

Was the cavalry saddling up?

Was it, Herbie? Is it?

I wasn't hearing the thunder of hooves heading in our direction.

I thought harder, like our lives depended on it.

Oh, yeah, right.

And that's when I popped a grin, the beneficiary of desperation.

I knew what I was going to tell Hartmann.

■ ■ ■ ■

The interior door slid into the wall and
Hartmann stepped into the room holding
the Beretta, his smile as phony as ever,
trailed by Popeye, who had traded in his
blazer, white linen slacks and wingtips for a
military-style outfit, a starched khaki shirt
with epaulets, pleated matching khaki
slacks, a Sam Browne belt and gleaming
jackboots. He was brandishing a Luger and
studying me with murderous intent.

Hartmann wasted no time or emotion.
"What have you decided, Mr. Blanchard?"

"It pains me to tell you this, Hartmann,
but Eve was speaking the truth and Marie
is the liar."

"How so?" I repeated the salient parts of
Marie's story. "And she said she doesn't
know where the photographs were taken or
what they show?"

"Right."

"Or where the photographs and negatives
are now?"

"Right."

"Very well, then. As I said, the liar would
be punished and you have the honor of being Miss MacDaniels' executioner." He
gestured for Popeye to turn over his Luger

to me and aimed his Beretta at my chest. "To prevent you from having any unwise ideas," he said, like I needed the explanation.

Marie sucked the oxygen out of the room, her eyes frozen on me.

I hadn't told her the gambit I'd concocted.

Why bother? There was no guarantee it would work.

I waved off Popeye's Luger.

Hartmann said, "You will take it and do your duty, if you know what's good for you as well, Mr. Blanchard."

"There's more for you to hear," I said. "It may change your mind."

"I'm listening." He showed he wasn't happy about it.

"She said she didn't know where the photographs and the negatives are, but she does know who has them."

Marie reared back, struggling to mask the confusion that had broken out on her face.

My pronouncement cracked Hartmann's rigid look. "Oh, and who would that be?"

"Her boyfriend."

"Her boyfriend, you say?"

"The latest blackmailer you've heard from, the one still alive and demanding your two hundred and fifty grand."

"Her boyfriend who is now demanding

my two hundred and fifty grand. Does this boyfriend even exist, or are you making up a story? Tell me, Miss MacDaniels, does this boyfriend of yours actually exist or is Mr. Blanchard making him up in an attempt to save your life?"

Marie said, "Yes," barely audible.

"Yes, he actually exists or, yes, Mr. Blanchard has invented him?"

She threw me a frantic look.

I said, "It's been one of the town's best-kept secrets."

"I love secrets," Hartmann said. "I'm waiting, Miss MacDaniels."

I answered for her: "Benjamin Siegel."

Hartmann's mocking smile evaporated. His eyebrows shot into his brow and his jaw opened wide, like he was welcoming a dentist. It took him a few moments to collect his surprise into a question: "Bugsy Siegel, *that* Benjamin Siegel, he's her boyfriend?"

"And my boyhood friend from the old neighborhood, how come I was one of the few he let in on the secret. Also, because Benny knew I worked at Metro and wanted me to keep an eye on Marie, keep her out of mischief, if you get my drift. A watchdog for the bulldog, that's me."

If I had a tic like Marie's, by now my face

would be sending out Morse code.

"You're such good friends, explain then the sharp exchange of words the two of you had and almost came to blows at the Coconut Grove. It was headline news in Hedda Hopper's column in the *Times.*"

"Hedda has a problem keeping her gaudy hats on straight, much less getting her facts straight. You want to know where I rank with Benny, ask your little friend Tyrone Powell. He had a real set-to with Benny, could have cost him his life if I hadn't stepped in and saved the day. Or, ask Benny himself. I'll be happy to introduce you to him."

"I know about Tyrone and Siegel, that business at the dog track," Hartmann said, like I'd challenged his intelligence. "If this one is the Jew's girlfriend, how do you explain why I read he's always out on the town with that floozy Virginia Hill?"

"In a nutshell — Esta is his wife, Ginny is his mistress and Marie's his girlfriend. Benny likes women as much as he likes to spill blood. Ask the town's ranking madam, Anne Forrester, the Black Widow, or her protégé, Brenda Allen, or any one of Anne's party girls. And he's very protective of them. Jerry the Sweater Sharell could verify that for you, only — after he roughed up one of

324

Benny's favorites at Madam Anne's — Jerry the Sweater disappeared. Hasn't been seen or heard from since. Something happens to Marie or to me, I guarantee Benny won't quit looking until his people have sniffed you out and introduced you to a block of cement and the deep blue."

Hartmann looked accusingly at Marie. "Why didn't you tell me this about the Jew gangster earlier?"

Marie, grown wise to my game, had no problem picking up on the cue.

"You didn't ask," she said.

Without another word, Hartmann retreated from the room, followed by Popeye.

The wall door slid out and Marie and I were alone again.

She said, "You got some imagination there, baby, but we're still stuck here."

I flashed her a smile. "And still alive."

"What now?"

"We wait — for Hartmann to decide what to do about us. If he's smart, he'll use us to help him get the negatives and photos from Benny, maybe even with you sweet-talking Benny into a deal that'll cost him less than two hundred and fifty smackers. Or, wait for Benny to contact him again and use us as bargaining chips to get the price down or make it disappear entirely, then — once he has his hands on the negatives and photos — kill us and risk outrunning Benny and the boys."

"Only Bugsy Siegel doesn't have the negatives and photographs and, besides, I've never laid my eyes on the man in person, or any other part of me."

"If he's working alphabetically, chances are Benny is still on A."

"Get serious, baby."

"I was serious. Anything you've heard about swordsmen like Errol Flynn, Freddie March or Leslie Howard, triple it about Benny Siegel. Even as a kid, all he had to do was bat his curly lashes and tune up his smile to get inside a pretty girl's bloomers, including the occasional teacher or two. Where his charm didn't work, his reputation did. Mobsters are still big time in the old neighborhood."

Marie shook her head and aimed a *Cut it out* hand at me. "Suppose Hartmann is trying to get hold of Siegel right this minute and Siegel tells him he doesn't know what in Hades he's talking about?"

I put a finger gun to my temple and fired. "Even if he did, you and I don't know everything, but we do know about this place and the place at Catalina. We know what's being cooked up by Hartmann and company isn't kosher. Just that adds up to too much knowledge — nothing Hartmann would want us to go tattletaling to the FBI about."

"Enough!" Marie said, turning her back and moving away from me, onto a chair against the far wall. She bowed her head, locked her hands in prayer. Her lips animated words I couldn't distinguish.

I wandered aimlessly, inventing happy endings to the scenarios I had spelled out for Marie, trying to do what my dear old grandma had always encouraged me to do when things weren't as rosy as I wanted — make lemonade from lemons. I laughed recalling what Grandpa always threw into the mix, telling me, "What your grandma means for you to do is scrape away the horseshit and find the horse, Christopher." He was also fond of saying, "They told me to smile because things could get worse, so I smiled and things got worse," where Grandma would quit her knitting long enough to remind him and me, "It's always darkest before the dawn, dear ones."

Well, Grandpa, if you're within hearing distance, I want you to know you got that one right.

Grandma, it couldn't get much darker than it is in here now, definitely too dark to find any lemons.

I spoke too soon, by about ten minutes.

An explosion knocked the steel entrance door off its hinges and almost on top of me. A second blast flattened the sliding door. Uniformed cops and FBI agents in ballistic vests, armed with handguns and assault rifles, charged into the room ahead of Ray Travis and Charles Cook, Travis shouting over the racket, "You two okay?"

Marie fled into his arms, like she'd discovered a lost lover.

Cook stepped over to me, understood the question on my face, and said, "The tiny fellow doesn't go anywhere we don't have him in our sights. He managed to signal us you and Miss MacDaniels were in a spot of serious trouble and needed help."

"In that case, what took you so long?"

"That's a joke, correct?" he said, like humor was forbidden by J. Edgar Hoover.

The Sanctorum was empty except for Marie and me by the time Travis and Cook had arrived with the rescue units. Everybody gone. No sign business had been conducted in any of the rooms for years. Card table chairs, mostly stacked and leaning against the wall. Cartons of Chinese food on otherwise clean desktops or in the waste baskets, much of it spoiled, and the walled-in acrid smell of cigarettes and cigars, whose remains overflowed ashtrays or had been heeled out on the tired hardwood floors. Empty pop bottles and milk cartons. Disconnected telephones, if they ever were connected at all. The Sanctorum was a rendezvous point, probably never anything more after Hartmann and his Bund buddies moved in.

"We won't know where they've landed until we hear from Tyrone or the agents I have on Tyrone's tail," Cook said.

"How'd Hartmann and company know to scram?"

"Same answer."

"Eve Whitney? They beat her up pretty bad."

"Best we can do for now is figure they took Miss Whitney with them."

"Beats the idea of her dumped and lying dead somewhere in Griffith Park."

"Or you and Miss MacDaniels there, keeping her company."

"You do have a sense of humor, Agent Cook."

"That was serious," he said. "They have come after you once, twice, and mark my words — there will be a third time and it could very well be the charm."

Travis joined us, supporting Marie with

an arm around her waist, a hand under her elbow. "Ready to move on," he said. "Got a car waiting for us outside."

Within the hour we were settling at the Ravenswood, a cop posted in the corridor outside my apartment door, another downstairs by the security desk in the lobby, two in an unmarked parked across Rossmore that gave them a bird's-eye view of the residential and parking garage entrances.

I ceded the bedroom to Marie, who flopped onto the bed and was asleep a minute later. I moved an armchair around to give me a direct view of the door and settled down with my .38 in my lap, my backup Colt pocket .32 automatic at instant reach on the side table.

I don't remember falling asleep, only that I woke up in bed, under the covers with Marie, both of us still fully clothed, her rhythmic breathing broken by an occasional snort and eerie noise, the morning light creeping into the room. The .38 under my pillow. The .32 on the nightstand.

I maneuvered from my side to my back trying not to wake her.

She'd been through plenty.

She deserved her sleep.

Maybe an hour passed before she roused, remembered where she was and reached over to verify she wasn't alone. She rolled onto her side facing me, smiled her movie star smile and whispered, "Thank you, baby. For everything."

"My pleasure."

"Not yet," she said. She slipped out of bed and undressed. "I need a shower," she said, and padded across the room. She stopped at the bathroom door, turned and struck a pose, legs spread and hands on hips. "You coming, baby?"

"Not yet," I said.

CHAPTER 19

Saturday, November 19, 1938

Marie and I spent Saturday making something that wasn't love and didn't have the tang of romance attached to it the way our bodies stayed attached, performing to wants and needs in consenting harmony. It definitely wasn't lust; we shared too much history to incite that kind of response. Passion passed between us most of the time; the kind of passion rooted in friendship and need. We needed each other — or somebody, anybody — given what we'd been going through together, our lives turned into one of those fifteen-chapter *Continued Next Week* cliffhangers, where every chapter ends with the good guys facing death, short of imminent rescue. We were rescuing each other, escaping into an emotion stronger than fear that we couldn't find a name for, so we quit talking about it or around it and practiced it, because it worked for us. *It.* As good a name as any for the emotion we shared, Marie replacing Clara Bow as the "It Girl" and me her "It Guy." We took it under submission as we stoked and stroked under the covers, taking occasional breaks to catch a second wind over a smoke, gobble down a snack or grab forty winks. We ignored the telephone, which rang on and off throughout the day. Whoever it was could wait. There were no passports into our sovereign state, Population Two, and neither citizen held any desire to exit, not until evening.

The phone rang while I was finishing up some basic housecleaning in the kitchen before rejoining Marie, who'd gone off to run another tub for us. I put down my beer and, without thinking, from force of habit, snatched up the receiver.

"Hey, flatfoot, Jimmy Timony here. Long time no speak. How you been?"

Jimmy was a longtime resident of the Ravenswood, Mae West's onetime live-in lover, who'd moved into his own apartment after he and the aging sex symbol broke up. They had remained close friends ever after, Mae clinging to him the same way she held onto George Raft after their affair was history — and never mind that Mae had never rid herself of Frank Wallace, her husband going on a quarter of a century, who was around, but never at the Ravenswood.

Jimmy and I kibitzed occasionally, whenever we bumped into one another in the garage, the lobby or the elevator, but phone calls were rare. I couldn't remember the last one. "The usual usual, Jimmy. How about you?"

"Still foolin' 'em, Chris. Win a few, lose a few."

"What can I do you for?"

"Playing messenger boy for my blonde beauty is all. Mae asked me to give you a jingle and invite you up to her place, you have some time to spare."

"When's that?"

"Now, and she apologizes for the short notice."

"Any idea why?"

"If it were me the lady was summoning, I'd know why. In your case, no, unless there's something heating up between the two of you." He put a laugh behind his words, but I read jealousy into it, maybe even a little resentment.

Marie's laugh was truer when I told her. "If I'm going to lose my man to anyone, nobody finer than Mae West," she said.

"Not a loss," I said. "A temporary loan."

"That being the case, how about one for

the road?"

The cop sitting guard in the corridor did a double-take when I told him who I was heading off to see and wanted to tag along, babbling something about an autograph. I told him, "You stick here looking after Miss MacDaniels. I doubt I have anything to fear from Miss West," and headed for the elevator. He called after me, "Don't do anything I'd do," a line dating back to the Garden of Eden.

The fellow who answered Mae's doorbell was unlike any of the young bucks who frequently called on her, good-looking muscle-bound types half her age taking time away from bodybuilding exhibitions down at Venice Beach. He was mid-forties, same as Mae, and stacked high, wide and heavy like a Greco-Roman wrestler, bald-headed, his beak of a nose off-center, almost like it was asleep on his fleshy cheek. "C'mon inside and make yourself comfy-cozy," he said, his gravel voice a perfect fit.

This was only my third visit to Mae's apartment, the first when she invited me up to meet the new neighbor, the other time when she threw a birthday gathering for Jimmy Timony, made memorable for me when she raised her crystal goblet of water

— Mae was not one for the hard stuff —
and recited one of her memorable movie
lines: *It ain't the men in my life that counts,
it's the life in my men,* adding as an afterthought, *Whoever it was claimed what goes
up must come down is nobody I'd ever care
to meet.*

Mae was currently between engagements,
five years removed from *She Done Him
Wrong,* the movie that cashed in big time at
the box-office and was credited with keeping Paramount from going bust. Last year's
Every Day's a Holiday wasn't one for the
studio, and they'd called it quits with her,
giving rise to a Parsons rumor that Mae was
heading to Universal and a comedy co-
starring W.C. Fields.

The parlor reeked of overstuffed comfort
and elegance, carried a regal air. It was easy
to imagine a Catherine the Great or a Marie Antoinette in this setting. The floor-to-
ceiling mirror against one wall reflected a
snowfall of off-white furniture and gold trim
that suggested another time, not an apartment in the heart of Hollywood. A nude
carved from white marble sat atop a white
piano, counterpoint to a painting on another
wall and elegantly framed photos on the
tables helping to create what amounted to a
worshipful shrine to the blonde, buxom

Miss West, whose beauty was as much or more in her sexy, stylish magnetism than in looks that spoke to different tastes in an earlier time.

The scent of perfumed air drifted into the room as the door to her bedroom eased open. I anticipated seeing Mae sweep in as she had last time, in a flowing, rose-colored gown that touched the vanilla rug and hid the fact she was walking on five or six-inch platforms attached to her shoes and meant to disguise the truth of her height, five-feet-one at best.

Instead, I got Benny Siegel's bodyguard Spikes, followed by Siegel himself.

The wrestler said, "I'll be hanging out with Mr. Timony until you're finished up here," aimed a salute at Siegel, and left the apartment.

"What the hell's this about?" I said, once I'd overcome my surprise.

"Same question I got for you," Benny said.

"You go first," I said, dropping onto a bridal white satin loveseat.

Siegel settled on the piano bench, his smoke angled out the corner of his mouth, and ran the keys with the backs of his fingers like Chico Marx was always doing, while studying me with his icebox eyes. "Miss West's a real dish," he said. "George got me use of the place while he run off with her to Warner Bros. for a wrap party for the picture he just done with Cagney, *Each Dawn I Die.*" He attached a smirk to the title and me. "You ever know that Cagney speaks Yiddish like a genuine Hebe? Grew up on the streets like me and you."

"Me on the streets, you in the gutter, Benny."

"That mouth of yours . . ." He shuttered his eyes and shook his head, slicked back his hair. He handed off his smoke to Spikes, who crushed it between his fingers without flinching and dropped it in a pocket. "Me and Spikes ducked out of sight in George's car coming into the garage and figure on leaving same way after me and you are done here, or don't you know you got cops covering you like a tarp, rainy days at Ebbets Field?"

"How *done here* do you have in mind?"

"Depends on how fast I hear from you what I come to find out."

"That being . . . ?"

"How *you* come to find out — whether we do it the easy way, like gents, or Spikes here practices some of his many skills on you."

He moved from the piano and hovered

over me with his hands on his hips — an intimidating figure I wasn't going to permit intimidating me, although with Benny you never knew. It was well known in the old neighborhood that looking at him cross-eyed could sometimes be enough to get you killed. I said, "Who's writing your lines for you, Benny? Or is it that you've seen one gangster movie too many?"

"More than one, but that's another story. Let's us stick to this one."

"Let's us."

"I'll spell it out for you in Technicolor."

"The *Reader's Digest* version, please. I got somewhere to be."

"Where's that?"

"Away from you."

"You do got balls, I'll say that much. . . . Spikes, my chum here, don't he got balls?" Spikes grunted his version of agreement. "So, as I was about to say, I get this phone call earlier today, a guy what got no business with my number or calling me. He says — you know what he says?"

"I can't wait to hear."

He made me wait while he hauled out a fresh smoke and gave it a good going over once Spikes lit it for him.

"He says he wants to make arrangements to finish up the sale I'd called him about. I say, *What sale might that be?* He gets sly with me, saying he has the two hundred and fifty gees I asked for and would like to know where and how we can make the exchange. I say, *What exchange?* The two hundred and fifty gees for the negatives and pictures, he says. I say, *What negatives and pictures?* Suddenly he's getting all uppity, climbing on a high horse, and he says maybe he was misinformed and is talking to the wrong person. I say, *Who would it be that misinformed you?* He gives me your name, Chris. He says it's Mr. Christopher Blanchard."

My pulse slowed to a gallop and I smiled. "Easy to explain, Benny."

"How easy?"

"That was a bad apple name of Nicky Hartmann who called you and —"

He cut me off. "Dammit, don't tell me what I already know. I know who it was. I need to know how you know. How you know I got the poor sap's negatives and pictures. I need to know how you found out about the two hundred and fifty grand asking price. I need to know who else knows, and you better make it snappy — here and now."

I used to know cops who confused bravery with stupidity.

A lot of them died in the line of duty.

Most of them.

I always promised myself I'd never be in a hurry to join them.

I caught my breath.

Lit my own smoke.

Spelled it out for Siegel —

The run-ins with Hartmann, going back to Avalon and pushing the story forward to yesterday, how I'd pulled his name out of the hat to stall chances of turning Marie and me into corpses. "No one in his right mind would run the risk of angering Ben Siegel," I said.

He liked that, although it played off his reputation for violence, maybe because it played off his reputation. Siegel was not without ego. He threw a nod and a half-smile at Spikes, who reciprocated in kind. "You're saying you didn't know I had cut myself in on Rothman and Covington's little blackmail business? That's *emmis?* The truth?"

"*Emmis*, Benny." I raised my hand like I was taking an oath. "On my mother's grave."

His sinister look turned sad. "Didn't hear. Sorry. I was always fond of your old lady. She always treated me regular like. *Aleha-ha-shalom.* May she rest in peace."

"On her grave, Benny, not on her. Mom's

341

still alive and kicking, feisty as ever."

Spikes laughed, and I realized too late I'd stepped over the line and embarrassed Siegel in front of his stooge. Siegel turned him off with an angry look and then turned it on me. He sucked hard on his smoke, raising an inch of tobacco ash that burned red hot. "Next time you dick with my head, I'm going to put this out in your eye, and then I am going to cut out your tongue, you got it? You unnerstan', Chris? Tell me you unnerstan'."

"Understood."

"Again." The bulging blue vein on his forehead looked ready to crash out.

"Better." He ran a hand across his temple and wiped the palm into his palm, then slicked back the other side. Ran his tongue over his lips. "I asked who else knows about this?"

"About Covington, Rothman and their blackmailing Hartmann, there's Marie and Eve Whitney. Hartmann himself. Tyrone Powell. Maybe some of the people at the Two Harbors house on Catalina." This did not feel like a good time to explain about the FBI and the Bund connection, so I left that part out.

"Tyrone Powell, you said got you and Marie to the island and shows up again at the place by Griffith Park, so one way the other he figures to be strong in the action. . . . I shudda stamped out that dwarf first time he got in my way at the dog track."

"Midget."

"I'm saying he's a dwarf," Siegel said, like he was Webster's Dictionary and the final authority. "You still owe me a big thank you for letting the dwarf off the hook, but no guarantee, he ever gets in my way again."

"Thanks, Benny."

"And an apology for our little set-to at the Grove."

"That, too."

"Yeah, good. Better. We're back to Even-Steven. . . . So what else? Where does that leave us?"

"It leaves me wondering how you finished up with Hartmann."

"His call left me wondering what else I needed to know, so I told him to ring me back tomorrow and we'd talk some more."

"And now that you know more?"

"One burning question still. I got no idea what makes the pictures worth a quarter mil and maybe I should be upping the ante to a half mil, maybe more, especially since it's not all going into my mattress. My friends back East are in for the skim, as usual. You got any ideas?"

"You never got an explanation from Roth-man or Covington?"

"Never got around to it, it so happens. I'll tell you about it sometime."

"Maybe if I saw the pictures?"

"Shots that belong in a family album, the best I make." He wandered over to the oil painting of Mae and studied it admiringly. "Yeah, some dish. Too much meat for my taste, but plenty appetizing." He padded back to me and rubbed his palms together. "You know what? You should have a look at the pictures, maybe see something I'm missing."

"When?"

"Over to my place soon as George gets back here with Miss West and his buggy."

"Tomorrow would be better, Benny. I have Marie waiting for me downstairs."

"So, she'll wait a little longer. You spot something makes a difference, I want to hear about it before Hartmann calls."

His look dared me to give him lip.

"I wasn't such a greedy bastard, I'd cut Garbo a piece of the pie," Siegel said, dig-ging an elbow into me. "It was her, after all, put me into this nice chunk of change." We were in the back seat of George's car, George driving and Spikes in the passenger seat, on our way to Siegel's place on the nine hundred block of Rexford Drive. He was renting it from Lawrence Tibbett, the opera singer, who, gossip had it, was inspired to move out after Siegel fell in love with the California casa-style spread and gave Tibbett his choice of packing and moving out or getting used for target practice. "I come out to the coast hoping to meet her while I'm here, maybe share some alone time with her, you unnerstand, but nothing was panning out until —"

"He mentioned it to me," Raft called over his shoulder. "Giving me a chance to do some payback, right, Ben?"

"As rain, George. . . . George here, he mentions to Jack Warner how I'm such a big fan of hers and Jack Warner, wanting to keep his star happy, puts in a call to L.B. Mayer. Next I know, I'm hearing from Mayer's fix-it man, Howard Strickling, who tells me Mr. George Cukor is inviting me to a Sunday blowout at his joint. This stops me in my size tens and I tell him, *Thank you and thank Mr. George Cukor for the invite, but I'm not one of those boys.* Howard Strickling says don't take it wrong, it's about meeting Greta Garbo. That takes some explaining, which he does. It seems she's been living in the guest house on Cukor's property and shows up regular-like on Sundays around the pool and the tennis court. I'd be a bone-head not to jump at that chance. I mean, Jesus! Greta Garbo!

"So it's Sunday, and I show up and get this big juicy welcome from Mr. George Cukor, a hug and *fegelah* kisses on both cheeks. One swell fella, he introduces me around and tells me to make myself at home. . . . An hour goes by, then another, and there's no sign of Greta Garbo. I figure to give it another thirty minutes and call it quits and am having a champagne cocktail at the bar setup outside when this guy in a bathing suit, all lathered-up in suntan lotion that smells like orange blossoms or some-thing, struts over to me and says, *I'm Day Covington,* like I'm supposed to know what that means. He sees I don't and says, *The movie star.* He holds out his hand. Some-thing else, I would-a popped him one. We shake, and I tell him, *I'm Ben Siegel.* He tells me he knows and how surprised he was to see me here. It's easy to see he's plas-tered, so I let it go. He brags how he's tak-ing a leaf from my book. I ask him what that's supposed to mean. He springs this story on me, how he and a photographer name of Otto Rothman have been running a successful blackmail operation that's about to put them in the chips, two hundred and fifty simoleons worth. I hear that, I know I have just made myself a new friend. Before I can pump him for more information, he gets stolen away by some giddy *fegelah* who's got on display a bulge as big as his biceps, you unnerstand?"

"You're saying Day Covington was a queer? Marie, his wife, said he was always welcome at Cukor's Sundays, where he'd drum up future business for him and Rothman." I could have told Siegel I had already heard that from Cukor, but I wanted to hear how he explained it.

"Baseball and football, they're both games, but they don't play by the same rules, either. Maybe Marie never knew he was a switch-hitter, but he was definitely into it that day." He stroked the air with an up-and-down hand motion. "Rothman, he didn't look any too straight arrow when I paid him a visit next day and told him the good news, how him and Covington had a new partner. He wised up fast that the New Deal Ben Siegel had to offer was as good for them as FDR's New Deal turned out to be good for the country, and Covington gave me no lip when he got the news. The three of us sat down like gentlemen and I got the straight skinny on their operation, small potatoes except for Hartmann, but it had room to grow once I got my feet wet. Why settle for chicken feed when you can have the whole chicken, you unnerstand?"

"And you walked off with the Hartmann negatives and pictures — for insurance?"

"I shudda, but instead I figured it was jake to leave 'em with Rothman, like a show of good faith and all that Shinola, once he gimme a tour of his files and filing system and I saw how safe it was, like in a Mosler. I shudda known better. It wasn't until Covington got himself murdered and I guessed what might be the cause that I sent Spikes for them. He saw Rothman's corpse, grabbed a bunch of coded files, wanting to be sure he had the right ones, and got the hell out of there. When I heard the news, I sent him back to burn down the joint, make it look like arson, so there'd be nothing around that could tie me to Rothman or Covington. That's where you showed up and stopped that from happening."

"You're saying you weren't behind Rothman's murder?"

"Or Covington. No reason. The three of us were getting along fine, like the Three Musketeers."

"That line you fed me that night at the Coconut Grove, about Rothmann and your friends from back East —"

"Yeah, a line. I didn't need you nosing around and maybe gumming up the works. You need to pin this on somebody — I say Hartmann's your guy."

"And you say you never got around to asking either Covington or Rothman what made the photographs so valuable?"

"What is it with you, the third degree? You already got my answer to that one."

George eased the car to a stop out front of the Tibbett house and announced our arrival.

Siegel thanked him as we piled out, adding, "You didn't hear any of this, that so, George?"

"Still deaf in both ears, Ben."

Easing up the walk, Siegel threw an arm around my shoulders and said, "Goes for you, too, Chris. Whatever happens next, you forget about, like it never happened. See no evil, hear no evil, speak no evil, *farshtey?* Unnerstand?"

So, I'd been a detective once and was playing one now, but I was a kid from the old neighborhood long before I became a detective and I would always be a kid from the old neighborhood. You can try, you can pretend, but you never stop breathing the air you grow up with. I knew the importance of keeping a button on your lip. I knew that silence was golden and stoolies were candidates for six feet under.

I said, "*Farshtey,* Benny."

"Of course, you do," he said, patting my back. "Only I gotta tell you — *Farshtey* — Jimmy Cagney pronounces it better. *Farshtey?*"

"*Farshtey.*"

Siegel hooted into the calm night air, raising the ire of several neighborhood dogs, and gave my cheek a few fatherly slaps. "Keep working on it," he said, "only my money's staying on Cagney. . . . Anyhow, you get what I was saying about Garbo before? She hadn't been expected at Mr. Cukor's joint, I never wudda gone and never wudda been this close to the quarter mil."

"*Farshtey,*" I said, the Mick in me not ready to quit trying —

About anything.

CHAPTER 20

We settled in the den, a comfortable room furnished hacienda style and full of tributes to Lawrence Tibbett. A framed certificate acknowledging his Academy Award nomination for his first movie, *Rogue Song*. Candid photos and studio portraits with co-stars like Lupe Velez, Virginia Bruce, Alice Brady, Jimmy Durante, Laurel and Hardy; all with fond inscriptions. Photos in costume for roles he sang at the Metropolitan Opera. Towering above the fireplace, an oil of Tibbett in costume for *The Emperor Jones.* The stucco wall papered with posters from various Met and movie appearances. Prominently displayed on the piano, his framed diploma from Manual Arts High School in south Los Angeles.

"Egos in this town, they spread like the plague," Siegel said, sweeping the room with a gesture while I removed Otto Rothman's photos from the file folder envelope and spread them out on the coffee table. "Not confined to the movie people, a *goniff* like that moron Jack Dragna being one example. He thinks he's running the rackets out here, he got another thing coming one-a these days soon.

"You want a drink, name your poison," he said, crossing to the bar. I waved off the offer. Siegel poured a tall cognac and settled on a barstool, studying me while I studied the photos. His shady lady, the brunette and bountiful Virginia Hill, sashayed in, in silk lounging pajamas that clung to her like butter on bread, pouting over the lack of attention she was receiving from her boyfriend. Siegel answered by thumbing her out. She sent him daggers and retreated. He said, "Talk about egos. She got one taller than the Empire State Building. Frankie Costello, Nitti, Charlie Fischetti, Joey Adonis, they all had a whack at her, but here she is with yours truly. You notice them gams of hers? Why I call her the Flamingo. She locks them gams around you and — " He kissed his fingers and threw them away.

I made a show of listening, but in fact I'd tuned Siegel out, the better to explore the Rothman photos. They were as advertised —

The type of candid picture people take on

trips and vacations; proof of places and landmarks visited; mementos to illustrate conversations at dinner parties and other social gatherings, eventually replaced by newer ones and consigned to keepsake albums.

I remembered some of the locations from Rothman's detailed ledger: Desert Hot Springs, Palm Springs, Lake Arrowhead, Yosemite National Park, San Diego and Hotel Del Coronado, where he'd noted sharing a room with a model, and —

Something went click.

I wasn't sure what.

I shuffled through the stack to find that one again, and studied the picture.

The model at the Del was a man, not some struggling starlet trading her body for a set of glamour shots.

Maybe somebody Rothman had hooked one sunny Sunday afternoon at Cukor's, but nobody I remembered seeing up there, only somebody who did look familiar from —

Yes!

The slab of beef who had been guarding the driveway entrance at the Sanctorum.

Maybe I was on to something.

I took a slower tour through the photos.

Most of them had been taken at places

outside California.

Never more than one photo taken at any single location.

From picture to picture, always a different man posing stone-faced in front of places like the Lincoln Memorial in Washington, D.C.; Constitution Hall in Philadelphia; Fenway Park in Boston; Union Station in Chicago; Frank Lloyd Wright's Taliesin West in Scottsdale, Arizona; the Hollywood Bowl . . .

Why?

There had to be a connection.

I wondered: Why pay a photographer to travel around the country when it would have been far less expensive to hire a photographer in each of the locations?

Charity?

Because Rothman needed the work?

Or because it was the kind of work that required a photographer Hartmann knew he could trust?

Why would he trust a photographer he didn't know until Rothman was suggested to him by Eve Whitney? Coincidence? Eve didn't know a link existed between Rothman and Hartmann, one her boyfriend thought better of mentioning to her?

Play it through again, Chris.

Come on, come on, come on.

What kind of link?

The love that dare not speak its name?

Hartmann didn't look or act the type.

He was more a Napoleon than a Josephine.

So was the side of beef at the Sanctorum.

If not that —

The German American Bund?

What if the German American Bund was the bonding agent?

Hartmann would certainly trust a fellow Nazi lover to —

Play it again, Chris.

What if all the people in the photographs were Bund members, maybe the same people who met with Hartmann on Catalina Island? What if they were posed on film in their hometowns?

Okay — take that as the *who, what* and *where* of it.

What about the *why* of it?

I went through the photos again, this time looking past the people, giving close examination to the backgrounds, and —

Landed on a theory that left only the *when* of it.

And it drained my face of color and I piped out a *Woof* that caused Siegel to shoot me a look, eyebrows askew. "You figure out something?" he said, easing off the barstool and padding over to have a look at the rows of photos stretched out on the coffee table. "I got a bigger payday going on with them or what?"

I wasn't inclined to share my suspicion with him.

Not yet.

Not before I checked out some things.

Not before I ran it past Charles Cook.

I said, "My stomach's acting up something fierce, Benny. An ulcer I got when I was on the force working vice."

"I hope that's all you got working vice." He smiled, so I smiled. "It got a name, your ulcer?"

"What do you mean?"

Siegel rubbed his stomach. "I named my ulcer Jack, after Dragna. I got the cure for it, though, and when the time's ripe —" His smile faded and he let the thought hang.

I said, "How about I head back home now, take the photos with me, so I can get a fresh start first thing in the A.M.; pick up where I left off?"

"Let the pictures out of my mitts?" Siegel looked at me like he was fitting me for a straitjacket. "You trying a game on me, Chris?"

"I've heard what happens to people who try games on you, Benny."

"Yeah. That'd put more than an ulcer in your belly." He scooped up the photos and packed the file folder under his arm. "I'll go tell Spikes to hustle you a taxi cab."

It was verging on eleven when the cab pulled up to the Ravenswood, the moon invisible behind another battery of rain clouds that exploded a moment or two before I cleared the canopy and ducked inside. I'd half expected to be hailed and halted by the cops in the unmarked parked across Vine, but that didn't happen. The cop at the lobby security desk was playing chess with Walter and too busy pondering his next move to bother turning and looking up as I quick-stepped past. The door to my apartment was being guarded by an empty chair.

My antenna went up.

Marie.

What about Marie?

Was she all right in there?

I heard the locks being played with and plastered myself against the wall, braced for battle, mentally prepared to make the element of surprise work for me when the door creaked open.

I gave myself a few seconds, then wheeled around and pushed it hard, throwing off balance whoever was doing the opening. He hit the floor, me instantly on top of him, playing knuckle ball with his face before recognizing I should have looked before I leaped.

Elmer Troy was cursing me out in a high-decibel shriek overriding my apology as I unsaddled from him. Eddie Vassily rounded inside from the corridor, his revolver in hand. Marie rushed over and grabbed hold of me like I was the original Second Coming. Behind us, an amused Ray Travis called, "You certainly know how to make an entrance, Blanchard. You learn that at the studio?"

Travis dropped his pipe in the hanky pocket of his suit and wandered over. "I do wish that one of these times you'll time your antics for normal working hours and I won't be rousted out of bed," he said.

"Talk about *antics.* How do you explain my being able to get back here without once being stopped by your people who are supposed to be protecting us?" I said. "Not outside. Not in the lobby. Not at the door. Not —"

Troy interrupted me, shouting, "I step inside for two minutes to take a dump and now I need to hear this crapola, boss?"

Vassily showed equal bother. "You're a

fine one to talk, Blanchard, leaving Miss MacDaniels alone by herself and afraid while you hotfoot it away, supposedly to go and see Mae West, only not so. Not so — ain't that so?"

"Is that what I did?" I wriggled free of Marie and stepped back from her, anxious to hear what she had to say.

She was wearing my bathrobe, unconsciously displaying enough cleavage and a trace of well-turned thigh to inspire a revolution. Realizing why the cops were staring at her, she drew the robe tighter to shut off the peep show. "When you were gone so long, I got crazy with worry," she said, her expression pleading for understanding. "I went up to Miss West's place. The fellow who answered the door said Miss West had retired after an evening away with George Raft, and he couldn't be any more help than that. That got me nuts, so I came back down and right away got on the phone to Captain Travis."

"So where did you disappear to, Blanchard? Care to explain how you managed to get in and out of the Ravenswood, past my men?"

"Raft gave me a lift in his buggy. A Bugatti 57 S Atalante, one of only seventeen made, and he had to pull strings to get his."

"Them damn wops, they *always* take care of their own," Vassily said, registering disgust.

"Ranft was the family name. He's German, not Italian," I said.

"Same difference," Troy said.

Travis said, "My men logged Raft coming and going, but no mention of you."

"George is a whiz behind the wheel."

"Where did you go?"

"He took me up to the Thrifty's on Vine for a tin of aspirin."

"Long line at the counter, was there?"

"A lot of migraine going around. We did coffee at the fountain, catching up on the good old days."

"And me so scared silly for you," Marie said, irritation building in her words.

Travis said, "Was this before Raft dropped you, Bugsy Siegel and Bugsy's trained ape Spikes off at the Tibbett house on Rexford?" He could not have shown more pleasure at my obvious surprise. "Face it, Blanchard, Mother Goose tells a better story than you. Besides which, the three of you weren't as invisible getting out of here as you may have thought."

"You lied about that?"

"What is it? You thought you owned the patent on lying?"

"That's what you call looking after me?" Marie said, and marched away, yelling, "I need to be anyplace but here!"

Twenty minutes later, while Travis and I waited for Charles Cook to arrive, Marie was on her way with Vassily and Troy to the Victor Hugo, an obscure four-story hotel on Sunset Boulevard west of Chinatown, one of several hotels downtown the LAPD used for witnesses and informants getting special protection.

I was glad to see her leave.

What I had to tell Cook and Travis about what I'd seen and what I thought might make her more paranoid than she already was. Meanwhile, I had to figure how to explain it all without revealing Benny Siegel's involvement in the blackmail scheme, breaking the old neighborhood's golden rule of silence and making me a candidate for an early casket if Siegel found out.

I'm no Einstein.

You ask me to explain his theory of relativity, best I could do is list my relatives in order of preference, starting with my sainted mother and a father who treated me and the rest of the brood like he was still in the King's Occupation Army.

I am, however, one of those people with a knack for finding the two in one plus one and getting my own theories right most of the time.

Make that *some* of the time.

This time, telling Cook and Travis about the photos, I felt as certain of my theory as I was about the sun coming up tomorrow.

I ignored the small talk and got right to the brass tacks after we settled over coffee at the kitchen table, telling them at some modest expense to the truth, "Siegel knows how close I've been to Marie over all the years, so he shanghaied me to his place thinking she might have said something to me that could shed light on a bunch of photographs he got from Day Covington."

"Siegel had the pictures to show you?" Cook said.

"Yes."

"Go on. This ought to be good," Travis said, loading his damn pipe.

"He said Covington dropped a bundle on the dogs and couldn't cover his marker, so he took the pictures and negatives to Siegel, offering them as security, telling Siegel they were worth a big, big bundle. He caught him in a good mood, because Siegel went for it. He gave Covington another month to make good without bothering to ask what it was that made the pictures so valuable, but with the usual vig attached, of course."

"Of course," Cook said. "Don't they all."

Travis said, "I don't buy it, Blanchard. It's more likely Covington had to tell him what the pictures meant, after which Siegel turned him into worm bait and himself into the new blackmailer on the block." He finished lighting the pipe, flew a line of smoke to the ceiling.

"Except, there'd still be Rothman to deal with."

"It's not as if Siegel would let a small detail like that bother him. He sweeps the deck clean by having Rothman bumped before he gets on the phone to Nicky Hartmann and tells him to cough up."

"Suspecting it is easy, Travis. Proving it — not so easy. I'm betting the last thing anyone pinned on Siegel was a note to his shirt, his kindergarten teacher telling Siegel's mama little Benny had been a bad boy in class again."

"Maybe easier than you think after we pay him a visit and pick up the pictures, put him in cuffs and deliver him downtown."

"Book him and then what? Rubber Hose Ray inspires Siegel to confess all?" I gave the concept the belly laugh it deserved.

Cook tapped his cup for attention.

"Enough, gentlemen, please. Please save it for the playground. I can tell you with certainty that, because of other investigations lately in progress, Mr. Hoover would not want to bring Siegel into this one and reveal our interest in his recent comings and goings."

Travis said, "For instance, the scuttlebutt I've been hearing about the mob and Las Vegas?"

Cook smiled politely. "If your curiosity gets the best of you, feel free to inquire of Mr. Hoover or our number two, Mr. Tolson." Travis rolled his eyes. "So, then, Chris, let's return to the overriding issue on our agenda, the significance of the photographs and what you said over the phone you suspect is a serious threat to our government."

"I think the Bund plans to inflict major damage around the country as a show of Nazi Party strength, superiority and determination in the states, as well as in Europe."

"And Chicken Little thought the sky was falling," Travis said, and patted a yawn.

"Ray, please . . . go on, Chris."

I fed them the rest of my theory, how the people in the photos were probably the Bund leaders in whatever city or state they're from, probably the same people

Hartmann had up at Two Harbors, where the planning was probably done. Posed by Rothman at the targets for attack they chose or the targets that were chosen for them.

Cook never took his eyes off me, like he was memorizing every word. "And you think Rothman got picked because he was trustworthy, also a Nazi sympathizer?"

"Or a Nazi, yes."

"Baloney!" Travis said, making it two words. *Buh-loney!* "I suppose you're saying the same about Day Covington?"

"Maybe, or maybe it didn't take more than greed to gas him up."

"So tell me this, wise guy — you're so smart, what days are they going to make this show of strength happen?"

"Not days, Travis. Day. Singular. *Day.* Planning to make it happen on one day."

"And I suppose you know which day that's going to be?"

I put space between his question and my answer, dropped my voice to draw in their complete attention before I said, "Next year, on February 19, to coincide with the rally the German American Bund is holding at Madison Square Garden in New York. They'll close out the rally the same way we celebrate the Fourth of July with fireworks, only their fireworks will be for real and possibly deadly."

Cook weighed my response. "You seem so certain of that. You know it for a fact?"

"No, but it jives with the Operation A Tyrone reported about to you, the date he said he overheard being mentioned. Maybe you should instruct him to follow up on that, see what kind of confirmation he can wangle out of Hartmann."

"An excellent idea, except Tyrone has failed to check in. We've not seen or heard from him since yesterday at the Sanctorum, when he disappeared with Hartmann, Miss Whitney and the others. It's not like him."

"Maybe he's now reporting straight to Hoover and Tolson?" Travis said, studying his pipe.

The sarcasm bounced off Cook. "Chris, is there some way for you to get your hands on those pictures without alarming Siegel, long enough for us to copy them? We need to identify those people and those locations in the photos before we do anything else."

"I can give it a try," I said, knowing that was the answer he was anxious to hear, so why tell him I'd already failed to pry them loose from Siegel? "Meanwhile, if it helps any, I can list for you the places I remember, just about all, and provide a fairly accurate description of some of the people."

"Excellent, Chris. I'll assign one of our sketch artists to meet with you."

"That won't be necessary," I said.

CHAPTER 21

Sunday, November 20, 1938

Nancy was ready to hang up the phone after I said hello, deterred only when I said I was calling to invite her to brunch at the Hillcrest Country Club, a place restricted to the wealthy or elite Jews of Hollywood and Beverly Hills, except by special invitation. I was none of the above, but I did know the power of a call to Howard Strickling, who got back to me in ten minutes. "You're down for eleven o'clock in the main dining room," he said, never once bothering to ask why I wanted to be there. We both knew I'd owe him a favor down the line.

"I suppose you want me to bring my sketchbook again?" Nancy said.

"If you don't mind."

"You're kidding. That's a gag, right?"

"I'd be lying if I said it was."

"You really are some piece of work," she

said, her irritation on display.

She was waiting for me in the foyer when I arrived fifteen minutes early, simply dressed, but looking as elegant and gorgeous as any of the women parading by in haute couture and diamonds. I had put on a tie and felt overdressed compared to the men, most of them in Sunday casual open-necked silk shirts, but sporting diamond pinky rings that put the Rock of Gibraltar to shame.

I recognized the show business faces in the crowd, especially the gang of comics at a round table directly off the dining room — Jack Benny, Georgie Jessel, Eddie Cantor, Harpo and Groucho Marx. A moment later, Al Jolson stopped by the table with his wife, Ruby Keeler, to trade jabs with Jessel.

"Is what I heard about them true?" Nancy said, while we were being escorted to a nearby table for four that gave us a clear view of everyone coming and leaving and close enough to get drunk on the smells emanating from a buffet spread the length of a football field, buckling under the weight of enough hot and cold dishes to feed the population of India, including mounds of smoked salmon, white fish, borscht, knishes, other traditional Jewish delicacies, and platters of fresh rye bread, pumpernickel and bagels.

It wasn't the kind of spread you'd find at any of the other country clubs around, all of them with bylaws that prohibited membership to Jews and were equally inhospitable to Negroes, Mexicans, Chinese, Japanese and anyone else wearing their minority status on their skin. At the Los Angeles Country Club, even actors weren't immune. Randy Scott loved to tell how he was accepted after telling the membership committee, *If you've seen any of my movies, you know I'm not an actor.*

Hillcrest came about when a bunch of Jewish stars tired of being discriminated against pooled their resources and purchased the hundred-and-forty-acre property across from 20th Century Fox on Pico Boulevard, built the country club, installed an eighteen-hole golf course, and only afterward discovered they were sitting pretty on an oilfield, a prime example of the rich getting richer.

I told Nancy, "Depends on who you mean and what you heard."

"How Jessel starred on Broadway in *The Jazz Singer,* but demanded too much money to do the movie, so the Warners asked Jolson, who took stock in the company instead of his usual salary."

"True, a decision that made it possible for Jolson to sail through the crash of '29 and the darkest days of our Great Depression like they never happened. And how it came to pass that his latest missus, Miss Keeler, was able to transfer her sparkling tap dancing shoes from the Broadway stage to movie stardom at Warner Bros."

"Their answer to MGM's Eleanor Powell. Who was it who said *Imitation is the sincerest form of flattery?* Mr. Jolson?"

"He would have said, *You ain't heard tap dancin' yet,* so probably Jack Warner."

She laughed like I was Groucho Marx, drawing stares from diners at surrounding tables and others busy invading the buffet, as well as a smile of recognition from David O. Selznick, who was with his wife, Irene, at a table presided over by his father-in-law, Louis B. Mayer, and Mrs. Mayer.

Selznick waved to her.

Her wave back was less enthusiastic, like she'd been found out at a grand, upper-crust ball where she clearly didn't belong, unmasked, unlike George Bernard Shaw's Eliza Doolittle in *Pygmalion,* who pulled off the masquerade engineered by Professor Higgins.

Mayer took note of Nancy and gave her a

nod of recognition before returning to his meal.

"How embarrassing," she said.

"Time to get the feed bag on," I said, anxious to erase her discomfort. I helped her from her chair and guided her to the buffet line. "You want to know what's embarrassing, I'll tell you what's embarrassing. It has to do with Mr. Mayer himself, here at Hillcrest." I held off until we were back at the table. "The way the story goes, Mr. Mayer and Samuel Goldwyn were in the steam room one afternoon and got into an argument over who knew more and better about producing motion pictures. Neither would give ground. Both grew increasingly red-faced and indignant as their tempers rose higher than the temperature in the room. Finally, Mayer had had enough. He punched Goldwyn in the nose and stalked out. It took a bit of doing for Strickling to cover that one up after somebody leaked word to Parsons. Then to Hopper. Then to Winchell."

"I knew Mr. Mayer was a tough businessman, but not tough that way. I hear it often enough when I meet with Mr. Selznick to show him my latest work for *Gone with the Wind* —"

"Tough what way?" We looked up to

372

discover Selznick was standing at our table. "Mind if I join you, only a minute. Let you know our meeting's on for tomorrow, Nancy, as per usual." He sat down. "So, the old boy's tough what way? What's it exactly you hear often enough from yours truly?" He sounded high on more than life or the champagne on ice at his table.

I repeated the Goldwyn story.

"Oh, yes, you're Mr. Know-it-All Ex-Cop, who thinks he knows everything about art and is now auditioning for gossip-monger, that it?" he said, trying to turn every word into a symphony.

"It's not gossip if it's true, Mr. Selznick."

"Some truths are better left unsaid, friend, but I'll tell you something else. That piece of gossip about my dear ball-busting father-in-law?" He slapped his hand over his heart. "True. Gave Goldwyn a nose to rival the Goodyear blimp. You know why? I'll tell you why. Because he could. Back in his junk man days, he became powerful lifting a lot of heavy metal. Like an ox powerful. Now, cut to Hollywood. He's turned to producing some of the junk his studio turns out and has become a power in town. So, one night he and a group of friends are dining downtown at the Alexandria Hotel. He notices Charlie Chaplin across the room.

373

He has a waiter deliver a nasty note to Chaplin, telling him he should be ashamed for the way he treated his soon-to-be ex-wife, Millie. Chaplin sends a nasty note back. Louie ignores the note, so Chaplin struts over to Louie and pokes him a good one that bounces off Louie like water off a duck's back, if you'll permit me to coin a cliché. . . . Big mistake, because Louie doesn't hesitate to haul off and deck Chaplin with a single blow that put out the little tramp's lights for five minutes or an hour, depending on who's reciting the story. No lost love there, to this day. Louie thinks Chaplin's a fucking Communist, so that keeps the pot boiling." He helped himself to my glass of water. "So, what brought the two of you together and here today? Romance in the air?"

Nancy seemed stuck for an answer.

I said, "She helped me and the studio out with a couple of sketches we needed. I thought Sunday at Hillcrest would be a nice payback for her services."

"Okay, then," Selznick said. "Be sure to try the kugel, it's particularly wonderful today." Rising, he patted Nancy on top of the head, reminded her, "Meeting tomorrow. Don't be late with the brilliant sketches

I expect to see," and drifted back to his table.

"Gone with the Windbag," I said when he was out of earshot.

About an hour and a half later, the brunch crowd had dissipated to barely a dozen couples, including the Mayers and the Selznicks, and the round table bunch was down to Cantor and Jessel. Nancy and I had spent the previous sixty minutes in an empty meeting room, Nancy playing off the descriptions I fed her with decisive strokes of her black and white charcoal pencils, displaying all the assuredness of a Norman Rockwell.

The results were — how better to say it than *picture perfect.*

I had concentrated on three faces in the Rothman photos that made the strongest impression on me, one because of the fat, pink dueling scar ripping across his cheek like a pipeline and a drooping mouth that limited him to a grotesque, gray-lipped half-smile, another by the ill-fitting Boy Scout leader's uniform he wore, the brown shirt full of merit badges at odds with the fact he was on crutches and lacked a leg.

The third sketch captured a face that looked like a younger version of the son of a bitch who had run away with my wife. I did a double-take when I spotted him last week at the home of George Cukor, where I planned on heading next.

It didn't work out that way.

Outside, waiting for the parking boy to bring around her car, Nancy and I traded awkward small talk, me kidding on the square about doing something like this again, she answering with the kind of *anything's possible* answer that sounded more like *anything's possible, but not this.* Her handshake was similarly ambivalent before she slid in behind the wheel and tooled off, leaving my dream romance in her dust.

I was about to surrender my parking ticket to the boy when a Mercedes eased up the circular drive honking its horn. The passenger side window lowered and Karl Mueller leaned out, motioning me over.

At the same time, Popeye gripped my shoulder from behind. "Don't try anything stupid, or I plant a bullet in your back and then I shoot the kid," he said, sounding far too happy about the possibility.

"I'm not packing," I said, starting forward. True, sort of. My shoulder rig and the .38 were in my glove compartment, and I felt no need to tell him my pocket .32 backup was strapped to my ankle.

"Chris! Chris Blanchard!"

I recognized the accent and froze.

Louis B. Mayer huffed and puffed over. He gave Popeye a polite but meaningless acknowledgment and turned his back on him. Popeye stepped aside and made a case for his gun hand in his jacket pocket while barely inching his head left and right. I visualized the headline:

GUNMAN MOWS DOWN MGM BOSS LOUIS B. MAYER, TWO OTHERS

Mayer said, "I'm glad I caught you before you got away, Chris. I meant to come over earlier, if only to escape for a minute or two from my ungrateful blabbermouth of a son-in-law. If you think he talks like there's a fire sale on words, you should see some of his memos and production notes. They're longer than a novel by Thomas Wolfe and half the time they make as much sense as Goofy from the Walt Disney cartoons."

"What can I do for you, Mr. Mayer? Is there something you need me for now?"

Popeye's expression signaled I was treading dangerously close to a bullet.

Mayer said, "A reminder for you to say something about the Tarzan girl to David for *Gone with the Wind,* only not where or who the idea is from, except for yourself."

"Do you mean go back inside and tell him that?"

Popeye began working his gun out of his pocket.

Mayer said, "No, definitely not now. You saw we got the girls with us in there, so it don't need to be now. Soon, whenever you can squeeze a word in edgewise."

"You can count on me, sir."

"Of course, I can," Mayer said. He gave me a fatherly smile, wheeled around and headed back inside.

Popeye said, "She's a pip, that Maureen O'Sullivan. I see what Mayer sees in her."

"Maybe come back in your next life as a talent scout."

"I'm not through living this one, so get your ass into the car," he said, joining me in the back seat after he'd stripped me of the envelope containing Nancy's three sketches and handed it over to Mueller.

We traveled in silence, except for a hissed *Shut up!* from Popeye whenever I asked a question, sometimes expressed as *Shut your mouth!* or *Shut your trap!,* other times as *Shut the fuck up!* They were easy questions, along the lines of *Where are we going?* and *Is Hartmann waiting for us?,* so I didn't test him with the tough ones, like *How'd you know where to find me?*

Mueller remained an inanimate silent object except when he took a gander at the sketches and grunted. Once. Twice. Three times.

"Anyone you recognize?" I said.

"Shut the fuck up!"

"That's his line," I said, indicating Popeye.

"Shut the fuck up!" Popeye said.

"See, Mueller, I told ya."

The driver, who resembled everybody's Uncle Joe the Accountant, had stolen glances at the sketches and now volunteered, "They're pretty jake, Karl, especially the one of poor Christian."

"Shut the fuck up!" Mueller said.

I said, "Which one is poor Christian?"

"Shut the fuck up!" Popeye said.

Uncle Joe the Accountant took the hint and remained silent for the rest of the trip up to Sunset Boulevard, then east past long stretches of undeveloped acreage into Pacific Palisades and north onto a winding canyon road, easy to miss if you weren't looking for it, that ended at a rustic ranch house in a virtual forest of towering trees — home to Will Rogers until three years ago, when the idolized entertainer was killed in a plane crash at Barrow, Alaska.

The two-hundred-acre spread included a barn, stables, an oval riding ring, a small golf course, hiking and riding trails that led to awe-inspiring views of the ocean and the mountains and what, it turns out, was our destination — the only regulation-size outdoor polo field in Los Angeles County.

I'd been here before, when one of our insecure stars intended to mount up for the all-star polo match that punctuated Sundays and drew a mixed crowd of industry people and who we referred to as "civilians," star-gawkers and actual fans of polo, many from the growing British population infiltrating L.A., who could tell you what a chukka was.

Gable and Tracy were polo regulars, their game skills not on par with their acting prowess, but they always managed to hold their own against the likes of Doug Fairbanks, Gary Cooper and Tyrone Power. David Niven was a brighter star than any of them on the field, if not in screen billing, but was too much the politician to ever outplay 20th Century Fox chief Darryl Zanuck, whose industry status was a more powerful weapon than his mallet.

I spotted Zanuck playing today, also Tim Holt and Walt Disney, as the car swung northeast past the grassy knoll, the picnic tables full of spectators, and around to an out-of-the-way, out-of-sight storage barn and pulled to a stop alongside a nondescript wood-paneled station wagon and an older, faded fire-engine red Chevy coupe.

The smell from tall stacks of packaged fertilizer hit me like the front line of the Washington Redskins NFL champs as Popeye guided me inside and around a maze of bundled hay and grain sacks to an open area, where I settled on one of the upended milk bottle cases being used as seats. He took one a few feet across from me, the Colt Police Positive on his lap.

"What now?" I said.

"Shut the fuck up!"

Based on the evidence, Popeye had no future writing dialogue for the screen.

After eight or ten minutes of silence plagued by flies and bees exploring the barn, the creak of floorboards announced company coming. Mueller circled into view followed by Hartmann, who was decked out in breeches, boots, knee guards and a helmet, and wielding a long-handled mallet.

"Mr. Blanchard, how very thoughtful of you to come," Hartmann said, propping up a boot on one of the milk cases. "I have only a few minutes between divisions, so I'll not waste time on gratuitous small talk and get straight to saying what needs to be said."

"Tell me about Eve Whitney. Is she all right?"

"You anticipate me, Mr. Blanchard," he said, swinging the mallet back and forth like he might be planning to use it on me.

"She is as fine as she'll ever be, for right now, all thanks to your exposing Miss MacDaniels as the liar in our midst before we were interrupted yesterday, but first things first. The envelope, Karl."

Mueller handed him the envelope containing Nancy's sketches. Hartmann set aside the mallet and pulled out the first sketch.

Nodded approval.

Did the same with the second and third sketches.

"Excellent representations," he said. "My compliments to your memory and to the girl with the drawing pad and utensils Willy saw you entertaining over lunch at Hillcrest. Miss Nancy Warren, correct?"

"Leave her out of this, Hartmann. She was doing me a favor, that's all. She has no idea what's going on."

"Good for you. There are too many people running around already who know too much." He returned the sketches to Karl and said, "Take care of these."

Mueller whipped out a flip-top lighter and set fire to the first sketch. Watched it begin turning grayish-white before releasing it to drift away. Repeated the process with the two other sketches. Was rewarded by Hartmann with a smile of approval.

"Now, then, I'm guessing you resorted to sketches because the photographs and negatives remain with that Jew criminal Siegel?"

"Yes."

"I've given the matter a great deal of thought, Mr. Blanchard. Your warning about the kike and his mistress whore yesterday continued to resonate overnight, and that's why I chose to meet with you today rather than chase after her. You said you were a boyhood friend and acting as Siegel's watchdog, fine. I'm leaving it to you to acquire the negatives and photos for me on terms no worse than the Jew's asking price of two hundred and fifty thousand dollars, and I'm giving you forty-eight hours to bring them to me."

"And if Siegel won't part with them at that price?"

"Eve Whitney, not the Jew's whore, will suffer the consequences."

"You'd kill her?"

"Of course not . . . I have people to do that for me."

Mueller and Popeye joined him in laughing.

"You're serious."

"Dead serious."

More laughter.

Herbie Duntz picked that moment to materialize, his expression curious about the laughter. "The next division is about to start, Nicky. They're calling for you on the field."

Hartmann said, "In fact, Mr. Blanchard, let me illustrate for you how serious I can be." He snapped his fingers at Mueller.

Mueller revealed the silenced Luger he'd been carrying under his jacket.

He turned on Herbie and fired.

The bullet hit Herbie in the chest and flew him backward into a stack of fertilizer that toppled over and onto him after he had landed face down. A trail of blood oozed out from under him.

Hartmann said, "Well done, Karl," retrieved his mallet and turned to go.

I called after him, "Why, Hartmann?"

He said, "I could recite several reasons, but simply put — along with the kikes and the queers, there is no place for dwarfs in our coming New Order."

"Not a dwarf, a midget, and you're a bastard, Hartmann."

"And you have forty-eight hours, Mr. Blanchard. Forty-eight hours, or you will have our lovely Eve Whitney's death forever on your conscience."

Uncle Joe the Accountant gunned the motor when he saw Popeye guiding me out of the storage barn. Popeye directed me to the front passenger seat of the Mercedes and climbed into the back, making certain I knew he had his gun out, ready to use on me if I tried anything stupid on the return trip to Hillcrest.

"*Kapish?* You get what I'm saying?" Popeye said.

It was all I could do to contain my anger over the murder of Herbie Duntz.

I wanted to go for my .32 ankle gun and put a bullet through him, make Popeye's eye pop for real, then take out Uncle Joe the Accountant, then charge back inside the barn and send Mueller on a slow ride to Hell, then find Hartmann on the polo field and spring a few permanent leaks in him.

"*Kapish.* I may be crazy, but I'm not stupid," I said.

"Shame," Popeye said, and I believed him.

Back at the country club, I waited for the Mercedes to disappear before I charged inside, got pointed to a phone, and dialed Charles Cook. He listened attentively and spent a modest guttural moan when I told him about Herbie.

"Mr. Powell recognized he was playing a most dangerous game," Cook said, "but he played it well, right up to the end."

"I don't consider getting shot and killed playing the game, Agent Cook."

"You certainly have made an excellent point there," he said, like he was reciting from an Emily Post book on pro forma FBI responses for all occasions.

"What are you going to do about it?"

"Dispatch a team to the Will Rogers ranch and investigate, of course."

"And arrest the bastards responsible?"

"Remains to be seen, Mr. Blanchard. It depends on what we find."

"Besides Herbie Duntz's dead body, you mean?"

"Wars don't end with the death of a single soldier, Mr. Blanchard. We still have bigger fish to fry."

"First you have to catch them," I said, and banged down the receiver.

There wasn't much of a crowd left at George Cukor's home by the time I got there, maybe a half dozen lounging around the pool, taking in what little sunshine remained of the day, while a dozen more guests were scattered inside, chattering away as houseboys cleaned up around them.

Cukor was holding court in the bar area, drawing laughter from a small circle that included one face I recognized, Ramon Novarro, the silent screen idol whose great claims to fame were the title role in *Ben-Hur* and, later, opposite Garbo in *Mata Hari*. There was a running gag at MGM, how the studio had trouble originally deciding whether Novarro should play "Ben" or "Her," so wound up casting him in both roles. He was approaching forty, but still hypnotically handsome and throwing off a giant allure far taller than his modest height.

Cukor noticed me, excused himself and rushed over. "Mr. Blanchard, to what do I owe this unexpected treat? Another sketch for me to peruse?"

"Not this time."

"Excellent. You just missed Billy Haines, who had lovely things to say about his meeting with you."

"Thank you for getting us together, Mr. Cukor. Mr. Haines was a great help, and now I'm hoping you can direct me to someone else."

"It's what I do for a living," he said, breaking out a smile and making a sweeping gesture with his Pall Mall.

"Have you ever had a Christian among your guests?" I said, hoping to pin down an ID on the person Uncle Joe the Accountant had mentioned by name when he looked over Nancy's three sketches.

"Dear boy, whatever else you've heard about me and my social circle, we are not exclusively Jewish." He laughed broadly to make certain I recognized the joke.

"It could be the name of a fellow I noticed when I was here last time," I said, and described the guy who resembled a younger version of the poor sap who thought he was getting a bargain when he stole my wife.

Cukor thought about it. "Your description fits no one I would call one of my regular guests, but he could be any one of a number of the twilight men and boys who wander in and out on somebody's arm." He gave it more thought, shook his head. "No, sorry, now excuse me, please, while I return to those of my guests who refuse to leave until the very last, fearing they'll otherwise quickly become the subject of tawdry gossip, as surely they would." He guffawed and danced off, but almost at once did an about-face and returned. "Describe this young man for me once more, will you?"

I described him.

Cukor made a clucking sound. "Before,

you didn't mention the port-wine stain on the lad's upper jaw."

"I didn't?"

"No, or I certainly would have remembered — and remembered the person you're asking about. For a very good reason you'll understand immediately, Mr. Blanchard. The first time, twice, in fact, he was accompanied by the late Mr. Covington. As monkey bait, I suspect."

"Day Covington?"

"Is there another? Times after that he came with Baxter Leeds, although last week he showed up alone."

"Baxter Leeds has been to your Sunday gatherings?"

"Come, come, Mr. Blanchard, you sound surprised. If you didn't know before this, now you can appreciate how convincing an actor Baxter Leeds is off the screen as well as on the screen, but not the Rhett Butler he fancies himself to be." He let the news settle in. "Something else to know — the lad introduces himself as Jeff or Jeffrey, not Christian, and that's an excellent hairpiece on him, so he may be older than he appears."

CHAPTER 22

Monday, November 21, 1938

The *Battling G-Men* set was between takes, Hal Bucquet running a camera setup with Johnny Seitz and calling out lighting cues, when I slipped onto the soundstage and went looking for Baxter Leeds. I found him in a corner, engaged in a game of chess with the picture's principal bad guy, Joe Calleia, who responded to a cautious move by Leeds quickly and aggressively, declared, "Checkmate!" and bared a triumphant smile.

George Zucco, who had been bent over Joe's shoulder observing, could not resist teasing Leeds. "Goodness, gracious, Baxter, until now I thought the hero always emerged triumphant."

Joe said, "We Maltese are not prepared to lose, ever, George. Ask the Turks, you don't want to take my word."

"The Turks? Ancient history. Joe, my good man, your tight little island's war with the

Turks was over three hundred years ago."

"So, ask Baxter, then. How many times have I defeated you so far, Baxter? I lost count after sixteen, or was it seventeen?"

Leeds got up from the table, fished out a handful of change from the coin pocket of his trousers, plucked out a quarter, and dropped it onto the game board. "Here's your victory, Joe. Now you're a four-bit actor," he said, and stalked off.

I caught up with him "Baxter, we need to talk."

"Fucking Calleia. The only Maltese actor in the business. Thinks that makes him special. And Zucco, with that holy-holy Brit accent — this is the first and last picture he's ever going to do with me, I have anything to say about it."

"Serious conversation, Baxter."

He said, "I'm not up for any serious conversation right this minute, buddy," and picked up the pace.

I called after him, "It's about Jeffrey."

He stopped so fast he almost tripped over his heels. Turned. Locked his arms and challenged me with a look. "Jeffrey? Jeffrey who?"

I joined him. "How many Jeffreys do you know?"

"Buddy, I don't know anybody by that name."

"What name *do* you know him by, Baxter?"

Leeds tried to read my eyes. I helped him out. "I mean your friend from Sundays at George Cukor's place, that Jeffrey." His face turned the color of a Moscow winter. He swished looks over his shoulders, imploring me, "For shit's sake, buddy. Will you please lower your voice?" He threw an arm across my back and steered us to an empty section of the soundstage. "You out to ruin my career, like it happened for Billy Haines and some others? I thought you were my friend, buddy. Nobody's supposed to know about me ever being at Cukor's. Strickling promised me personally it would never leak. Jesus, Hedda or Parsons to print that, Mayer would have me on the first train out of town."

"Definitely not my intention, Baxter. I heard something that ties him to the death of Day Covington. He might know something that'll help get Marie off the hot seat."

"That's it?"

"What else could it be?" It could be Leeds's connection through Jeffrey to Nicky Hartmann, of course, but I was saving that for later.

"No, nothing. Fine. Now I understand, buddy." His words stopped traveling like the Twentieth Century Limited. "And I can trust your discretion?"

"Scout's honor," I said, and gave him the Boy Scout sign, about the only thing I'd mastered in the two weeks before the Scoutmaster sent me home with instructions never to come back. I hadn't meant to break Dickie Russo's jaw, but he had no business saying what he did about my mother, the little prick.

Leeds said, "I'll be honest with you, buddy. He was another trick in my life and that's all. He caught my eye one Sunday and one Sunday led to another and a few more before I moved on. Last time I noticed him, he was licking dick underwater in George's pool. Not mine. Okay, so now you know what I know."

"Still could use a last name and where I can find him, Baxter."

"He told me it was Jeffries, that his folks decided calling him Jeffrey would make him stand out in the crowd. Jeffrey Jeffries. We'd meet at George's and later he'd trail me to the California, an out-of-the-way, no-questions-asked hotel across from Westlake Park. Wham, bam and goodbye." I refrained from telling Leeds he was as good a liar as he was an actor. "You want to know one more thing, buddy? It wasn't until we were breaking up that that spiteful tramp confessed he'd never once seen any of my pictures."

First thing when I got to my office, I phoned the Department of Motor Vehicles and asked for a department manager whose fifteen-year-old son I once extricated from a felony situation that could have landed him on trial as an adult. The way I saw it, the kid was only guilty of hanging out with the wrong people, but that was by my alphabet, not by the letter of the law. He deserved a second chance and a fresh start, not enough years to put him back on the street as a hard-case criminal.

I opened the conversation with a question, "How's Peter doing, Andy?"

"About to graduate Stanford with honors, and he's been accepted by Harvard Law, Chris, all because of you and what you saw in him. I'll never be able to repay you for that in my lifetime."

"I didn't put a price tag on it, Andy, but maybe there's something you could do for me now, a favor."

"Not a favor, Chris. A privilege."

"I need the address that goes with a name

— Jeffrey Jeffries."

"Don't go anywhere." He was back in five. "If he has a driving license, it's not on our books, Chris. Nothing even close."

I played a hunch with the name Uncle Joe the Accountant had said. "How about Jeffrey Christian? Try that, please."

Five minutes later, Andy blew an appreciative whistle in my ear and said, "You got a winner this time, Chris. It doesn't get much ritzier than Windsor Square."

I made him repeat the address, to be sure I'd heard him right the first time.

And because my memory was telling me I knew the house.

Baxter Leeds lived there.

The two-story Tudor-style home was on Irving Boulevard between Wilshire and Sixth, set back from a street lined with tall, wind-bent trees and fancy automobiles. I had been inside twice, both times for the same reason, after Leeds got rubber-legged, potty-mouth, pass-out drunk at end-of-shoot set parties for *Battling G-Men in New Orleans* and *Battling G-Men in Paris*. I was delegated to maneuver him the hell home while Strickling guided the invited Hollywood press heavyweights to interviews with Marie MacDaniels and Eve Whitney over tall drinks, jumbo shrimps and other tempting hors d'oeuvres.

The house was among the most impressive on both sides of the block, but inside it gave truth to the whisper that Leeds, cash poor after investing in a public showcase that suited his oversized ego, filled the place with furniture borrowed from the MGM warehouse. In fact, only three or four of the rooms were furnished, the others empty and collecting dust, something I discovered on a quick tour after the first time I maneuvered Leeds upstairs to the master bedroom and struggled loading him onto a classic, king-sized four-poster that made me think of *Dinner at Eight.*

Big Ben chimed when I pressed the doorbell and waited hat in hand for somebody to respond. The door window opened a minute or two after my second try and I could feel myself being studied before a disembodied man's voice said, "Didn't you see the sign out front on the gate, by the mailbox, mister? It says *No salesmen or peddlers.*"

"An excellent policy," I said, "but I don't fit either category."

"How so?"

"I'm from the studio, delivering a package for Mr. Leeds."

"Nice try, friend, but Mr. Leeds is at the studio right now."

"I'm delivering a package *from* Mr. Leeds *for* Mr. Christian. Is that better, or are you going to tell me Mr. Christian is on Pitcairn Island?"

"I'm not going to tell you how many times I've heard that gag since *Mutiny on the Bounty*," he said, opening the door. "C'mon in."

I stepped inside, for a few seconds uncertain whether I'd found my ex-wife's son of a bitch, because of his bald head, until I flashed on George Cukor's notion that Jeffrey might wear a hairpiece. He wasn't naturally bald. There was a darker coloration to areas where he had shaved off what remained of hair. He looked ten or twelve years older than the face I saw in the Rothman photo and described to Nancy Warren. He was taller and bulkier than the photo suggested, his voice deeper than I would have guessed, but it was Jeffrey all right, down to the port-wine stain, wearing a hand-tailored silk Chinese lounging robe over ink-black silk pajamas.

He closed and locked the door and, turning back to me, said, "So?"

"So?"

He held out a hand. "So, where's the

package from Mr. Leeds?"

"Oh, yes, that. I'm the package."

"What's that supposed to mean?"

"It means I little white fibbed you," I said, drawing out my .38. "I could've said I was the Fuller Brush Man, but that would have done me no good. Same for a Jehovah's Witness. You don't look like you'd get anything out of reading the *Watch Tower*."

"Who are you? How did you know my name?"

"I came for answers, not questions, Mr. Christian."

"That gun makes me nervous."

"No answers and it could make you dead."

"Like what? What kind of answers?"

"Are you and Baxter Leeds lovers?"

"I can't say. Baxter would kill me if he learned I said anything." I cocked the .38. "Oh, yes, well, all right, okay, yes we are."

"How long?" Christian gave me a funny look, like he wasn't sure how I meant the question. "How long have you been lovers?"

"Oh. Months."

"How'd you meet?"

"We were introduced at a social gathering. Can we sit down somewhere?"

I had him lead me into the living room. Motioned Christian to take one of the mismatched armchairs sagging from frequent use and settled into the one across from him that faced the hallway entrance.

"Tell me about the social gathering."

"At the home of a wonderful and important director, George Cukor. I was taken there by a friend on this particular Sunday afternoon. I was hoping to be discovered for the movies and I found love instead."

"Who was the friend?"

"An actor. He's recently deceased."

"But I'm guessing still alive when he took you there. Did he have a name?"

"Covington. Day Covington."

"Covington, yeah. I've heard people say he gave acting a bad name."

"Given the right role in a movie that matched his talent, he'd've proven all of them wrong."

"Was Covington your boyfriend at the time?"

"Not really my boyfriend."

"What then?"

"A benefactor out to do me a good turn. I met him through a photographer who is also deceased now."

"Mr. Christian, you're beginning to sound like an advance man for Forest Lawn."

Christian made a sour face and turned it on me. "A fine gentleman, Otto Rothman. Before his untimely death, Mr. Rothman had been using me regularly in his assignments for magazines like *Touring Topics,* the Automobile Club magazine."

"And maybe using you for his private French postcards? Sex stuff, maybe?"

"What a horrible thing to suggest. No. Absolutely not. I'm not that kind of a boy. Besides, I don't talk French."

"Nicky Hartmann. What can you tell me about him?"

"Nicky Hartmann? I don't know any Nicky Hartmann."

"How do you explain being in one of the photos Otto Rothman took for him?"

"You think I knew all of his clients he was taking pictures for? I did not, so there's your answer. When Mr. Rothman phoned, he told me where and when to show up, what I should wear, and how much the job would pay."

"What would you say if I told you Hartmann was a good friend of your boyfriend Baxter?"

"Baxter doesn't introduce me to his friends, ever, except for some we bump into at George Cukor's."

"What would you say if I told you the pictures ordered by Nicky Hartmann were for the German American Bund and that your boyfriend Baxter is also part of that

400

Nazi-loving collection of miscreants?"

He broke out an arrogant grin and aimed it past me. "I'd say it's about time you showed your face, darling."

Turning, I saw Baxter Leeds in the seconds before he brought down on my skull the butt of a Luger he had gripped by the barrel and was using as a club.

I roused chilled to the bone, unsure where I was or how long I'd been out, bound hand and foot to a chair by thick hemp digging hard into me. A dim bulb dangled from a high ceiling, sending out enough light to reveal concrete walls that suggested this was a cellar. The back of my head ached where I had been clubbed and my eyes had to work at keeping focus, maybe because of a mild concussion.

Maybe worse than mild?

And my nose itched.

And I couldn't do anything about it, because of the damn hemp.

I replayed my conversation with Christian, gave him points for staying calm in the face of my .38 and tough guy approach. Not tough enough, maybe? He'd sucker-punched me with his fairy attitude, bought time stretching out his answers until Leeds came riding to his rescue, before I could get him to spill about Leeds's connection to Hartmann and the German American Bund.

Maybe an hour passed before footsteps that sounded like they were descending a stairway grew louder and became moving shadows that materialized as Jeffrey Christian and Baxter Leeds, in lockstep and holding hands, while Nicky Hartmann trailed them by several steps.

Leeds, still in his *Battling G-Men* costume, said, "I suspected you might go and try something like this, buddy, so I got right on the phone to warn Jeffrey and let Nicky know. . . . See, Nicky, I told you you'd always be able to count on me."

"Never in doubt, my good man, never in doubt," Hartmann said. He had traded in yesterday's polo outfit for a sweater and casual slacks, while Christian had his hairpiece in place and was dressed like a page out of *Esquire.* "But you, Mr. Blanchard, shame on you, playing Nosey Parker instead of more wisely applying the forty-eight hours I gave you to making my deal with your Yid friend Siegel."

"In the third place, I was curious."

"Haven't you heard? Curiosity killed the cat."

"With you people, I heard it was Katz who

got killed. And Mrs. Katz."

"One day your ugly mouth will get you in serious trouble, Mr. Blanchard."

"What do you call this?"

"I haven't made up my mind yet. You said *In the third place.* What was in the first place and in the second place?"

"In the first place, I talked to Ben Siegel before heading over. In the second place, he's agreed to make the exchange tomorrow night."

"Tomorrow night is past forty-eight hours, Mr. Blanchard."

"You called the terms, Ben Siegel is calling the play. You want to argue, you can take it up with Benny. Be my guest. I know better."

Hartmann waved it off. "You're saying he agreed to accept two hundred and fifty thousand dollars for the negatives and photographs?"

"Yes."

"*All* the negatives and photographs?"

"Everything. A one-time-only transaction."

"Where do we meet for the exchange?"

"Downtown. Olympic Auditorium. Henry Armstrong is heading the card, and it's a fight Benny doesn't want to miss. Armstrong and Chalky Wright. And one other thing:

It's not *we,* it's *me.* Benny is expecting me to personally make the delivery or it's a no-go."

Inventing as I went along.

Siegel was a regular at the Olympic and the Hollywood Legion, especially for the big bouts, where he'd bet and win big time, like he'd known going in how the score cards would add up.

Everything else I said — buying time.

"Pushy, like every Jew I've ever met," Hartmann said, shaking his head. "His day will come, along with all the rest of them, isn't that so, Baxter?"

"If you mean like Mayer and Thalberg, others who have stood in the way and kept me from achieving the kind of stardom I deserve, yes, absolutely," Leeds said, rocking a clenched fist. "Commies, the lot of them."

"Your reward, I guarantee you, once we're running the show."

Leeds beamed, like he'd just won Boardwalk and Park Place.

"Nobody deserves it more," Christian said, embracing him.

I said, "Hartmann, I recall you mentioning there'd be no place in your New Order for fairies and other misfits."

Leeds and Christian looked at Hartmann aghast.

He answered them with a smile that turned sour on me. "You genuinely are one for stirring up trouble with your nasty lies, Mr. Blanchard." Stepping closer, he slapped me on the cheek, then reversed direction and caught the other cheek with the back of his hand, setting off a ringing in my ears. "There's your answer, gentlemen, if he raised any doubts that our victory will serve all who join with us now, not later, when we will have triumphed."

I struggled against giving him the pleasure of seeing my pain and said, "There's one more thing you should know. I want Eve with me when I head downtown to make the exchange with Benny."

He snorted, dismissed the idea with a gesture. "Afterward. Once everything has gone well and I've examined the merchandise, Eve will be returned to you in excellent condition."

"Speaking of liars, why should I believe you?"

"Consider the alternative."

"Not good enough. I'm making the delivery. Eve is my tip."

Hartmann studied me for the bluff, gulped down a gallon of dusty air and blew it loose.

"Well, then, Mr. Blanchard, you will have the pleasure of her company tomorrow night, but you'll stay Baxter's guest here until it's time to leave. I'm sure you understand I can't have you running around, making more mischief. . . . Anything else?"

"My damn nose needs scratching," I said, and flashed him a grin.

The three of them left.

Maybe an hour passed, every minute adding to the grief my bladder was feeling, before I had company again —

Mueller and Popeye.

Popeye kept a gun on me while Mueller cut me loose, explaining, "Through that door, a toilet. Rollaway's over there. Bag we're leaving got enough food to last you until next time. You're a damn nuisance. Up to me, I'd kill you and dance on your grave."

"You strike me as more the marching type, Mueller."

"Wait and see," he said, sounding like he knew something I didn't want to know about the future Hartmann was fitting me for, which was no future at all.

I didn't need his help.

I'd already sized that up without any prompting from Mueller, anticipating a last scene that didn't end with me living happily ever after. It would have to come sometime soon after I traded Siegel the money for the photos, which wouldn't necessarily be at the Olympic tomorrow night.

First things first —

I needed to figure my way out of here, connect with Siegel and convince him the deal I'd invented on his behalf was one he could live with.

Me, too.

CHAPTER 23

Tuesday, November 22, 1938

Sometime after midnight, the creaking stairs half-awakened me from a troubled sleep and seeing it was Eve took me the rest of the way. She tiptoed over to the rollaway and gave me a gentle nudge. "You awake, Chris?"

The poor lighting softened the black eye and bruises the Bund beasts had inflicted on her last Friday. A bandage covered her swollen nose. Her lips rested crookedly on her face and distorted her voice. It would take a miracle of makeup to allow her in front of a movie camera anytime soon.

I rolled into a sitting position. She settled alongside me, understood my look, and cuddled my face in her hands. "It's not all that bad, kiddo," she said. "You saved my life, so that says something."

"Not enough, Evie. This mess never should have involved you."

"It wasn't my idea or yours, but it is what it is. Where do we go from here?"

I told her about the deal I'd cooked up, how she'd be going with me tonight to the Olympic. I left out the rest of it, how my arrival would be a big surprise for Siegel — if he was there — and how I expected Hartmann to make short work of us afterward.

She was no dummy.

"All this trouble because of some cheesy blackmail business?" she said, adjusting the Peter Pan collar and buttons of a bland housedress that further disrupted her glamour girl persona. " 'Fess up, Chris. You know better than ever to kid a kidder, especially when the kidder's me, not to mention that Nicky Hartmann didn't exactly turn out to be the man of my dreams, did he?"

I couldn't bring myself to try a line on her under current circumstance.

"Not unless the man of your dreams was a Nazi shitheel," I said, and spelled out my history with Hartmann, how the murders of Covington and Rothman figured in, about Marie and Herbie Duntz, about Benny Siegel. I said, "He romanced you like a conduit, to get close to people who could do him or his phony-baloney cause some good, like Baxter Leeds."

"Ouch," she said. "Never once did I suspect Nicky was screwing me while he was screwing me. Or Baxter screwing me by never screwing me and ending my perfect record with leading men. I could never pull him into my trailer for a quickie, and I tried, so help me, I tried. I never even suspected he was goose-stepping to a different drummer."

Eve rambled on like that for a few more minutes, using sex grounded in humor as a cover for the fear she had to be feeling, before she admitted as much. "You and me, we know too much. We're excess baggage, dead pigeons once they don't need you anymore, right, Chris?"

See?

She was no dummy.

I stumbled through an answer that was unconvincing, even to me, but it made her laugh. She stroked my hair appreciatively and added a little sister kiss of appreciation that nicked the side of my mouth.

"Funny," she said, "how there's always been more'n that available to you, going all the way back to Echo Park. When was that, Detective Blanchard?"

"Five, six years ago. You were in over your head then, still a teenager, celebrating your option pick-up the wrong way, the booze and the Benzedrine sending out the wrong message."

"Five, six . . . yeah. The rest of it —" she shook her head "—I was only nineteen, but already a not-so-choosy-floozy, if you want the truth. I liked the boys and the boys liked me, so if you rescued me from anybody, it wasn't necessarily those horny boys in blue, it was from me, myself, and I. I still do, but I don't have to tell you that part."

"Save it for when you graduate to the important movies, maybe surprise yourself by winning an Academy Award, finally believe in yourself and your talent the way a lot of others already do."

"If I live that long, you mean. Besides, the new kid on the lot's no longer me. It's Turner. Lana, she's a peach, but she's a younger, blonder, bigger-titted version of yours truly. She's got Billy Wilkerson from the *Hollywood Reporter* pulling favors for her with the bigwigs, Strickling pumping up a fake glamour history, calling her *The Sweater Girl* and how Lana was discovered by Wilkerson sipping a soda at a drugstore counter. She's stolen my reputation for inviting into my dressing room any gent around in tight pants and muscles bulging in all the right places, no difference whether they're stagehands or stars. . . . Well, that part's true, anyway . . ."

"My money's on you, Evie."

"Don't go crazy, Chris. Anytime you want it, it's yours for nothing," she said. "So, anyway, tell me true — is tonight the end of the line for bright-eyed and bubbly Miss Eve, the starlet harlot herself?"

Before I could manufacture an answer, she closed her eyes and fell asleep nesting against my shoulder. A good thing. My eternal optimism understood a hopeless situation, and this situation was definitely hopeless.

For now.

Any chance she and I had for escaping the inevitable would need to come at the Olympic, not here, us fighting for our lives while Henry Armstrong and Chalky Wright batted each other's brains out in the ring.

Exhausted, I eased myself away from Eve, gently guided her onto the rollaway, covered her with one of the horse blankets, took the other one for myself, settled on the floor beside her, and was asleep within minutes.

Shortly past six in the evening, Popeye woke me up by toe-tapping my sick ribs and said, "Time to rise and shine, make yourself presentable, so we can be on our way."

I'd slept away the day.

Mueller, standing guard a few feet from me, said, "And be quick about it. We're late enough as it is."

I tossed aside the blanket and pulled onto my feet.

The rollaway was empty.

I said, "Where's Eve?"

"Don't worry about her."

"I'll worry about who I want to worry about. Where is she?"

"I'd be more worried about myself, I was you," Popeye said.

"Unfortunately, the best you can ever aspire to is yourself. Where is she?"

"All present and accounted for," Eve said, stepping out of the toilet and pushing the door shut. Hearing what I perceived as a smile in her voice was enough to settle my nerves. "Takes a girl longer than it does a man to get herself ready for an evening on the town, Mr. Blanchard. I thought you'd appreciate that by now."

She looked spiffy, wearing men's clothing the way Dietrich had started a trend by doing, only a looser fit, everything in white, the shirt and the tie, baggy slacks with rolled cuffs, a tapered blazer, even shoes; her hair piled high on her head under a raffish beret. It was an outfit that drew attention from the tan created by a layer or two of makeup she had lathered on to disguise all the facial bruises. Thick-framed dark glasses hid the damage to her eyes.

"What do you think?" she said, striking a few poses. "All from the sissy G-Man's well-stocked closet and his array of Max Factor pan-cake. The perfume is stronger than I like, but what's a girl to do under these circumstances?"

"It beats the smell these altar boys brought with them," I said, nodding approval as I headed for the toilet, pausing to give her a wink and a friendly poke on the arm.

"A-men to that, brother," she said. "A-men."

"Nicky, he is already at the Olympic, waiting for us," Mueller said, answering my question. We were heading downtown, Uncle Joe the Accountant behind the wheel of the Mercedes, Mueller in the passenger seat, Eve and I in the back seat with Popeye.

"And Hartmann has the money with him, the two hundred and fifty grand?"

"Of course, all nicely and neatly packaged in a briefcase. After I get the high-sign from him, we drop off you and the girl. She will wait with Nicky in the auditorium lobby while you locate the Jew and bring him.

Nicky will inspect the negatives and the photos and, once he is satisfied, he will hand over the briefcase. Presently, you and the girl will be set free with nothing more to fear from us."

I believed that, right up there with Santa Claus, the Easter Bunny and the Tooth Fairy. "Where will you and your playmates be while all this is happening?" I said.

"Let's just say, enjoying a frankfurter and a cold beer."

Sure, with Santa Claus, the Easter Bunny and the Tooth Fairy.

"Let's just say, what if Siegel wants to see the money before he lets loose of the negatives and photographs, not the other way around?" I said.

"Let's just say, I would urge you to convince him otherwise. Nicky is not one to change his horses mid-stream."

"And if Hartmann's not satisfied? If Siegel doesn't have the negatives and photos on him?"

"That would be immediately unfortunate, for you and the girl, as well as for the Jew," Mueller said, and let it go at that.

So did I.

I used the rest of the ride trying to figure my way out of the situation, imagining myself in a cliffhanger, same as I'd done a few days ago, only this time *Continued Next Week* was *Continued Now.*

What would Dick Tracy do?

Or Flash Gordon?

Or The Lone Ranger?

Better —

Spy Smasher.

What would Spy Smasher do to rescue himself and the fair damsel in distress as the ceiling slowly lowered to the floor, the clock ticked away the last seconds before the bomb exploded, the train derailed and plunged off the suspension bridge into the murky waters below, the airplane's engines burst and the plane went into a tailspin, the . . .

What else?

What next?

What now?

The Olympic Auditorium, built in '32 for the Summer Olympic Games, was a tall concrete fortress that covered most of a city block at Eighteenth and Grand and, after the Games, had been transformed into the country's largest indoor arena, pulling in capacity crowds for some of the most important boxing matches staged anywhere.

Tonight's card headed by reigning feather-weight champion Henry Armstrong and

Chalky Wright, a major contender for the crown, was expected to fill all fifteen thousand seats. Wright was a local kid, the pride of the Mexican community, and Armstrong was a popular favorite, who had not fought locally since March, when he beat Baby Arizmendi on points.

There'd be the usual turnout of celebrities, a mix of legitimate fight fans and the famous faces who knew these events drew gossip column mentions and their pictures in the fan magazines, guaranteed first call on the best ringside seats by the Olympic's fight card promoter, Tom Gallery, a former silent screen star and the ex-husband of Zasu Pitts, the screen comedienne with the saucer-sized eyes in a state of constant wonderment.

He was a good egg to deal with, as I had many times for the likes of Bob Taylor, the Barrymore brothers, Spencer Tracy, Gable and Wally Beery, who used the occasions to remind the fans he had starred in *The Champ*, a title role that brought him an Academy Award as Best Actor, tied with Freddie March, who'd played both halves of *Dr. Jekyll and Mr. Hyde.* (Actually, what I heard inside the studio walls — Beery had trailed March by a vote or two in the final count, but when Strickling heard this, he made a few calls and a few promises to the right people and that was that.)

Street and lot parking was impossible by the time we got there, by my reckoning about halfway through the preliminary bouts leading up to the main event. The sidewalk was empty, except for a dozen or so late arrivals racing for the entrance doors, the usual congregation of ticket scalpers, souvenir hawkers, and panhandlers, beat cops relaxing over smokes and jokes, and Nicky Hartmann.

He was standing at the corner, curbside, clutching the briefcase and doing an edgy dance. When he spotted the Mercedes, he waved the car over.

"Did Karl explain how this will work?" Hartmann said, as Eve and I stepped out.

"Every detail, right down to the sharp-shooters who'll have us in their sights from start to finish," I said.

Hartmann flinched and threw a nasty look at Mueller, whose head was swinging like all the neck screws had come loose. "No, not true, Nicky," Mueller said. "I spoke not a word about that."

Hartmann managed a laugh. "Mr. Blanchard, I have the greatest respect for your macabre sense of humor."

"Tell me that tomorrow."

He laughed again. "Shall we be on our way?"

"What if I say no?"

He shrugged. "Then tomorrow never comes."

One of the street bums had shuffled up behind Hartmann and tapped him on the shoulder. "Buddy, spare the price of a meal?" he said, his voice sandpaper on stone. "I ain't had nothing in my belly going on two days."

Hartmann fooled me by digging into his pocket and coming up with a few coins, which he blindly handed over to the bum, who appeared equally surprised by Hartmann's generosity. "God bless you," he said, and turning to Eve before he hurried off, "And God bless you, too, Miss Dietrich."

Hartmann handed over three tickets to the swarthy doorman, whose flattened nose and cauliflower ears illustrated an earlier career inside the ring, and we were directed to a two-lane stairway leading to the cheap balcony seats.

"Here's where we'll be waiting for you," Hartmann said, stopping halfway there, at a long wooden bench near an exit door and a wall lined with framed posters hawking boxing attractions dating back a dozen years and battlers like Newsboy Brown, Sammy Shack, Frankie Grandetta, and Young Nationalista. He motioned Eve to sit and sat down beside her with the briefcase parked on his lap.

I headed for one of the doors leading into the ground-level seats.

The guard there, another boxing wreck, said in a thick European accent, "Your ticket takes you to upstairs, not through here."

I smiled and said, "I'm supposed to meet Mr. Siegel here."

"Mr. Benjamin Siegel, him?"

"Him."

"You're welcome, go ahead," he said, stepping aside. "You tell him Zaslavsky, he sends hello. That's me, Zaslavsky."

"Can you point out where he's sitting, Mr. Zaslavsky?"

"I don't see him come in tonight, Mr. Benjamin Siegel, so, no."

Maybe Siegel wasn't here tonight?

Jesus!

I didn't know if that was good news or bad news made worse.

The noise level and the nose-punishing sweat stink overtook the hanging aroma of hot dogs and mustard, cigars, cigarettes and spilled beer as I passed into the smoke-filled auditorium and headed down toward the ringside seats. Two middleweights were toe-to-toe in the center of the ring, bloodying the canvas in a furious exchange of punches that drew roars of approval from the crowd. The bell clanged, ending the six-round bout, but they kept pounding away until the ref managed to squeeze between them and elbow them back to their corners.

The crowd was on its feet, screaming support for one or the other boxer while the judges' ballots were collected and counted, making it tougher for me to scout the ringside for Siegel.

I spotted Jolson and Ruby Keeler hobnobbing with Eddie Cantor.

Bob Taylor with his latest flame, Barbara Stanwyck.

Johnny Weissmuller squandering hugs and kisses on his hot-tempered wife, Lupe Velez, leading me to wonder if Strickling had sent our Tarzan here to pour water on the rumor, however true, that he and Lupe were on the verge of a divorce, a truth that might dethrone the King of the Jungle at the box office.

A number of familiar faces belonged to local politicians and civic leaders, several collected around D.A. Davidson, who three days ago had replaced "Two Gun" Davis as

L.A.'s chief of police, pumping Davidson's hand or backslapping congratulations.

The time-keeper made trolley noises with the bell and the ring announcer strode out to announce an unpopular split decision that caused a thunder of hisses and booing and pitched beer bottles and cups. Dozens of unruly types flooded the aisles massing for an attack, but the uprising was quickly halted by uniformed cops who surrounded the ring and locked arms.

Seeing them massed like that rekindled an idea I'd dismissed earlier, but suddenly seemed doable.

Charge down to the nearest cop.

Quickly describe the situation.

Lose myself in the crowd while the cop pulls together a team to charge the lobby, rescue Eve and arrest the bad guys.

The idea definitely made far more sense than shouting *Fire!*

I started on my way, but had barely traveled a dozen steps when Mueller moved out from a row, blocking my way, and said, "Nicky wanted me to remind you not to try anything stupid. We have friends all over the auditorium. One false move and it will be your last move forever."

Maybe Mueller was bluffing, but his presence alone was enough to put a damper on my rekindled idea.

He stepped aside and I resumed moving down through the aisle traffic, which now included one of the boxers on the undercard and his retinue of corner men. He was a tall, muscular Negro kid, who responded to cries of support with a bright smile lacking two or three teeth while pumping air victory-style with his hand-wrapped mitts.

I sensed Mueller tracking my back about the same time I saw George Raft on the other side of the auditorium, trading talk with Mickey Cohen, the mobster sent out here by East Coast bosses Meyer Lansky and Lou Rothkopf to serve as Siegel's lieutenant. I had to believe that Siegel would be with them if he was anywhere in the hall.

I navigated around to them, blanking out the ring introductions and the partisan roars of the crowd while I tested words to satisfactorily explain the situation to my old and unpredictable neighborhood nut case.

Siegel was there, in a front row seat, sucking on a cigar, his arm around Virginia Hill, both dressed to the nines. Spikes was sitting watchdog directly behind them, and a couple of rows back, adding a dash of the surreal to the real, "Little Caesar," Edward G. Robinson, stagging it with his close friend and fellow fine art connoisseur Sam Jaffe.

I glanced over my shoulder.

Mueller had taken an aisle seat alongside Popeye.

Both looked at me stone-faced.

Mueller patted his jacket, a reminder I didn't need that he was packing lead.

Popeye duplicated Mueller's gesture.

"Hey, it's the ex-detective," Mickey Cohen said. "Hey, Benny, see who's here? It's the ex-detective what's now on MGM's pad. So, what's the story, ex? You come on by to make a social call?"

Raft threw me a nod of recognition, which I answered in kind as Siegel lifted out of his seat, stepped over and gave my shoulder a few welcoming pats. "Chris, my old pal, what kept you?"

"What?"

"I was just saying to Georgie, Wha'd'ya think is keeping my old pal, Chris? Ya think he got himself lost or something? So, we jake, Chris? We ready to roll?"

"What?"

Siegel snapped his fingers at Spikes, who stood and handed him a thick manila envelope the size of others I'd seen in Otto Rothman's studio.

Siegel, in turn, handed over the envelope to me.

Raising his voice to be heard above the crowd cheering the ring action, he said, "Here ya are, the negatives and photographs like the doctor ordered. Now, where's the bastard you're fronting for? Let's us go and get this *mishigash* out of the way so we can settle down and enjoy the main event."

I pressed the envelope to my chest like precious treasure and headed off, Siegel on my heels. Mueller and Popeye rose as we were passing and kept a respectful distance. Out of a corner of my eye I saw Spikes angle onto the aisle and fall in behind them.

"My money's heavy on Henry tonight," Siegel said, pulling even with me. "Last year he won twenty-two in a row, twenty-one by kayo, and he got seven more going into this year, before he had to settle for a decision when Arizmendi managed to go the whole ten rounds against him. That cost me a hunk-a cabbage, but I'm counting on better results this time around, ya understand?"

"I hear Chalky's in line for a title fight if he manages to look good tonight," I said, as the crowd exploded to a knockdown. The colored boy was flat on his back. The other fighter, darker and heavier by a good ten pounds, watched from a neutral corner as the ref got to an eight-count before the boy managed to get back onto his feet.

I used the distraction to ask, "Benny, what's going on, how'd you get wise to the jam I'm in?"

Either he didn't hear me or he ignored the question.

CHAPTER 24

Hartmann settled the briefcase on the bench beside Eve and rose when he saw us approaching. He waited until Mueller and Popeye responded to his silent question with nods of confirmation before stepping forward to join Siegel in an indifferent handshake, afterward rubbing his palm on the hem of his jacket.

"Let's get this thing done, so I can get back in to the real main event," Siegel said. "That it over there?" He indicated the briefcase.

"I'm sure you won't mind if I go first," Hartmann said, pointing at the envelope.

"Mind?" Siegel closed his eyes against the concept. "The pictures, the negatives, they're all in there as advertised, friend. You got my word."

"Seeing is believing, Mr. Siegel."

"I couldn't agree with you more."

Words evolved into a staring contest that

lasted a minute or two, neither inclined to budge before Siegel shrugged and said, "What the fuck. Hand him over the envelope, Chris."

Hartmann may have sensed he could be creating a problem for himself down the line. "On reflection, your word is certainly good enough for me," he said. He dug a key out of his pocket and gestured toward the briefcase. "Help yourself, Mr. Siegel."

Siegel accepted the key and said, "Spikes, the briefcase." Spikes walked over, picked up the briefcase and waited for further instructions. "You know what?" Siegel said to Hartmann. "Changing your mind the way you did shows me you are one savvy bastard, so I'm gonna take your word for it on the contents and the count."

"That's generous of you, Mr. Siegel."

Generous? Generous had never been a word I heard anybody pair with Siegel. I couldn't guess what game he was playing with Hartmann, but he was definitely playing a game.

"Go on and check out the package," Siegel said. "I don't want to hear later about any problems whatsoever, you catch my drift?"

"Entirely."

Hartmann took the envelope from me, sat down and emptied it onto his lap. He rifled through the photos one by one and spot-checked the negatives against the sad neon light of the lobby.

Siegel flashed me a wink.

Hartmann said, "All in order, I'm pleased to say," and returned everything to the envelope as doors opened and people spilled out, buzzing loudly and angrily about the split decision that had ended the prelim bout. "We'll be on our way now. Come," he said, summoning Eve and me.

Siegel took my arm. "I been saving two ringside seats for you and her, remember, Chris? After the fight, I got a taste for some of that Frenchie food at the Troc. Mickey's already reserved a table for us."

"Definitely, if Eve's up for it. Evie, you up for it?" I said, responding to a memory I'd never had because it had never existed.

Eve caught on, too. She looked up from the program book she was about to sign for a chubby Mexican fan who had raced over begging for her autograph and said, "Jake by me."

"Eve? Why's he calling you Eve?" the chubby fan said in Spanish-tinted words. He took back his program book and pencil from her and checked what she had written. "Eve Whitney? Hell, I thought you was Marlene Dietrich," he said, and stalked off.

Hartmann said, "Unfortunately, Mr. Siegel, they have some important unfinished business with me that must be resolved tonight." No flab in the pronouncement. No room for argument in his taut expression.

Mueller and Popeye slid their hands inside their jackets in perfect synchronization, inspiring Spikes to make the same move with his gun hand.

Siegel's eyes narrowed into nasty slits. "Ya got something against Frenchie food?"

Hartmann stood his ground. "What I don't have an appetite for is trouble with you, Mr. Siegel, not in this setting, this crowd, or under these circumstances."

"Under any circumstances in the end wouldn't turn out too good for your health."

"Maybe not today, Mr. Siegel, but a whole new world is on its way."

A voice called, "Mr. Benjamin Siegel!" It was Zaslavsky, the door guard, guiding Virginia Hill and Mickey Cohen to us. "Your friends, they come out looking for you, Mr. Benjamin Siegel, so I bring them over."

Cohen sized up the situation in a hurry. "Trouble, Benny?"

"Nothing I can't handle, Mickey."

"Trouble, what I'm here for, to turn fire

into smoke," Zaslavsky said. "Anything I can do for you, I do, Mr. Benjamin Siegel."

"Thanks, Zaslavsky," Siegel said. He pulled a thick roll of bills from his pocket and slipped the guard two Andrew Jacksons. "There is something," he said, and added a third Jackson.

"You bet, whatever," Zaslavsky said, bowing appreciatively and stashing the three twenties. "Every time."

Turning to his girlfriend, Siegel said, "Ginny, I need for you to take that briefcase from Spikes and head back to our seats. Zaslavsky, you see that she gets there safely and keep her company until I return."

"Done for absolute certain, Mr. Benjamin Siegel."

"Mickey, you go along to protect the merchandise."

"You sure about this, Benny?"

"I got Spikes here to keep me company. *Farshteif?*"

"When do you know Benny to not be certain?" Virginia Hill said, smiling a honey-drip smile to go with her southern-flavored accent. She took possession of the briefcase, and the three of them joined the thinning crowd feeding back inside the auditorium.

Siegel watched them go. When the corridor was almost empty again, except for a few stragglers at the tag end of the concession counter, he said, "Where do we go from here, friend? What's your next play?"

"Depends on yours, doesn't it, Mr. Siegel. Frankly, I've never been one to tolerate being ordered around by pushy Yids like you."

"Watch your tongue, friend."

"No friend of yours or any of your kind, ever, that's my sworn promise."

Spikes looked ready to leap for Hartmann's throat. His hand started withdrawing from inside his jacket. Mueller and Popeye were faster on the draw. They had their guns out before Spikes finished his move and came out empty-handed.

"Now, if you kikes will excuse us, we'll be on our way," Hartmann said. "All of us," he said, and — turning his disgust on Eve and me — "that includes your kike-loving friends."

He motioned for us to lead the way.

Mueller and Popeye trailed behind him, keeping watchful eyes and half-hidden weapons on Siegel and Spikes, ready to engage any false moves.

It was precisely then that a sampling of hell broke loose.

It began with the echo of shouts ordering Siegel and Spikes to their knees from a pair of cops in protective vests who'd burst out of the toilet and rounded the corner armed with Police Positives.

The three customers at the concession counter wheeled around aiming Mausers.

Auditorium doors crashed open, and heavily armed plainclothes and uniformed cops charged through yelling to be heard over the raw crowd sounds serenading the ring action.

One of the plainclothes closed in on Hartmann.

Mueller and Popeye dropped their weapons and threw their hands skyward.

Seconds later, the three of them were on their knees being cuffed.

Ray Travis and Charles Cook emerged from behind a nearby arch and marched over like conquering heroes, smiles to match their strut.

Travis let Hartmann know he, Mueller and Popeye were under arrest and rattled off a list of charges that included suspicion of murder, attempted murder, kidnapping, attempted kidnapping, assault and battery, assault with a deadly weapon, breaking and entering and carrying unlicensed and concealed firearms.

One of Cook's people picked up the package of negatives and photographs that sprang loose from Hartmann's grip when he hit the ground and handed it over.

Cook made a show of the package. "Add to that treason and conspiring to commit treasonous acts, you Nazi-spewing buckets of garbage. They're federal offenses that carry the death penalty."

Hartmann responded with a cold-eyed smile and added a wad of spit to the gum, candy wrappers and cigarette butt residue on the concrete floor. "I salute your stupidity, all of you," he said, before a team of feds lifted Mueller and him up and led them away.

A uniform standing guard over Siegel and Spikes called to Travis, "They're both clean as a whistle, Captain."

Travis signaled him to help them to their feet and removed the cuffs. "You're free to go," he said.

Siegel rubbed his wrists, brushed himself off and said, "Your boys didn't have to play so rough with me, Mr. Policeman."

"Old habits are hard to break," Travis said, lighting his pipe and shipping off a set of smoke rings.

"That's the thanks I get?"

"The most you'll ever get from me, Bugsy."

Siegel winced at hearing himself called by his nickname, then broke into laughter. "I'll remember that," he said, sounding like it was the kind of memory I wouldn't ever wish on my worst enemy. "Let's go, Spikes. We got us the real main event coming up." He threw me a wave. "Catch you later, Chris. Don't take any wooden nickels from these bums."

Cook stepped over to us. "Are you all right, Miss Whitney? Mr. Blanchard?"

"I am now," Eve said, clinging to me adoringly, like we were Powell and Loy. "I don't know how you managed to pull it off, but I owe you big time, Chris."

"Not any of my doing," I said.

"Then how?" she said, wonder creeping into her voice.

"I'm pretty sure the answer's on the way to ringside."

"Only half the answer," Cook said, "and not the most important half."

"Care to explain?"

"In time, perhaps," Cook said, as Travis joined us.

Travis and Cook agreed there was no hurry in taking statements from us after Eve, overcome by the relief that arrived with her freedom from danger, pleaded to be taken home and permitted to collapse in her own bed. Both were fine with tomorrow or the day after.

My curiosity was feeding on an adrenaline rush. I waived the offer of a ride to my place, passed around a bundle of thank yous, and headed inside an auditorium thundering welcomes to Henry Armstrong and Chalky Wright as they entered the ring to handshakes and hugs from celebrities who'd been called up to take a bow by the ring announcer.

Raft, behaving like all the cheers were for him, did some fancy footwork on the canvas before dipping out through the ropes and stepping back to his front row seat next to Siegel.

When I reached them, Siegel gave me a few playful pats on the cheek and ordered Raft to slide over one. Raft grumbled, but did as he was told.

"Benny, there's something I have to know," I said.

"Save it for later," he said. "I got money on the line here."

Virginia Hill, sitting on the other side of Siegel, leaned across asking, "Does your lady friend, Miss Whitney, always copycat the way Miss Marlene Dietrich dresses?"

"Sometimes it's like Miss Joan Crawford," I said, an answer that satisfied her a moment before the ring announcer brought up

436

the main event's referee, Jack Dempsey, whose name was enough to inspire a standing ovation that rattled the Olympic's walls.

Even Siegel was on his feet.

"I met the champ," he said, like he was pinning on a medal of honor. "I seen him one time when me and Meyer was at his restaurant in Times Square with Charlie Lucky, who walked us over to the champ's table for a hello and a handshake. This hand. Didn't wash it for a year."

Less than fifteen minutes later, Dempsey was raising Armstrong's gloved hand in victory, the winner by a third-round knockout. Wright was dragging himself up from the canvas, and the auditorium was suffering a sea of outrage from an audience that had been rooting and chanting for the hometown boy.

"Nice payday for me," Siegel said. "Ya find bettors acting on emotion instead of the statistics, ya grab all the action you can, and ya score big time, like tonight. Easier'n fixing a fight. Chalky Wright's an up-and-comer, champion material, but he's no Henry Armstrong, not yet, maybe a year from now."

Driving to the Trocadero, I couldn't pin down Siegel about his potentially lethal encounter with Hartmann and Hartmann's bully boys, why he could walk away free and clear and two hundred and fifty thousand bucks richer. He kept feeding me the same old refrain — *Save it for later* — and resumed dissecting the fight, discussing every punch and counterpunch Armstrong and Wright threw, like he had memorized the bout in progress.

He was comparing Armstrong favorably to Joe Louis as Spikes pulled up to the Troc. "I was there at the Garden when the Brown Bomber polished off Schmeling in one and brought the heavyweight title back home to the U.S. of A.," he said. "A whole lot of difference for how I felt back in '35 at Yankee Stadium, when I saw him deck one of our own tribe, Maxie Baer, in the fourth. Next day, the old neighborhood was dolled in black and sitting shiva."

Raft said, "How much you drop on that one, Benny?"

Siegel arched back and raised an eyebrow. "What are you, Georgie, some kind of wisenheimer? My bundle was riding on Louis. How many times I have to say it? Go with the statistics, not emotion, and you'll die a rich man."

"I'm all for statistics," Virginia Hill said, and leaned over to lap Siegel's ear with her tongue, before she allowed the parking boy to help her from the car.

Mickey Cohen was waiting for us under the entrance canopy. He snapped away his cigarette and rushed over, fed the parking boy a ten spot, and after Spikes drove off let Siegel know, "We scored the best table in the joint and champagne's already icing, compliments of Billy Wilkerson."

Wilkerson owned the Trocadero as well as the *Hollywood Reporter.* He'd opened the nightclub four years ago and turned it into what everybody called "The Jewel of the Sunset Strip," even after a particularly unsavory incident last year involving the death of Ted Healy, the vaudevillian-turned-movie-comic, whose stage act had spawned the Three Stooges, Larry, Moe and Shemp.

According to the widely reported version, Healy, who was an obnoxious drunk, got into a loud argument at the Troc with three college students and was ordered to leave. Outside on the street, they jumped Healy, knocked him to the ground and kicked him in the head, ribs and stomach. Healy's buddy, the stuttering comic Joe Frisco, picked up his unconscious friend from the sidewalk and got him home to his apartment, where he died, never having regained consciousness, from what the coroner ruled acute toxic nephritis — inflammation of the kidneys.

The version that circulated only in whispers as rumor or truth — take your pick — among Hollywood insiders claimed the three college students were never found because they never existed. They were invented by Howard Strickling and his fellow MGM fixer Eddie Mannix, to protect Wally Beery. It was Beery, another foul-tempered boozer, who had argued with Healy at the Troc, tracked him outside and beat him to death. Strickling and Mannix sent Beery on a European vacation while they engineered the cover-up.

Did I have a hand in any of this, acting on a direct order from Mr. Mayer?

I don't remember.

I caught myself stealing glances at Fred Astaire, Bing Crosby and Cary Grant as the maitre d' guided us past tables and booths that put their occupants on display. Astaire and Crosby were with their wives, but it was only Crosby's I could put a name to, the actress-singer Dixie Lee.

Grant was sharing a booth with Randy Scott, his roommate at the Malibu beach house they called Bachelor Hall, and a well-endowed, titian-haired starlet, who looked like an aging refugee from the last group of Wampas Baby Stars a few years ago and a more recent round of casting couch auditions.

The distractions delayed my astonishment at discovering who already was seated at Siegel's table, debating with himself over which Havana to choose from the cigarette girl's tray before the sound of our approach caused him to turn around and call out to me.

"Friend Chris!" Herbie Duntz said.

I was too stunned to speak.

The dead come back to life in the movies, not in the Trocadero.

Siegel, laughing uproariously at my reaction, slapped me on the back and said, "I think you already know my little pal, the dwarf."

"Midget," I said.

"We came to a meeting of the minds, smoked a peace pipe and now we're living happily ever after," Herbie said. "He wants to call me a dwarf, he can call me a dwarf. He can call me anything he wants. In turn, I can call him anything I want." Siegel fired up an ominous look. "As long as it's Mr. Siegel." Siegel relaxed.

"First things first," I said.

"Oh, that," Herbie said, recognizing I meant his return among the living. "Up at Will Rogers, when Hartmann wanted to make certain you believed he would kill Eve if he didn't get his way? I was rigged with a pill capsule they'd spooned full of fake blood. Mueller hit me with a blank bullet and I popped the squib. First chance after, I got a red flag to Agent Cook, same as I managed after you and Marie MacDaniels got locked in at the Sanctorum."

"A regular Superman, the little guy," Siegel said, genuinely impressed. "Tell him the rest, how you showed up on my doorstep and all, a gutsy thing to do knowing how I felt about ever seeing you again."

"I get wind of the story you fed my creeps-in-arms at Baxter Leeds's place, about trading the money for the pictures at the Olympic, and it hit me like a bellyache, friend Chris. Knowing Mr. Siegel's reputation, I figured he'd want someplace more isolated and private, where he'd have more control, you know what I mean? The Olympic made sense only if you were looking for a crowd that you and Eve could somehow escape into."

Siegel slammed the table. "Tell me the dwarf doesn't have brains as well as guts, I dare ya."

Herbie acknowledged the compliment and continued. "Hartmann started having his own doubts almost immediately, so I asked him, *What's the worst could happen? He doesn't show up? That comes up the case, we still have Blanchard and Eve Whitney, we know who has the pictures and the negatives and we build ourselves a better mousetrap.* He thinks about it, grinding his teeth like an angry gorilla, and I figure he isn't buying the pitch until his head starts bobbing for apples. He says, *Blanchard or Siegel, if either one's playing angles, so what? I'll have my own angle ready to play.*

"Karl Mueller, looking strained, like he desperately needs a bowel movement, reminds Hartmann he's up against Ben Siegel and what that means, given that Ben Siegel is — and here he's not so polite about you, Mr. Siegel."

"Fuck him," Siegel said. "What's this angle he mentions?"

"He never said, Mr. Siegel, and I never asked. I was too anxious to come up with an excuse to find you and square friend Chris's story with you, if I could, but first I needed to explain the situation to Agent Cook at the FBI."

Siegel shook his head in admiration. "You could-a bowled me over with a feather when the little guy announces he works for the feds and knocking on behalf of them sons of bitches with a deal he says I can't refuse. I tell him to beat it before the beating turns on him, but he won't budge, not an inch, until I hear him out. Moxie like that ya gotta respect and give the time-a day to."

"In a nutshell, I explained what Agent Cook was planning to happen tonight and what was being asked of Mr. Siegel."

"I work the trade with this Nazi, I walk off with the two hundred and fifty gees. I don't got to give it up afterward. I get to keep it free and clear. Never any worry about the IRS dropping by for the kind of bon voyage they once give to Capone in Chicago. I'm in, and there you have it. Another reason we're out celebrating."

Garwood Van's orchestra had settled on the bandstand and Van was leading into a fresh set with "Cornfed," his ten-year-old hit recording.

Virginia Hill looked at Siegel with begging eyes and said she wanted to dance.

"Can't-cha see I'm talking here?" he said, and turned to Cohen. "Dance with her, Mickey."

Cohen looked less than thrilled with the idea.

Same with her.

Raft said, "I'll be happy to take Ginny for a spin, Ben."

Ginny's eyes lit up.

Siegel said, "I wanted that, I would-a asked for that. I said for you to dance with her, Mickey."

Cohen helped Ginny Hill from her seat and guided her to the dance floor.

Raft turned away from the table and surveyed the room. Broke into a smile and excused himself to zigzag to a second-rate table shared by Paramount's up-and-coming star, Dorothy Lamour, and a pale imitation of Gary Cooper, in what smacked of one of those typical studio-arranged dates designed by the Paramount publicity boys for the fan magazines and gossip columnists. Another minute and he was helping her from the table to the dance floor.

Herbie, who had followed Raft's progress, wondered, "Why am I thinking he has more on his mind than a fancy fox-trot?"

Siegel snickered. "He's had this itch about her since when he made *Spawn of the North* with Hank Fonda and her last year. This is the closest she's come to giving him a tumble. George has this problem, always falling for his leading lady, not that they ever fall back for him. You remember Harvey Geller from the old neighborhood, who's now a song plugger? Harvey used to lay a line on every girl he ever crossed paths with, figuring to score with at least one in five, and he did. Had a real gift of gab, that boy. He played the statistics and they worked for him up until the day he met his future wife and let his heart rule his head."

"So there can be a payoff for emotion over statistics," I said.

"You mean how they lived happily ever after? Yeah, up until the night she caught him in bed with somebody who wasn't herself and told him what she thought by burying a pair of scissors in his chest. The *schlemiel* would-a been better off sticking strictly with the statistics."

Siegel launched another lecture.

He had dovetailed from Harvey Geller to the comeback victory of Don Budge over Baron Gottfried von Cramm last year in the Davis Cup zone finals when Spikes showed up at the table and whispered something in his ear.

He didn't like what he was hearing.

His eyes tightened and his mouth formed a grim slash across his face.

He pushed up from his seat.

"Tell Mickey he should take Ginny home," Siegel said. He wheeled around and did a

double-time out of the Trocadero, Spikes
racing to keep pace.

CHAPTER 25

Wednesday, November 23, 1938

I got to the studio early and discovered Strickling had made a home for himself behind my desk. The telephone was tucked between his chin and shoulder and his hand was clutching a cup of java. There were dark circles under his eyes and a grim set to his mouth, but his tie was perfectly knotted and not a wrinkle on his gray pinstripe. He gave me a limp smile and hand-signaled me to wait a minute while he finished the call.

He was on with Hopper, so it was more like five minutes before he cooed a love note at her and hung up, shaking his head as he rose and ceded the desk back to me.

"What was that all about?" I said, settling into my chair.

"What it's always about, sweeping up after the elephants."

"Any elephant in particular?"

"Baxter Leeds. Denying, denying, denying

he's on the run from police and federal agents, who are chasing after him with warrants on unspecified charges. Hedda's playing the game my way, of course, and so is Louella, the wires, even Winchell. It's going to be an expensive Christmas."

"You're not lying with your denying, Strick. Cook called me to say they caught Leeds in bed playing bury-the-boner with his boyfriend and hauled both downtown for sweating. If they agree to spill everything they know about the Bund — about the people and locations in Rothman's photographs, the Madison Square Garden rally on February 19, Operation A, everything — Leeds and Christian draw Get Out of Jail Free cards."

"I heard all that on a wake-up call from Travis. That won't happen. What they're not being told by the feds is that LAPD will immediately re-arrest them. One way or the other, their goose-step is cooked." He muffled a smile, appreciating his little joke. "Until then, the line I'm feeding everyone is that Leeds wrapped his role in the new *Battling G-Men* and has disappeared to parts unknown for a well-earned vacation. Dropped in to let you know how you also should play the story."

"Doesn't Leeds still have scenes to shoot?"

"Not any longer. He's finished here, for good. The studio is invoking the morals clause in Leeds's contract and Mr. Mayer will be spreading the word around town where it matters. Meanwhile, we have Freddie Faust working on new script pages that will explain how Agent Thomas Harrison Two died bravely fighting off the bad guys in Havana. Scott Fitzgerald is also trying his hand at a rewrite, but my money is on Freddie, who holds his booze better than Fitzgerald."

"So, a traitor in real life will die a hero's death in reel life."

"A typical Hollywood ending," Strickling said.

"We have us a situation," Herbie Duntz said.

He'd found me handholding the playwright Clare Luce on the set of *The Women,* where her international stage hit was being directed to the big screen by George Cukor. I excused myself and left Luce to the tea and gossip she was sharing with Norma Shearer, Joan Crawford, Roz Russell and Paulette Goddard between takes, Joanie, as usual, doing her damnedest to steal the conversation and attention away from her arch rival, Shearer.

Aiming for an empty corner of the soundstage, he said, "If this was *Little Women* I'd be up for a leading role as one of the little men."

"Herbie, spare me the jokes."

"Hartmann, Mueller and the others, including Baxter Leeds and Jeffrey Christian, they were all sprung from custody in the wee hours of the morning."

"T'ain't funny, McGee."

"I ain't no Fibber, friend Chris." He raised one hand and placed the other on an invisible Bible. "The German Consulate General in L.A. showed up with proof they're official members of the German diplomatic corps and entitled to diplomatic immunity."

"You're serious."

"Cook and Travis had no choice. They had to let 'em go. Cook sent me to let you know and Travis is telling Strickling. By now there's round-the-clock surveillance on the two ladies, just in case."

"Just in case? That's like saying Hartmann can still order a murder and get away with it."

"Not if Mr. Siegel gets to Hartmann first."

"What's that supposed to mean, Herbie? What else do you have to tell me?"

He gave it a moment before answering, like he was rupturing a confidence.

"You remember last night, how Mr. Siegel

scrammed from the Trocadero after his guy Spikes said something to him?"

"Go on."

"Spikes was late arriving because Mr. Siegel had him doing a count on the payoff in the briefcase. It came up like me — short."

"How short?"

"A fraction over four feet."

"Herbie, dammit!"

He threw his arms between us like he was defending himself against attack. "Give or take, two hundred and fifty thousand dollars short. Mr. Siegel was played for a sap by Hartmann."

"That doesn't sound like Hartmann. He'd be too smart to try any kind of trick on Siegel. Besides, there was no way he could know in front that Siegel wouldn't insist on opening the briefcase to check the contents before handing over the photos and negatives."

"If he'd checked, he would have seen the greenbacks there in nice little bundles, only they were all counterfeit, funny money, every last one phony as a three-dollar bill. Spikes knew it the minute he set his eyes on them, Mr. Siegel told me when he showed up an hour ago at the Culver Hotel, hotter than a Texas tamale. He knew Hartmann had been sprung from custody and figured I might know where to find him."

"What did you tell him?"

"I said Hartmann talked about everyone meeting again on Catalina after he took possession of the pictures and the negatives. Mr. Siegel asked if that included me. I said yes, although I hadn't heard from Hartmann since the FBI had to cut him loose. I said it would also take Agent Cook deciding it's still safe for me, that Hartmann hasn't figured out my connection. Mr. Siegel gives me a long, hard look and he says, *Don't you go under no circumstances. I want for you to steer clear of the island.*"

"Did Siegel say why?"

"No, and I didn't ask."

"What do you think?"

Herbie pushed out a pound of air. "I think it was smart of me not to ask."

"What did Cook say when you told him?"

He appeared to be debating with himself about how to answer the question when we were joined by one of Cukor's hip-wiggling gofers, breathless and pointing at me like he'd found Judge Crater.

"There you are," he said. "Mr. Cukor's ready to shoot the next scene with Miss Shearer and Miss Crawford and needs you to rescue them away from Miss Luce."

"Why can't he do that?"

The gofer grew five inches, like someone had rammed a pole up his ass, and gave me a sanctimonious look. "Because he's George Cukor, of course."

"Of course," Herbie said.

"Of course," I said, and told Herbie to stick around.

I was back ten minutes later, having maneuvered Shearer and Crawford away and filled their canvas chairs around the tea table with Joan Fontaine and Mary Boland.

Herbie had disappeared.

I spent the rest of the day expecting him to show up again. He hadn't by the time I'd loaded Luce and her writer friends Anita Loos and Jane Murfin, who had adapted *The Women* for the screen, into one of the half-dozen limousines caravanning to Riverside for the first sneak preview of Garbo's latest, *Ninotchka*. The director, Ernst Lubitsch, was in the lead limo making the sixty-mile trip east, guarding the canisters of film with three of his screenwriters, Charlie Brackett, Billy Wilder, and Walter Reisch. A nervous Melvyn Douglas was in another limo with Strickling, who was playing nursemaid to Garbo's new leading man, who'd taken Garbo's absence as a sign the movie was a disaster and he was destined to drop back to low-budget pictures and secondary roles.

The audience screamed approval when Garbo's name and the name of the film flashed on the screen, as if it were their reward for gambling on a theater marquee that had allowed no more information than MAJOR STUDIO PREVIEW TONIGHT.

The screening played to laughter and applause in all the right places.

The lobby opinion cards soliciting reaction and suggestions that would help shape the final cut were unanimous in their scribbled praise, Lubitsch was predicting *Ninotchka* would be Garbo's biggest hit, and Wilder was strolling around with a straight face telling anybody who'd listen, "All the Swede wants is to be alone and that bastard Lubitsch goes and does this to her."

Strickling caught my eye and stepped away from a beaming Douglas, who was engulfed by autograph seekers, leaving him to the care of studio publicist Emily Torchia.

"We need to get back to town and modify our story about Leeds," he said, his stutter heavier than usual. "Dietz will cover for you with Luce. He's with her now."

"What's to amend?"

"Leeds is dead. Murdered." He pointed

455

to Ray Travis, angled against the silver La-Salle parked out front in a red zone, his hat pulled low and his coat collar turned up against a breeze dancing in from the desert. "Come on."

Five minutes later we were speeding west on the 60, past acres of tumbleweed and modest patches of farmland, a stretch or two of roadside storefronts, Travis's driver diligent about dodging the frequent potholes and swerving to avoid an occasional rabbit his headlights caught scampering across the lanes.

"The shooter was waiting for Leeds and his boyfriend, Christian, when they got home and pulled into the driveway, sometime after the feds released them from custody," Travis said. "Both popped twice execution-style, the kill shot and a second time for good measure, probably with a silenced weapon, since no neighbors reported hearing anything. They were discovered in the front seat of the car hours later, by Leeds's gardener when he showed up mid-afternoon."

"A professional hit?" I said, my mind toying with the notion Siegel was behind the murders.

"Or made to look like one," Travis said.

"Take your pick."

"Cook? What's his take?"

"He doesn't want the feds involved at this time, not while they have bigger fish to fry." Turning to Strickling, Travis said, "We haven't released anything about the murders to the news boys yet, Strick. I figured it was important to make the drive to Riverside and get your suggestions first."

"Extremely thoughtful of you, Ray. I'm certain Mr. Mayer will want me to show MGM's appreciation in due course." Travis waved him off and took a deep suck from his unlit briar. After we'd gone a few more miles, Strickling said, "I do have a suggestion to make." He paused and held onto the silence, his brows knitted, eyes angled on a distant planet, until he nodded confirmation to himself. "The Communists," he said, launching his suggestion.

It was a simple corruption of the truth meant to disguise the truth, built on Baxter Leeds's outspoken, well-publicized and frequently quoted loathing of Communism and its threat to basic American values. Those damned Commies were tired of Leeds's outbursts and finally decided to put a stop to them. They were lying in wait when he arrived home with Christian, who was meeting with him to create a new organization they planned to call "Americans Against the Red Menace." Christian was shot first, Leeds after putting up a battle to save both of them, as valiant as battles he had fought many times before in his popular *Battling G-Men* series of films, only this time with tragic results.

Strickling kept going, his passion building, gesturing dramatically as he injected the story with more and more plugs for the studio, foremost, how a grief-stricken Louis B. Mayer would continue the *Battling G-Men* series in Leeds's memory and as a lasting tribute to their shared vision of a Communist-free America. "The press will eat it up," he said, "especially the Winchells and the Hoppers out there, and the box office for *Battling G-Men in Havana* will swell as the public feels it's their patriotic duty to see the picture." He took a deep breath. "What do you think, Ray?"

Travis applauded him. "You're a fucking genius, Strick. That's definitely the way we'll play it."

"Simply a professional who knows his business, Ray, same as you do. Chris, how about you?"

"You heard the man," I said, hoping he wouldn't spot the sarcasm under a smile a mile wide. "All that's missing is a special

Academy Award."

"Fine one, Chris, fine, indeed. Something to put our muscle behind after the Nazi stooge is six feet under."

Chapter 26

Thursday, November 24, 1938

By morning it was evident the Fixer had worked his magic again.

Baxter Leeds's murder had stolen every front-page banner headline from a fire that broke out Wednesday in the Trippet Ranch area three miles from the mouth of Topanga Canyon and was now raging out of control. The stories, especially in Hearst's morning *Examiner* and afternoon *Herald Express,* painted Leeds as a modern-day Custer, who'd engaged in one last, brave stand against assassins identified as most likely Communist-inspired by a police spokesman, Captain Ray Travis.

Strickling wasn't finished.

In the absence of any family members stepping forward, he'd taken command of final rites for Leeds. A service was scheduled for Hollywood Memorial Park Cemetery, whose plots and crypts were occupied by the famous and infamous of the movies, from the legendary Valentino to the notorious Virginia Rappe, whose sex-charged death had destroyed the career of Roscoe Arbuckle, and kinky director William Desmond Taylor, whose murderer had never been found.

The cemetery was spread out over a hundred acres adjacent to the back wall of the Paramount and RKO studios in the heart of Hollywood, at Santa Monica Boulevard and Gower Street. Strickling had his choice of prime locations, of course, so I figured it was him exercising an under-employed morbid sense of humor when I learned he had picked a plot in the south-western section, called Beth Olam and set aside exclusively for members of Holly-wood's Jewish community.

A memo he composed and distributed over Mayer's signature announced that the studio flag would be flying at half-mast for the duration and urged stars, producers and directors to attend Leeds's memorial service in words that barely fell short of a com-mand. Not one to leave anything to chance, he had the publicity department call Central Casting and order enough mourners and bystanders to overflow the cemetery chapel and impress the press photographers and newsreel boys.

Jeffrey Christian, for all the attention he was receiving, could have been Claude Rains in *The Invisible Man,* but an unexpected call from Travis put him in the center of my universe.

"I have something you'll want to see," Travis said.

"Do I get a hint?"

"The files that were missing from Otto Rothman's studio? I got 'em."

We met in Travis's office downtown at police headquarters, cozy space with all the ceremonial trappings of his rank on the paneled walls and display shelves, a few framed citations for bravery prominently featured, along with show cards from movies in which he had appeared and autographed photos of him posing on the set with their stars, looking happier than a kid with a box of Cracker Jack.

"Sorry you had to wait," he said, rising from his desk chair, not sounding sorry at all or bothering to explain the twenty minutes he'd kept me hanging in the anteroom. His handshake was as insincere as his words, but I hadn't broken a couple of speed limits or run a few stop signs hurrying here to replace our distaste for one another with friendship.

Travis made it clear he shared the sentiment. "I invited you down strictly because of Charles Cook," he said. "He felt you're entitled to know because of the part you played in the FBI's Bund sting, but it's nothing we're going public with for reasons that'll become obvious once you take a gander." He pulled a pack of file folders from a desk drawer and pushed them toward me as I settled in a chair across from him.

Rothman's coding system was unmistakable. I recognized immediately these had to be the files dated July to November I'd discovered missing from his studio the day of his murder. They contained dozens of photos of Jeffrey Christian grappling sexually with Baxter Leeds in a variety of settings and vulgar poses beyond any I remembered from the *Kama Sutra.*

They weren't always alone.

Men.

Women.

Animals.

One series involving a frightened child in perversions that took me to the brink of vomiting.

"Makes you want to strike medals for whoever punched their ticket," Travis said, sounding as emotionally disturbed as I'd ever heard him about anything or anybody, me included. "It makes their deaths and Rothman's murder mercy killings." He signaled for me to return the folders and replaced them in the desk drawer.

"What sewer did you find these in?"

"Christian's dump of a flat over by Hollywood High, behind the Roosevelt, during a by-the-book check for possible leads to his killer. My boys discovered them in a carton he'd tucked away in the back of the bedroom closet, along with some other sick shit that gives the impression he was street trade before he went exclusive with Leeds. You follow what that means, Blanchard?"

"Try me."

"Instead of a lead to Leeds's killer, we uncovered strong evidence it was Christian who murdered Otto Rothman, probably pushed to it by Leeds, the motive as obvious as your Adam's apple. Leeds wakes up one fine morning and realizes being blackmailed by Rothman has a beginning and a middle, but no end; how damaging the photographs can be to his career and his ambitions, if they ever get out. Maybe Christian has ambitions of his own that go beyond Leeds as a meal ticket. They talk about it, and the windup is that Christian goes after the photos at gunpoint. Rothman isn't about to cooperate. Bang, bang, and that takes care of Rothman. Christian searches for the pictures, finds them, takes off and there you have it."

His words were too pat, his attitude too matter-of-fact. "There *you* have it, Travis. Nix on strong evidence. Circumstantial at best."

"Better than any other best floating around, and it's the one we're going with. Otto Rothman's murder solved. Case closed. Over and out."

"And Day Covington's murder? You also pinning that one on Christian?"

"Of course, but not yet and certainly not publicly, only sub-rosa and unofficially."

"Explained away how?"

Travis made it sound obvious. "Christian tried Covington first. He moved on to Rothman when he couldn't find the negatives and photos at Covington's bungalow."

"I don't think so."

"I don't remember asking what you think, Blanchard."

"Different weapon. Different M.O. Adds up to a different shooter where I come from, Travis."

"Where you came from I still am, Blanchard, still working homicide for LAPD, and for me it adds up to a shooter who knows that variety is the spice of life."

"It's Strickling," I said, snapping my fingers. "You're doing this for Strickling, right, Travis? Saying Covington's murder was Christian's handiwork lets you close the book on the investigation and takes Marie MacDaniels off the hook as a murder suspect."

"That's what you think, take it up with Strick," Travis said, looking at me like dirt under his fingernails. "You have any other bright ideas, leave them in the Suggestion Box on your way out."

Back at MGM, I headed straight for Strickling's office.

He listened patiently, fiddling with his tie and shirt collar, while I described the meeting with Travis and afterward said, "I heard. The good captain of detectives got on the horn to me the second you left his office."

"So why didn't you stop me?"

"I was interested in hearing your take."

"And?"

"The same as his, only without his concern bordering on hysterics that you might not be the loyal MGM employee Mr. Mayer and I know you to be and, instead, run off to the press and make us out to be liars."

"The truth already beat me to it, Strick.

While there's evidence Christian may have killed Rothman, it's pure fantasy to link him to Covington's murder."

"I know you have strong feelings for her, but I'm no fan of Marie MacDaniels, so remember this, we are in the fantasy business, Chris. If a little make-believe gets her out from under the web of suspicion, that's more important than my personal feeling. She's a studio asset of growing value and importance. Protecting her is as vital to our interests as the story about Leeds and Christian we've fed to the media is important to the FBI and the country."

"Does she know?"

"Not yet. Travis is leaving it to me to break the news to her." He thought about it. "Why don't you, Chris? I think she'd rather get the glad tidings from you. I'll call Travis and advise him there's been a casting change."

The Victor Hugo Hotel was originally one of the nondescript stucco apartment buildings that shared the working-class Victor Heights streets with faded bungalows and neighborhood merchants on a first-name basis with their customers. It catered to resident tenants who paid by the month and kept to themselves, not transient traffic, making it an ideal location for the LAPD to warehouse people in the modestly furnished one-bedroom unit on the fourth floor that the department maintained on a year-around basis.

Eddie Vassily answered my knock.

"It's Chris Blanchard, as advertised," he called out. He holstered his weapon and thumbed me inside. "The captain called to tell us you were on the way over, Blanchard. He said for Elmer and me to pretend you were welcome."

"About as welcome as cholera," Elmer Troy said. He was sitting over a cup of java, his shirtsleeves rolled up, at a card table set up in the middle of the room. "Make yourself homely. She's in the other room making herself pretty for you."

Vassily wandered back to the chair across from him, rescued the filter tip parked on the edge of the table, and took a last drag before mashing it out in an ashtray begging to be emptied. He picked up some cards and studied them. "Any eights?" he said.

Troy looked at the cards he was holding and announced, "Fish."

I crossed the room, past the kitchenette, to the view window and pulled aside the faded curtain enough to see there was a fire escape down to the hotel's unlit parking lot on the other side of window bars that could be opened only from inside the apartment.

"How's it been, any problems?" I said.

Vassily said, "Besides her, you mean? She spends half her time singing the blues about being here, another half singing the blues about being here, and another half doing that funny praying routine she's got going, probably praying to be anywhere but here."

"You blame her? This isn't exactly the Biltmore."

Troy said, "Any queens?"

"Besides her," I said, indicating Marie, who'd chosen this moment to join us.

She was barefoot, floating inside a brandy-colored cotton dress with a neckline that made the curve of her naked breasts the centerpiece of attention, wearing her hair pulled back and knotted at the nape of her neck, fully exposing the distress on her face that a thick layer of makeup, mascara and lipstick couldn't disguise. Black sacks under her eyes testified to sleepless nights. She looked like she'd dropped at least ten pounds since Day Covington's murder two weeks ago.

Marie answered my smile with one as real as Tinker Bell's and flew at me. She slapped a hand across my mouth. "Not a word," she said.

She took me by the hand.

Led me into the other room, closed the door to Vassily and Troy and turned the key in the lock.

"Make love to me, baby," she said, fumbling at my belt. "I need that more than anything, baby."

She latched onto my wrist and pulled me toward the bed, stopping short to wiggle out of her dress and toss it across the room.

A minute later, she had me out of my jacket and was unbuttoning my pants. They dropped to the carpet and she dropped to her knees, lowering my resistance as I rose to a foregone conclusion.

Afterward, stretched naked on the bed with her face nesting on my chest, sharing a Lucky, we substituted smoke rings for conversation until, after about twenty minutes, she said, "It's wonderful how you always show up when I need you most, a true friend. Thank you, baby, a million times over. I felt your love, spiritually as well as physically."

Saying *You're welcome* was inappropriate, since I hadn't been a willing convert to her cause, anyway, not at first. Not that the news I was bringing wouldn't be cause for her to celebrate, but it would have made more sense to celebrate afterward, and I told her so.

"We can still do that," she said, pouring on a real smile. She put out the cigarette, rolled off me and into her cross-legged yoga position, began chanting.

"It's about Day," I said, raising my voice to be heard. "The cops have worked out who murdered him." Marie took a sharp breath and quit chanting. "A man named Jeffrey Christian, who also killed Otto Rothman."

"No, definitely not," she said, like a child refusing her morning Pablum.

"He was Baxter Leeds's boyfriend. They were probably in it together."

"Baxter's boyfriend?" Marie appeared startled. "Baxter's lover?" Her eyes played the room, navigating the walls and ceilings, unable to find a place to land. "I never knew that about Baxter or even suspected . . . or did I?"

"There's more, kitten," I said, and told her the rest, revealing their connection to Hartmann and the German American Bund before I fed her what would be the official police account of Day's death and allow Travis to stamp the case closed.

"But it's not true," she said, unwilling to accept the lie. "You don't understand."

"What's not to understand? They're dead

471

and good riddance to them. They were bad people. Nazis. I'll learn to live with the lie because it's getting you out from under, and so should you, Marie — for the same reason."

"I can't do that," she said, "for reasons of my own."

"I'm listening."

"This," she said, outlining her body with her hands. "My yoga has put me in touch with my spiritual core, my innermost nature, that which I truly am. My yoga has freed me to let my personal experience shape my understanding. It has led me to explore the depth of human nature, to plumb the mysteries of the body and the mind. It has me committed to a rebirth of myself and my soul, to a life now dedicated to non-harming, compassion, charity, tolerance, freedom from greed, anger and jealousy, and truthfulness. It leaves no room for a lie, no matter how well-meant, Chris."

Her moist stare begged understanding.

"I get it," I said, "but it's not your lie, Marie. It's the LAPD's lie. An FBI lie. A Strickling lie. By adoption, my lie. You can ignore it, pretend it doesn't exist, but you can't make the lie go away by ignoring it."

"I'm not ignoring it, Chris. It's not that lie I'm talking about. It's the lie I built on truth and burdened you with, the one that got you caught up in this horrible mess. I can't live with it any longer, baby. I can't."

"Spell it out for me, kitten."

She laced her fingers and spent a minute picking at her thumbnails with her teeth. "Okay, here goes . . . forget everything else I said — I did kill Day. That was the truth, how we argued that night about his gambling and what it was doing to our lives, how he came after me and how I shot him."

"Tell me you're joking."

"Life is a joke, Chris. You have to learn when to laugh. This is not one of those times."

I waved her quiet. "You're letting your emotions run away with you. I told you already — you shot the picture of a deer hanging on your wall with that peashooter Vest Pocket Colt of yours. The weapon that put half a dozen slugs into Day Covington was a larger caliber. Somebody else killed Day. Jeffrey Christian killed Day."

"That weapon also was mine. I worked a switch and shot the deer afterward, after I figured out how I could get away with murder, starting with you. I gave one of my best performances at your place, certain you'd want to protect me once you were convinced of my innocence. Certain it wouldn't take much and it didn't. The gag with the Colt. Going downtown to the Biltmore to meet up with Eve and her dinner date before showing up at your door, a mental mess and not as snookered as I made you believe. Isn't that so, Chris? Isn't it?"

"Instead of me, why not an SOS to Strickling? He's buried as big or bigger messes than this with the law, the courts, the press."

"You remember my history with him. I was scared, baby, scared I'd be the one he would bury. He'd find a way to pull it off without any damage to his precious MGM, while my career would be over and out and I'd be sitting in some filthy cell getting mauled by horny guards until it was time to march me off and strap me into the chair."

"So, instead, you played me for a fool."

"I played you for a friend, Chris, and now I'm sorry. I'm sorry for lying. I'm sorry for everything. I'm asking you to forgive me, so I can start forgiving myself."

I'd never seen her looking or sounding this fragile, or was it that I'd never noticed before? "Of course," I said. "It's nothing you have to ask."

"Thank you," she said. "In my heart of hearts I knew you wouldn't disappoint me. One more favor — I'd like you to be with me when I tell the police. I'm not strong enough to do it alone."

"I don't think you should, Marie. There's nothing to be gained by telling the cops. They have a truth that satisfies them. Let it be. Put this sad, ugly business behind you and get on with your life."

"Nothing to be gained?" She cracked a troubled smile. "Haven't you heard a word I've said, Chris? I can't live the lie anymore, not with anyone. It's a weed in the garden. It has to be pulled."

"At the expense of your future?"

"I have no future as long as that part of my past continues to exist. *Sarvam ekam,* Chris. *All is one.* Will you or won't you come with me?"

"Do I need to give you an answer now?"

It wasn't what Marie wanted to hear. "You don't need to give me an answer at all, and that would be your answer," she said.

"I'll sleep on it and let you know tomorrow."

Marie reassembled herself into her yoga position. "Go, then. The faster you leave me today, the sooner our tomorrow will come." She began chanting, only now it seemed to carry deep undertones of depression.

I left feeling her guilt as my own.

■ ■ ■ ■

I was still awake when Strickling called well past my bedtime to ask, "How did it go today with our Miss MacDaniels?"

I had been alternately squatting and pacing the apartment, my mind well oiled and my innards pleasantly pickled by straight shots of vodka and, after the vodka ran out, gin, while I tortured myself over Marie. I wanted to do right by her, but I had an obligation to do right by the studio that underwrote my booze. Did I hold her hand while she confessed all to the cops or did I try again to talk her out of it?

Under more sober circumstances, I'd have dodged Strick's question with a lie of some sort, a delaying action that would satisfy him temporarily, but I may have been infected by Marie's whatchamacallit. What had Miss Yoga of 1938 called it? *Spiritual core,* that was it. *Her spiritual core.*

A lie wouldn't come.

I put life into a wooden match, lit a fresh Lucky, and breathed out the truth in a river of smoke, chased it with a slug of gin from the bottle.

Strickling didn't receive the truth well.

"Chris, I'm certain I speak for Mr. Mayer

as well as myself when I urge you to do better with her tomorrow," he said. "Bear down. Make her understand and accept the fact that Jeffrey Christian murdered Day Covington."

"And if I can't make it happen?"

"Make it happen," he said, and disconnected.

I raised the gin bottle and replenished my spiritual core.

CHAPTER 27

Friday, November 25, 1938

When the phone rang like it was calling the fire department to a five-alarm fire, I'd been asleep for maybe an hour, on the floor in an upright position, my back pressed against the wall, hugging the bottle of gin. My eyes clicked open and were momentarily blinded by the morning light pouring through the living room curtains and playing on my eyelids. I crawled to the phone, fumbled finding my ear with the receiver, and said, "This better be damn good."

"Sorry for the interruption, sir." It was the Ravenswood's daytime doorman, Jack Johnson Smith. "I'm downstairs in the lobby with a dwarf insisting he gotta see you."

Herbie Duntz's voice boomed in the background: "A midget, Uncle Remus. I'm a midget."

"He says he's a midget, Mr. Blanchard."

"Short guy?"

"And nasty."

"He grows on you, Jack Johnson. Send him up."

I let Herbie in.

"You look like shit," he said, scooting past me. "Smell like it, too." He hopped onto the couch and tucked himself into a corner. "I was your girlfriend, I'd be afraid to kiss you, you know what I mean?"

"Thank you for bringing me to my attention," I said. "Any other reason for the unexpected treat of your visit?"

"You don't sound sincere, friend Chris."

"There's a reason."

"There's a bigger reason I'm here."

"Considering the source, how big could that possibly be?"

He locked his arms and hit me with an imperious smirk. "How big would you like it to be? It's from Mr. Siegel."

"Okay. Big enough."

Herbie studied the room like the walls might have ears. Satisfied, he motioned me closer and said, "Anybody comes around asking, he wants you to say he was hanging out here with you and Raft, talking up old times."

"Why would I want to do that?"

"Because he's asking?"

I dismissed his answer with a gesture. "I think you know better and can do better."

"Friend Chris, don't give me higher billing than I deserve."

"Either *better* or thanks for dropping over and goodbye, Herbie."

He juggled his palms like he was weighing a decision before lowering his voice another decibel. "If he was here with you, he couldn't have been over on Catalina same time. That help?"

"More would help better."

"Talking about more, you have any more of the hooch you've been guzzling?" I pointed him to the gin bottle. He took a long swallow, then another. Wiped his mouth with his fingers. "High-grade fuel. If it's what you're planning to dispense as Christmas gifts, put me down for a bottle or two."

"More, Herbie."

"Appreciate your generosity," he said, and took another swallow. Used the back of his hand to dry his lips. "Where were we? Oh, yes. You're going to be hearing on the news how they found a bunch of bodies up at a remote villa at Two Harbors on Catalina. Murder victims. Nicky Hartmann. Karl Mueller. Some others that you ran into recently. Beaten to bloody pulps before being shot to death. No immediate clues to who might be behind it or why. Blah, blah, blah."

"Siegel and his boys getting even for the funny money Hartmann passed off on him. Is that what I'm reading into this, Herbie?"

"Better you should stick to the *Reader's Digest*. Mr. Siegel told me that wasn't the case at all, but he wanted to have a story backed up by a solid citizen like you, in case the feds come banging on his door."

"As they most certainly will, given they know about Siegel and Hartmann. What about the others who were supposed to be meeting there?"

Herbie shrugged. "Mr. Siegel didn't say anything about them being around."

"Of course, especially since he wasn't there, so he couldn't possibly know."

"I'll drink to that," Herbie said.

And he did.

He emptied the bottle and smiled like a contest winner before he abruptly pushed off from the couch, covered his mouth and staggered across the room to what he thought was the bathroom, only to recognize too late that he was about to throw up in the hallway closet.

Herbie didn't let that stop him.

He dropped to his knees and heaved.

A second time.

Groaned contentedly.

Began a crawl back, his skin the color of chalk, and managed half the distance before his arms and legs quit on him.

Closed his eyes and was snoring in seconds.

Something about Herbie's visit bothered me more than my having to clean up his mess. It wasn't the message he'd delivered from Ben Siegel. It was because he'd brought the message.

This was uncharacteristic of the Ben Siegel I knew, except for times he wanted to pound his message home, in the truest sense of the word. On those occasions he'd unleash some of his pet bulls. Otherwise, he'd show up himself, to take personal delight in scaring the poor bonehead behind in his payback, payoffs or whatever with a quiet word, a subtle gesture, or by demonstrating the fine art of kneecapping.

It bothered me enough that I picked up the phone and called Siegel.

Spikes answered on the first ring.

"It's Chris Blanchard. Put him on the line."

"Can I tell him what it's about?"

"If you know, go ahead. Otherwise, put him on."

I heard muffled voices trading words in my ear before Siegel said, "I'm busy here, so make it snappy. What?"

"Thought I'd let you know I got your message, Benny, and not to worry about me playing along. I'm good with it."

"What message? Good with what?" he said after a brief silence.

"Delivered in person by Tyrone Powell. About the island? Catalina?"

"I hope you know what you're talking about, because I don't. The dwarf must've been yanking your chain for some reason. I had anything at all needed saying to you, I'd say it the hell myself."

The connection clicked off, leaving me unsure who the liar was, Herbie or Siegel.

I had to know.

When Herbie didn't respond after I punctured his eardrum demanding he wake up, I filled a pitcher with water from the kitchen tap and poured it on him. He bolted upright, looked around, told me it had started raining and I should close the windows and settled back to sleep.

Larger measures were called for.

I went to the bathroom and filled the tub,

lugged Herbie there and dropped him clothes and all into the water.

That did the trick.

He attacked me with a cavalcade of nasty names and tried climbing out.

I pushed him back and shoved his head underwater.

He sputtered to the surface demanding to be let out.

"Not until I hear the truth, the whole truth and nothing but the truth," I said, and repeated my conversation with Siegel.

Herbie stopped struggling, resigned to co-operating.

"It sounds to me like your detective friend Travis was there," he said. "He was due about the same time Mr. Siegel sent me to deliver his message — nothing he would want to talk about in front of a cop, especially since the cop had phoned saying he was heading over and had questions about that."

"That's not how you told it to me before, Herbie. Before, you said it was a cover in case the feds came calling on me. Nothing about Travis."

"How Mr. Siegel wanted it said. He's keeping his distance from the feds, because they made the deal with him. The detective wasn't in on the deal."

"The deal? Tell me about the deal."

"How about you let me out of here first, before I catch pneumonia and die, and you have to live your remaining days with the knowledge my death was your fault?"

"How about you go first?"

Herbie grimaced and splashed a handful of water at me. "It starts before the deal," he said.

He said he had overheard gossip at a Café Berlin meeting in Glendale about an "Operation Goebbels," a plan to destabilize the United States economy by flooding the country with millions of dollars in counterfeit bills of various denominations. Hartmann would be among group leaders receiving test money smuggled into the country through Canada.

Herbie passed along the gossip to Cook, and that was that until Hartmann used a large chunk of his funny money to work the trade with Siegel and Siegel went bonkers. Cook met with Siegel within hours after Hartmann and the others were sprung loose by the law, because of diplomatic immunity. He offered Siegel a legitimate two hundred and fifty thousand dollars in exchange for services rendered.

"Next I knew, Leeds and Christian were practicing rigor mortis and Mr. Siegel was coming at me, wondering if I could point him to Hartmann and the others," Herbie said. "Agent Cook had told me what to tell him in that event, so I steered Mr. Siegel to Catalina. . . . You know what happened over there." He ran a finger across his throat.

"That was the deal, the FBI underwriting those murders?"

"Not in so many words. All I ever heard Cook say was *services rendered.*"

"Not what for?"

"No."

"Or why?"

"No, but if I had to guess —" He scrubbed his hands and held them up. "See how clean they are, daddy?"

"What else can you tell me, Herbie?"

"I'm freezing my nuts off in here."

After Herbie left, those questions still unanswered, I showered, shaved, dressed and took off for the Victor Hugo Hotel to deliver the answer I had promised Marie.

I was still uncertain what it would be.

I'd wrestled with myself the entire drive over.

It didn't matter.

Marie was dead.

I knew it before it was confirmed for me, a sixth sense lit by the row of LAPD squad cars rimming the street in front of the hotel and the uniformed cops guarding the entrance and the walkways leading to the rear of the building.

I found parking two blocks away, trotted back and weaved through the crowd, but couldn't get past the baton-wielding cops maintaining sidewalk control inside the wooden horse barriers until I spotted Ray Travis exiting the building and shouted for him.

Travis signaled the cop to let me through.

I said, "Marie MacDaniels."

A statement more than a question.

"A suicide," Travis said, without emotion, and went after his tobacco pouch and pipe, a meerschaum. Had the hand-carved ceramic bowl shaped like a lion packed and lit by the time I'd recovered my voice.

"I don't believe it," I said. "I was with her here yesterday. There wasn't a sign of any kind that Marie had suicide on her mind."

"Suicides don't advertise," Travis said, like he was Franklin P. Adams answering one of Clifton Fadiman's questions on *Information Please.* "Without warning they pick up and do it. . . . What was on her mind, what'd you two talk about?"

"Suicide how?"

"A swan dive from her bedroom window

487

sometime during the night. Landed in the parking lot. A post office worker coming home from his swing shift discovered her. You haven't answered my question. What'd the two of you talk about?"

"Her yoga. How it was changing her. How she was being reborn body and soul because of it."

"Doesn't that tell you something else, get rid of any doubts you have? For Christ's sake, Blanchard — you have to die before you can be reborn. She was letting you in on her sad little secret while she had the chance."

"She leave a note?"

"No. No note. Nothing."

"I want to see her."

"It's not the way you'd want to remember her."

"I said I want to see her."

He hesitated, staring at the meerschaum like it held the answer until he recognized where I intended to stow the pipe if he didn't take me to her.

He wheezed a sigh of resignation and said, "This way."

Marie had cracked her skull when she hit the parking lot concrete and was resting on a pillow of brownish-red drying blood, her limbs twisted at impossible angles inside a chalk outline. The lab boys in white jackets marked by old stains were still working her fully clothed body. The detectives were standing nearby in a semi-circle, under a heavy nicotine cloud, competing for laughs with bad taste observations meant to dull the ugly image they'd be taking home today.

I wanted to tell them to shut up and show some respect for the dead, but I was one of them once. I'd behaved the same way. It came with the job. It helped get you to twenty years and your pension — provided you didn't crack first and perform a tonsillectomy with your gun.

I scanned the scene, working from the ground to the window of her bedroom. The window bars that could only be opened from inside were pressed against the exterior wall of the hotel. I visualized Marie stepping up to the sill and, maybe, saying some kind of a yoga prayer or maybe crossing herself before closing her eyes and jumping. Or did Marie welcome death with open eyes on the short flight down?

I watched her fall.

Watched her fall again.

Something was wrong.

I thought I knew what, but I couldn't be sure.

I told Travis I wanted to go upstairs to the room.

He shrugged indifference.

The uniform at the door stepped aside for us.

Vassily and Troy, the only detectives around, were at the card table laboring over investigation report forms. Travis wandered over and joined them while I headed for the bedroom, where two lab boys were packing up.

Red Callendar I knew — we'd worked many a case, shared many a round together back when — but not his partner, a gloomy-looking, towheaded kid who was Red's junior by at least a dozen years.

"If you've come to get a movie star's autograph, you're too late for this one," Red said, punctuating his wisecrack with gnarled laughter that was exclusively his, impossible to forget once you'd heard it.

I smiled politely and said, "Anything special I should know, Red?"

"Committing suicide can be injurious to your health," he said, and laughed again. "Teddy here agrees, don't you, Teddy?"

"What's not to agree?" Teddy said, but the look burning in his eyes told a different story.

"See for yourself," Red said. He snapped the locks on his satchel, preparing to leave. "Only, if you're of a mind to follow in her footsteps, be sure to look before you leap," he said. No laughter this time. Moving his head like he was sending me a coded message.

I waited until they were gone before heading to the window.

I didn't have to be careful about touching the sill. The surfaces had been dusted, revealing a sloppy mess of finger and foot prints that defied analysis or identification. I leaned out and looked down, catching the smell of garbage burning and sending up black smoke from the backyard incinerators, watching as Marie's body was bagged and loaded into the coroner's van.

And confirmed what I'd been thinking down there.

If Marie had fallen or jumped from the window, she would have landed closer to the building, most likely in the parking space immediately below.

Not even a giant leap would have carried her as far out as her landing point.

The angle of trajectory said Marie had either been thrown or pushed to her death.

She was no suicide.

She was a murder victim.

That's what Red wanted me to see and take into account, so why couldn't he come right out and say it? I charged back into the parlor, anxious to put the question to Vassily and Troy, who were supposed to be guarding her. To Travis, who'd been too quick to say it was an over-and-out clear case of suicide.

Vassily and Troy had disappeared.

Travis was sharing the card table with Charles Cook and Howard Strickling.

"Pull up a chair and join us," Travis called, unnecessarily.

I was on them with the evangelical fury of a Billy Sunday.

They listened politely.

Their expressions gave nothing away.

When I was done, they conferred silently among themselves for a minute or two before Travis spoke up.

He said, "Vassily and Troy were sitting where we're sitting from the time you saw them last night to the time they left a few minutes ago, Blanchard. For anybody to get in here and toss her out the window, he would have to get past them — by coming in through the door or climbing up the fire escape and through the window. Then, out the same way he got in once he'd given Marie MacDaniels her flying lesson. It didn't happen, it couldn't happen like that, or do you mean to accuse Vassily and Troy of her murder or of looking the other way and permitting her murder to happen?"

"You have a better scenario, Travis?"

"You still haven't given us a motive, Blanchard."

"Why tell you what you already know?"

Cook said, "Humor us, Chris." Travis started to object. "No, please, Ray. Let's hear him out."

"It starts for me where it ends up," I said, "with Marie in a panic over the murder of Day Covington. Telling me she killed him. Me convinced otherwise and out to prove it, finding myself more deeply involved when I stumble over the body of Otto Rothman."

Certain I had their attention, I threw out what facts I knew, indifferent to where or how they would land, hoping to provoke Travis, Cook and Strickling into revealing truths that completed a whole truth they seemed bent on keeping to themselves.

How Otto Rothman's murder led to discovering the blackmail business he ran with Covington, and how the collection of squalid photographs drew panic and profits from faggot celebrities in the Homowood suburb of Hollywoodland, including George Cukor, Billy Haines, Baxter Leeds and others in the MGM stable so well protected by Howard Strickling.

How their business came to involve Nicky Hartmann and the German American Bund, threatening whatever the Nazi bootlickers were calling Operation A and planning for a Madison Square Garden rally in February, making it imperative Hartmann retrieve negatives and photographs that could prove destructive to the cause.

How those two worlds intersected and collided, ultimately drawing in Ben Siegel, George Raft, Tyrone Powell, Eve Whitney, Mickey Cohen and Jeffrey Christian, along with a grubby bunch of bad actors you'd never want to cast anywhere but behind bars — Karl Mueller, Popeye, Uncle Joe the Accountant, Spikes.

I tossed in a few more names for flavor and taste, like I was inventing a Blanchard Salad the way Bob Cobb, owner of the Brown Derby on Wilshire, had come up with his Cobb Salad last year — by accident — when he went on the prowl for a late evening snack in the Derby kitchen, chopping and dumping everything into a salad bowl and pouring on French dressing. Lettuce, avocado, romaine, watercress, tomatoes, hardboiled eggs, cold breast of chicken, chives, cheese, crisp strips of bacon and, *voila!,* a star was born.

"And the motive?" I said. "To stop Marie from following through on her need to clear her conscience by confessing it was she, not Jeffrey Christian, who murdered Day Covington. That would bring the house of cards built by the three of you gents tumbling down, put a fatal crimp in your conspiracy of silence. Destroy the idea that Baxter Leeds and Jeffrey Christian were gunned down by Communist agents. Reveal the truth behind Otto Rothman's murder and implicate the real killer. Further tarnish the reputation of the LAPD and probably end your career, Travis. Cripple your ability to manipulate the town to the advantage of the studio, Strick, the Fixer unfixed once and for all time. You, Agent Cook, you risk the greatest fatal exposure. How do you think Mr. Hoover will react after he learns you turned the FBI into an assassination bureau through the deal you made with Ben Siegel?"

Cook laughed in my face. "He'll congratulate me and move me up first in line for a promotion. Mr. Hoover has the greatest respect for agents who not only follow orders, but exceed expectations. You think he didn't know? You think I'd take any action without his approval? If anyone's on the brink of disaster, it's you, Chris, not the three of us."

Cook took a walk around the room, paused at the window to swallow a lungful of dirty air and cough it out before rejoining us. He settled his elbows on the table and made a pyramid of his hands, the top of the triangle supporting his schnozzola, and stared at me menacingly.

"You're not a man of modest intelligence, so I'll be as candid, straightforward and blunt with you as I can be," he said, as calm as a hound dog in the sun. He turned first to Travis, then Strickling for a vote of confirmation. Both nodded. "You need to step aside, stop asking questions, stop making idle threats, and get back to your usual bidness at the MGM studio. I'm saying this for your own good and welfare, Chris."

"In other words, you're threatening me."

"Your words, not mine, but understand this — we come to a meeting of the minds at this table or I can't vouch for your safety in the future, or for the continued well-being of Eve Whitney and Tyrone Powell, anybody else who might know too much or say too much and risk the success of the mission Mr. Hoover and your government entrusted to me."

"Keeping Ben Siegel busy, that part of your mission?"

"Mr. Siegel has become a useful tool and a trusted ally, who has put himself and his organization behind us like a true patriot. Whatever his faults, and I know they exist, as part of our bidness arrangement he'll not be maligned or prosecuted for any services in our behalf."

"Like bumping off Leeds and Christian?"

"The work of the damned Communists," Strickling said, spoken like he believed his invention.

"Like what happened here with Marie?"

"Suicide," Travis said. "Isn't that so, Strick?"

Strickling donned a mourner's face. "I heard from her in the early morning hours. Marie called me and —"

I interrupted him. "That was me on the phone, Strick, and it wasn't so early."

He ignored me.

"I heard the despondency in Marie's voice over Baxter Leeds's murder," he said. "He was more than her co-star in the studio's popular *Battling G-Men* series. Baxter and Marie were long-term lovers. I was helping them arrange a secret getaway to Reno after shooting was completed on *Battling G-Men in Havana.* She couldn't stop sobbing. She said without Baxter she had no reason to go on living. I pleaded with her that he'd want her to get on with her career, achieve the artistic heights she was capable of reaching. I thought I had her convinced by the time I said I would come see her later, to talk some more, and we traded phone kisses." Tears had welled in Strickling's eyes. "Dear Lord, maybe there'd have been a different, happier ending if I had come right over."

"Jesus Christ! You've outdone yourself, Strick. The Fixer goes highbrow with his flack, rewriting Shakespeare."

He accepted the comparison as his due. "AP, UP and INS are already carrying the tragic news. Hedda will be going with an exclusive quote from Mr. Mayer. Parsons will have exclusives from a grieving Norma Shearer and Leslie Howard."

"And you'll see to it that Marie is buried alongside Leeds at Hollywood Memorial Park Cemetery, all for the greater promotional good and box office of Metro."

"Working out the final arrangements now, Jack Barrymore delivering the eulogy, if we can keep him sober long enough."

"Answer me this, Strick — have you ever had a moment where you've felt the least bit ashamed for what you do?"

"No, never."

Cook tapped the table for attention. "You answer me this, Chris. Can I count on your future cooperation?" I hesitated. "Come, come, Chris. A simple yes or no, preferably a yes, is all I need to hear before sending confirming assurance to Washington."

"First I need to hear something else. Once you got your photographs, why was it necessary for Hartmann and the others to die? Why couldn't the government simply have them deported, sent back to Germany where they belonged?"

"The deaths send a warning to the people in the photographs that we're on to them and their plans for the day of the Bund rally at Madison Square Garden, February 19, or three days later on Washington's Birthday, this so-called Operation A. Beyond that I am not at liberty to say. You will have to accept that it's a matter of critical national security, where the life of one or a few innocents is a small price to pay when measured against a situation that could cause the deaths of thousands, perhaps hundreds of thousands, if we don't nip it in the bud." Cook leaned forward and hugged me with his eyes. "So, what's it going to be, Chris, the lady or the tiger?"

CHAPTER 28

Saturday, November 26, 1938

The MGM lion logo towering above the lot had been dressed in a mourner's band of black and the flag outside the administration building was at half-mast when I arrived at the studio and pulled into my parking slot. Otherwise, it was production as usual in an industry that practiced a rain-or-shine six-day work week.

Work was the last thing on my mind.

I was here because misery loves company.

My company had already arrived —

Mickey Cohen.

Nearby, half-in and half-out the rear of a nondescript Studebaker coupe parked curbside.

Smartly dressed from his snap-brimmed fedora to his elevator-heeled wingtips, everything in-between custom-built to honor his stocky frame, the image of perfection sullied only by his indelible five o'clock shadow and a fondness for expensive cigars that diminished the smell of his perfumed aftershave.

"Climb in," he called.

It wasn't an invitation.

I climbed in.

He tapped his driver on the shoulder and said, "Hit 'em on all six, Schmaya."

I said, "Where we heading?"

"You'll know when we get there," Cohen said, and filled the cabin with smoke.

Less than an hour later, we were traveling north on Ventura Boulevard, the two-lane gateway to the San Fernando Valley, a collection of dairy farms, horse ranches and orange and lemon groves, the occasional pumpkin field, and miles of empty acreage.

At a point somewhere around Tarzana, named after the jungle cowboy created by the farmland area's first, most famous and wealthiest settler, Edgar Rice Burroughs, the Studebaker pulled off the boulevard and onto a bumpy, easy to miss dirt road, sending up clouds of dust as it sped past walnut groves and wasteland overgrown with weeds, finally pulling to a stop at a desolate and rundown Spanish Colonial-style ranch house.

Schmaya made music with the horn.

The front door squeaked open and Ben

Siegel stepped onto the porch, regal-looking in a double-breasted camel hair topcoat and matching fedora, his eyes hiding behind a pair of Foster Grants.

He waved and aimed for the car, Spikes following in his wake.

Cohen and I joined them.

"Whaddaya think?" Siegel said, throwing his arms to the wind. "I bought me a hundred acres out here as an investment before I got to thinking maybe I can do better over in Nevada. Las Vegas."

"What's there that isn't here, Benny?"

"My imagination," he said. "But right here and now, me and you, we got us some unfinished business, *kapish?*"

"You do what you have to do," I said, and steeled myself against what I knew was coming.

"That's what's in the cards." He took out a pair of brown kidskin gloves from the topcoat, pulled them on, and monitored the fit to his satisfaction. "Okay, Spikes," he said.

Spikes stepped over and handed over a junk gun he had holstered inside his belt, a .22 automatic, the handle wrapped in electric tape.

Siegel studied the weapon and tried it on for fit. "It'll do the trick nicely," he said, checking the barrel sights against some sparrows flying by, tracking them until they flew past Spikes, at which point he lowered the .22 and fired.

The bullet caught Spikes between the eyes.

He staggered backward a few feet, twisted and hit the ground on his belly.

Siegel advanced on him and put two fast shots into the back of Spike's head.

"Yeah, it did the trick nicely," he said, no pleasure in his words or in the look he turned on me. "They don't come more loyal than Spikes always was, but a deal is a deal, and you don't got your word, you don't got nothing. Back in town, you make sure Cook knows I come through for him again, and then go fuck yourself, Chris."

"Spikes murdered Marie MacDaniels, Benny. He pitched her out a window. He got what was coming to him."

"No, you got what was coming to you as part of your own deal with Cook and who-ever else it took to get your nose back in joint. You had the guts, you would-a come after Spikes yourself, your finger on the trig-ger, not mine."

"Don't think I wouldn't have under other circumstances."

"Other circumstances." He coughed up a wad and spit on the ground. "That's what I think of other circumstances. All's I know, my boy Spikes is dead and I don't never need to hear about your fucking other circumstances."

Siegel tossed the junk gun aside and turned to Cohen, who had been playing silent witness. "You and Schmaya need to clean up around here like usual," he said. "I'll get this prick back over the hill." He turned away and headed for a jalopy parked across the yard. "C'mon, prick, let's go for a ride." He laughed. "Don't I wish."

The note on my desk announced in large, bold, block letters that Mr. Mayer was waiting to see me. Ida Koverman threw out her slender hands in relief. "Go on straight in. You're the only reason he's still here instead of at the track," she said.

Mayer was pacing furiously behind his desk, hands behind his back, irritation on full view until he heard the door click open and saw me entering. His irritation dissolved into a Bunyanesque smile. He raced around the desk and locked me in an embrace like I was a long-lost child.

"My boy, my boy, my boy. I wasn't going nowhere with people waiting for me at the track until I saw you," Mayer said. "Isn't that the God's honest truth, Strick?"

"The God's honest truth," Strickling said. He was parked in his usual chair by the desk. "I didn't have to explain more than once that you were engaged in a very important meeting with government representatives. After that, Mr. Mayer refused to leave, though I assured him I could deliver his good news to you on his behalf."

Mayer released me and quick-stepped back to the desk, easing onto the cushion in his chair like he was defending against a hemorrhoids attack. "Definitely. Patriotism like yours deserves the top man, especially knowing how much you been doing to help stamp out Communism in our beloved country. Same as when Mr. John Edgar Hoover, himself a top man, got on the long-distance to me personally this morning to commend you for a job well done." He picked up a sheet of paper from his desk and offered it to me. "Go on and read," he said. "It's the announcement Strick will be planting after we give ourselves a little time once we get out from the way the memorial services for Baxter Leeds and our precious darling Marie MacDaniels."

The publicity release announced my promotion to unit producer in glowing terms, Mayer's quote praising my dedicated and devoted creative services to the studio without explaining what those creative services were. Effective immediately, I'd be taking over MGM's popular *Battling G-Men* series, being continued to honor the memory of its late, lamented co-stars Baxter Leeds and Marie MacDaniels, with the leading roles now to be played by rising ingénue Eve Whitney and MGM's latest star discovery, Tyrone Powell, the most original, one-of-a-kind talent since Lon Chaney.

"So how do you like it? What do you think, Chris, my boy?"

"I couldn't have asked for more," I said.

Strickling resisted a smile, waiting until after Mayer gave me a last hug, added a kiss on my forehead, and fled the office for the track, to say, "More is what it's all about in the movie business. Enough is never enough for anybody. It's a word that doesn't exist, Chris. Of course you could have asked for more."

I suppose.

I'd made a pact with the devil in the name of patriotism to serve our country, help protect our country from the enemy threat posed by the German American Bund, while I was at it move Eve and Herbie out of harm's way, and me, too, reward the three of us for our silence.

Patriotism.

Was that really it?

Really?

Could patriotism also explain why Spikes was dead and buried in some invisible grave somewhere in the San Fernando Valley?

No.

I needed more and wanted more, that was the reason.

And the reason I was feeling so dirty.

After Strickling left, I phoned Nancy Warren.

I was hungry to hear her voice.

She'd never been far from my mind.

She said, "What's it this time, fella? Need another sketch?"

I laughed, pretending I'd heard the humor in her voice, although uncertain if it was there. "I received some great news earlier, great news for me that also translates into great news for you."

"Swell. I'm always in the market for great news."

I read the publicity release to her.

"Congratulations. Onward and upward, but I don't follow why you say that's also good for me."

"I want to steal you away from the art department and put you exclusively on my pictures, the *Battling G-Men* pictures and everything that comes after."

"Your generosity is overwhelming," she said.

"How about celebrating tomorrow at Hillcrest? It'll be a week since we were there for brunch, so we can also celebrate our one-week anniversary."

"I don't think so, Chris."

"A prior engagement?" I said, salvaging my ego.

"It's more than that," Nancy said, after a lingering silence, like she was weighing a decision. "Dave Selznick was not too happy about discovering me out with you last week and —"

"He may rule your roost on *Gone with the Wind,* but what you do on your own time is your own business. . . . Nancy, you hear me? You still on the line?"

"You don't get it, Chris. I've been seeing Dave since before he put me on *Gone with the Wind.* I'll be on his next one, too, *Rebecca.* He's bringing Hitchcock over from England to direct Laurence Olivier and Joan Fontaine. I'm moving from MGM down the street to Selznick Productions. It's the kind of opportunity I've been aiming and working for ever since I came to town."

I made a joke of it. "Anybody who'd choose Olivier and Fontaine over Powell and Whitney deserves what she gets."

Her laugh was genuine. "You're a fine gent, Chris, fun to be with, but Dave — he's my future."

"And that makes me gone with the wind," I said.

"At least for the present," Nancy said. "Who can predict what'll happen after the future becomes the past?"

This time we laughed together.

I brooded for about fifteen or twenty minutes after hanging up, until I flashed on a saying attributed to Napoleon that I'd once read: *Victory belongs to the most persevering.*

Waterloo be damned.

Impulsively, I dialed Eve Whitney's number.

"I've been worrying sick about you," she said, sounding it. "Tell me everything's jake, Chris."

I read her the publicity release.

Eve let out a whoop. "This calls for a celebration," she said. "How you fixed for time? C'mon over and we'll celebrate together, pop a few corks."

"I'm on my way," I said.

CHAPTER 29

February 1939

Eve, Herbie and I were in New York for the world premiere of *Battling G-Men in London* at the Roxy the week the German American Bund staged its attention-grabbing rally at Madison Square Garden. Other than protest demonstrations outside that led to a few arrests and the bunk diatribes inside by Fritz Kuhn and others that had thousands of miscreants on their feet cheering the Nazi party line, there were no incidents anyplace in the country involving any of the people or locations the FBI had managed to identify in the Rothman photos.

February 19 passed without incident.

On the February 22 holiday observance of Washington's Birthday, the FBI again stationed armed security teams at those locations.

The day passed without incident.

We were back in L.A. five days later, on

Saturday, February 27, in bed satisfying our sexual appetites, when we heard about the bomb explosions that destroyed synagogues in three dozen modest-sized communities in the Midwest, killing and injuring thousands of worshippers celebrating the Sabbath.

The news bulletin that cut into the Metropolitan Opera live broadcast of Mozart's "The Marriage of Figaro" compared it to *Kristallnacht,* the "Night of Broken Glass," in Germany earlier in the month, the Nazi wave of pogroms that targeted Jewish-owned stores, destroyed more than three hundred synagogues, murdered almost a hundred Jews, and arrested and deported thirty thousand more.

I rolled away from Eve, grabbed the phone and called Herbie, who'd been keeping close ties with the feds, expecting he might know more than what the radio was reporting.

I was right.

"Just got off with Cook," he said. "Besides having the date and target in common, there's nothing to link the bombings to the Bund or anyone in the Rothman photographs, to any so-called Operation A, Cook said. He said it's ugly out there. He said they're still counting the bodies. I'll give you a buzz, I learn any more."

I cradled the receiver and shared the information with Eve.

She broke into tears, sat up and begged for a hug.

We hugged for the longest time, seeking comfort from Mozart.

"Figaro" concluded, and the announcer commented on the opera's original title: "The Day of Madness."

So appropriate, I thought, at the same time fearing more days like today were on the way.

NOTES FROM THE AUTHOR

This is a work of fiction. Certain historical facts, dates and details were adjusted or moved in time to better serve the story.

For instance:

• Ben Siegel did not arrive in Los Angeles on behalf of his mob undertakings until 1940.

• Henry Armstrong fought Chalky Wright earlier than November 1938 at the Olympic Auditorium. Jack Dempsey did not referee the bout.

• Operation Goebbels was inspired by "Operation Bernhard," the Nazi plot to savage the British economy by flooding the country with counterfeit Bank of England notes.

ABOUT THE AUTHOR

Robert S. Levinson is the bestselling author of eight prior novels, *The Traitor in Us All, In the Key of Death, Where the Lies Begin, Ask a Dead Man, Hot Paint, The James Dean Affair, The John Lennon Affair,* and *The Elvis and Marilyn Affair.* His short stories appear frequently in the *Ellery Queen* and *Alfred Hitchcock* mystery magazines. He is a Derringer award winner, has won *Ellery Queen* Readers Award recognition three times, and is regularly included in "year's best" anthologies. His nonfiction has appeared in *Rolling Stone,* the *Los Angeles Times* Magazine, *Written By* Magazine of the Writers Guild of America-West, *Westways,* and *Los Angeles* Magazine. His plays "Transcript" and "Murder Times Two" had their world premieres at RiverPark Center's International Mystery Writers Festivals in Owensboro, Kentucky. Bob served four years on Mystery Writers of America's (MWA) national board of directors. He wrote and produced two MWA annual "Edgar Awards" shows and two International Thriller Writers "Thriller Awards" shows. His work has been praised by Nelson DeMille, Clive Cussler, T. Jefferson Parker, David Morrell, Heather Graham, John Lescroart, Gayle Lynds, Michael Palmer, James Rollins and others. He resides in Los Angeles with his wife, Sandra. Visit him at *www .rslevinson.com.*

The employees of Thorndike Press hope you have enjoyed this Large Print book. All our Thorndike, Wheeler, and Kennebec Large Print titles are designed for easy reading, and all our books are made to last. Other Thorndike Press Large Print books are available at your library, through selected bookstores, or directly from us.

For information about titles, please call:
  (800) 223-1244

or visit our Web site at:
  http://gale.cengage.com/thorndike

To share your comments, please write:
  Publisher
  Thorndike Press
  10 Water St., Suite 310
  Waterville, ME 04901